# A Year at Nethercombe Ley

# A Year At Nethercombe Ley

## Tony Hopes

Matador
9 Priory Business Park,
Wistow Road, Kibworth Beauchamp,
Leicestershire. LE8 0RX
Tel: (+44) 116 279 2299
Fax: (+44) 116 279 2277
Email: books@troubador.co.uk
Web: www.troubador.co.uk/matador


ISBN 9781783061419

British Library Cataloguing in Publication Data.
A catalogue record for this book is available from the British Library.


Printed and bound in the UK by TJ International, Padstow, Cornwall
Typeset by Troubador Publishing Ltd, Leicester, UK

Matador is an imprint of Troubador Publishing Ltd

*For Olive*

With gratitude and special thanks to Anne and Trevor Bannister, without whose encouragement, support and determination, this book would never have progressed beyond the random scribbling of someone 'who would be a writer'.

My debt to Trevor, for his invaluable guidance, patience and sympathetic editing, is immeasurable.

I also offer my heartfelt thanks to Wendy, my long suffering wife, who has supported me throughout this project.

Last, but by no means least, I thank family and friends for their encouragement.

This story unfolds in a county dear to the author's heart. It is, in part, an expression of affection for the glorious county of Dorset and its people.

Places and establishments in the county are described from memory and recollections of them at the time they were last visited. Any departures from current reality will hopefully be excused as resulting from the passage of time and/or the author's imperfect memory.

The story is fiction. It is not intended to relate to, or refer to, any incident or occurrence which may have actually taken place at any time, in Dorset or anywhere else.

The Advisory Council for the Co-ordination of Regional Services (ACCORS) and the Pan African Volunteers Trust (PAVT) are imaginary, as are La Terrazza and L'Isola della Pizza restaurants. None is based on or represents any actual organisation or establishment which may exist.

The villages and the hamlets where this story is set, together with the Beldene Valley, where they lie, exist solely in the imagination of the author. All the characters in the story are fictitious, and are neither based on nor represent anyone living, or who has ever lived. Their beliefs and opinions, as expressed in the narrative, are not meant to reflect those of the author or anyone associated with this book.

Hopefully, you will enjoy meeting them and getting to know them, during the course of:

**A Year at Nethercombe Ley**

# CONTENTS

# JANUARY

## A New Start

The pale winter sun had lost its struggle with encroaching dusk, and lights already glowed through closed curtains around the village green, as Harry emerged from the trees and neatly trimmed hedges lining Manor Hill. A Christmas tree still twinkled in a window, defying the cheerless mid winter gloom, as if unwilling to acknowledge the passing of the festive season.

Light spilled from the windows of *The Black Bull*, but the village shop was in darkness as he drove past, peering intently to read a sign half hidden by an overgrown bush. He made out '*The Pound*' through the foliage and turned into the narrow lane, reflecting on how different everything looked from that summer day when the estate agent had first shown him May Cottage. Calling it a cottage was stretching a point. The deeds confirmed it to be a Victorian villa, which its decorative brick facade and slate roof suggested. It was a good deal larger than the older cottages on either side and set further back from the lane, at the end of a gravelled drive. A five-bedroomed house was too big for someone living alone, but the previous owners had needed a quick sale, and the asking price had been tempting. He only intended it to be a stop-gap, so whatever it was, it would suit him for the present.

Harry recognised the large, unkempt magnolia at the entrance to his new home and looked up as his headlights swept across the patterned brickwork and the tyres crunched on the gravelled driveway. The dark, lifeless house seemed to exude the depression he felt, and he switched off the engine, to sit for a few moments in quiet contemplation before going in.

He was now nearer fifty than forty. After twenty-two years of marriage, Sally had left him for a new life and a new love. His daughter was at university and his son had turned his back on him. He was alone.

He could remember the dread he felt as he had approached his fortieth birthday, and realised that he could no longer think of himself as a young man. But little did he know that his contented and comfortable life with Sally and his adored children was destined to fall apart.

Sally had been his only serious girlfriend, so perhaps he had allowed himself to become too comfortable; even taken her for granted. A modestly successful businessman, who enjoyed golf, the theatre, visits to restaurants and dinner parties with their circle of friends; he could now see how dull and complacent he had become.

Why had he not noticed the signs of Sally's frustration? Once the children were virtually off their hands, her dissatisfaction with her own unfulfilled ambitions had crystallised into resentment at being, what she considered, little more than the supportive wife. Having been the secretary of a company director before the children arrived, she had begun to hanker for something more challenging than her part-time job at a local garden centre. She had eventually been offered a position as a secretary in a local firm of media consultants. Never one to do things by half, she had embraced the opportunity whole-heartedly. Promotion to the position of PA to a senior executive had soon followed; and it was then that Harry's world had started to crumble.

At first, the occasional evening she worked late had hardly registered, and he had been happy to support her in a career that was obviously important to her. But the occasional late evening had soon become the norm, interspersed with nights away, when she was *needed at a conference*. Harry was not sure when it had first dawned on him, but all the small clues; the stylish new clothes and hairdos; the disappearance of the little touches and caresses, and the absence of simple endearments, each in themselves insignificant, had soon added up to one terrifying conclusion. Sick with foreboding, he had eventually forced himself to confront her; longing for her to angrily reject his accusation. But she had tearfully confessed. She was in love with Jonathan Robertson, her company's legal consultant. To compound his misery, she had even expressed relief that he had spared her the anguish of having to find a way to break it to him. It had been the final straw. He had broken down and cried in a way he had not done since his teenage years, and the death of his much-loved grandmother. Sally had cried too; with remorse for his pain and confusion. Overcome with grief, he had clung to her, holding her for the last time; his tears glistening in her hair.

He had not begged her to stay, as he had desperately wanted to. Had he done so, she may have taken pity on him and relented. But for how long, and at what price to her happiness and his self-respect? She was no longer in love with him. Soon afterwards she had moved in with her lover, leaving Harry in despair, and with his emotions in turmoil. His relationship with their son Adam had been the major casualty of the misery and heartache that had consumed him.

Adam had borne the brunt of his father's moodiness and what he referred to as 'gutlessness'; rebuking Harry for 'not putting up a fight to save his marriage and the family', and 'standing by pathetically, while another man took his wife.' Harry had reacted angrily; what did a kid with no experience of life know? What did the young fool expect him to do, drag his mother back by her hair? Thankfully, their daughter, Debbie, had been at university in Reading, and was spared the sudden mood changes and aura of helplessness surrounding her father.

The arguments had become more uncompromising. Adam had eventually moved in with his mother for a short while, until he had taken his exams and found a summer job on the east coast with one of his friends. Harry rarely heard from him now.

He had not been able to summon up the will or the energy to contest the divorce. However, Sally had protected his interests far more effectively than he had been prepared to, and had settled for a fair split of everything, except for his business partnership. Ignoring the advice of Jonathan and her solicitor, she had insisted that it remain entirely his.

She and Jonathan had been married just before Christmas, which for Harry, had made it just as miserable as the previous one. His parents had celebrated their fiftieth wedding anniversary earlier in the year, but the shock of his marriage breakup and his distress had constrained his mother's ability to celebrate wholeheartedly. His father had said little, which was his way of coping with anything he found difficult to deal with.

Adam had put in a brief appearance on Christmas Day, but it had been Debbie who had provided the only joy of the so-called festive season. She had tried to lift Harry's spirits with her sunny smile and youthful exuberance, but seeing Sally in so many of her gestures and mannerisms had also served as a poignant reminder of his loss.

\* \* \*

The *tick ... tick* of the cooling engine was the only sound to break the stillness as Harry shifted his unfocused gaze from the dull reflection of his BMW in a window, to look up at the dark, unwelcoming building that was his new home; the one he had chosen as a sanctuary from the wreckage of his life and the job that no longer gave him satisfaction.

The sympathy of colleagues and the few friends who remained in contact had been unbearable, and he had soon tired of being invited to dinner out of sympathy or a sense of duty. Worse still were the invitations from acquaintances wanting all the 'lurid details' of the break-up. On one occasion he had found an unattached female seated next to him, and he had suffered the embarrassment of trying to be polite, without conveying the impression that he wanted anything more.

He did not want a relationship; not yet! He needed time to piece his life back together. A new start.

Harry woke the following morning to the trill of a bird outside the window. He felt stiff from having slept on the camp bed he had brought with him, and slightly disorientated by the unfamiliar surroundings. It was so different from the traffic noise that used to assault his ears each morning, and for a few moments he lay contentedly enjoying the comparative silence. The beam of watery sunshine lighting up one wall of his bedroom reminded him that he needed to put up a curtain rail and hang the curtains his mother had made.

He had wanted change, and this was it; almost complete silence. No traffic; no radio blaring out thumping rhythms; no unbearable morning cheer of programme presenters; no need to hurry. In fact no need to get up. For the first time in years, he was free to do as he liked, which in itself was a problem. He had no idea what he was going to do to fill the day.

The bedside clock showed almost seven-thirty. There had been no reason to set the alarm the previous night and he had slept a full hour past the time he normally got up. Getting out of bed and stretching, he was in time to see the sun disappear behind an ominous cloudbank, and the branches of the magnolia sway in a gust of wind that bent the spindly tops of the tall conifers bordering his neighbour's property. The lane beyond the shrubbery at the front of the house was devoid of traffic, and the house opposite hidden behind hedges and trees.

"Well, Harry my boy; you wanted peace and quiet, and you've got it," he said to himself, as he pulled out a t-shirt and jeans from one of his suitcases and searched in vain for his slippers.

He shivered as he entered the bathroom. He would have to find someone to look at the central heating. The room was small compared to what he had been used to, with a shower over the bath instead of a separate cubicle, but it was perfectly adequate for his needs. At least there was a separate W.C. on both floors. There was no need to shave. What a luxury!

The kitchen seemed even larger than he remembered and was what he had always imagined a typical country kitchen should be, with a flagstone floor and windows almost the length of one wall. It looked out on a large, overgrown garden that Sally would love. He could imagine her eyes lighting up at the thought of "re-doing it", as she would put it. But Sally would never see it. Steeling himself, he fought back the tears pricking the backs of his eyes, triggered by the empty house and his solitude.

Breakfast! That was it! Where was that coffee and bread he had brought with him? He had put bacon, eggs, sausages and milk and butter in the fridge last night. Now, where was the damned thing? The fridge-freezer and dish-washer were hidden behind wooden facades which matched the cupboard doors, and together with the worktops and the varnished oak table and chairs he had purchased from the previous owners, reminded him of a deserted bar-room. He found the fridge; a huge, American-style affair. All he needed now were the kettle and the toaster. Now, what had he done with those?

He had his breakfast sizzling nicely in the pan, when the door-bell rang. The *ding-dong* was slightly off-key and he made a mental note to change the batteries. He opened the front door, expecting it to be the removal men bringing his furniture from storage, but found a slim woman, wearing a dark raincoat and a bright red rain hat with a floppy brim, standing in the small porch, shaking raindrops from a multi-coloured umbrella. Harry guessed she was probably in her mid forties.

"Yes?" he asked tentatively.

"Oh hello, I'm Marjorie Alders," she announced in a light, nasal voice, as if she thought he ought to be expecting her.

"Hello," Harry replied. "I'm Harry Simmonds."

"Pleased to meet you, Mr. Simmonds. I hope you don't mind me calling so early, but I'm on my way to work."

"Not at all. What can I do for you Mrs. Alders?"

"Didn't Mr. Clarkson mention me?"

"Mr. Clarkson?"

"Yes; the estate agent," she prompted hopefully.

"Oh, yes; of course!" Harry exclaimed, as the penny dropped. "No he didn't I'm afraid."

"I live near the Memorial Hall," she continued. "I used to clean for

Mr. and Mrs. Williams, the previous owners; two mornings and one afternoon a week. Mr. Clarkson promised to speak to you about whether you wanted me to carry on."

"I'm afraid he hasn't said anything about it," Harry said, to her evident disappointment. "But it sounds like a good idea. Would you like to come in and discuss it?"

Mrs. Alder's face brightened. "I'm afraid I can't stop; I'm on my way to work. My husband's waiting out in the car. I work Mondays and Wednesdays in the shop at the service station up on the high road. I saw the light on and thought I'd pop in to see what the situation was, while I was passing."

"I'm glad you did," Harry replied.

"Would it be alright to come back tomorrow morning?" she asked hopefully.

"Yes, please do."

A smile broke out on the woman's face for the first time, as she backed out of the porch and raised her umbrella.

"See you tomorrow then," she called.

Harry closed the door, and then remembering his breakfast, rushed to the kitchen.

"Well, I've made a start. Got a cleaner already," he said out loud. Sally would be impressed. Damn! He had to stop thinking about what Sally would do or say!"

His furniture arrived soon after breakfast. Each item and packing case had been labelled to indicate the room allocated to it, so he put on a thick sweater and left the removal men to get on with it, while he made the short walk to the village shop for a newspaper. Despite the recent shower and the ominous dark clouds, it was not particularly cold; except when the occasional sharp gust swayed the bare branches of the oaks bordering the village green. Behind *The Black Bull*, the church spire rose above the treetops, its weathered stone dappled by rain. He felt invigorated by the clear, fresh air on his face and the comforting sigh of the wind in the branches overhead.

The interior of the shop was surprisingly modern; belying its drab exterior. It was laid out like a small supermarket, and brightly lit, with central shelving and a post office counter at the far end. There were only two other customers; a young mother with a toddler in a push-chair and an elderly chap in a heavy coat, who was unloading the contents of a wire basket beside the till. He and the white-coated woman behind the counter broke off their conversation as Harry entered.

"Good morning," Harry said and picked up a copy of *The Daily Telegraph* from the rack inside the door. The elderly man nodded and the woman smiled.

"We 'aven't seen you before." She spoke with a strong West Country accent, and the statement was obviously more in the nature of a question.

"I'm Harry Simmonds. I've just moved into May Cottage ... in *The Pound*," Harry said.

"Oh well; welcome to Nethercombe," said the woman with a smile. "I hope you'll be very 'appy here."

"Thank you, I'm sure I will." Harry replied, concealing his amusement at her inconsistent use of 'aitches'.

"I'm Peggy Flowers," she continued. "If you want to order your papers, we can keep them for you, but we can't deliver, I'm afraid. We can't get nobody to take over Wayne's paper round, now the Burtons have gone."

Harry thought of asking if they had '*gone for a burton*', but thought better of it. "Do I need to order them?" he asked. "There are plenty in the rack."

"It's safer to," Peggy replied. "They're sometimes gone by mid-day."

"Thass right!" The elderly man was suddenly animated. "I come for my *Echo* last Friday and some bugger'd taken it."

"Now, now Albert, I wasn't 'ere last week, and Lisa forgot to keep yours back. But I let you read mine, didn't I?"

"Thass not the point. I always 'as the *Echo*!"

"In that case, I'd like the *Telegraph* and the *Sunday Telegraph* please," said Harry, adding, "Is *The Echo* a local paper?"

"There's two," Peggy replied, opening a ledger on the counter. "There's *The Daily Echo* and *The Dorset Echo*."

"Well I'd better order a copy of both for the time being," Harry replied. "As I don't know Dorset, it will keep me up to date on what's going on."

I likes *The Dorset Echo!*" Albert suggested.

Peggy began writing in her ledger. "Ted, my 'usband, prefers *The Daily Echo*. 'E likes the sport. 'E's from Bournemouth; 'e follows the football team."

"I see," said Harry.

"Will there be anything else?" Peggy asked, looking up.

"I need batteries for my doorbell; AA size I think."

"The batteries are over by the door. Will you or your wife be wantin' any magazines ordered?"

"No thanks … I'm on my own," Harry answered quietly.

"Oh," was all Peggy said, but it spoke volumes.

Suspecting that he was in the presence of an experienced interrogator, Harry paid for the newspaper and a carton of batteries, and left, before anything more could be extracted from him.

* * *

The gusting wind rose steadily through the morning, driving brief, but heavy showers before it. After the removal men had left, Harry started to arrange items of his furniture in what the estate agent's brochure had described as '*a generously proportioned sitting room of distinctive character*'.

He had earmarked the room between the sitting room and the kitchen, which was technically the dining room, as his study. The '*generous proportions*' of the sitting room easily accommodated his furniture; the raised floor in front of the french windows at the far end, being ideal for the dining table and chairs.

The wardrobes and drawers in the main bedroom were fitted, and all he needed to do was make the bed. There was no urgency about putting up pictures or arranging the furniture in the other bedrooms, so he left everything else where the removal men had put it, and leaving the unpacked boxes stacked against one wall of the sitting room, settled in his favourite armchair with a mug of coffee, to read the newspaper.

By mid afternoon the squally showers had given way to a pale blue sky, streaked with the tattered remnants of purple and magnolia tinted clouds. After a late lunch, Harry decided to start exploring his new surroundings, in the brief remaining daylight. Slipping on his shower-proof jacket and the hiking boots he had once bought on a family holiday in the Lake District, he made his way along the lane in the direction of the hills he could see from his kitchen window.

Walking steadily away from the village, between the grass verges of the lane, brought him to a wooden signpost, one arm of which denoted that straight ahead led to Garstone and Belmont Lovall. Another, bearing the legend *Garstone Farm*, indicated a rutted track, which meandered across a boggy field towards a cluster of barns. The third pointed towards a path between two grey-stone cottages, with the words *Hallows Hill.*

The garden on one side of the narrow path was unkempt and neglected, with an old bathtub and various abandoned household appliances half buried amongst the weeds. At the far end, a rusty, corrugated-iron hut was fighting an unequal battle with waist high nettles. On the other side the garden was well tended. In the centre of a lawn, surrounded by shrubs and plants, a child's swing swayed in the breeze, with a few brightly coloured plastic toys scattered across the grass beneath it.

It reminded Harry of the carefree, golden days when Debbie and Adam had been toddlers playing in the sunshine; all so long ago. He swallowed hard to clear the lump in his throat. Would he ever be happy again?

At the end of the gardens, the track rose steadily between briar and brambles towards a copse, just below the summit of the hill. Harry was breathing heavily by the time he reached it; a reminder of how sedentary his life had become. Gusts of wind tormented the overhanging branches, showering him with cascades of moisture, as he made his way along the steep, muddy path towards a stile set in an overgrown hedgerow.

Beyond the stile, the copse gave way to scrubland, interspersed with gorse and an occasional tree, whose bare branches raked the blue, rain-washed sky like wizened claws. The wind was stronger at the summit, gusting and moaning sibilantly, and tugging at Harry's clothes. He turned his back to it and gazed out at the barren fields, spread below in a mosaic of browns, greens and russet hues. A solitary shaft of pale sunlight reflected off water somewhere beyond the glistening rooftops lining Manor Hill, and below him a wisp of smoke floated lazily from a cottage chimney, swirling and dispersing on the wind as it rose above the surrounding treetops.

He had dreamed of a life in the country, with its quieter and gentler rhythm of life, but he had never imagined it without Sally. Perhaps if he had made it happen, instead of indulging in pipe dreams, Sally would be here with him. He shook his head. The idyllic rural backwater was his dream, not hers. She had left him because she had sacrificed so much for him and their children, in exchange for what she saw as a life of unfulfilled ambition.

He had asked himself endlessly how he had managed to miss the change in her; without ever really reaching an answer. But had she changed, or had he never really known her? At first, he had attributed it all to the stimulation of her new job, and a sense of release from years of the responsibilities of motherhood. But, in his heart, he knew it was more than that. Sally was not that shallow.

In contrast to his own contentment and, as he would now admit, complacency, she had no longer found their marriage satisfying or fulfilling. His pain and confusion had been compounded by the thought of her with another man. Even now, and especially when his spirits were at a low ebb, the anguish returned; a dull ache that bruised his soul.

Dark, menacing clouds on the horizon and the fading light suggested it was time to start back. He had almost reached the stile, when a dull rumble seemed to emanate from beneath his feet. Rasping snorts were getting closer, and suspecting the presence of an unseen bull, he made a dash for the stile. He had just thrown his leg across it, when the crown of a red and black quartered helmet appeared above the brow of the hill, followed by the tufted tips of a horse's ears.

11

The horse slowed to a walk as it crested the rise, and like its rider, turned its head towards him. Feeling a little foolish at his momentary panic, he watched them approach, fascinated by the grace of the animal and the sinuous power of its muscles as it moved.

But it was the rider that held his attention. She was tall and slim, and handled her mount with elegant ease, as she guided it towards him. When she leaned forward to pat its neck, wisps of hair, the colour of harvest corn, fluttered at the nape of her neck, where the tail of a braided plait hung, tied with a blue ribbon.

Harry's pulse quickened as her blue eyes met his and she greeted him with an engaging smile. "Hi! We don't see many hikers at this time of year."

Harry felt his cheeks redden, betraying his innate shyness. "Actually, I'm not hiking. I've just moved in at Nethercombe Ley," he said, remembering to pronounce it 'Nethercum Lee', as the locals did.

"Oh, then you'll be getting a visit from my brother soon," she chuckled.

"Will I?" Harry replied, puzzled.

She grinned impishly. "Yes, he's the rector of St. Luke's. Simon likes to introduce himself to potential new customers."

Harry smiled. "I see. Well, I'll look forward to his visit. I'm Harry Simmonds. I live at May Cottage … in The Pound."

"Oh, the Williams old place." She pulled off her glove and extended a slim, well-manicured hand. "I'm Rachel; Rachel Cornish."

"Nice to meet you Rachel," Harry replied, careful not to squeeze or hold on for more than a moment.

The horse snorted and stamped, tossing its head restlessly, and she ruffled its forelock. "Steady Monty," she murmured, before turning back to Harry. "He's impatient to get home, I'm afraid."

"I'd better be getting back," Harry replied. "I've still got a lot of unpacking to do."

"It was nice meeting you, Harry," she said, turning the horse away from the stile. "If you're ever at a loose end, we're often in *The Black Bull* at weekends, when I'm staying with Simon."

"Thanks," Harry replied, and as she urged her mount into a trot, he stifled a childish impulse to wave.

Mrs. Alders appeared the next morning, while Harry was having his breakfast. It surprised him to notice, that without the restraining rain hat, her hair was shoulder length, black and wavy, with the merest hint of grey at her temples. She wore a light, quilted jacket over a white t-shirt and jeans, which accentuated the slimness of her figure.

Harry led her into the kitchen.

"Oh, I didn't mean to interrupt your breakfast!" she exclaimed.

"It's no problem," Harry replied."I've almost finished anyway. Why don't we have a coffee while you fill me in on anything you think I ought to know or do, and when I need to do it. But more importantly, what I should pay you. Please, take a seat."

Mrs. Alders hesitated before pulling out a chair, while Harry lifted a mug from the mug-tree and poured from the cafetiere. "Help yourself to milk," he said. "I don't think I have any sugar, I'm afraid."

"Thank you. I don't take sugar," she replied.

"What did you do for the former owners?" Harry asked.

"I used to do the downstairs and toilets and bathroom on Tuesdays and Friday mornings," she replied. "I did upstairs on Thursday afternoons. I usually gave the lounge another quick hoover and dust as well, if there was time."

"That's sounds fine," Harry said. "Look, I don't have much experience of this sort of thing; my wife used to handle it. I'm divorced by the way."

"I see," she replied, giving him the impression he had not told her anything she did not already know.

"How should I pay you?" he continued.

"Well … Mrs. Williams paid me on Fridays."

"In cash?" Harry prompted.

"Usually," she said, clearly uncomfortable discussing the subject.

"How much?" Harry asked.

Mrs. Alders hesitated, "Thirty pounds."

"For three days?" he asked incredulously.

She looked down at her coffee, avoiding his gaze. "Well, if it's too much?"

"No; of course not!" Harry replied quickly. "It doesn't seem enough. How many hours did you work?"

She looked up in surprise. "Between two and two-and-a-half hours a day; it depended."

Harry did some quick mental arithmetic. "That's only four pounds an hour. It's well below the minimum wage!"

"But it was unofficial, as Mrs Williams used to say. I'm happy with that."

"If you say so," said Harry, doubtfully.

"Well, if you're satisfied, shall I make a start?" she suggested, and stood up, cradling her mug in both hands.

"Yes, if it's alright with you. I'm perfectly happy," Harry replied.

Knowing her way around the house, she made her way to the tall cupboard in the lobby that led off the kitchen to the garden. Hanging up her coat, she opened the cupboard door, took one look and turned towards him. "I don't suppose you've had time to unpack your cleaning stuff?"

"Oh, I'm sorry; it's in there," Harry said, and pointed to a cardboard box behind her.

Mrs. Alders squatted on her haunches and opened the flaps. "Is this all of it?"

"I'm afraid so," Harry replied sheepishly.

"Have you got a hoover or a broom?" she asked.

"Yes, the hoover's in the sitting room; the broom is upstairs, somewhere." He stood up and pushed away his chair. "I'll go and get them."

"No, you carry on with your breakfast. I'll get them when I'm ready," she said, and began unloading the box and placing its meagre contents in the cupboard. Harry stood up with the intention of clearing the table.

"Leave that to me," she ordered. "I'm sure you've got more important things to do."

Harry did not have the heart to tell her he hadn't.

"What do we need by way of cleaning things?" he asked. "Can you make up a list?"

"I can get them if you like," she answered. "It might be easier."

"Thanks, I'll get my wallet,"

"There's no need; you can pay me on Friday," she replied, already loading the dishwasher. "There is one thing," she added, tentatively.

"What's that?"

"I was wondering how I'll get in if you're not here."

"I hadn't thought of that," Harry replied. "How did it work before?"

"I had a key," she said tentatively. "But it's a bit too soon for that."

Harry shook his head. "No; that'll be fine."

"Are you sure?" she asked.

"Yes; there are a couple of spare sets on the window sill. Please take one."

He decided to look purposeful by inspecting the garden. The estate agent's 'blurb' had described it as '*extensive, with fruit trees and panoramic views*', but he had not really taken a great deal of notice during his previous visits.

The initial impression was uninspiring. Weeds were growing between the grubby flagstones on the patio that stretched the length of the house, and on which stood one or two randomly placed terra-cotta pots containing the ragged remains of unidentifiable plants. At either end of the patio, two wide steps led down to a large, unkempt lawn, studded with dandelions and patches of moss and clover. The shrubs and plants bordering the grass were just as unappealing, but he was relieved to observe that the overgrown leylandii, that formed an ugly, straggling barrier along one side, were rooted on his neighbour's side of the wire fence. The boundary on the other side of his garden was marked by a wooden fence, topped by a neatly clipped privet hedge.

The rest of the garden, beyond the lawn, was screened by a trellis entangled with the winter deadwood of what appeared to be a well-established clematis, and pierced by an arched gateway. Walking across the damp grass, he realised he was still wearing his slippers, but decided against returning to the house to change them. Beyond the gate, a small aluminium-framed greenhouse and a wooden shed, both appearing to be in reasonable condition, stood on either side of a weed infested patch of ground that bore a few nondescript fruit bushes.

The rotted remains of windfall apples and leaves lay at the foot of a line of trees which seemed to stand at the extremity of his property. But as he approached, he could see another grassy area beyond them. In the farthest corner, stone steps led up to a raised, paved area, where a wooden park bench faced meadows and the distant hills. A tangled, shoulder-high hedge of hawthorn and briar marked the true limit of his domain. He could imagine the pleasure of sitting on the bench on summer evenings, and with a contented smile, carefully made his way back towards the house.

"Mornin'."

Harry looked up in surprise as he ducked under a branch and emerged from the trees. The owner of the voice was leaning on the adjoining fence, where the dividing privet ended. Harry judged him to be seventy-ish, and from the ruddy face, topped by a flat cap, that he had spent his working life on the land.

Conscious that his slippers and socks were soaking wet, Harry made his way gingerly over to the fence and held out his hand. "Good morning! I'm Harry Simmonds. I've just moved in."

His neighbour nodded and grasped his hand. He did not offer his name in reply, but the firm handshake from a rough, calloused hand reinforced Harry's initial impression.

"The missus an' me seen you about. On yer own are yuh?"

"Yes," Harry replied, and to head off the obvious follow-up question, he continued; "I was just having a look at the garden. There seems to be a fair bit to do to bring it up to scratch."

"Right you are. The Williamses weren't much o' gardeners. She 'ad a go, but 'e weren't that bothered. Let it all go, 'e did."

"You appear to be quite an expert," Harry replied, gesturing towards his neighbour's well-tended vegetable patch. "I'd be grateful for some advice. Being a pen-pusher, I don't know much about growing things. My wife was the gardener." He had said it without thinking, but, to his relief, there was no reaction or indication that the old chap was curious about his wife's whereabouts.

"I dunno about expert, but Ellen an' me been 'ere nigh on forty year. We picked it up by trial an' error."

"Were you a farmer?" Harry asked.

"No, I worked fer the council … on the roads."

Harry suppressed a smile, as his assumption crashed in flames.

"But if you want them trees looked at, you oughtta talk to Alfie Cox. 'E worked in the council parks fer years after 'e left the army. What 'e don't know ain't worth worryin' about."

"Thanks, I will," Harry replied. "Where can I reach him?"

"*The Kings 'Ead*, up on the 'igh road's yer best bet. Enjoys a pint does Alfie."

"Thanks very much," Harry repeated. "I'll have to do something about those leylandii too."

"Damn nuisance they are," the old chap said. "You gotta keep 'em trimmed back. I can't abide 'em."

"Do you think the people on that side would mind if I cut them back?" Harry asked.

"Don't matter if they do. You got the right to cut off whatever grows over on your side."

"Have I?"

"That's the law. As long as you gives 'em back what you cut off, or at least offers it to 'em. I doubt they'd want it though."

"What are they like?" Harry asked.

"'Bout your age, I suppose. Don't 'ave much to do with 'em. They moved in two or three year ago. They're both out at work all day; on'y sees 'em weekends. They seems alright. Don't mix a lot … leastways, not

17

with the likes of us. They're chummy wi' that lot on t'other side o'the green."

"I see," Harry said, aware that his wet feet were becoming numb with cold. "It's been nice meeting you, but I'd better go in and get my feet dry."

The old chap looked down at his sodden slippers and chuckled. "It's wellies weather this time a'year," he said.

For the rest of the month, most of Harry's time was occupied with his resignation from Eldon Management Services and settling into his new home. He unpacked and stowed away his possessions, arranged his furniture, and purchased and put together a flat-pack desk in his study. He organised the installation of cable TV and made arrangements for broadband access.

The curtains in the sitting room and bedrooms were eventually hung with the invaluable help of Marjorie Alders, who was turning out to be what his mother would call 'a treasure'. Under her *regime*, May Cottage sparkled, down to the gleaming brass knocker on the front door. She had even taken over his laundry, mildly chastising him for using the tumble dryer on a fine day, instead of 'hanging things out for a good blow' as she put it.

Among the cards he received, was one from Sally, with the simple message '*Wishing you happiness in your new home*', which he knew to be sincere, but it still tore at his heart strings. Her mother, Grace, also sent a card, with a simple reminder to '*keep in touch*'.

His mother's rambling letter had been full of 'chin up' and 'keep smiling' clichés; intended to cheer him up, although it only served to depress him. However much she pretended otherwise, he suspected that she would never be able to bring herself to forgive Sally.

A couple of days after his conversation with his neighbour, Harry answered the door to a plump, grey haired woman, with an engaging smile, who introduced herself as 'Rob's wife from next door'. She presented him with a covered porcelain dish.

"I thought you might like this," she said. "Rob said you was on your own. We was given a leg o'lamb; too much fer just the two of us, so I made the rest into shepherd's pie. I thought you might like some."

She politely refused his invitation to come in for coffee, but Harry was touched by the gesture, and promised himself that he would return the kindness, whenever an opportunity arose. The shepherd's pie was, as he expected, delicious.

The high spot was one Friday afternoon, when he happened to look out of one of the sitting room windows, and saw Debbie walking up the drive, wearing a backpack and a sunny smile. He dashed to the front door and yanked it open just as she reached it and threw herself into his arms.

"Hello dad; how are you?" she exclaimed, as he hugged her.

"All the better for this wonderful surprise!" he mumbled into her hair. "Why didn't you tell me you were coming? I would have picked you up!"

"I wanted to surprise you!"

"It's a lovely surprise, but how did you get here?" he asked, helping her off with her coat.

"I caught the train. I had to change at Basingstoke. I got the bus from Dorchester. The driver told me where to get off … near the shops by the housing estate. It's a long walk down that hill, but worth it, to see you."

"You should have called me. I could have picked you up at the station!" Harry protested.

"Never mind, I'm here now; I'm hungry though."

Debbie's appetite was usually modest, but she demolished an omelette with obvious relish and even managed a slice of Grandma Marian's sponge cake. With a mixture of pride and wonder, Harry was content to watch while she ate, and listen to her chatter about university life, her friends, and what was going on in Reading. She was obviously happy, which, as he had come to realise, was the most important thing in life.

"Why don't you let me help you buy a car?" he asked, during a brief lull in their decidedly one-sided conversation.

"Dad; we've been through all that!" she replied emphatically. "I don't need one and I've got nowhere to park it. It's only twenty minutes to most of my lectures; I'm on a good bus route. Melinta's got a car if we're going anywhere. You've done enough for me already. I won't have a huge debt hanging round my neck when I graduate; unlike most of the others."

"Well, at least let me give you a lift home."

"I've got a return ticket! At that price, I've got no intention of wasting it!"

Harry laughed. She was her mother's daughter where value for money was concerned. "Well to Dorchester then."

"OK; cool. I've brought some clothes in my bag; I wasn't planning on going back until Monday, if that's alright with you."

"Of course it is!" he replied delightedly. "Stay as long as you like!"

They spent the rest of the day in the sitting room, with their feet up in front of the log fire, catching up on each other's news, which in Harry's case was not all that much. Inevitably, the conversation came round to Adam. But Harry's hopes that Debbie had more current news of her brother were unfulfilled.

"The last time I spoke to him was at Christmas," she said wistfully. "He hardly ever calls me these days. I've tried calling him, but I think he may have a new mobile, because I can never get through."

Harry sighed. "Christmas was the only time I've spoken to him in months. I don't know where he's living or what he doing; not that it's any great surprise. I think he's finished with me once and for all."

"Don't say that, dad. He'll get over it eventually; you'll see."

Harry had intended to take her to *The Black Bull* for dinner, but by early evening an unrelenting, icy drizzle had set in, so they were content to eat at home.

The following day dawned dry, but dull and cold, and after breakfast they donned coats and scarves for a tour of the village. Debbie looked fresh and lovely in a fetching, white, knitted beret, topped by a red pompom. Buoyed up with paternal pride, Harry played the proud father, missing no opportunity to 'show her off' to anyone they met; in particular Ted and Peggy, when they called in at the shop to pick up his newspaper.

"I wouldn't a'thought your dad was old enough to 'ave a grown up daughter," Peggy said flatteringly, as Harry introduced her.

"Well, she can be thankful she didn't get her looks from 'im," Ted interjected with a wicked grin. "I presume she 'as her mother to thank for that."

"I came here for a newspaper, not to be insulted," Harry reposted.

"So where d'you usually go then?" Ted chuckled.

Harry laughed and looked at Debbie. "Forget what I said about it being a friendly place."

"You can give as good as you get!" she giggled.

"So what are you studying at university, Debbie?" Ted asked.

"I'm doing a BSc in Meteorology and Climatology."

"So, are we goin' t'see you on telly, waving your 'ands about in front of a map?"

Debbie laughed. "I shouldn't think so. The Met Office is one option when I graduate, but there are others."

"Oh, I see," said Ted, and raising his eyebrows at Harry, he grinned. "Intelligent women frighten me. I can't imagine being married to one."

"Thanks very much!" Peggy exclaimed, and Ted rolled his eyes. "Oh God! In the dog 'ouse again!"

"I think we'd better go and leave Ted to finish digging his own grave," Harry chuckled.

When they left the shop, Debbie tucked her hand under her father's arm, and circling the village green, they made their way between the aged cottages lining the gentle slope of Church Lane. In the trees behind the churchyard, the rooks kept up a raucous chorus among the skeletal branches, like a coven of demented witches. A squirrel stared at them from the eaves of the lychgate roof, twitching its tail in agitation as they passed.

"It's very pretty here, isn't it!" Debbie exclaimed, as they strolled between the manicured hedges and lawns of a lane known as *The Meadowcroft*. Admiring the impressive residences on either side, she added, "I'll bet some of these places cost a packet."

"I wouldn't think you'd get much change from a million for even the small ones," Harry replied, returning the wave of an attractive woman with short blond hair, who was raking up leaves from her expansive lawn.

"Who's that?" Debbie asked.

"Mrs. Spenser-Smith; I think her name's Cheryl. I've spoken to her once or twice in the shop. She seems friendly. I've no idea what her husband does to be able to afford a place like that."

"So that's what you get up to!" she replied mischievously, "Chatting up your neighbours' wives. You should be looking for a rich widow."

"You can cut that out!" Harry chuckled. "I don't need you *and* your Grandma trying to get me married off again."

Their morning ramble led to the discovery that, after half a mile or so, *The Meadowcroft* gave way to a narrow track. They followed it along the side of a large barn, skirting sloping fields, until they came to a wooden footbridge over a stream. On the other side, a pathway led into Mill Lane and back between more modest dwellings to the village green.

* * *

By midday, the dull overcast had given way to periods of pale sunshine, which afforded little warmth, but nevertheless made everything look more cheerful. After a lunchtime snack, Harry suggested a trip to Sherborne, where they spent a pleasant afternoon 'mooching' around the shops in and around Cheap Street and the town centre. Harry thought it one of the nicest and most appealing places to do so … if you enjoy that sort of thing.

They found the Priory fascinating, and were intrigued by the curious mediaeval structure known as The Conduit. The only disappointment was finding the museum closed. However, both of them considered the town delightful and well worth another visit. With the light fading, they enjoyed tea and homemade cake at *Kafe Fontana*, before starting for home.

Knowing Debbie loved Chinese food, Harry suggested dinner at *The Golden Lantern* that evening. It was situated on the high road, and although it had been open for only a few months, it had acquired an excellent reputation.

Watching Debbie's deft use of chopsticks bemused him. He had never been able to eat with them. His attempts to do so usually achieved nothing more than cramp in the heel of his hand; much to the amusement of his family. So deciding that 'lack of cool' was preferable to hunger and pain, he opted for a fork.

Reading his expression, Debbie grinned and her eyes sparkled mischievously.

"You can laugh, but at least I'll get more in my mouth than in my lap!" he said.

He waited for her to stop laughing before he asked the question which had been on his mind for some time. "Have you given serious thought to what you want to do when you graduate, and where you might live?"

"I'm trying to keep my options open," she replied thoughtfully. "But I'm looking quite seriously at the Environment Agency. There seem to be possibilities there that could be interesting."

"I'm not trying to interfere. Whatever you choose to do is fine with me; as long as you're happy," Harry said quietly. "The reason I ask is you've worked damned hard and I'm very proud of you. So if you want to take your time before deciding, there's no rush. If you want to let your hair down; take a sabbatical or something …"

"You've done enough already dad. I can never repay you."

"Who said anything about repaying me? You're my daughter; my own flesh and blood. I've done no more than I should do … or wish to."

She patted his arm. "I know, but it's time I stood on my own feet. Some of us are thinking of going on holiday after we graduate, but only for a week. It depends on what job opportunities come up. But I want to start work and put my studies to good use. I don't know where I'm going to live; it will depend on where the job is."

"I know it's not what you'd choose, but you know you're always welcome here; if only as a stop-gap."

"I know. Thanks dad. I *will* come and stay with you from time to time, but I'm not going to sponge off you … or mum."

"It's nothing of the sort!"

"I know you'll always be there for me. Deep down, so does Adam."

"I doubt that!" Harry retorted.

"Alright; let's change the subject," she said firmly. "Let's talk about you. What are you going to do with yourself; apart from chatting up rich men's wives in the local shop?"

"I was thinking of making a career of it," he answered, eliciting a splutter of laughter that reminded him once again of her mother.

The next morning, Harry had collected his *Sunday Telegraph* from the shop, and with all its sections spread out on the kitchen table, was finishing his breakfast, when Debbie put in an appearance. She drowsily lowered herself onto a chair opposite him, as he looked up from the paper.

"Sleep well?" he asked, and received a yawn and a nod in reply. "Tea and toast?"

24

"I don't suppose you have any muesli?" she replied.

"I don't keep rabbits," he said with a grin.

"I'll settle for toast," she said and stood up to peer out of the kitchen window. "What's the weather like?"

"Dry, but no good for the beach. You'll get chilblains if you go for a paddle."

"I'll give it a miss then," she replied, adding as an afterthought, "Your garden's a bit of a mess, dad!"

"So, do you fancy a day's gardening?"

"Dream on," she giggled and dropped two slices of bread into the toaster.

Later that morning, they took a leisurely drive along the narrow tree-lined lanes, passing the track leading to Hallows Hill. Harry began to describe it, but Debbie's attention had been captured by a sign for '*Garstone Riding School*'. At Garstone Green, he took the right fork, and after a few miles, the trees receded to reveal a village green, larger than the one at Nethercombe Ley, with a cricket square roped off at the centre and a small wooden pavilion and sightscreen at one end. The board beneath the thirty-mph-limit sign read '*Garstone - twinned with Beauchapelle Sous Bois*'.

"Where's Nethercombe Ley twinned with?" Debbie asked.

"I've no idea; nowhere, as far as I know," Harry replied.

Noticing what appeared to be a charmingly rustic and typically English, country pub on the far side of the green, he asked, "How about trying *The Cricketers* for lunch?"

The charm and appeal of the pub to a visitor from *Beauchapelle Sous Bois*, or anywhere else for that matter, would evaporate the moment they crossed the threshold into the poorly lit interior. The bar to the left of the entrance was crowded and noisy; the deafening babble of raised voices constantly pierced by an incessant cacophony of bleeps, burps, and other dissonant warbling emanating from the fruit machines. The other bar was quieter, but dingy and, to Harry, equally unappealing.

He was all for leaving and trying somewhere else, but Debbie, being younger and less fastidious, insisted, "It's OK; we're here now. Let's check out the menu."

It consisted of the usual three-course basic Sunday roast, with a choice of chicken, pork or beef. The only alternative for vegetarians being something called 'Mushroom Bake'; its unappetising name endorsed by the glutinous mound delivered to a table nearby.

Harry's leek and potato soup was appetizing and turned out to be the best part of the meal. Debbie felt the same about her breaded mushrooms. They both chose chicken for the main course, but it looked and tasted as if it may have been pre-cooked and re-heated. It came with pebble sized baked potatoes and baby Yorkshire puddings, so brittle they shattered like shrapnel on contact with cutlery. The vegetables, although attractively presented in individual serving dishes, were limp and tasteless; leading Harry to wonder aloud if they were leftovers from Christmas, and if the gravy had been supplied by Halfords.

Debbie chided him light-heartedly. "Stop whinging and eat what you can! That's what you used to tell Adam and me!"

They both settled for ice cream as the safest option to finish.

"Well that was an experience; but then, so is toothache!" Harry exclaimed, as they skirted the crushed cigarette ends strewn around a small, open-fronted shelter on one side of the car park. Two shivering girls wearing flimsy dresses sheltered inside, puffing at cigarettes and swigging from bottles of Mangers cider. Their curious conversation, littered with four-letter words, apparently required neither of them to pay any attention to what the other was saying.

"I wonder what happened to civilisation," Harry mused.

"Dad, don't be such a grouch," Debbie giggled.

For a while, they strolled arm-in-arm around the village. The larger houses suggested that their owners were as affluent as those in *The Meadowcroft* at Nethercombe Ley, although, in Harry's opinion, Garstone lacked Nethercombe's charm.

When they arrived back at May Cottage, the fading light and low, threatening clouds led Harry to abandon his idea of taking Debbie for a walk to Hallows Hill. Instead, they settled in front of the sitting room fire for the rest of the day, chatting, half-watching television and enjoying several hot drinks; "To take away the taste of that God-awful meal!" as Harry put it. Neither of them needed much for tea or supper, because as Harry said, "What their lunch lacked in flavour it made up for in density."

It would be a wrench to wave goodbye to his daughter the following morning. Their short time together had been precious. She had lifted his spirits, and he knew it would be a while before he readjusted to the stillness and emptiness of May Cottage, devoid of her chatter and laughter.

Harry eventually received the promised visit from the local vicar, one cold, windy evening at the end of his first month at May Cottage. The tall, broad-shouldered figure, muffled against the biting north easterly, all but filled his porch. In Harry's opinion, he looked more like a rugby flank-forward than his idea of a cleric. Harry guessed he was in his mid-thirties.

A broad smile lit up his handsome face, as he held out a large hand. "Hi, I hope it's not an inconvenient time. I'm Simon Cornish; Rector of St. Luke's."

"No, of course not." Harry grasped his hand. "Harry Simmonds … come in!"

Harry had been looking forward to meeting Reverend Cornish, although he had to admit it had less to do with religious conviction than the possibility of renewing his acquaintance with Rachel.

Even after removing the heavy jacket and enveloping scarf, the rector was still a big man; almost filling the fireside armchair. He wore jeans and a plain, dark sweater over his shirt and dog collar.

"Can I offer you coffee or tea?"

"Oh, coffee please; no sugar!" Simon replied gratefully. "It's a little parky out there."

When Harry returned from the kitchen with two steaming mugs, Simon was gazing around the sitting room, no doubt hoping to glean an impression of his new parishioner.

"Thank you," he said, and taking the mug from Harry, wrapped his large hands around it, before looking up. "I'm here to welcome you to the parish, but not to browbeat you into coming to church," he began.

"Thank you," Harry replied. "I'm afraid I'm not particularly religious."

Simon smiled. "No problem. I'm available when needed, regardless of whether or not people choose to endure my sermons."

Harry grinned. "If you don't mind me saying so, you don't look like the average person's idea of a clergyman."

A broad smile lit up Simon's face. "I suppose not. My sister, Rachel, says I should have played basketball or been a wrestler; they're better paid. What do you do, Harry?" he asked, casting his eyes towards the open laptop.

"I am … or was a management consultant. I'm also an accountant. Very dull," Harry replied.

"Are those your children?" Simon asked, glancing at the framed photographs of Debbie and Adam on a side table. The question seemed to hang in the air.

"Yes, Debbie's nearly twenty-one. Adam is eighteen. Their mother and I are divorced." It still sounded odd to say it.

"I didn't mean to pry," said Simon, apologetically.

"No need to apologise. Sally has re-married."

Simon nodded sympathetically.

Harry continued. "I came here because I needed to get away from it all; my job and everything that was getting me down."

"I see," Simon said quietly. "And how are things working out?"

"Pretty well," Harry replied. "I know my neighbours on one side, the people at the shop are friendly … and I have a cleaner; Marjorie Alders."

"Oh, good," was all Simon said, giving no indication that he recognised the name.

"Are you married?" Harry asked.

"I was. Zoe was killed in a road accident four years ago."

"Oh God, I'm sorry!" Harry exclaimed.

"We'd only been married for six months," Simon added wistfully.

"Didn't it shake your faith?" Harry asked.

"Yes; at first," Simon replied honestly. "It's sometimes hard to divine or appreciate God's purpose. I suppose it was His will. I drew some comfort from that."

"Rachel told me you frequent *The Black Bull*," Harry said, anxious to change the subject.

"Yes. Rachel works in London all week, but she comes down quite a few weekends; more to see her horse than me, I suspect."

"Monty," Harry chuckled. "I've met him."

"So I understand," Simon said with a grin. Rachel keeps him at Garstone Riding School. Laura … Laura Caxton runs it. She's a friend of ours. She mucks him out and feeds and grooms him. She gives him the odd canter during the week, as well."

The diffident way Simon had mentioned Laura, made Harry wonder if she was perhaps more than a friend.

After another half an hour or so of small talk, Simon stood up. "Look, I've taken up enough of your time. I'd best be off".

"Not at all," Harry replied, but Simon was already shrugging on his coat. He produced a printed sheet from his pocket. "This is all the info; times of our services; names, ranks and serial numbers, etc. You're not religious, I know, and I'm not trying to put pressure on you in any way, but it just might come in handy; if only to light the fire."

Harry laughed. "I not sure about religion, but I'm not really an atheist," he said.

"Well, there you are," Simon replied. "But anyway, you know where I am if you need me."

"Thanks," said Harry.

"My telephone and mobile numbers are on the sheet," Simon added more seriously. "And my e-mail address. You see; the church can be up to date. Just think what Jesus and his disciples could have achieved with modern technology."

"The Gospels in textspeak?" Harry suggested, making Simon chuckle.

Harry had taken an instinctive liking to the unconventional cleric, and decided he would like to know him better; with or without the added attraction of his sister.

'I might just venture a trip to *The Black Bull* one evening,' he thought, when Simon had left.

Feeling relaxed, he flopped into his armchair and stretched out his legs, daring to believe he had taken the first steps on the road to contentment; until the telephone rang.

"Hi dad; it's me ... Adam."

# FEBRUARY

## *One Step at a Time*

Patches of frost; remnants of a bitterly cold few days, clung on defiantly in the shadows and hollows on either side of the road, as Harry reached the outskirts of Wareham. Catching sight of the NatWest Bank as he approached the cross roads in the centre of town, he turned into South Street looking for somewhere to park. A little way past the pillared portico of *The Black Bear Hotel*, he found a car park beside a bridge.

The low winter sun glinted on windows and windscreens, sparkling on the river in myriad darting lights as he stopped in front of *The Old Granary* restaurant. One or two boats, cocooned in their hoar-frosted, winter covers, were moored against the far bank, and behind the riverside buildings, the square tower of a church loomed majestic and imposing against the winter-blue sky. All Harry knew of Wareham was something he recalled about it having been fortified against the Vikings, somewhere around the time of King Alfred.

The air was crisp and cold despite the sunshine, and he put on his heavy coat for the short walk into the town centre. There were few people about, but as Wareham lay en route to the Purbeck coast, he could imagine it thronged with visitors in summer.

He had not managed to find the forge that his neighbour, Rob, had assured him was somewhere on the outskirts of town, so the wrought iron gate he had hoped to have repaired remained in the boot of the car. With no on-line access until he managed to get a broadband connection, he had driven into Wareham to find a bank and make a transfer to Adam's account.

* * *

The call from his son had been as disturbing as it was unexpected. Adam was in debt; to a degree that had shocked Harry. He had barely been given a chance to reply to Adam's cursory, "How's it going dad?" before he had launched into, "Dad, can you lend me some money?"

Harry's first instinct had been to ask what had happened to the allowance he sent him each month. However, the tension in Adam's voice had made him loath to appear confrontational, especially as he had not heard from his son for some time. His question; "What do you want it for?" had met with evasion.

"I need to like ... pay some bills ... and stuff."

"You mean your rent and household bills?"

"Well ... yeh. I'm like, three months behind with my share of the rent. I need to pay my mobile phone account and stuff like that, right?"

"How much do you need?"

There had been a pause before Adam answered. "About five hundred ... maybe six?"

"How much?" Harry had been unable to restrain himself any longer, "What's happened to the allowance I send you every month?"

Adam's anger had surfaced quickly, as it had all too often in recent years. "Well, right ... OK; forget it!"

"Wait a minute, Adam. That's a hell of a lot of money on top of what you already get. Just tell me the truth!"

There had been another pause before Adam's reply. "It's like ... I owe some guys."

"What guys?" Harry had asked flatly.

"Just some guys. Guys that Steve and I like, hang out with."

"Why do you owe them money?"

Adam's in-drawn breath had been clearly audible before he spoke. "Well, we like, play a friendly game of poker now and then."

Harry had felt the hair stand up on the back of his neck. "How much do you owe them, Adam?"

"About three hundred or so … I guess."

"You play poker for that kind of money and you call it friendly? Who the hell are these *guys*?" Harry had asked incredulously.

"Just guys that Steve knows. They hang out and play poker once a week. They like, invited us to join in, right."

"They must have seen you coming! How much does Steve owe them?"

"He's OK. I think he's about quits."

It had been Harry's turn to pause, as an unpleasant thought came into his mind. He had never managed to bring himself to like Stephen Edmunds, during all the years that Adam and he had been friends. It was not anything he could put his finger on, but he had never taken to the boy and could never bring himself to totally trust him.

He had been tempted to say, '*Don't you think it's odd that it's only you that's losing?*', but what he had actually said was, "Does your mother know about this?"

"No way!" Adam had retorted. "Think what her precious Jonathan would say!"

"Don't you trust her, of all people?" Harry had retorted. "Do you think her feelings for you would change because of anything Jonathan … or anybody else might say? You're still her son, Adam. Whatever's happened between your mother and me, we both love you. When do you need this money?"

"As soon as possible," Adam had answered, more subdued.

"Are *these guys* threatening you for this money?"

"No!" Adam's response had sounded hollow. "We're cool; but I owe them. So I want to like … pay my debts."

Harry had felt a knot in his stomach. "Is this all, Adam? If I send you this money, will it sort this mess out, once and for all?"

"Yes dad." The relief in his son's voice had been unmistakable.

"This is the end of it, Adam! No more poker or any other gambling! Is that understood?"

There had been no immediate response.

"Adam?"

"OK dad."

"Alright; I'll transfer the money to your account."

He had heard Adam's sigh of relief. "Thanks dad."

"How are you … apart from this mess, I mean?"

"Yeh; I'm good."

"Are you still working at the amusement park?"

"Well, no. It's out of season. It's hard to like, find anything at this time of year."

Again Harry had sensed evasiveness in Adam's response. "Have you got my new address?"

"Yeh. Debs gave it to me when I called her for your number."

"You know where I am then, if you need me?" Harry had felt heartsick that he could sense no real connection with his son. "Take care of yourself, Adam."

"Cheers dad; I will."

Another awkward pause had followed. There had been so much Harry had wanted to say, but he had sensed it would mean little to Adam, other than embarrassment.

It was Adam who had broken the silence. "Well, I have to split. Bye dad. Thanks again."

"Bye son."

No, *'How are you dad? How are you settling into your new home? I'll come and see you as soon as I can, dad.'* To the little boy who had once run to him when he came home from work; who had cuddled up to him in the armchair for a bedtime story; and who used tell him everything he did, or thought, he was now no more than 'the bank of last resort'. Worst of all was the thought that he had only himself to blame.

\* \* \*

The bright sunlight was dazzling after the dim interior of the bank, and Harry regretted leaving his sunglasses in the car. He turned away from the blinding glare, low in the winter sky, as he stood at the crossroads, trying to decide whether to have another go at finding the forge or cut his losses and buy a new gate.

"Harry Simmonds; by all the saints!"

Harry turned towards the voice. Against the glare, he could make out little more than the silhouette of a man wearing an overcoat and a flat cap, beneath which, a pair of prominent ears were made comically translucent by the harsh backlight. The voice was vaguely familiar.

"Harry, old son! What on earth are you doing here?"

The shadow of a passing bus allowed Harry to recognise the figure approaching with a broad smile and his hand outstretched.

Harry smiled back and grasped his hand. "Hello Guy; how are you!"

"Oh you know; not so bad," Guy replied, shaking Harry's hand vigorously. "Long time; no see! So what brings you to these parts?"

"I live in Dorset now; at Nethercombe Ley."

Guy frowned thoughtfully. "Afraid I can't place it."

"It's north of here … a bit off the beaten track. I've only just moved in."

"How's that lovely wife of yours?" Guy asked.

"We're divorced," Harry said quietly.

Guy's mouth opened; his face registering disbelief. "My God! You are joking?"

"I'm afraid not. Sally's remarried."

Guy's lips moved soundlessly, before he exclaimed, "I can't believe it! I would have bet The Bank of England on you two celebrating your golden wedding!"

"We never even made silver," Harry said with a weak smile.

Guy still looked shaken. "What on earth? Oh God, I'm sorry Harry! It's none of my business."

"That's OK Guy. I get the same reaction from everyone. It took me a long time to come to terms with it myself."

"Look, have you got time for a cup of coffee?" Guy asked. Then holding up both hands, he added, "Don't worry I'm not trying to pry. Like I say, it's none of my business. But it's been years since you left Bennetts. It's good to see you again after all this time."

35

"That sounds great," Harry replied. "I've got plenty of time these days."

Guy led the way to a cafe tucked away in a small precinct off the main road. In spite of the chill winter air, two young women sat at a table outside smoking, both with a toddler in a pushchair parked beside them. The cafe was almost empty; the only other customers were an elderly couple, who like strangers, sat silently staring out of the window. 'Is that what it would have come to with Sally and me?' Harry thought.

It was pleasantly warm inside, so they shed their heavy coats and hung them over the backs of chairs. Guy's dark overcoat was tailored and stylish, as were his navy blue business suit, pale blue shirt and silk tie. It did not surprise Harry in the least. Guy had always been a snappy dresser. He had a way with the ladies, which he proved by dropping his scarf and tweed cap onto the table, and turning to bestow a smile on the woman behind the counter; the smile that Jean, Harry's secretary at A.J. Bennett and Co, had dubbed 'Guy's elastic snapper'.

Harry smiled to himself at the thought that even now, eleven years on, it still worked. Had he done the same, it would have been met with indifference rather than a flutter of eyelashes.

"This is on me. What's your fancy?" said Guy, gazing up at a board displaying a list of available beverages.

"Coffee; plain black for me, please."

"I think I'll have a cappuccino," Guy said, and began inspecting the pastries in the display case, while the woman turned to a row of chrome dials and handles behind her.

In Harry's opinion the years had not been especially kind to Guy, who by his calculation had to be fifty-ish. Guy's hair had been thin and prematurely grey eleven years ago, but now it had all but receded from his dome-like skull. Like so many balding men, he had let what remained grow overly long around his ears and at the back of his head. However, despite the laughter lines, his eyes still held their old mischievous sparkle, which, as he had just demonstrated, still had the same effect on women.

How it worked Harry would never understand. With ears like those, hair like that ... and that nose, how on earth did he get women eating out of his hand?

"Do you fancy a cake, Harry?" Guy called, peering down at the display case, and no doubt the ample cleavage hovering at eye level across the counter.

"No thanks."

"See anything that takes your fancy?" the woman asked.

"Yes! Your buns are tempting," he said, and with an impish grin, pointed to the far end of the cabinet.

A flicker of a smile played at the corners of the woman's mouth, as she leaned across with her tongs. "Just the one?" she asked, her eyebrows arching, as her eyes met his.

"I think it's all I can manage for now," Guy answered.

The woman dropped an iced bun onto a plate, her eyes twinkling, and Harry lost the struggle to keep a straight face. With a beaker in each hand and the plate balanced on one them, Guy turned towards him with a wink.

"You never change do you Mr. Wolstencroft?" Harry murmured, as Guy approached.

"Just letting a little sunlight into this weary toil," Guy replied, placing the mugs and plate carefully on the table, before sitting down opposite Harry. "So, what are you doing with yourself now?" he asked, sipping the froth on his coffee.

"Not much really," Harry replied. "I recently resigned my partnership in the management consultancy I've been with for the past eleven years. When that's all settled, I'll look around for something to keep me occupied."

Guy lifted his eyes from the rim of his mug. "Any idea how soon that's likely to be?" he asked.

"Not really; why?"

"Well, I might have something that's right up your street."

"How do you mean?" Harry asked.

"Well, I'm involved with a nationwide project," Guy began, "although I'm only concerned with the south west. As usual there are millions being sprayed around by people who couldn't organise the proverbial in a brewery."

"So you work for the government?"

"Not as such," Guy replied. "I work for a quango; ACCORS. That's The Advisory Council for the Co-ordination of Regional Services," he explained in response to Harry's bemused expression. "I'm based in Poole; near the harbour."

"I'm afraid I don't know Poole," Harry replied. "So where are you suggesting I would fit in?"

Guy swallowed a mouthful of bun, and wiped his hands carefully on a paper napkin. "Well let me put it this way. What I've come to realise after six years in the public sector is this; every few years a new minister, eager to make his mark, or some other dozy prat in a suit, will dream up *'an initiative'* that costs millions, creates chaos and upheaval, and in the end achieves bugger all!"

Recognising one of Guy's preliminary outbursts, Harry waited while he took a swig of coffee and dabbed the foam from his lips.

"So far, after eighteen months of umpteen committee meetings, workshops and steering groups, all we seem to have achieved is tons of bumph for NHS Trusts, local authorities and God knows how many other quangos and NGOs … that's Non Government Organisations by the way."

"What would I be expected to do?" Harry asked in amusement.

"Organisation Harry! It's your forte. We were always well organised at Bennett's; at least we were before you left."

"They were taken over a few years ago weren't they?"

"Yes; the Yanks bought us out. A lot of us were given a nice fat cheque and shown the door. Anyway, back to the point. One thing that *was* agreed at the last Directors' meeting was that we need to sort out our administration structure. We've got people working as part of one team, but reporting to the director or a manager of another; sometimes more than one. The whole thing's got out of hand. You know; vested interests and little empires resisting change. It needs an outsider. Someone with your ability and experience could give the organisation the kick up the arse it needs, and get some changes pushed through."

The idea of battling against internal politics struck Harry as less than appealing, but he asked, "Why would they appoint me?"

"On my recommendation," Guy replied. "I'm Deputy Director of Corporate Affairs; and don't ask how many I've had!" he added with a grin. "We're one of the smaller quangos. The directors know we have to do something about it, but want to keep it fairly low key. I'm pretty certain they'd prefer you to the hassle and expense of a big international organisation."

"I'm not sure it's for me, but thanks anyway," Harry replied.

Guy pulled out a small notebook and pen and perched a pair of square, rimless glasses on the end of his nose. "At least think about it, Harry. It would be a contract for say six months … maybe longer if you thought it necessary. I'm not asking you to say *yeh* or *nay* at this moment. Here's my mobile number in case you have any questions; give me yours and I'll give you a buzz in a week or so. If you change your mind, we can talk more about it then. How's that?"

"OK. I'll think about it." Harry took Guy's pen and wrote his number in the notebook.

"So how are things?" Guy asked, removing his glasses.

"Well, I'm getting used to being on my own," Harry began. "Sally got married again last November. She's become very much a career woman. Debbie, our eldest, is at Reading University, and Adam is somewhere on the east coast doing I'm not sure what."

Guy's eyebrows rose. "Debbie's at university? My God! She was still at primary school the last time I saw her."

"I know; the years fly by. She's a young woman now; twenty-one in May," Harry said, absently stirring his coffee. "Sally decided she wanted more than routine domesticity," he added, half to himself.

"I'm sorry mate," Guy said quietly.

"It's OK. I'm used to it now. I came to Dorset looking for a fresh start."

"Is it working?"

"I don't know. It's too early to tell. Nethercombe Ley is certainly different to anything I've been used to."

"Anyone in your life at the moment?" Guy asked tentatively.

"No," Harry chuckled. "I'm not ready for that yet. I'm not exactly God's gift to women, so I don't have any great expectations, anyway."

Guy patted his shoulder. "Don't put yourself down. You're a good man, Harry."

Harry shrugged. 'A good man', he thought; 'Women don't fall for good men do they? They seem to prefer rogues and charmers.'

"How about you? Is there someone special in your life?" he enquired, never doubting the answer.

Guy smiled. "Yes; there's Emma. We've been together for over a year now. She's quite a bit younger than me, but it doesn't seem to bother her. And it certainly doesn't bother me!"

They spent half an hour or so reminiscing, after which Guy walked with Harry to his car, extracting a promise that he would seriously consider the consultancy offer.

Harry left Wareham in a light hearted mood, having come to the conclusion that the more he saw of Dorset, the more he liked it.

"Mrs. Alders; could I have a quick word?"

She looked up from cleaning the cooker with a concerned look, as Harry entered the kitchen.

"Don't look so worried; it's pay day," he said with a grin, and held up an envelope. "That's one of things I want to talk to you about."

Still looking apprehensive, she stopped wiping to turn towards him, twisting the J-cloth around her fingers.

"Mrs. Alders; my father taught me the maxim of *a fair day's pay for a fair day's work,*" Harry said quietly. "And over the past few weeks you've more than kept your side of the bargain. In fact you do a lot more than we agreed. We both know what this place would be like if it was left to me. You've taken on my laundry as well!"

"It's no trouble," she replied.

Harry went on undeterred. "I can't go on paying you a measly thirty pounds a week. It's daylight robbery, and not on as far as I'm concerned. "There's sixty pounds in there," he said, holding out the envelope. "It's still a bargain, as far as I'm concerned."

She looked at him, clearly nonplussed. "Thirty pounds is all I expected."

"My wife used to pay a woman that for four hours; one day a week," he added.

Mrs. Alders put her hand to her throat. "Are you sure?"

"Positive," Harry replied. "Are you happy with it?"

"Good grief, yes! Thank you Mr. Simmonds," she almost whispered, smiling for the first time since their conversation began. "It's very kind of you. I never expected anything like this."

"There's one other thing," said Harry.

"Yes?"

"Please call me Harry, and would you mind if I called you Marjorie? Mrs. Alders this and Mr. Simmonds that sounds so Dickension."

She looked surprised, and perhaps even apprehensive, he thought.

"There's no need to worry, I'm not trying to … well, get over familiar." He felt his cheeks burn, but a smile lit up her face. "I never thought you were," she giggled.

"I just thought calling each other Mr. and Mrs. all the time seemed a bit overly formal."

"Alright," she replied, her eyes still sparkling with mirth.

The doorbell rescued Harry from further embarrassment, and he hurried to answer it. A slim, elegant woman in a pale blue, tailored suit smiled at him as he opened the door. "Grace!" he exclaimed. "How lovely to see you; come in!"

"Hello Harry! I've been staying with my sister Bea in Taunton; you remember Bea don't you?" Harry nodded. "Well, I couldn't go home without calling in to poke my nose and have a look at your new house." She held out a gift-wrapped box. "A belated little house-warming present."

"Thank you," said Harry, kissing her cheek.

Marjorie appeared in the kitchen doorway, and Harry gestured towards her. "This is Marjorie, my Girl Friday. Marjorie; this is Grace, my moth … ex-mother-in-law."

Marjorie's expression registered momentary surprise.

"I would imagine most married men think they're the best kind," Grace chuckled and held out her hand. "Hello Marjorie. I can see Harry is being well looked after."

"Thank you. Pleased to meet you," Marjorie replied.

"Right!" said Harry "Would you like the ten quid tour before or after coffee?"

"Oh, let's do the tour first."

Half an hour or so later, with Grace settled in an armchair beside the fire in the sitting room, Harry opened her gift. "Oh, Grace, thank you, what a super present!" he exclaimed.

Grace crossed one elegant leg over the other. "I wasn't sure about buying a vase for a man, but I didn't think you'd have one; and I always think flowers make a room look more cheerful."

The cut glass glistened as Harry held it up to the window. "You're right; I haven't got one. It was very thoughtful."

Marjorie appeared in the doorway and exclaimed, "That's lovely! Are you ready for coffee now?"

"I wasn't expecting you to make it," Harry answered.

"It's already brewing. Would you like a biscuit with it?"

"I don't think I have any," Harry said.

"I bought some a few days ago," Marjorie replied. "They're in the cupboard with the crackers and water biscuits."

Harry grinned and shook his head in bemusement. "Would you like a biscuit, Grace?"

The two women looked at each other and smiled. "I would love one, please," she replied.

"Where did you find her?" Grace asked when Marjorie had left the room.

"She found me, actually," Harry replied, and went on to describe Marjorie's early morning call on his first day.

"Can you stay for lunch?" he asked.

Grace's eyebrows rose. "She doesn't cook your meals too, does she?"

"No," he laughed. "There's a pub on the other side of the green. The food is supposed to be good, but I haven't tried it yet."

"That sounds marvellous!"

Marjorie came in bearing a tray with a plate of carefully arranged biscuits and cups and saucers, with a matching coffee pot, sugar bowl and milk jug.

She politely refused Harry's invitation to join them. "I'll get on, if you don't mind and leave you to have a chat," she said.

"Now!" said Grace. "Tell me what you've been getting up to. Shall I pour?"

At lunchtime, they made the short walk around the village green. The spire of St. Luke's, rising graceful and imposing above the cluster of trees and cottages behind *The Black Bull*, brought an appreciative exclamation from Grace. "How delightful! It must look absolutely lovely on a summer's day."

Unsurprisingly, the rustic tables and benches outside the pub were deserted, but Harry noticed several vehicles in the car park at the rear. He had to duck his head at the entrance to the dim, narrow lobby, which opened onto a bar on one side and a small dining room on the other.

Harry ushered Grace into the dining room, whose plain, pine furniture and stainless steel fittings contrasted incongruously with the dark oak beams, fake mediaeval escutcheons and carefully applied rough plaster. 'IKEA meets Merry England', Harry mused. Half of the dozen or so tables were occupied, and as their eyes became accustomed to the subdued lighting, a girl appeared through a swing door carrying fully-laden plates.

She threw them a welcoming smile. "Make yourselves comfortable, I'll be with you in just a second."

Grace made for a table in the corner of the room, while Harry hung up his coat and her woollen shawl. She was studying the 'specials' on the board on the far side of the room when Harry took his seat opposite her.

"It all looks very tempting," she said.

The smiling girl returned with menu cards. "Hello, I'm Mandy. Can I get you something to drink?"

"I'm driving. Just a tonic water for me," Grace replied, fishing in her handbag for her glasses.

"What bitter do you have?" Harry asked.

"We have *Piddle* and *Jimmy Riddle*," Mandy replied with a wide grin, eliciting a giggle from Grace. "They're local real ales. We've got *Tanglefoot* and *Badger's Original* as well."

"Oh, I'll try a pint of *Jimmy Riddle*, if I may," Harry replied with a grin.

"Probably very appropriately named, if my dear Reggie was anything to go by," Grace chuckled.

Mandy left them to peruse the menu while she fetched their drinks.

"So what's Adam up to these days?" Grace asked without lifting her eyes.

"Your guess is as good as mine," Harry replied. "But I have to admit, I'm worried, Grace. He's been gambling and getting himself in debt."

"Gambling?" Grace looked up from the menu, her eyebrows arched in surprise.

"Yes; he rang me a couple of weeks ago to ask for money."

"I thought you gave him an allowance every month."

"I do, but that little *rat*, Steve Edmunds, got him playing poker with '*some guys*', as he calls them. They took him for over three hundred quid!"

"How much?" The shock had made Grace's exclamation louder than she had intended, and several diners at other tables looked across at them.

"He says three hundred," Harry replied quietly. "But I have a nasty suspicion it could be more."

"Good grief! Do you know where he is?" Grace asked, almost in a whisper.

"Not exactly. He was somewhere in the Great Yarmouth area the last I heard. That was a few months ago. My first inclination was to go up there and try to find him, but as you know, we aren't close these days. I blame myself, but there's not much I can do. He's an adult and he can make his own decisions now."

"Yes, but you're still his father!" Grace replied.

"I don't think that means much to him anymore," Harry sighed.

"But you can't keep bailing him out, Harry."

"I know. I told him this was the first and last time. But I'm still worried. He's not working now, either."

The arrival of Mandy with their drinks created a hiatus in the conversation. "Are you ready to order?" she asked.

Grace pointed to the board. "I think I'll have the spaghetti carbonara, if I may."

"Steak and ale pie for me, please," said Harry.

Grace waited until the waitress was out of earshot, before she asked, "Have you spoken to Sally?"

"No," Harry replied. "I haven't got her number. I haven't mentioned it to anyone before now. I don't want to worry Debbie, now she's so close to her finals. I thought of getting in touch with Sally, but what can she do? Neither of us can force him to do anything he doesn't want to."

"I suppose not," Grace replied. "But we can't just let him ruin his life. He's always been such a loving boy. We have to hope he sorts himself out, or find some way of doing it for him."

"I guess so. But I'm damned if I know how, Grace."

"Thank you Harry; that was a lovely meal!" Grace exclaimed, as he shepherded her from the dining room into the dimly lit lobby.

"My pleasure. You know you're always welcome," he replied.

He was distracted by a voice calling, "Hi Harry!" which made him look back in surprise. The door to the barroom stood open, and he could see someone waving from the group of people at the bar.

"Hello Rachel," he said, with a tingle of pleasure.

She was wearing a fairisle sweater and jeans, and her hair was pulled back in a pony-tail, emphasising her classic cheekbones. Detaching herself from her companions, she came towards him, smiling broadly. Aware of the curious stares and Grace's amused interest, he felt his cheeks burn.

"So you made it here at last," she exclaimed. Turning to Grace, she said, "You must be Harry's mother."

"Not quite," Grace replied with a mischievous grin.

"This is Grace; my *ex-wife's* mother," said Harry, enjoying the sudden reddening of Rachel's cheeks.

"Oh!" Rachel was clearly taken aback. "I'm so sorry …"

"That's quite alright, and perfectly understandable," said Grace, holding out her hand. "I just came to visit Harry and see his new home. It's a bit unusual, I have to admit."

"I think it great," Rachel replied, regaining her composure and shaking Grace's hand. `"Come and have a drink and meet the gang."

"Thank you, but I really must be getting home," said Grace. "But don't let me stop you Harry; you go ahead."

"I have a few things to do; but thanks anyway," he replied.

Rachel was undeterred. "Simon and I will be in here for supper tomorrow evening, if you care to join us."

"OK, thanks. I might just do that," he said.

As Harry read the email from Grace, thanking him for lunch the previous day, he could not suppress a mischievous grin at the thought of his mother using the internet in the same way, or funnier still, texting. Her 'thank you' letters were pages long. The idea of her trying to cram everything into a text made him laugh out loud; the sudden sound a reminder of the stillness and his solitude.

He had not really intended to take up Rachel's offer, but with the lights already on by late afternoon, having a meal in company suddenly seemed infinitely preferable to spending another dreary evening alone in front of the TV.

He fell to speculating about her. She obviously assumed he lived alone, although he had not mentioned it when they had met on Hallows Hill. It made him wonder how much Simon had told her about him. Simon had not said anything about her having a partner, and she stayed with him at weekends, so it seemed unlikely that there was anyone permanent in her life.

"Steady on," he said to himself. "Don't get carried away. She's an attractive young woman, and she won't be short of admirers. So let's keep our feet on the ground."

He made himself wait until around eight o'clock before setting out, so that, if they were not already there, he would not have to wait too long for them.

The dining room was almost full when he arrived, but he could not see them. He was pondering whether to claim a table or wait in the bar with his new-found friend *Jimmy Riddle*, when the waitress approached. Her badge introduced her as Carla. "Is it just for one?" she asked.

"I'm expecting some friends," he said. "They may have booked … in the name of Cornish."

"Oh, Rachel and the Rev'll be in the bar," Carla replied. "We do bar meals, as well."

Thanking her, Harry turned to the door opposite. As he opened it, he was met by piped music and the buzz of conversation, the loudest of which emanated from a group at the bar. They stared at him as he went in, making him feel he was intruding.

To his relief, he heard someone call his name. Looking across the room, he saw Rachel and Simon sitting with a young woman in one of three back-to-back booths that ran the length of the far wall; each booth consisting of a table between high-backed benches.

All three stood up to greet him and Simon held out his hand. "Harry, what a pleasure. We were hoping you could make it."

"It was kind of Rachel to invite me," he replied.

Rachel turned to the young woman beside her. "Have you met Laura?"

Laura gazed at him through the large round lenses of a pair of fashion spectacles. Her rose-bud mouth and copper tinted hair, spilling across one broad shoulder and reaching halfway down her back, gave her an almost adolescent charm. Harry guessed she was around thirty, and remembering his conversation with Simon, attributed the firmness of her well toned figure to the benefits of spending a good deal of time on a horse.

She answered Rachel's question for him, her voice light and girlish. "No we haven't met. Hi Harry; nice to meet you."

"Nice to meet you Laura," Harry replied. "What are you all drinking?" he asked, shedding his heavy coat.

"Thank you: Laura and I are on the house white," Rachel replied.

"We've got a tab going. We were about to order food, so I'll come with you," said Simon.

One of the women at the bar called, "Hi Simon", and the group turned and opened ranks as they approached.

"Hello Miranda … everyone," Simon replied. "Let me introduce Harry. He recently moved into May Cottage, in The Pound."

Harry nodded in response to a chorus of greetings; the volume and heartiness of which he attributed to the alcohol they had already consumed. Though he absorbed no more than a 'Gerald' and a 'Jessica' from Simon's introductions, his innate politeness prevailed, and he asked, "Can I get anyone a drink?"

They declined courteously; except for a woman whose glassy expression as she drained her glass, suggested that it was by no means the first time it had been refilled that evening. Despite the unseasonal tan, dyed blond hair, silk chemise and skin-tight leggings that clung to her lean body, the inexorable march of time was betrayed by her hands and neck and the creases around her eyes and mouth.

She smiled, revealing even, white teeth. "Thank you Harry," and bestowing a smile on the young barman, she added, "Dimitri knows what I like."

From Dimitri's smug expression, Harry formed the impression that he probably knew more than he should about what she liked. Noticing the gold ring on the third finger of her left hand, the word 'cougar' popped into Harry's mind, which he thought was the word in current parlance to describe a predatory older woman.

As she edged closer and touched his arm, he caught the pleasing fragrance of what he assumed to be an expensive perfume. "It's nice to have another unattached male in the village," she purred.

'So everybody knows!' he thought, grateful for Dimitri's prompt return with a large glass of wine. As *the cougar* bestowed a disconcerting smile of thanks on him, Harry turned to Simon for support, but to his relief, her attention was diverted by one of her companions.

Dimitri waited expectantly. "That's two house whites, a pint of *Jimmy Riddle* and whatever you're having Simon," Harry said.

"Why don't we put it all on the tab?" Simon replied. "We can sort it all out later. Are you eating?"

"Yes, I think I'll have the chilli."

"I'll stick to lemonade," Simon said. "Can't have me slurring the sermon tomorrow, can we?"

"I don't know; it might be entertaining if the subject's the evils of the demon drink," Harry replied mischievously.

Simon laughed heartily, and the short, balding man behind the bar grinned as he looked up from his order pad. Simon made the formal introduction in his own inimitable style. "Bob, this is Harry Simmonds, of May Cottage Estate; Harry … Bob Andrews, mine host and proprietor extraordinaire of *Ye Black Bull* hostelry."

They shook hands, and Bob called over his shoulder, "Dimitri, these are on the house!" Turning back to Harry he added, "Welcome to Nethercombe Ley."

"Thanks very much," Harry replied.

Returning to the booth, they edged in opposite the girls; Simon easing his large frame in carefully. As they settled, Rachel chuckled. "I see you've met Stella."

"Is that her name?"

"Didn't you ask?" she teased.

"Not me! She scared the life out of me!" he replied, eliciting a giggle from Laura.

"She's married to Colin, the tubby guy in the checked shirt," Rachel explained. "He's absolutely loaded!"

"So's she, by the look of it," Harry reposted, enjoying the trill of laughter from both girls.

"I meant *financially!*" Rachel replied in playful reproach.

"Doesn't he mind … you know, the way she carries on?" Harry asked.

Rachel grimaced. "I think he's past caring. He seems to turn a blind eye to it all."

"She's left him twice; run off with some chap or other, but he's taken her back both times," Laura added.

"I see," said Harry, although he did not really see at all.

"By the way, I'm so sorry I mistook that lady for your mother. I hope I didn't offend her," Rachel said.

In reply to Laura's puzzled look, Harry explained. "I brought my ex-wife's mother here for lunch yesterday. Rachel naturally assumed she was *my* mother. It's not the first time it's happened, and she wasn't at all offended. In fact she saw the funny side of it. She possesses quite a sense of humour."

"It's nice that you're still on such good terms with her," Laura said.

"She's a very special person. I'm very fond of her," he replied. "She was a tremendous support to me when Sally and I broke up."

Recognising a mischievous twinkle in Rachel's eyes, he grinned. "Yes: we had to suffer jokes about *'When Harry Met Sally'*; especially poor Sally. She had to put up with all the ribbing and dares from our friends when we were in a restaurant."

Rachel giggled. "I'm sorry, I didn't mean to be rude, but I must admit it did occur to me."

Harry laughed, and she looked at him, as if in appraisal. Holding her glass in both hands with her elbows propped on the table, she asked, "What do you do for a living?"

"I am, or was, a management consultant," he said. "But I'm getting out and selling my share of the business. I came to Dorset looking for a little peace and tranquillity; to give me time to sort myself out, I suppose."

Sitting close and directly opposite her, Harry realised she was probably older than he had at first thought; probably late thirties. Her looks were more classically striking than pretty, but nevertheless she was a very attractive woman. She was also self confident and aware of her looks; holding his gaze with her arresting blue eyes as she spoke.

"Do you have any children?" Laura asked.

"Yes, two. Deborah is coming up for twenty-one; she's at university. My son, Adam, is eighteen. My wife has remarried, by the way."

"I didn't mean to be nosey," Laura said defensively.

Harry smiled. "I know, Laura. It was a perfectly natural question to ask. I don't mind telling you about myself … as long as I'm not boring you."

"Of course not."

Simon had said nothing, leaving the girls to ask questions and Harry to answer as he saw fit, which suggested he had not divulged anything significant about their previous conversation.

"So what have you got planned for the future?" Rachel asked.

"Not much," he replied. "I bumped into an old colleague in Wareham recently. He wants me to do some work for an organisation based in Poole, but I'm not sure I'm ready to get back into harness yet."

"It might be good for you," Rachel suggested.

"It's up to Harry to decide that," Simon interjected quietly.

Rachel flashed her brother a glance that bore the hallmarks of irritation, but she smiled and replied, "Of course it is."

"So, what do *you* do?" Harry asked, looking across at the girls.

Laura answered immediately. "I have a riding school and stables at Garstone. You know, liveries and hacks and all that. I'm hoping to get an '*own a pony for a week*' scheme up and running in time for the school holidays. It'll give youngsters the experience and fun of riding and looking after a pony for a week or so, without the expense of owning one full-time. I hope it'll bring in some very welcome extra cash, too."

"It sounds like a very good idea," Harry replied. "I don't think I've known many young girls who weren't mad on horses. My daughter and her friends were."

It was obviously the reply Laura had hoped for, because her pretty face lit up with a broad smile.

The *Jimmy Riddle* and the congenial company were obviously having a beneficial effect, because he began to relax, and turning his gaze to the captivating blue eyes opposite him, he asked, "What about you?"

Rachel pulled a face, as she held his gaze. "Me? I work for one of those investment banks that everyone hates. You know, the ones that gamble with people's hard earned savings and pensions, and pay obscene bonuses to their staff ... I *wish*!"

"Good grief, you sound like my mother!" Harry replied. "I sometimes think she writes *The Daily Mail* editorials."

Rachel's shoulders began to tremble and she burst out laughing, but before he had a chance to wallow in his triumph, Simon interjected playfully with, "What about me?"

"I thought you said you were thinking of taking up wrestling," Harry reposted.

Their laughter was interrupted by the arrival of the food, born on a large tray by a girl with a strong East European accent. "Von Lasagne, von cheeli, and tow reezotto," she chanted melodically.

Two hours and another pint of *Jimmy Riddle* later, Harry made his way home, having enjoyed the beer and the '*cheeli*', but the company even more. It felt as if he had spent the evening with old friends, which he hoped they soon would be.

Hearing the rattle of the letter box, Harry got up from his breakfast and went out into the hall. Two or three envelopes, a couple of flyers and the local newsletter lay on the doormat. He could tell that two of them were cards, and suddenly realised what day it was.

The handwriting and the postmark on one of the envelopes gave away the sender's identity. The card bore a large red heart and the legend: 'Love You Forever'. Inside Debbie had written simply *Always your girl*.

He had received a Valentine card from her every year since she had been five or six years old; many of which, during her school days, she had made herself. She had never missed, even when she reached her teens and started to receive her own from hopeful admirers. In recent years the underlying sentiment of her cards had become especially poignant, and he even more appreciative of her thoughtfulness.

The other card was an invitation. It read:

> *Nick and Sue Holding*
> *Request the pleasure of the company*
> *of*
> *Mr. Harry Simmonds and Partner*
> *On the occasion of the celebration of*
> *the 25ᵗʰ Anniversary of their Wedding*

Harry noted the date was in May and skimmed over the details of the venues for the renewal of the vows and the reception afterwards. His immediate inclination was to send his regrets, claiming a 'prior engagement'. He had no one to go with and could not face turning up on his own. It was not something he felt proud of. Nick and Sue were old friends, who had been guests at his and Sally's wedding. Unlike several couples he had once considered friends, they had kept in touch and regularly emailed him with updates about their lives, their family and pictures of their grandchild. They had sent him a card when he moved in and had even been pleased to accept his emailed invitation to visit him for a weekend, when he was settled.

The invitation was another painful reminder of the change in his life. It was not that he did not want to celebrate with them. They had remained true friends; uncritical and unbiased towards Sally or him. He was certain that she and Jonathan would be invited too, which was not a problem … in principle. But he was not sure he was ready to cope with the reality, even if he did find someone to go with. It was a few moments before the obvious solution occurred to him, and he called Debbie.

"I'd love to," she replied, as he had anticipated. "I'd love to see Uncle Nick and Aunty Sue again!"

Harry was a little easier in his mind when he put the phone down. Going with Debbie would not dispel the pain of seeing Sally with her new husband, but it might ease the awkwardness of the situation.

He settled at his desk with the intention of dealing with the paperwork concerning his resignation from Eldon Management Services, but the solicitor's letter setting out the settlement terms for him to agree in principle was turgid and lengthy, and he had to force himself to wade through it, adding pencil notes and comments against points he felt needed clarification.

For a few moments of light relief, he glanced through *The Valley Voice*; the Beldene Valley magazine. It was the first one he had received since his next-door-neighbour, Alan Anderson, had persuaded him to subscribe. Alan's editorial was both witty and well written, and countered the official reason for the impending removal of the phone box in Witsnell Green, with the suggestion that its lack of use might have something to do with the fact that it had been *out of order* for months.

There were the usual notices of meetings of The Parish Council, times of church services, meetings of The Women's Institute, The Ramblers Society, The Scouts, allotment societies and various other local associations and clubs. Some of the advertisements were intriguing. In addition to the orthodox; such as pubs and restaurants, builders and decorators, Laura's riding school, a couple of vets and a garden designer, there were some less conventional services on offer, including dog sitting, cat grooming and something called *meditative aromatherapy.*

Not so long ago, he would have dismissed a publication like this as quaint and parochial, but the more he read, the more interested he became; and more to the point, surprised by how much was going on in the area.

Apparently Saint Agnes' church in Belmott Meade needed bell ringers, which made him ponder the fact that he had never heard bells being rung at Saint Luke's. He made a mental note to mention it to Simon.

There were several pieces written by local clerics, including one by Simon. His 'View from the Vestry' dealt with the relevance of faith in our material world. In a reasoned and thought provoking manner, he offered the premise that 'material possessions bestow only fleeting satisfaction; and without faith, there is no hope; and without hope there is no joy or contentment'.

Harry could empathise with those sentiments. He was better off than he had ever been. After he sold his partnership in Eldon Management Services, there would no real necessity for him to work. However, he would gladly give it up to go back to the way he and Sally were when they had been newly married; hard up, happy and full of hope for the future. Which brought him back to the problem of what to do about Adam.

What could he do? His instincts told him that his son's troubles went deeper than gambling debts. Simply bailing him out was only dealing with the symptoms; not the cause. He had even considered employing a private investigator to find out Adam's whereabouts, but dismissed it. Neither he nor Sally had the power to force their son to come home, or do anything he did not want to. If, by chance, Adam were to find out, he would undoubtedly accuse them of spying on him, and become even more estranged.

Harry sighed resignedly, reflecting on the irrefutable fact that, no matter what material success he had achieved, his private life was a mess.

"Harry?" His heart missed a beat at the sound of the voice on the line.

"Hello Sally."

She came straight to the point, without preamble. "Harry, I've just been speaking to mum. She tells me you've sent money to Adam, to pay off gambling debts! Is that true?"

"Yes, I'm afraid so."

"I can't believe it! What on earth's going on?"

"I wish I knew," he replied. "He called me, asking to borrow six hundred quid."

"Six hundred?"

"Yes. Apparently that little swine Steve Edmunds has got him playing poker with some characters who must think all their birthdays and Christmasses have come at once! I didn't know what else to do! I warned him it was the last time."

Sally's indrawn breath betrayed her anxiety. "He called me earlier this week asking for a loan; at least that's what he called it. He wanted a hundred and fifty pounds. He told me it was to pay his rent! He never mentioned asking you for money!"

"Did you send it to him?"

"No; I was worried. You already give him an allowance. I told him I wanted to meet him. I'm going up there this weekend."

"Where is he?"

"Bury St. Edmunds. Didn't you know?"

"No, I didn't," Harry replied uncomfortably. "I can't get anything out of him these days. What's he doing there?"

"Gambling obviously!" she retorted curtly, then added, "I'm sorry, that was uncalled for."

"That's OK, Sally. I'm worried sick too," he replied. "I'd have him here, but he wouldn't come. He doesn't want anything to do with me these days … unless it's money. It's all my own fault I know, but that's the way it is."

"Harry, it's not all your fault. I'm the one he blames for walking out on him! But there's no point in us competing to take the blame. He's obviously in trouble. Did you manage to get any more out of him than that?"

"Very little. But he sounded 'up tight' as he himself would put it. I got the impression that whoever he owed the money to was threatening him, or at least putting pressure on him. He's not working now, either."

"All the more reason why I need to talk to him," Sally replied. "He told me he'd been laid off and needed the loan to tide him over. I guessed there was more to it than that. But gambling!"

"Just be careful Sally. We don't know who these characters are. Do you want me to come with you?"

"No. Don't take this the wrong way Harry, but I think I might get more out of him on my own. Don't worry; I don't intend doing any more than talk to him at this stage, to see if I can find out what the hell's going on."

"Will you let me know how you get on?" he asked.

"Of course; I'll call you after I've seen him."

"Thanks, Sally. I'm not offended; I agree with you. You stand more chance of getting him to tell the truth than me. But I'm more concerned than ever now."

"So am I. We'll have to make up our minds what to do after I've seen him."

"Yes, that's the best idea."

"So, how are you settling in?" she asked. "Mum said the village is pretty. Apparently you've got yourself a 'Girl Friday'."

Harry laughed. "Yes. But she's hardly a girl. She's got two grown up sons. She and your mum seemed to get on pretty well. I'm settling in fine. Thanks for your card. I'll have been here two months tomorrow. I know some of my neighbours … and I met Guy Wolstencroft a week or two ago; in Wareham of all places."

"Oh, that rogue. What's he up to these days?"

"He's employed by some quango or other. He wants me to do some work for them. How about you?"

"I'm fine thanks; at least I was, before Adam called me. Thank God Debbie seems happy enough though. I can't believe she's twenty-one in a few months."

"Tell me about it!" said Harry. "The years have flown by."

"We're thinking of moving too," Sally said. "Jonathan's running his company's office in Windsor now. It's a real drag for him driving back and forth from Bromley every day; the M25 gets worse. We're thinking of looking for somewhere around Byfleet or Weybridge. It should take me about thirty to forty minutes to get to Kingston and Jonathan about the same time to Windsor."

"I see; onward and upward."

"I don't know about that," she chuckled. "But we're both pretty busy these days. By the way, have you got my mobile number?"

"I can see it in the display," he said. "Do you want my mobile number?"

"Yes; we ought to be able get in touch if we need to talk. As I said, I'll let you know what happens when I've spoken to Adam."

Harry recited his mobile number; repeating it to make sure she had taken it down correctly.

"Do you know how long he's been gambling?" Sally asked.

"No, but I would imagine it's been for some time, if he's racked up debts like that. If he's asked you for money as well, he's obviously still doing it!"

"Oh God, Harry! What on earth are we going to do?"

"I don't know, Sally. All we can do is try to get him away from there as soon as possible, I guess."

"I suppose so," she said wistfully. "Well; take care of yourself. I'll be in touch. Bye."

Harry could hear The Beatles '*It's A Long and Winding Road*', coming from the kitchen radio, as he put down the handset. "It certainly is," he sighed; the tears he had been fighting back suddenly coursing down his cheeks.

# MARCH

## *Making Progress*

The overnight snow had covered the village in a crisp, white blanket three or four inches deep, reminding Harry that he really ought to get someone to examine his central heating. Bleeding the radiators had made little difference, and although the kitchen was warm and the log fire made the sitting room cosy, the rest of the house would have felt decidedly chilly without the portable heaters he had brought with him.

He had mentioned it to Marjorie, in the hope she might know someone who could give him practical advice, but it was one of the few domestic problems she did not appear to have an answer for. Perhaps Simon would know someone; one of his parishioners perhaps. He must remember to ask him.

After breakfast, he dug out his camera and wellington boots and trudged to the village green, revelling in the crisp, cold air, the crunch of the snow beneath his feet and the almost ethereal stillness. The pristine surface in the lane had already been disturbed by the tracks of a vehicle and several sets of footprints leading to the shop. As he reached the village green, he stopped abruptly; captivated by the incomparable beauty of nature.

Like icing on a Yule-log, the stark, bare branches of the oaks were crowned with white; their trunks frosted and dappled with a lacework of driven snow. Below them stretched a glistening carpet, marked only by a few unidentifiable paw prints. Around the village green, lights glowed in windows, bringing to mind visits to his grandparents, and the delicately painted porcelain lamps, in the form of snow covered cottages, that stood on their polished sideboard at Christmas.

Above the glistening rooftops and snow-laden trees loomed the spire of St. Luke's, the cross at its apex silhouetted against the slate-grey sky.

As he paused to take pictures, he imagined how things might look from Hallows Hill, and made up his mind to take his camera up there after breakfast. However, his plans were delayed. A little later, while he was standing at his sitting room window, with a slice of toast in one hand and a mug of coffee in the other, he caught sight of Ellen Hardy gingerly making her way towards her gateway.

She was taking one faltering step at a time, while hanging onto the fence for grim death. Harry rushed to the front door and called to her, but muffled by the upturned collar of her heavy coat and the thick woollen scarf wound around her head, she did not hear him. He went out to her, heedless of the fact that he was wearing his slippers.

"Are you alright?" he asked.

The fear in her eyes was unmistakable. "I don't like the snow, Mr. Simmonds. I'm terrified of fallin' over an' breakin' a leg or somethin'."

"Anything I can do to help?" Harry said.

Ellen turned towards him slowly, gripping the fence with both hands. "Rob's got a nasty cough, Mr. Simmonds. It's all this cold weather. It's gone straight to 'is chest. I'm on me way to the shop t'get 'im some cough medicine."

"I'll do that for you," said Harry. "You go back inside in the warm. I'll go and get my wellies on and come round to you."

Ellen's expression registered gratitude and relief. "Bless you," she said. "That's very kind of you. Peggy'll know what t'give you."

Harry could hear Rob's rasping cough when Ellen opened the door to him a few minutes later. "Come along in for a minute," she said. "Rob's in the parlour."

Harry found him sitting in a large, comfortable armchair beside a log fire, watching breakfast TV. Looking up, he nodded in acknowledgement as Harry stepped into the overheated room. He just managed, "Much appreciated," before he was wracked by another bout of coughing.

"No problem. I'm happy to help," Harry answered.

Harry turned to Ellen as she came in carrying a large purse. "I don't want to interfere, but wouldn't it be better to call the doctor?"

Rob intervened, red faced and watery-eyed. "I d'want no doctor. I'll be right as rain when it warms up a bit."

"If you say so," Harry replied doubtfully.

"Stubborn as a mule 'e is Mr. Simmonds," said Ellen.

"Why don't you call me Harry? We are neighbours, after all."

As Rob nodded and launched into another fit of coughing, Ellen replied, "Well then, you call 'im Rob an' me Ellen. I must say we're glad to 'ave you as a neighbour Mr. ... er, Harry."

"Is there anything else you need, Ellen?" Harry asked.

"I was goin' t'get some milk, as well; two pints should do it. Oh; and if you could get Rob a paper, we'd be much obliged to you."

"Of course," said Harry.

"I always 'as *The Sun*," Rob chimed in.

Ellen opened her purse, but Harry held up his hand. "You can pay me when I get back."

"Thank you. I'm so grateful to you," said Ellen. "I don't mind tellin' you, I was frightened out'a my wits tryin' t'walk on that snow."

"My pleasure," Harry repeated.

Rob smiled and turned his attention to the TV weather girl.

Ellen led Harry out of the room and called to Rob. "I'll just see Mr. ... um ... Harry out, then I'll go an' get one or two more logs in."

Harry remembered the low, open-fronted shed at the end of Rob's vegetable garden, where the Hardy's housed their log supply. "I'll fetch them for you when I come back," he said. "Stay indoors and keep warm, Ellen."

Behind them in the parlour, Rob was convulsed by another bout of coughing. Ellen smiled in gratitude. "We shall never be out of your debt."

"Don't be silly," Harry replied. "What about the cake you baked for me and that delicious shepherd's pie … and the advice Rob gives me in the garden. Don't risk going out in this weather; I'm only next door. If there's anything I can do; any time, you only have to ask. You both know that."

Ellen's face broke into a smile. "We counts ourselves lucky the day you moved in next to us Harry," she replied.

Lisa was behind the counter with her mobile phone clasped to her ear, deep in conversation, when Harry entered the shop. She was a plump, pleasant girl, with a ready smile and a friendly nature, but in Harry's opinion, not a contender for *'Brain of Britain'*. She greeted him cheerfully as he entered the shop, but immediately returned to her conversation, emitting exclamations of, "Did she? … What'd she say? … and what did 'e say? … 'E never!"

He had to wait at the counter, clutching the milk and glancing at *The Sun*, while Lisa awaited the final denouement of the saga being relating to her. Eventually, he caught her attention. "I need cough medicine. It's for Rob Hardy," he said.

Lisa waved her hand towards the shelves. "It's over there on the top shelf."

"I know," Harry replied, "but there are three or four different kinds. Apparently Peggy knows which kind he usually needs."

" 'Ang on a minute!" Lisa exclaimed, and reluctantly took the phone from her ear. "She's upstairs."

"Is it possible to have a very quick word?" he asked.

"I suppose so," Lisa said vaguely.

"Well, could you ask her for me?" Harry suggested.

"Oh, right! Yeh," Lisa replied, as the light came on behind her eyes. She moved to the doorway and shouted up the stairs. "Peg! Mr. Whassname from round the corner wants 'ave a word with you!"

A muffled reply was all Harry could make out.

"She'll be down in a minute," said Lisa and pressed the mobile to her ear once more. "So anyway, what'd 'e say to that?"

Peggy appeared from the doorway behind the counter a few moments later.

"Sorry to keep you waitin'. I was just seeing to Ted. He's not at all well," she said.

"I'm sorry to hear that," Harry replied. "Sorry to trouble you Peggy."

"That's alright, Ted's asleep now. I was just about to come down anyway. 'E can't keep nothin' down. He's been complainin' about his stomach for weeks, but 'e wouldn't go an' get it seen to. I'm waitin' for the doctor now. His own doctor don't come out no more; they've got what they call an '*out of hour's service*'. Somebody's comin' from there. I expect 'e'll 'ave a problem gettin' through the snow."

"Give Ted my best wishes and tell him I hope he's up and well again soon," said Harry.

"Thanks, I'll tell 'im you asked after 'im," Peggy replied.

"The reason I asked to speak to you is because I need some cough medicine for Rob Hardy. Ellen said you'd know which one," Harry explained.

Peggy pointed towards the shelves. " 'E usually needs the one for bronchial coughs; it's the one with the green label."

"Thanks," said Harry. "Let's hope the doctor can sort Ted out quickly."

When he left the shop, a line of vehicles had formed on the other side of the village green; the tail end disappearing into Church Lane, as each driver waited in turn to tackle the treacherously steep slope of Manor Hill. The only other access to the *high road*, as the villagers called it, was through the more convoluted route along the narrow, tree-lined lanes through Garstone, Beaumott Meade and Monks Harcourt. But in this weather, nothing short of a tractor was likely to manage it. Harry felt comfortably smug at the thought that he no longer needed to be part of the morning rush, and trudged home with a spring in his step.

It was mid morning before he was able to make his way to the summit of Hallows Hill. Ellen had insisted that he stay for a cup of tea, and during the ensuing conversation, he had learned a great deal more about his neighbours.

In reply to Ellen's enquiry about his children, Harry had mentioned his estrangement from Adam, without going into too much detail. Her reaction had been instantaneous and forthright.

"You make it up with him, Harry," she had insisted. "Don't you let it fester. Life's too short, an' you can't *never* go back."

The remark had taken Harry by surprise, until Ellen had explained that it was twenty-six years since their only son had drowned while on holiday; three weeks before his twenty-first birthday. Tears had filled Ellen's eyes as she gazed at the framed photograph of a smiling young man in the full flush of youth.

Harry had felt humbled by her sorrow, and grateful that, despite his troubled relationship with Adam, he had been spared such tragedy. It was food for thought.

The hike to Hallows Hill was invigorating and despite the slippery and strenuous trudge up through the copse, well worth the effort. As he expected, the view was breathtaking.

The sun emerged briefly from behind the slate grey clouds, to create a vista of dazzling white and cobalt blue, pierced by the black, eerie profiles of trees and hedges bordering the fields. Here and there, he could see the dark, angular outline of a cottage or farm building half hidden beneath a gleaming, wintery quilt.

A sharp, glacial wind swept across the exposed hill, freezing Harry's breath in drifting clouds. However, it was not enough to constrain the exuberance of the youngsters tobogganing on the slopes below him.

It reminded him of a winter when Debbie and Adam had been children, and he and Sally had taken them to a nearby hillside, to slide down the gentle snow covered slope on a cheap plastic sled. Nothing money can buy could have delighted them more. In his mind's eye, he recalled their laughter and shrieks of joy, and saw them again, rosy cheeked, with their noses and the tips of their ears glowing pink.

But as Ellen had said, 'You can't never go back'.

Gingerly skirting the snow laden copse, he looked down on the heart-lifting vista of Nethercombe Ley, nestling peaceful and ageless under its winter coat. Above it, silhouetted against the gleaming, white landscape, towered the dark spire of St Luke's. Blue-grey smudges spiralled from several chimneys around the green, and Harry could detect the pungent hint of wood smoke on the wind.

He stood for some time gazing out across the valley, swathed in its downy winter blanket, occasionally attempting to capture its breathtaking splendour with his camera. He found it uplifting, but at the same time, a poignant reminder of his solitude; the raucous chorus of the crows in the tree-tops behind him seeming to echo a silent cry from his soul.

Harry was fighting his way through a particularly unappetising supermarket curry, when his mobile demanded attention. He knew instinctively that it would be Sally, and heart in mouth, he answered the call.

Filled with foreboding, he asked, "Hi Sally, how did it go?"

Sally sounded upbeat. "Well, first the good news; Adam's coming back to live with Jonathan and me for a while."

"You're sure he's really coming?" Harry asked.

"Quite sure," she replied. "He hasn't got much choice really. His flatmates have thrown him and Steve out. They've had enough of the pair of them and some obnoxious little slug, who calls himself Rosco. They've been getting drunk and leaving the place in a mess. Adam owes money for his rent too."

"And that's the good news?" Harry said sardonically. "How many of them are there in this flat, for goodness sake?"

"God knows. There are *two* girls there. The flat's quite large; three or four bedrooms, I think. I made Adam take me back there. Harry, it's squalid. The place is old and looks a ruin. I should think it's about ready for demolition … that's if it doesn't fall down first. It smells of dry or wet rot; I don't know which. There's mould on the walls and ceilings, too."

"How on earth did he let himself get to that state?" Harry asked, half rhetorically.

"Well apart from the poker losses, he's got the sack from a couple of jobs; probably through opening his mouth. He tried *coming the Smart Alec* with me in front of his flatmates, but I wasn't having any of that!"

Knowing Sally's no-nonsense attitude, Harry did not doubt her ability to take their son down a peg or two. "So what's the bad news?" he asked with trepidation.

"I haven't told you all of it. There's a reason he's ready to come home with me. It was that or an ASBO."

"A what!" Harry exclaimed. "What the hell has he done?"

"Drunken vandalism and resisting arrest; that's the gist of it," Sally replied with a heavy sigh. "I'm calling from outside his flat; he's just getting his things."

Harry exhaled with a long sigh of his own. "My God! Why didn't you tell me?"

"I'm sorry, Harry. I know I should have told you before. But honestly, I only found out a day or so before I got here. I knew you'd insist on coming. I was afraid there'd be a row between the two of you. We wanted Adam as calm as possible and on his best behaviour in front of the magistrate."

"We?"

"Jonathan arranged for someone local to represent him."

"Oh, I see. And there was a real danger of him getting an ASBO?"

"Yes," she said. "His solicitor was very good."

"I should imagine he was."

"It was a she," Sally replied flatly. "She stressed Adam's background and explained about our divorce and the influences on him where he was living. In the end, she managed to persuade the magistrate to fine him and bind him over instead of issuing an ASBO. But he's got to live with one of us for the next six months … and keep out of trouble." She sighed audibly. "So I suppose things could have been worse. He's unharmed … physically anyway."

"You're right," said Harry. "Give Jonathan my thanks, won't you."

"Yes, I will," Sally replied. "It's still going to need quite a bit of money to clear up this mess though," she added tentatively.

"Do you know how much?" he asked.

"Not exactly, but several hundred, I would think. There's the solicitor's fee on top of the fine; plus whatever else he owes. I'll take care of what I can, but I can't expect Jonathan to contribute. I know Adam's cost you a packet already. If you could perhaps help out a little."

"A little?" Harry exclaimed. "Sal, you've done more than your share. Leave that to me."

"No, I'll contribute," she argued.

"Look, you're going to have your hands full with him for a while by the sound of things, so please leave the money side of it to me. Just let me know how much and who to pay."

"Thanks Harry." She sounded relieved. "But make sure you cancel his allowance. The little sod's not living the *life of Riley* under my roof!"

Harry could not help chuckling. Sally only used strong language when she felt stressed.

"I will," he replied. "You did great Sally; I appreciate it."

"I doubt if our son does," she said. "I gave him a piece of my mind just now. He's feeling pretty sorry for himself at the moment; especially as his mother as good as tanned his backside in front of his cronies."

Harry laughed. "It won't do him any harm, if it's only his pride that's hurt."

The snow lasted for little more than two days, before it was washed away by a week of persistent downpours, which delayed Harry's plans to make a start on the garden.

After checking if Rob and Ellen needed anything, he made his way to the shop; shoulders hunched against the stinging rain that slanted almost horizontally into his face.

The shop was more crowded than he had ever seen it, and the atmosphere decidedly humid and steamy. As he collected his newspaper from the 'Reserved' rack, he spotted Mrs. Keates, his neighbour from the large house opposite, queuing at the post office counter. He had not had the chance to exchange more than a few words with her and her almost permanently absent husband since he had moved in to May Cottage. He nodded and she smiled in acknowledgement.

Ahead of her, he recognised the unmistakeable figure of the Reverend Simon Cornish; taller than anyone around him, and appearing even bulkier in his grey duffel coat.

Simon spotted him as he turned away from the counter. "Hello Harry; just the chap I want to speak to."

With his curiosity aroused, Harry answered, "Really?"

"Can you spare a few minutes? I can run to a coffee at my place."

"Yes," Harry replied. "Just let me pay for my paper and grab something for lunch."

Simon peered through the film of condensation on the window. "I think it may have stopped raining," he said hopefully. "I'll wait outside, but if I'm wrong, I'm afraid we'll have to make a dash for it."

"Can't you put in a special request to your boss to move this weather somewhere else?" Harry quipped, pointing skyward.

Simon grinned ruefully. "I think someone must have beaten me to it."

They hurried across the green and up the gentle slope of Church Lane, which ran between aged thatched cottages, some of whose ancient walls and roofs bulged and sagged alarmingly. The vicarage stood beside the walled churchyard, screened by birch trees which crowned a crescent shaped grassy bank. The hedge-lined lanes that led off from the crescent, were, according to Rob Hardy, '*Where all the money was*'. From what Harry had seen of the impressive cottages and villas nestling amongst manicured lawns and foliage, that was not far short of the truth.

As they approached the vicarage, Harry took an appraising look. Tall sash windows on either side of a pillared porch, and the fanlight above the wide, panelled door, suggested that Church House was Georgian in origin. The room Simon showed him into was surprisingly light, and comfortably furnished with well-worn, leather settees on either side of a wide, stone fireplace, where several logs were burning brightly in a large fire-basket. The shelves in the alcoves on either side of the fireplace were crammed with books, many of which looked as if they could be as old as the building.

A paper-strewn pedestal desk stood under the window, and one or two well padded armchairs and polished side tables were placed around the walls, beneath hanging landscapes mounted in heavy, guilt frames.

"Make yourself comfortable, while I rustle up some coffee," Simon said, leaving Harry to settle himself on one of the settees, where he could enjoy the warmth and fragrance of the log fire.

Except for the slow, steady *tuck-tuck* of the pendulum clock on the mantelpiece, the room was still and quiet, and set him wondering about Simon's predecessors. Who were those clerics, who had ministered to past generations of the sons and daughters of Nethercombe Ley? What hopes and fears, triumphs and disappointments had befallen them through the centuries?

A venomous gust of wind swept through the straggling shrubs outside the window, tormenting the foliage into a thrashing frenzy and cascading raindrops across the narrow panes. A puff of smoke floated out from the fireplace and hung over the mantelpiece in a thin, blue haze. Looking up, Harry noticed a silver frame containing a photograph of a radiant bride; petite and delicate. Beside her stood Simon; resplendent in morning dress, smiling down at her.

Harry was inspecting the bookshelves when Simon returned with two steaming mugs of coffee. He placed one on the small drum table beside Harry, and set the other one down in the hearth, before seating himself opposite him.

"I hope a beaker's alright?" he asked.

"Perfectly alright, thank you," Harry replied. "I was looking at your books; you seem to be something of a history buff."

Simon laughed. "They're not all mine. I inherited many of them with the house. But yes, bygone days do hold a certain fascination for me, although I wouldn't claim any expertise in the field. I'm just an enthusiastic amateur."

"Me too," said Harry. "I was just speculating on the history of this place."

"This building dates from 1758," Simon replied.

"That would make it ... George the Second?" Harry suggested.

"Yes," said Simon. "I had a look at the records. The previous house burned down three years earlier. I think that predated the Tudors. Incidentally, the village pound used to be roughly where May Cottage stands now."

"I didn't realise that!" Harry exclaimed. "So Nethercombe Ley has quite a history."

"It certainly has. It was inhabited before the Norman invasion, but there wasn't a church until the late fourteenth century."

Noticing Harry's surprise, Simon continued. "The church and the most prosperous village used to be at the other end of the valley, until the Black Death decimated the population. Apparently, many died, including the priest, so they abandoned the church, and took to praying in the open air; probably on Hallows Hill, or so it's thought."

"I suppose that's how it got its name," Harry mused.

Simon nodded. "It seems the most likely explanation. About twenty years ago, archaeologists discovered the foundations of a church and the remains of a village, just the other side of Motts End. They uncovered a plague pit, too. It's possible that this end of the valley was spared the worst ravages of the disease, for some reason, so the survivors shifted here ... and eventually built St.Luke's."

"That's fascinating!" Harry exclaimed.

Encouraged by his interest, Simon continued. "The spire was added in the early nineteenth century. Apparently the local squire felt it ought to have one, and was good enough to pay for it."

"Very magnanimous of him," said Harry. "I was wondering how Manor Hill got its name; there doesn't seem any sign of one."

"A manor house stood at the foot of the hill in Tudor times," Simon explained. "But it was abandoned at the beginning of the eighteenth century and a new house built; around where the new estate is now. Both of them have been built-over long since. There are the remains of a mediaeval barn in the garden of the Treadgold's place, a few doors along from *The Black Bull*. Nearly all the existing records are at Dorchester Record Office now, but there are a few documents still here; mostly accounts and the like. I'll dig them out and let you have a look at them sometime."

"I'd like that," Harry replied, enthusiastically.

Simon stood up and moved to his desk. "But I didn't get you here for a history lesson. I was wondering if you'd mind having a look at these."

He passed a number of thin folders to Harry, each bearing the title:

## Annual Financial Statements
## Relating to the Affairs of
## The Friends of the Parish Church of St. Luke the Evangelist

"Of course," Harry said. "Do you want me to look at them now?"

"No; there's no hurry," Simon replied. "In your own time. It's just that … well, it's a little delicate and I wanted to speak to you in private. You see, Roger Smailwood, who used to be one of my parishioners, was the FOSL's treasurer." He pronounced it fossils.

"The what's treasurer?"

Simon grinned and spelled it out. "F … O … S … L; Friends of Saint Luke's. It's a group of parishioners, who donate time and money to the church; towards its upkeep and various charitable deeds within the parish. I don't know where we would be without them. Anyway, Roger was treasurer; he had been for years before I became rector. Last December he and his wife, Sybil, moved to Spain."

Harry smiled knowingly. "And you want me to hold the fort, until you cajole somebody else into doing it?"

"Well, I was hoping for a bit more than that," Simon said, cagily. "I was wondering if you'd perhaps give the figures a bit of a once over. I must confess we've never bothered much with the accounts. Everything seemed alright, and there's always been money in the bank. But we've been discussing one or two pet projects recently and, to be honest, we can't quite figure out where the money's gone. Putting it bluntly, there's less than we thought we had."

"How much less, would you say?" Harry asked.

"Several thousand."

Harry blew out his cheeks. "That's a lot of sangria."

"We may be wrong; I really hope we are," Simon sighed. "Needless to say you're the only one, apart from me and a few other trusted FOSLs, who are aware of this … at the moment."

Harry replied with a nod. "Of course; that's understood. But I'll need to look at the bank statements, cheque books and invoices that relate to these accounts."

"No problem, I'll turf them out and let you have them."

"Would you prefer me to do the work here, for confidentiality?" Harry asked.

"That's a good thought. Thanks Harry. If it wouldn't be inconvenient?"

"No; it's no problem."

Simon settled back on the settee and stretched out his legs. "So, enough business; how are things with you?"

"Oh, a bit like the curate's egg," Harry chuckled. "You know; good in parts. Marjorie, my cleaning lady, has got the house running like clockwork, and I'm gradually getting to know people here. But my son is a worry."

Thankful for the chance to unburden his cares to a sympathetic ear, Harry explained the background to his troubled relationship with Adam, and his son's recent brush with the law.

Simon listened without comment or interruption, occasionally nodding, until Harry had finished. "It's distressing, but not that unusual in the circumstances," he said. "But at least Adam's mother is keeping her eye on him now; and you've got him away from those bad influences. The fact that he was brought up in a loving home is probably an important factor in why he's finding it so difficult to come to terms with his parents splitting up. But that can also work in his favour. Love is a redemptive and healing emotion. I'm sure that in spite of everything, he knows he's loved, by both of you."

"I hope you're right," Harry said ruefully.

"I also think you're too self critical," said Simon. "It isn't all your fault, Harry!"

"Isn't it?" Harry retorted. "When he needed me, I wasn't there for him. I fell apart. I was blind drunk a lot of the time!"

"Talk to him, Harry. However hostile or indifferent his response may be. Don't give up. It means too much to you. You know it does."

Harry smiled. "You're not the first one to tell me that. My neighbour, Ellen Hardy, said very much the same thing. She and Rob lost their son just before his twenty-first birthday. She said life's too short."

"And she's absolutely right, isn't she?" said Simon.

Harry was looking out dejectedly at the steady drizzle falling on his bedraggled garden, when the phone rang. The number in the display was unfamiliar, but he guessed it might be Guy ringing once again to persuade him to accept the consultancy offer. He had called the previous week, but lacking the willpower to give an outright 'no' in the face of Guy's silver tongue, Harry had played for time and won himself another week or so.

"Hello, am I speaking to Harry Simmonds?" The caller's voice was unmistakeably female, with traces of an accent that, from the way she pronounced his name, suggested Australia, or perhaps New Zealand.

"Yes," he replied cautiously.

"Hi Harry; my name's Emma. I'm Guy's partner."

"Oh, I see," was all he could think of as a reply.

"Guy told me about meeting up with you again. He was really thrilled about it. He said you'd recently moved to Dorset."

"Yes, that's right," said Harry, enjoying the pleasant lilt of her voice.

"It's beautiful isn't it?" she continued. "I've lived here for almost five years now and I still can't get over how pretty it is."

"Whereabouts in Dorset do you live?" Harry asked.

"Just outside Wareham; where you met Guy, but I work in Swanage. Do you know it?"

"No, I'm afraid not," Harry replied. Falling back on the stock British topic of conversation, he asked, "Have you had much snow recently?"

"We didn't get much where I live; just a few flakes that came and went overnight. I'm not sure about here. I'm calling from Guy's flat in Ringwood."

"We had a few inches here in Nethercombe." He had already adopted the local habit of dropping the 'Ley'. "I took some pictures. The village looked like a Christmas card."

"I've never been there, but I can imagine it," Emma replied.

"Yes …" Having reached the limits of his ability to chat with what he took to be an attractive young woman, Harry dried up.

Emma broke the brief silence. "Look Harry, it's Guy's birthday on the fourth of April. He'll be fifty, but don't tell him I told you." Her chuckle was infectious. "He's a bit sensitive about '*Old Father Time* stalking him', as he puts it. So I'm arranging a little party for him, to cheer him up. He'd really love you to come."

Harry hesitated. "Fourth of April? … I'm not sure I can make it. I'll need to check my diary."

"It would be great if you could," Emma persisted. "It would really please Guy. It's not going to be a big thing. Guy hasn't got much in the way of family; just his cousin. There'll be a few friends and neighbours, as well. Guy said to tell you that Laurence Todd will be there. You can bring someone, if you like."

"I will if I can," Harry lied. "As I said, I'll need to check the diary first. Can I get back to you? When do you need to know?"

"There's no need; just turn up. Have you got a pen handy? I'll give you directions."

Harry wrote, with no intention of using what she was dictating. "What time?" he asked, to support his deceit.

"Any time from about seven-thirty."

"That sounds great; thanks," said Harry, as convincingly as he could.

"Please come if you can Harry." Emma's tone suggested, to his embarrassment, that she had not been fooled. "And bring the pictures of the snow. I'd love to see them."

"I will," he answered.

"Look forward to meeting you then. Bye Harry!"

What was the matter with him? Why couldn't he be like a normal person? In his heart he wanted to go. He needed company, and he would love to know what the owner of that delightful voice looked like. But he would not go.

He could envisage it all too well. He would arrive nervous and ill at ease. After the introductions and handshakes: an allocation of Guy's time; a brief, self-conscious conversation with Emma and a few awkward reminiscences with Laurence, whom he had not known that well at Bennett's, he would drift unnoticed to one side, to spend the rest of the evening nursing an empty glass, listening to other people's conversations, and waiting for an opportune moment to politely take his leave.

He sighed and finished his coffee. He was what he was.

As Harry neared his parent's home, the snowdrops and rippling waves of bluebells carpeting the woods on either side of the road were reminders of the carefree joys of his childhood. It saddened him that a visit to his parents was now as much a chore as a pleasure; not because he did not love them, but simply that they chose to remain within their self-imposed purdah of familiarity and routine, while he and the rest of the world moved on.

The three-up-three-down semi they had moved into soon after they were married had once been one of only a handful of homes looking out across fields and woodland. Now, it was all but besieged by the hideous red-brick sprawl of a modern estate. Despite their distress when the latest development had removed almost all of their view of the woods, his entreaties to move had met with stubborn resistance, given voice by his mother's repeated mantra, "Why should we move? This is our home; we've always lived here!"

His divorce had been beyond her comprehension. He could smile now, as he remembered her initial reaction, and in particular her opinion of Sally's part in it. "She should remember she made a promise ... *in church*!" The irony eluded her that, in her life, religion only assumed such mystical reverence at weddings, christenings and funerals.

He pulled onto the hardstanding beside his father's gleaming car; 'polished more than driven' as Adam had once remarked. His mother opened the front door almost before he had pulled on the handbrake.

He managed to keep a straight face at her exclamation, "Harry! What a lovely surprise!" As if he did not visit her on her birthday every year, and as if she had not been sitting at the window waiting for him.

"Happy seventieth mum," he called, lifting her cards, a bouquet and two gift wrapped parcels from the back seat; her favourite perfume from him, and a gardening trowel he had bought on Adam's behalf. After a hug and a kiss, she led the way into the house.

"Alex; look who's here!"

'You should have been an actress mum,' he thought.

His father greeted him with a broad smile. "How are you Harry?"

"Fine thanks, dad; and you?"

"Make Harry a cup of tea," came the command from behind the cupboard door, where his mother was searching for a suitable vase. His father mouthed, "She Who Must Be Obeyed!" and they both grinned conspiratorially.

"Are you looking after yourself properly?" his mother asked, as she invariably did. Harry had been waiting for it, but he still had to bite his tongue, while he watched her fussily arranging the flowers in a tall vase.

"Yes mum, I'm fine." He almost added, 'Grace bought me a lovely vase as a housewarming present,' but stopped himself in time to avoid the inevitable questions about how, when and why his ex-wife's mother should have visited him before his own parents. Reminding her of the unavoidable fact that it was because Grace had taken the trouble, would not have helped. Grace had tried to preserve the friendship she and her late husband had enjoyed with his parents since he and Sally had married, but although polite and courteous in return, his mother had done little to reciprocate.

"You'd prefer coffee wouldn't you, Harry?" his father asked.

"Please, dad."

"You shouldn't drink so much coffee! It said in *The Daily Mail*, it's bad for your heart."

"OK. Mum." Harry followed her into the lounge, where she placed the flowers on the windowsill and turned to her cards and presents.

"Thank you darling, it's beautiful," she said, placing his card prominently among the others arranged on the mantelpiece, next to one with overlapping hearts and the sentiment, *'A Birthday wish for My Darling Wife'.*

Harry smiled. Was she still his 'darling' after fifty years of marriage, and before that, a couple of years of 'courting' as his father would put it? Probably, he thought. Although a man of few words, his father was capable of deep emotions and enduring loyalty. Any passion there may have been between them had undoubtedly long since been replaced by devotion. But he would never doubt his father's love for his mother, or him.

Would he and Sally have been like them after fifty years of marriage? Would an ember of the fire that had once consumed them have remained?

"I see you had to write Adam's card," his mother said. "I suppose you bought it, as well. We never hear from him these days. Where is he?"

"Somewhere on the east coast," Harry replied. He had decided to keep his parents in the dark about Adam's problems and whereabouts for the time being, partly to shield them from the shock and distress he knew it would cause, but also to avoid what he knew would be an enervating conversation about why Adam had gone off the rails. Debbie had been of the same mind. She had agreed to leave it to him to decide when and what to tell them, when he felt the time was right.

"What's he doing there?" his father asked, placing a tray loaded with crockery on the low coffee table.

"I think he works in an amusement park," Harry replied vaguely.

"What kind of job is that, with all those GCEs, or whatever they are these days?" his mother retorted.

"Well, at least he's working," his father said. "And you're only young once."

"Debbie calls us. She comes to see us regularly. The last time was last week, wasn't it Alex?" His father nodded.

"We haven't heard from her today though," she added wistfully.

"You'll see her at lunchtime," Harry said.

His mother's expression brightened immediately. "Is she coming to see us?"

"No, the other way round," Harry replied. "We're picking her up. As it's your seventieth birthday, we're all having lunch together."

He could not have caused more pandemonium if he had set off a fire alarm. "Oh, my goodness! Why didn't you say? I'd better get ready. Go and get shaved Alex!"

"I already have!" his father replied, indignantly.

"There's plenty of time," Harry said soothingly. "I arranged to pick Debbie up at a quarter-to-one. It will only take us twenty minutes or so to get to Reading, so you've got over an hour before we need to leave."

Harry could hardly take his eyes off the lovely young woman chatting animatedly with her grandparents, both of whom gazed back at her with undisguised adoration. Where had the years gone? She was so like her mother at that age; waves of chestnut hair tumbling to her shoulders, eyes like dark pools, sparkling in the reflected light, and white, even teeth, framed by ever smiling lips.

"Isn't that right dad?"

"What?" Harry was brought from his reverie to find all three of them gazing at him. "I'm sorry …" he began.

"Dad, you weren't listening; you were day dreaming!" his daughter teased. "You weren't looking for Dominika were you?"

"Who?"

"Dominika; that little Polish waitress who served us the last time we came here. I'm sure you haven't forgotten." Turning to her grandparents, she added conspiratorially, "I think she quite fancied dad."

"She was your age!" Harry replied with feigned indignation.

"Whatever! C'est la vie, or whatever the equivalent is in Polish!" Debbie giggled and, to his delight, his mother joined in.

'It's amazing what a glass or two of white wine can do,' Harry thought. "So what was the question?" he asked.

"What? Oh yes!" Debbie flapped her hands, the way her mother did. "I was just telling Grandma and Gramps; Nethercombe Ley dates back to mediaeval times. And May Cottage is where the village pound was."

"That's right," said Harry. "Some of the locals look as if they've been around since then."

Everyone laughed dutifully.

"I was just thinking; Grandma and Gramps haven't seen your new house yet."

"They know they're welcome, any time. You all are."

"It's a long way for dad to drive," his mother said.

"It's not that far! I'm not senile yet!" his father retorted. "How long did it take you to get to us, Harry?"

"About two hours."

"It'll take us a lot longer," his mother said pointedly. "Harry drives a lot faster than you Alex."

"I'll pick you up if you like," said Harry.

"There's no need. I'm quite capable of driving to Dorset!" his father insisted.

"Boys! Boys!" Debbie interjected, her eyes twinkling. "Play nicely!"

Harry met his father's gaze and they both grinned. "Anyway, all I'm saying is, I would be pleased to see you. You can stay if you like. I've got four spare bedrooms … well three and a big cupboard with a window," he chuckled.

"Can I bring someone?" Debbie asked.

"Of course; they'll be more than welcome."

"Especially if it's Dominika!" his mother suggested impishly, sending them into surprised laughter.

It was time for the cake, and catching the waiter's eye, Harry gave the signal. His mother's eyes were moist with emotion as she blew out the seven candles that represented her seventy years, to cheers and a chorus of 'Happy Birthday' from around the restaurant. Debbie turned the envious stare of the children at a neighbouring table to smiles, as she cut the cake and toured the room, offering slices to other diners.

'It's just what her mother would have done,' Harry thought.

Debbie was unusually quiet as Harry drove her back to the rented house she shared with three other students. She had been her usual, cheerful self when they had taken his parents home and shared a parting cup of tea with them, but now she seemed pensive. He had been loath to discuss Adam's situation with her, although she was fully aware of her brother's problems. He realised that he could not stop her being concerned, but it worried him that she might be brooding on it, and become distracted at such a critical time for her.

"Dad," she said suddenly.

"Yes?"

"About my twenty-first."

"What about it?"

"Would you be upset if I said I didn't want a party? It could be awkward, couldn't it?"

"No I wouldn't be upset," Harry replied. "And I can't see why it should be awkward. But if you genuinely don't want one, that's fine with me."

"You can't deny that seeing mum with Jonathan would upset you. Grandma and Gramps wouldn't be comfortable either, would they?"

"It's your birthday; that's all that matters. I'd survive, and your grandparents will have to get used to the situation sometime."

"It's not only that. I just don't want a party. I had one for my eighteenth and that was great, but I don't want one this time."

"This doesn't have anything to do with Adam, does it?" he asked cautiously.

"No, of course not!"

"So, what do you want to do?"

"I thought I'd come and stay with you for a few days. We could go out for a meal and whatever."

"That's fine with me. Are you sure?"

"Yes, positive."

"Have you mentioned this to your mother?" Harry asked.

"Yeh; she's cool with it. She suggested a girls' day out in London; shopping … with Grandma Grace."

"If that's what you want, it's perfectly OK with me," said Harry.

"You're sure you don't mind?"

"Yes, of course," he replied. "When are you thinking of coming to stay?"

"I thought I'd stay with mum for the weekend before my birthday, and come down to you after that."

"That's fine. I think the May Fayre is around that time," Harry replied.

After a pause, she said, "You will come to my graduation, won't you, dad?"

"Wild horses couldn't keep me away. Your mum and I are very proud of you."

Debbie's eyes moistened. "I'm proud of you too Dad. I know how hard it's been for you. Not many men would have accepted it all the way you have."

Harry smiled ruefully. "I didn't have much choice did I?"

"You know what I mean," she replied, and dabbing her eyes, she leaned across to kiss his cheek.

"It's called life, my love," said Harry.

The door opened with a laboured groan, and Simon appeared holding a large mug. "I thought you might be ready for coffee," he said.

"Perfect timing," Harry replied.

"How's it going ... so far?" Simon asked tentatively.

Harry pushed his laptop away and pointed to the wallets stuffed with bank statements. "Have you got any other statements, beside these?"

"I don't think so," Simon replied. "Are there some missing?"

"Not from those bank accounts," Harry said. "They're all there and in sequence. But there are transfers from the Projects Reserve Account to an account at Lloyds TSB that you haven't given me statements for."

"I see," said Simon, settling on the arm of a settee. "I'll have another look, but I don't recall having seen any." As an afterthought, he added, "How much is involved ... roughly."

"Eighteen thousand, four hundred pounds, *exactly*," Harry replied. "Transferred over a period of six months. I can't identify which branch or account the money went to, but you should be able to find out from your own bank."

Simon sucked in a deep breath. "I'm not a finance man, but I can't understand why we didn't spot it from the financial statements."

Harry pointed to one of the folders. "Only your current account balance shows separately on the balance sheet. The others are all amalgamated into the heading of 'Reserve Accounts'. The eighteen-grand has been included in that total."

"I suppose you might say we've been a bit naïve," Simon said.

"Just a bit," said Harry. "I presume you don't have your accounts audited."

Simon spread his hands. "It's not obligatory. Roger was always steady and reliable; a pillar of the church. He's made regular donations to the Friends."

Harry sipped his coffee. "I take it Roger was an authorised signatory for FOSL transactions."

"Yes, but it needs two signatures for cheques or transfers," Simon replied.

"How many other people are authorised?" Harry asked.

"There are four others besides Roger: Lady Lauderham, Sir George Woodleigh, David Casson, who replaced Wallace Debenham; he died last year, and me."

"Are they all well heeled?" Harry asked.

"Apart from me, absolutely!" Simon replied. "I can see what you're getting at, but eighteen grand would be peanuts to them. They've donated more than that to the Friends anyway."

"So the mystery deepens," Harry mused. "Well, everything else is neat and in order, so if you can find the statements or trace the missing account, there might be nothing to worry about."

They were distracted by the snarl of a red Range Rover Sport, as it swung around the birch trees and drew up beside Simon's more modest Ford Focus.

Simon smiled. "Ah; my big sister!"

Harry closed his laptop and began tidying the files and papers on the desk, while watching a long, elegant leg stretch towards the ground, as Rachel lowered herself from the car. She came towards the house briskly; her shoulder-length hair swinging and her hips swaying. Her eyebrows rose in surprise as she spotted Harry at the desk.

To his delight, her face broke into a smile and she gave him a little wave, before disappearing behind the shrubs by the porch. He heard brother and sister greet each other in the hall, before the door opened and in she came, radiant and full of vitality.

"Hello Harry, what a lovely surprise! Have you suddenly got religion?" she teased.

"Not exactly," he replied with a diffident smile.

"Harry has been helping me sort out the FOSLs accounts," Simon explained.

"Oh I see," said Rachel, and lowered herself onto a settee beside the fire. "Roger hasn't been fiddling the books, has he?" she added flippantly.

Simon laughed, but his look was an unmistakable warning to Harry. "Roger and Sybil went off to live in Spain, if you remember," he said.

"Yes, of course!" Rachel replied. "Lucky them!" Then, as an afterthought, she exclaimed, "I'm not interrupting anything, am I?"

"No, I think we've just about wrapped it up, for now," said Harry.

"So, what's everyone doing for lunch?" she asked.

"I'm afraid I have an appointment in Belmont Lovall in an hour or so," Simon replied apologetically.

"OK. What about you Harry? Or are you going to stand me up, too?"

Harry laughed. "No, I'm more than happy to have lunch with you, if you don't mind my company."

"Oh, I think I could force myself," she chuckled.

The bar of *The Black Bull* was almost deserted when they arrived, forty minutes later, and seated themselves in the same booth they had occupied on Harry's first visit. Alone with Rachel for the first time, he felt awkward and lost for words.

She studied him over her wine glass with a quizzical smile. "So, Simon's put you to work already?"

Harry grinned. "Yes, Nethercombe must be short of accountants."

"I'd hardly have thought so! Accountants, bankers, lawyers and captains of industry are things it's definitely not short of!" she exclaimed. "It must be because he feels he can trust you."

"He hardly knows me."

"Simon's a pretty good judge of character," she said. "He's taken to you."

"I like him too. Your brother's very easy to get on with."

Her cornflower-blue eyes twinkled playfully. "What about me; aren't I?"

Harry felt himself blush. "Yes; when you're not making fun of me."

"Harry, please!" she exclaimed. "I'm not making fun of you, I'm having fun *with* you; there's a difference."

"If you say so."

"You're very self-conscious about your shyness aren't you?" she said.

"Yes, I am," he answered flatly.

"Don't say it like that. It's a refreshing change from guys who think they're God's gift."

"I'll take your word for it. But all the same, I'd rather I wasn't. It's a barrier to so many things."

"Such as?"

"Well, meeting people; making new friends. For instance, I've been invited to a friend's fiftieth birthday party, but there's no chance of me going."

Rachel's eyes widened. "Why ever not?"

"I'm not a party person. I don't like turning up on my own. I find it difficult to just walk up to people and start a conversation."

"Why don't you ask your friend if you can bring someone?" she suggested.

"Oh, I can."

"So?"

"I can't think of anybody to ask. I'm a bit out of the swim after all these years."

"You know me," she said.

Harry laughed nervously.

"I'm serious!"

"I couldn't expect you to do that! I'm sure you've got a damned sight more interesting things to do than nursemaid me for an evening!"

"When is it?" she asked, fishing a diary from her bag.

"Rachel; no! It's very kind of you, but that's not why I mentioned it."

"I know. Just tell me where it is and when!"

"Next Friday week … in Ringwood."

"Let's see … I've got nothing special on, so I can come down straight from the office. It should take us about forty-five minutes to an hour from here. As long as we don't have to be there before eight-thirty, I'm game if you are."

"Rachel!"

She screwed up her nose puckishly. "What's the matter, don't you like the idea of being seen with me?"

"Are you kidding?" and spreading his hands, Harry shook his head. "OK. But if you change your mind or get a better offer, just let me know; understood?"

"Oh, I'll drop you like hot coals," she retorted playfully. Pushing her empty glass towards him, she said "You can express your gratitude by getting me a refill."

No-one was serving when Harry reached the bar, and while he waited for someone to appear, his eyes were drawn to a folder on the counter beside a chap he guessed to be about his own age. He wore an olive green sports jacket and cavalry twill trousers, and was sitting alone at the bar, tucking into a ploughman's lunch and reading *The Dorset Echo.*

The folder held a stack of flyers, each headed by a turquoise banner proclaiming:

*Gerald Spenser-Smith*
*Your Candidate for Local Issues*

Below this was a picture of Gerald beaming benevolently. Harry recognised the face as a member of what he had come to think of as '*The Cougar Pack*'; Stella's cronies, who could usually be found, clustered around the bar at weekends.

Noticing Harry's interest, the chap looked up from his newspaper, revealing a large turquoise rosette pinned to his lapel, with the legend '*Vote Smith*' on the central button. 'Presumably Gerald's name was too much of a mouthful to include all of it', Harry thought mischievously.

"Do you live locally?" the man enquired.

"Yes, I do," Harry replied with scarcely concealed amusement.

"So you'll know about the election for the Parish Council."

"I've seen the notices and flyers," Harry replied. "I understand the vacant seat is being contested by three people."

"That's right. I'm Gerald Spenser-Smith's campaign manager."

"Really?" Harry said incredulously.

The man picked up a flyer. "Yes. Would you be interested in putting one of these in your window?"

"Not really," Harry replied. "No-one would see it from the road, anyway."

The door opened and Harry's neighbours, Jill and Alan Anderson, appeared. Jill smiled at Harry, and spotting Rachel, went over to greet her with the ritual Gallic *kiss … kiss* on each cheek. Alan, taking in the flyers and rosette with a brief glance, asked, "What's this? Is the circus coming to town?"

Thankfully the distraction of Carla appearing behind the bar allowed Harry to stifle the laughter bubbling up within him. Alan pointed to the glasses Harry held. "Let me do this; what can I get you and Rachel?"

"Thanks. Just a half of *JR* and the house white for Rachel, please."

"Right; plus another house white and a large red for me, please Carla."

Anticipating more fun from his neighbour's acerbic humour, Harry said, "It's to do with the Parish Council elections. This is Gerald Spenser-Smith's campaign manager."

"Good Lord!" Alan exclaimed. "I must have missed the cameras and the 'Battle Bus' when I came in." He leaned on the bar, his face expressionless, as he peered at the name badge pinned below the garish rosette. "Well Chris; when can we expect a visit from '*Call Me Dave*', or will it be, '*I'm Not Really Red, Ed*?'"

"I beg your pardon?" Chris replied nonplussed.

"What's the Torrid Turquoise Party's position on the Euro and the European Court of Human Rights?"

"Alan; stop it!" Jill called with ill-disguised mirth. Harry did not dare to look at her or Alan.

"We're campaigning on purely local issues," Chris replied innocently.

"What; like Home Rule for the Beldene Valley? Some of us are very keen on that!"

"No; we're concentrating on local issues and amenities!" Chris replied deliberately, as if suspecting he was dealing with the village idiot.

"We've got some of those," Alan sighed. "We've got a phone box, but unfortunately no phone. They took it away when it was vandalised two years ago … to mend it, so we were told. They seem to have forgotten to bring it back. We've got a bus stop too, but sadly we're a bit short of buses. In fact the last one we set eyes on was in 2003. So what's our Gerry proposing to do about it … *if* we trust him with our vote? And I must just point out my friend here and I are not averse to being offered inducements."

Fortunately for the bemused Chris, Carla interrupted by placing the drinks on the bar. "Are you intending to eat, Alan?" she asked. "Do you want me open up a tab?"

"Yes we are. Thanks Carla."

Chris drained his glass, folded his newspaper and with a nod to Carla, left with his folder tucked under his arm

"You shouldn't have wound that poor man up like that," Jill chided, her dark eyes twinkling with amusement, as Alan and Harry joined them at the table.

"They're as bad as each other," said Rachel. "Harry was egging Alan on."

Jill could not restrain her infectious giggle. "I know; I don't think we should let them out together."

"Surely a campaign manager is a bit over the top for a parish council election?" Harry chuckled. "It smacks a bit of *The Vicar of Dibley*, doesn't it?"

"Yes, but all the candidates take it very seriously," Alan replied.

"What's Gerald Spenser-Smith like?" Harry asked.

"You've met him in here," Rachel said.

"I know, but only to say hello and goodbye to. I've spoken to his wife a couple of times. She seems very pleasant."

"Yes, Cheryl's lovely," Jill agreed.

"Gerry's alright," Alan answered. "He takes himself and things like this election a bit too seriously. It's dead easy to take the rise out of him; he does ask for it at times. But he's a nice bloke really. He actually cares a lot about Nethercombe Ley and this area."

"The name Spenser-Smith is made up of course," Jill added.

"Yes, I heard that," said Rachel. "I forget who told me; it may have been Colin Merrick." Looking mischievously at Harry, she added, "Your friend Stella's husband." Turning to Jill, she asked, "Wasn't his name just plain Smith before he changed it?"

Jill nodded. "Yes; apparently Spenser was his grandmother's or an aunt's maiden name; something like that."

"He added it, because he thought a double-barrelled moniker would sound more impressive," Alan added. "It seems to have worked too. He's done pretty well for himself."

"What does he do for a living?" Harry asked.

"*Drakes*; the supermarket chain," Alan replied. "Worked his way up from an assistant branch manager to the board."

"Very impressive," said Harry. "It must have taken more than a hyphenated name to achieve that."

Alan took a generous swig of wine. "Anyway, enough of Gerry and politics. Are we all eating together , or were you two young things hoping to be alone?"

Feeling his cheeks burn, Harry replied quickly, and a little too loudly, "No; Simon should have joined us for lunch, but he has an appointment."

"I'm too hungry for romance, anyway," said Rachel, casting an impish grin at Harry.

"Quite right, Rachel," Alan replied. "Never make love on an empty stomach. It plays havoc with the digestion."

"Alan!" Jill exclaimed. Amid the laughter, he grinned and looked at Harry questioningly. "There's just one other serious matter to get cleared up. Do you play golf, Harry?"

# APRIL

## *A Breath of Spring*

The sorry state of Harry's lawn brought to mind the old proverb '*A rolling stone gathers no moss*'. It seemed to consist almost entirely of moss, interspersed with clumps of clover and a liberal scattering of dandelions. 'Perhaps a few rolling stones wouldn't go amiss,' he thought wistfully.

His parents had finally paid him a visit the previous afternoon, and he had been almost too ashamed to show them the garden. But, true to form, his father had chosen to emphasise its potential; expressing envy of the fruit trees, and enchantment with the view of the sunlit hills, dappled by the shadows of drifting clouds.

They had been delighted by the brief tour of Nethercombe Ley Harry gave them. Typically, his mother had been full of praise for the cleanliness and tidiness of the house. Her only criticism had been its size. "It's much too big for you on your own. When are you going to find someone to settle down with again?"

They had declined his offer of dinner at *The Black Bull*, his mother asserting, to his father's evident surprise, "We don't want to be too late. Your dad doesn't want to be driving home in the dark on that motorway." They had settled instead for tea and sandwiches, which she had insisted on making, and the chocolate sponge-cake she had brought with her. Nevertheless, he had enjoyed their company and the opportunity to show off his house. The thought that, even in his forties, he still sought his parents' approval, brought a wry smile to his face.

Having invested in a pressure washer, he spent the morning cleaning the patio, leaving it gleaming and spotless. However, his sense of achievement was short lived, when he realised that the french windows were spattered with the dirt and lichen blasted from the paving stones. With the thought, 'Marjorie will have a seizure if she sees this,' he set about cleaning them.

He would need to do something about the leylandii, before their encroachment became too intrusive. His neighbours, Alan and Jill, had no concerns about him lopping them back on his side of the fence, and his offer to return anything he trimmed off, had been declined with good natured amusement.

It was while he was inspecting the barren wasteland of what he euphemistically called his 'vegetable garden', that he became aware of voices on the other side of the fence. He looked up as Rob exclaimed, "'Ere 'e is! This is the feller what wants t'ave a word with you, Alfie."

The slim, dapper man standing beside him was a good deal shorter than Rob. His hair was light grey, almost white and neatly trimmed, above a face lined and weathered by the seasons. A regimental crest was proudly prominent on the tie, neatly knotted at the collar of the crisp, white shirt he wore beneath an olive green anorak.

"This is Alfie; the chap I was tellin' you about, if you wants some 'elp with them trees, 'Arry."

Harry held out his hand over the fence. "Hello; I'm Harry Simmonds. As Rob said, I would appreciate some advice."

Alfie's eyes were masked by the smoky-blue lenses of his gold-rimmed glasses, as he gripped Harry's hand.

"Alf Cox," he said, taking in the condition of Harry's garden with a lingering appraisal. "You got a job on there," he declared.

"I know," Harry replied. "Not only do I not know where to begin, I haven't much idea what to do about it when I do."

"Them apple tress need prunin' for a start."

Harry nodded. "How do I go about it?"

"You'll need t'be careful, or you'll do more damage than good. You'd be better off lettin' somebody who knows what they're doin' have a go at 'em."

"Do you know anybody?" Harry asked.

Alfie grinned. "Well, there's me, I suppose."

"Would you be prepared to take it on?"

"I reckon sommat like this'd just suit you Alfie," Rob suggested. Looking at Harry he explained, "Alfie retired last year. 'Es bin lookin' fer a bit a'gardenin' work t'keep 'im occupied."

"Would you be interested?" Harry enquired hopefully.

"Well, I could 'ave a go at them trees, for a start. We can take it from there. See 'ow it goes."

"Excellent!" Harry exclaimed. "You can work as and when it suits you. There are one or two tools in the shed. You'd better tell me if there are any others you need. I'd buy a mower too … if I had any grass."

Alfie chuckled. "We'll 'ave a look at that, as well. But there's no need to worry; I got all me own tools."

"Access won't be a problem. Marjorie or I will be here most days, but if we're not, the side gate isn't locked."

"Oh, I know young Marjorie!" Alfie exclaimed. "Billy Prickett's eldest. Ellen was tellin' me she cleans for yuh. You got a little diamond there!"

"Don't I know it?" Harry replied.

Alfie took a lingering look at Harry's garden and stroked his chin. "What if I pop round later in the week an' 'ave a proper look? We can go from there?"

It was music to Harry's ears. "Fine; whenever it suits you. We can sort out what you're going to charge me, too."

"Well I dunno. I've never done nothin' like this before."

"It might be useful to find out what the local gardening firms charge," Harry suggested.

Alfie shook his head. "Good Lord; I'm not gonna charge them prices! I'm not lookin' for a fortune. No; you an' me can come to an arrangement that suits the both of us."

"Tea up!" Ellen called from the house.

"D'you fancy a cup. 'Arry?" Rob asked.

"Thanks, Rob. But I need to go into Dorchester before lunch, so I'd best be off. Many thanks. See you soon!" he called to Alfie and went back into the house in high spirits.

There was no need to scrutinise the numbers and name plates beside the door of each flat. The faint throb of bass notes identified their destination, even before the lift doors opened. A glance at the tall, elegant woman beside him calmed the familiar flutter of nerves he always experienced when arriving at a party. Her poise and confidence was enough for both of them.

Clutching a bottle of vintage Bollinger, Guy's favourite tipple, Harry pushed the button beside the brass plate bearing the number 17 and G.R.F. Wolstencroft, while Rachel rested her clutch bag and a bouquet of flowers on a hall table. She brushed a wisp of golden hair from over one eye and made a final check on her appearance in a tall mirror.

In Harry's opinion, she had no reason for the slightest concern. The burgundy cocktail dress she wore beneath the white, woollen jacket suited her to perfection; hugging her pencil-slim figure, and ending high enough above the knee to draw appreciative attention to her endless legs, without straying beyond the bounds of good taste. A gold watch, drop earrings and simple gold chains at her throat and on one wrist, completed the image of chic and elegance.

Aware of his attention in the mirror, she raised an eyebrow; to which he responded by placing the tips of his thumb and forefinger together in the time honoured gesture of appreciation. Her husky chuckle was drowned by the music, as the door opened.

"Hello; come on in!" The Antipodean accent was more pronounced than Harry remembered from the phone call, and the appearance of the chubby woman who greeted them not what he had envisaged or expected from experience of Guy's previous girlfriends. Without waiting for them to introduce themselves, she turned and called across the crowded room. "Guy, you've got more guests!"

Heads turned as they went in; male eyes homing in on Rachel.

Guy appeared from a group in one corner of the stylishly furnished room. A broad smile lit up his face as he spotted Harry, only for it to be replaced by surprise as he saw Rachel beside him. Guy's gaze left her for only a second as Harry helped her off with her coat.

He took the coat and shook Harry's hand. "Wow, vintage Bollinger! Thanks Harry. It's great of you to come!"

"Happy birthday Guy; this is Rachel … Rachel, meet the birthday boy."

She smiled, clearly aware of Guy's appreciative scrutiny. "Happy birthday Guy; I hope you don't mind me coming with Harry."

"*Hello* Rachel!" Guy exclaimed. "Of course not; you're very welcome. A *very* pleasant surprise." Gesturing towards the bouquet, he asked impishly, "Are those for me?"

She treated him to one of her disarming giggles and held out the flowers. "No, these are for Emma."

"Oh! I'm not Emma!" the plump young woman exclaimed in surprise. "I'm Chrissie; Emma's in the kitchen."

"Would you be a dear and get her, Chrissie?" Guy asked. Waiting until she had left them, he looked at Harry with a pained expression.

Harry lost the struggle to keep a straight face. "Sorry; it was the accent. We just naturally assumed …"

Guy grimaced. "Give me *some* credit!" he replied in mock indignation. "That's Emma's cousin from *Ad … el … aide*." He pronounced it in an excruciating parody of Chrissie's accent.

Harry chuckled. "I did wonder."

"Anyway, let me take the flowers off this lovely lady, and get you something to drink. But first of all, let's introduce you." Guy clapped his hands loudly, at which the babble of voices tailed off and the music was turned down by an unseen hand. "Everyone … this is the lovely Rachel and her escort, Harry!" he announced, adding archly, "Rachel's the blonde one, by the way!"

He received a dutiful ripple of laughter in response, which was accompanied by a ragged chorus of, "Hi Rachel! Hi Harry!"

"Rachel … Harry, this is everybody. I won't bother with their names. By the time I've got through them, you'll have forgotten and be none the wiser, anyway. So I'll leave you to work it out for yourselves. Now, what can I get you to drink?"

As the volume of the music and chatter increased again, Rachel brushed another errant wisp of hair from her eye. "I'd love a glass of white wine, if I may?"

"You can have anything you like my dear," Guy replied deliberately. "But let me guess; would I be right in assuming you'd prefer champagne?"

Rachel rewarded him with a dazzling smile. "Please!"

"And, for your escort? My guess would be a beer. Is that correct Mr. … er?"

"Yes please, waiter." They grinned at each other like schoolboys after a juvenile prank.

"Well, hello. Glad you could make it!"

Recognising the voice from the telephone call, Harry turned to discover its owner was entirely in keeping with his expectations. Although not as tall as Rachel, she was equally eye-catching and, in Harry's estimation, a few years younger. Her luxuriant, titian hair fell to her shoulders in loose waves and curls, sweeping across her forehead above a pair of striking green eyes. Her mouth, with its full top lip and prominent front teeth, reminded him of a poster of Brigitte Bardot he had once seen on the wall of a Paris brasserie. Like Rachel, she wore little jewellery; a gold locket around her neck, a large, white fashion watch, and a ring, with what Harry took to be an opal at its centre, on the third finger of her right hand. A sleeveless, cream dress hugged her eye-catching figure, complimenting the light, golden tan of her shoulders and arms.

Guy poured the champagne and made the introductions in his own inimitable style. "Rachel … Harry, this is Emma. You'd never guess, but she's not from around here."

Emma pulled a face at him. "It's good to meet you," she said. "We're so pleased you could make it."

Harry took the hand she offered, enjoying the touch of her long slender fingers. The two women shook hands and did the fashionable kiss on the cheek routine, greeting each other with a smile and a swift, all encompassing glance of appraisal; the way attractive women do when they meet.

Rachel picked up the bouquet. "These are for you," she said.

"Thanks Rachel; they're gorgeous!"

Rachel chuckled. "You're welcome. I almost gave them to Chrissie, thinking she was you."

Chrissie grinned nervously. "We're cousins. My dad and Em's dad were brothers."

"Nice to meet you Chrissie," Harry said, sensing her embarrassment.

Guy reappeared with a brimming champagne flute. "Here we go, bubbly for Rachel; and I think if we ask Chrissie nicely, she'll fetch young Harry a cold tinny from the fridge."

"No probs!" Chrissie trilled. "Shall I take those and put them in water, Em?"

"If you wouldn't mind, Chrissie," Emma replied, burying her nose in the bouquet, before handing it over. "They're lovely." Looking up, she asked, "Did you bring the pictures Harry?"

Harry was momentarily perplexed. "Pictures?"

"Yes; the ones you took in the snow. You promised to bring them. Do you remember?"

"Oh yes! No I haven't. I forgot them, I'm afraid," he replied clumsily.

"Never mind; perhaps another time."

"I'm sure he won't forget next time, will you Harry?" Rachel added pointedly.

"No," he replied, thankful for Chrissie's swift return with his beer. He accepted the ice cold glass and raised it to Guy. "Here's to you; happy fiftieth."

"Don't rub it in," Guy groaned, grinning ruefully.

"I'm sure I recognise that face!" Rachel turned towards the

overweight middle-aged man, whose boldly striped open-necked shirt barely constrained his well developed paunch. He introduced himself with a self assurance bordering on arrogance. "Bob Richardson. I'm with NBH. You were at the Manchester IBD Conference weren't you?"

"Yes, I was," Rachel replied.

"I never forget a face; especially a pretty one."

"Were you speaking there?" Rachel asked politely, although her expression betrayed barely concealed annoyance at what she clearly suspected was an unwelcome advance.

"No-oo! I was there to hear Eddie Markham speak."

"Oh; you mean Sir Edward Markham," Rachel replied flatly. "Know him well do you? I'm not on first name terms with him myself!"

"Well … no … not exactly," Bob replied awkwardly.

Recognising her irritation, Guy intervened. "No shop talk, Bob," he said jovially. Taking Rachel's elbow, he ushered her towards the group behind them. "Come and meet this gang of ne'er-do-wells, Rachel."

True to form, when left alone with an attractive woman, Harry was apprehensive. Emma seemed to sense his nervousness, and asked, "So, how are you settling into your new home, Harry?"

Her accent was less overt and more mellow than Chrissie's, which Harry assumed was due to the years spent away from her homeland. He found it engaging; especially the way she pronounced his name.

"Slowly, but surely … I think," he replied. "Village life is a lot different to Croydon. Everyone seems to know your business as soon as you do."

Emma laughed. "I can imagine. It's not quite that bad in Swanage."

"I've never been there," Harry replied. "I don't know Dorset very well at all."

"You'd like Swanage," she said. "It's quite small as seaside towns go, but very popular and pretty crowded during the season. It's not as brash and brassy as a lot of other resorts … very family friendly."

Beginning to feel a little more comfortable, Harry asked, "Where do you work?"

"I've got a shop in Swanage. We sell mostly women's clothes and accessories. You know; sweaters and jumpers, skirts and coats. We stock a few items of menswear too … sweaters and polo shirts, and that sort of thing."

"And all of it bloody expensive!" Guy interjected mischievously, as he reached for the champagne bottle on the table behind her.

"I should hope so. It's all top quality!" Emma retorted. "Cashmere and silk don't come cheap!"

"You should see Emma's knickers!" Guy said, and raised his eyebrows suggestively, before turning to top up the glasses of the group gathered around Rachel.

Harry felt his cheeks redden; unsure if he had heard correctly.

Emma's face adopted a pained expression. "I also stock a range of lingerie," she explained. "It's designed by a friend of mine. It's very feminine and …"

"Expensive!" said Guy, replacing the bottle.

Harry laughed, more from relief than amusement, and became aware of a thin, balding figure in a plaid sweater, hovering at his elbow.

"Hello Harry; it's been a long time."

Harry shook the outstretched hand. "Hello Laurence."

In Harry's opinion, time had been even less kind to Laurence than Guy. His pale complexion and thinning hair made him appear a good ten years older than the forty-ish Harry knew him to be.

"Of course; you two were colleagues, weren't you?" Emma exclaimed. "Well, do you mind if I leave you to chat about old times, while I check out the food?"

Harry cast a furtive and appreciative glance at the swaying hips as Emma made her way to the kitchen, then turned his attention to Laurence and the vaguely familiar young woman beside him. She was idly surveying the room with a look that implied she would rather be somewhere else. Delving into the recesses of his memory, Harry recalled the raven-haired young tartar from accounts, whose zealous scrutiny of expenses claims had led her to acquire the epithet 'Lil the Enforcer'.

"Hello Lillian," he said, suppressing a mischievous urge to ask if she had made a note of the mileage from home.

"Hello Harry," she replied, with a smile that pleasantly banished her dour expression.

Laurence beamed. "Lillian and I got married after you left, Harry."

"I see," Harry replied, adding by way of a pleasantry, "Do you have any children?"

"Yes; a boy, Jason. He's five."

"That's not your wife, what's her name … Sarah, is it?" Lillian asked pointedly.

"Sally," Harry replied in amusement, in no doubt that she had heard Guy's introduction when they arrived. "No, that's Rachel. Sally and I are divorced." Guessing what they were thinking, he was about to add, 'No, she's not the reason for the divorce', but decided it was more fun to let them wonder.

"Really!" Laurence exclaimed, his gaze lingering on Rachel, who appeared perfectly at ease amongst people she had only just met. "So, what are you doing now, Harry?"

"Not much at present," Harry replied. "Until recently, I was a partner in a company specialising in management consultancy. But I decided I'd had enough. I've only just moved to Dorset; that's how I came across Guy."

"I see," said Laurence. "Lillian and I are still with Everson Quinlan." Noticing Harry's bemused expression, he added, "They took over A.J. Bennett and Co. after you left. Lillian is Controller of Staff Imbursements now."

"That's American for payroll," Lillian quipped.

Harry grinned with amusement. "Oh, right."

"I have to find the little boys' room," Laurence announced. "Will you excuse me for a moment?"

Lillian broke what could have been an awkward silence. "I presume you're wondering about Laurence."

"In what way?" Harry asked disingenuously.

She smiled. "Come on Harry; there's no need to pretend. Laurence is still in *Technical Planning*. He's got the title '*Head of Section*', but it's only four guys at drawing boards. He's been passed over for department manager and deputy manager more than once. He'll never go any further and he knows it."

"Does it really matter?" Harry replied. "He seems happy. He's a nice guy; and if my memory serves me well, good at what he does."

Lillian sipped at what appeared to be tonic water. "It doesn't matter to me; not any more. He's a good husband … he dotes on Jason. But he's too *'nice'*, as you put it. He's far too deferential and won't push himself. I used to think you were a bit like that. You were always polite and never tried to fiddle your expenses. *Lil the Enforcer* never had to chuck them back at you!"

Harry laughed out loud. "I didn't realise you knew about that!"

"How could I not know?" Lillian giggled. "You all called me it."

"Not in your hearing," he replied. "We didn't dare!"

"That bugger did!" Lillian nodded towards Guy. "In fact I wouldn't be surprised to know he started it."

"You could well be right," Harry chuckled.

"So, do you and Rachel have any marriage plans?" she asked, in the disarmingly direct way he remembered.

"Good Lord, no! I've only just met her. Believe it or not, her brother's the local vicar."

Lillian's eyes widened. "She's not exactly shy and retiring, is she?"

Harry grinned. "No, Rachel is anything but a wallflower."

Guy clapped his hands once more and the music faded. "OK everybody! Emma tells me the tucker is fair dinkum. It's all in the kitchen, so please help yourselves … and enjoy!"

Contrary to Harry's initial fears, he *was* enjoying himself, and did not feel isolated or out of his depth. Lillian Todd had either matured, or his recollection of her was flawed, because he found her both amusing and self deprecating. However, her husband proved to be a different proposition. Although pleasant and amiable, Laurence was still as dull and devoid of personality as Harry remembered.

After the excellent buffet, Emma produced a cake, topped by a blaze of candles. Guy blew them out with a flourish, and then gave a typically witty and amusing thank you speech, while Emma and Chrissie distributed the cake and champagne.

Guy and Emma were perfect hosts; circulating independently, chatting and re-filling glasses. Rachel mingled effortlessly, with *Bob the Banker* dogging her heels. His voice and raucous laughter were often audible above the general ebb and flow of conversation. When Harry managed to penetrate the group clustered around her, she asked, "Are you OK?" He was happy to reply that he was.

He was chatting to Jean and Ray, a charming couple who had recently retired after selling their business, when Guy appeared with a champagne bottle to top up their glasses. "Encore un bier pour Monsieur?" he enquired.

"Merci non, garcon," Harry replied in kind. "Je suis le conducteur."

"Well as long as you're only punching bloody tickets, what's the problem?" Guy retorted waggishly.

"I take it you've known each other for *some time*," Jean giggled.

"Far too many years," Harry replied with a wry smile. "Thanks anyway Guy. I've already had a couple of beers and some champagne."

"Why drive all the way back to Nettley Cowpats, or wherever it is, tonight?" Guy countered. "I'm afraid I can't offer to put you and Rachel up. I've got Chrissie and my cousin Clive and his wife staying overnight." Arching his eyebrows, he nodded suggestively towards Rachel. "But there are some decent hotels around here."

To Harry's acute embarrassment, she overheard and looked at Guy and then at him questioningly. "Did I hear my name mentioned … and something about hotels?" she asked.

Before Harry could reply, Guy intervened. "I was just suggesting to Harry that you ought to find a hotel for the night. He's been practically tee total all evening!" Guy's forehead creased, and he added archly. "He deserves a little fun, don't you think?"

Harry blushed to the roots of his hair. "No, it's OK Rachel; ignore him."

"Oh, Harry, I'm sorry!" she exclaimed contritely. "I've been so inconsiderate! You're the invited guest. I ought to have offered to drive home, but I've been selfishly guzzling Guy's bubbly all evening."

"It's OK," Harry replied awkwardly. "I don't have a problem with that."

Rachel put a hand on his arm. "Now I feel guilty! We can check into a hotel, if you like."

Harry avoided eye contact. "No! One of us would still have to drive there."

"Ever heard of taxis?" Guy interjected. "I take it you parked in the courtyard. You can leave the car there overnight. It'll be quite safe."

"Neither of us has brought anything for an overnight stay, anyway," Harry said.

Guy chuckled mischievously. "I'm sure you can manage without your jim-jams for *one* night!"

Irritated by Guy's persistence, Harry retorted sharply, "I'm perfectly happy with a soft drink!" Moving closer to avoid Rachel overhearing, he hissed, "I've only just met her, for Christ's sake! God knows what she thinks we're up to! She probably suspects this is some juvenile stunt we cooked up to get her into bed with me!"

"We hardly qualify as juveniles," Guy chortled.

Uncomfortably aware of Jean and Ray's amused interest, Harry snapped loudly, "Look, I'm driving home, and that's all there is to it!" Embarrassed by his outburst, he excused himself on the pretext of needing the toilet.

He returned a few moments later, chastened and feeling decidedly foolish. Rachel had resumed her interrupted conversation, while Ray and Jean had drifted to a group on the other side of the room. Even the Todds were happily exchanging parental anecdotes with another young couple.

Standing by the kitchen door, Harry watched the clusters of guests nodding and laughing in animated conversation. It had been such a promising start. But here he was, just as he had anticipated, watching everyone else enjoy themselves. He would have liked to leave, but shied away from the further embarrassment of trying to justify an early exit to Rachel and Guy.

Wandering into the deserted kitchen, he absently took a cocktail sausage from a plate. It was relatively quiet; the buzz of conversation and occasional burst of laughter muted and barely registering above the muffled beat of the music. He was not looking forward to the journey home, now that Rachel undoubtedly suspected him of enlisting Guy in a ploy to get her to a hotel.

The volume of the music and the babble of voices suddenly increased as the door opened. "Fancy a coffee?"

He turned to find Emma, standing in the doorway. "I wouldn't mind, if you're having one," he answered.

"You seemed to be miles away," she said, and began filling the kettle.

"I suppose I was."

"You don't look as if you're having a very good time."

"I am. It's just that … well; I suppose I'm not very good at mixing."

"You've been doing fine," she insisted.

Harry sighed, and leaning against a worktop, looked down at his shoes. "I made a bit of a fool of myself just now. That's something I *am* good at."

"No you didn't!"

Harry looked up into her striking, green eyes. "Oh; you saw."

"Yes I did," Emma said quietly. "Guy can be bloody insensitive at times."

"It's not his fault. Guy is Guy. I've known him a long time. I should know what to expect. I ought to have made a joke of it, or something … anything but the stupid scene I made."

"Don't be silly," Emma said soothingly. "You did nothing of the sort. You were embarrassed." Taking a jar of coffee from a cupboard, she asked, "Will instant be OK?"

"Fine thanks." Harry grinned self-consciously. "God knows what Rachel's thinking. She only came along to give me moral support. I didn't have the bottle to come on my own; and now …"

"It's not a crime to be shy, Harry," Emma said softly. "And I wouldn't worry about Rachel. From what I can see, she's no fool. She handled Bob Richardson without batting an eyelid. I'll bet she's got Guy's measure too. She'll realise it was nothing more than Guy playing the fool."

"I hope you're right," Harry said doubtfully.

The door opened again. "Hello! Hello! What goes on in here?" Guy enquired suggestively.

"For God's sake Guy!" Emma retorted. "When are you going to learn to pull y'head in? Haven't you caused enough mischief?"

Guy's expression became a picture of injured innocence. "Me?" he asked in feigned surprise. Then, just as suddenly he was serious. "Look Harry, I'm sorry, mate. I didn't mean to embarrass you. I meant it as a bit of fun, but it was a serious suggestion. I don't think Rachel's put out about it. All the same I'm sorry. I'm glad you came."

Harry smiled. "I'm the one who should apologise. I shouldn't have made such a song and dance about it. Rachel's probably convinced I'm a complete prat now."

Emma handed him a mug of coffee and tugged at his arm. "Come on, let's go and meet a few people. I haven't spoken to Laurence and his wife yet; or that pair from downstairs who seem obsessed with their kids. I need some moral support."

Harry followed Emma towards the door, turning to Guy as they reached it. "By the way, do you still want to talk about that contract?"

"You bet!" Guy replied.

Emma took a welcome lead and drew him into mingling with the other guests. He found Linda, the wife of Guy's cousin, Clive, particularly entertaining. She worked in an upmarket health clinic, and was not only amusingly tipsy, but delightfully indiscreet about the clinic's clientele; one or two of whom were minor celebrities. Harry would find it difficult to take the predictions of a certain TV weather girl seriously in future.

Guy and Emma seemed loathe to let Rachel and Harry go. They stayed chatting until well past midnight, and were the last to leave. No-one mentioned the *hotel incident*, and from her demeanour, Rachel gave the impression she had forgotten it; although Harry was not convinced.

They finally left with Harry agreeing to let Guy set up a preliminary meeting with the directors of ACCORS, and an invitation to Emma and Guy to join Rachel and him for dinner at *The Black Bull*, sometime in the near future.

As the lift doors closed, Rachel looked at him questioningly. "Had a good time?" she asked.

"Yes thank you," he replied. "Thanks for coming with me."

"I enjoyed it. It was a nice party," she said. "Guy's fun, isn't he?"

"Oh he's a scream!" Harry replied acidly.

The doors opened onto the lobby, and Rachel's heels clicked on the marble floor as they made their way to the exit. "Emma's quite something, isn't she?" she said.

"Yes, she's very nice," Harry replied.

"Very nice?" Rachel laughed. "You couldn't take your eyes off her!"

"Don't be stupid!" Harry exclaimed defensively.

She ignored his petulance. "Not that anyone could blame you. She's got a great figure. Terrific boobs … not like my poor excuses."

Harry considered it wiser to refrain from comment. He pushed the button on the key-fob to unlock the car and held the door open, enjoying the display of elegant leg, as she lowered herself onto the seat.

He waited until he had started to pull away, before beginning a halting apology. "Look Rachel … whatever you think … that hotel thing … It wasn't my idea. It wasn't what Guy made it look like, with his grubby innuendos."

"Really?" she replied, with a playful smile.

"It wasn't!" he protested. "I swear to God, it wasn't! I was quite happy with one or two beers."

"I know," she giggled. "The look on your face was enough; not to mention the colour. You were bright red."

"I could have bloody well killed Guy!" he exclaimed.

She laughed. "Oh Harry, you are funny. It's just his way. Surely you know that! Some men would've gone along with it, hoping to get lucky … assuming they fancied me of course," she added archly.

"What do you mean, assuming?" Harry said. "Even that sap who couldn't stop talking about his kids was eying you up. I can't imagine you've met many men who didn't fancy you."

"It seems I have now."

"And what does that mean?"

"Well, it's not very flattering to be turned down in front of room full of people, when you offer to spend the night with a fella."

"Stop taking the piss!" Harry retorted, thankful that he needed to keep his eyes straight ahead.

"I'm not!" she chuckled.

"Yes you are! Look Rachel, I don't need reminding of my shortcomings. I was going to say I'm out of practice after twenty-odd years of marriage. But the truth is, I was never bloody-well *in* practice. I spent my adolescence at an all-boys school. I hardly knew any girls! I wouldn't know how to seduce a woman, even if I had the guts to try; especially one like you!"

"One like me?"

"Don't go all coy," Harry replied. "You're hardly a schoolgirl!"

"Thanks for reminding me!"

"You know what I mean!"

"Alright, I do," she relented. "Of course I know you didn't plan it. I'm not a schoolgirl, as you so chivalrously mentioned."

"I never meant it like that!"

She gave him no chance to finish. "I can see forty looming, and I've been around the block, as they say; so I've learned a bit about men. Most women my age have. Of course I know you weren't trying it on! And it's not about being too shy is it? You're too honourable and decent to try something shoddy like that."

Harry could think of no reply to what he took to be a euphemism for 'dull and boring'.

"But for what it's worth," she continued. "It wouldn't have been so terrible to share a bed with you ... if that's what you wanted."

Misinterpreting his surprised expression, she added, "Don't look so worried. I'm not desperate to snare a man. I'm not after a husband. I've already got one."

Harry's astonishment registered clearly on his face. "You're married?"

"Yes; I have been for six years."

"So where's your husband?"

"New York. I met him when I worked on Wall Street. He's a pilot with an American airline."

Harry was nonplussed. "You're here and he's in New York?" He was aware that she was watching him, probably trying to gauge his reaction.

"Yes," she replied. "It's all over between us. We just haven't got round to a divorce."

"Would it be impertinent to ask why?"

"He wouldn't agree to it. I wanted to come home; the job and the marriage weren't working out, but Karl turned it into a war. When I wouldn't go back to him, he did everything he could to make it hard for me. In fact he was an utter shit! I had to go to court to get my things from our apartment."

"When was this?"

"Nearly three years ago. I was … still am technically, Mrs. Karl Bannichinski."

"Good grief!" Harry exclaimed, to which she replied with one of her chuckles.

"So you could say we've both been through the matrimonial mill," she sighed.

"What if you ever wanted to marry again?" he asked.

"Oh, I dare say I could persuade Karl to give me a divorce now, if I wanted one."

"Do you ever see him?"

"*No!*" she answered emphatically. "I haven't been in contact with him for two years."

Harry could not help wondering what her brother made of it all.

As if reading his mind, she said, "Simon's been a brick; especially as it wasn't that long after he lost Zoe. But he took me in and gave me a bolt hole, until I got back on my feet again."

"And I thought I was hard done by!" Harry exclaimed. "I've got nothing on you two!"

Rachel chuckled huskily. "So, are we still friends?"

"I sincerely hope so."

"Good," she said, "Have you got any plans for next weekend? It's Easter."

"Not really. I'm not a churchgoer, I'm afraid."

"Neither am I," she replied, "I've never been able to believe the way Simon does. Bless his heart; he doesn't have a problem with that."

"I see," said Harry. "Anyway, if the weather's not too bad, I thought I'd have a wander around Dorset. I like what little I've seen so far."

"That's sounds interesting. Were you intending to do it alone?"

"I guess so."

"You don't fancy some company, I suppose?"

Harry's pulse quickened. "I'd like that very much."

Harry was unsure what to expect when Simon ushered him into the now familiar room at Church House. Although he had no vested interest in the outcome of the meeting, he still felt apprehensive. After all, isn't the harbinger of bad tidings often given as hard a time as the perpetrator?

David Casson looked the epitome of a senior civil servant, from the tailored suit and silk tie to the polished leather shoes. His calm, quiet manner suggested self-confidence, but without arrogance. He greeted Harry politely.

Jeremy Radford was very tall and slim, with thinning grey hair. He was casually dressed in a tweed jacket, corduroy trousers and a checked shirt, of the kind beloved by country gentlemen. His greeting was affable and friendly.

Sir George Woodleigh was large and burly, with a florid, weather-beaten complexion, suggesting an outdoor life; probably involving farming, Harry thought. His manner seemed brusque, but his handshake was firm and reassuring.

Any preconceptions Harry had entertained regarding Lady Diana Lauderham were dispelled on sight. He had half expected tweed, twin-set and brogues. Instead he found himself shaking hands with a woman of indeterminate age, with frizzy, dyed blond hair and what his father would call a *well upholstered figure*, barely contained within a bright red dress.

Creases appeared at the corners of her eyes and mouth as she smiled. "Thank you so much for coming, Mr. Simmonds," she said.

"You're welcome," Harry replied. Declining Simon's offer of refreshment, he seated himself on the settee beside him. The other three male FOSLs sat opposite; Lady Lauderham occupying an upright chair facing all five of them.

"Shall we begin gentlemen?" she said, crossing her sturdy legs and donning a pair of spectacles with heavy tortoiseshell frames. She opened the folder on her lap. "As this is an unofficial meeting, I suggest we dispense with agreeing minutes of previous ones. We can leave that for the next scheduled meeting in June. Agreed?"

To murmurs and nods of assent she continued. "I think the best way to start is by thanking Mr. Simmonds for his work, and asking him to expand on his investigation into our finances. If you would be so kind, Mr. Simmonds."

Harry cleared his throat and began cautiously. "Well, as you know, Simon … Reverend Cornish, asked me to conduct an unofficial audit of the accounts produced by your treasurer. I'm afraid there's an apparent discrepancy."

"I can't see that there's any *apparent* about it!" Sir George growled.

"Can we let Mr. Simmonds finish before we comment, George?" Lady Lauderham interjected firmly. "Please continue."

"Unfortunately, it seems that Sir George may be right," said Harry. "As I understand it, Reverend Cornish's investigations haven't managed to trace the transfers from the Projects Reserve Account."

Simon nodded in agreement, and Harry continued. "There's no account in the Friends' name at the bank the funds were transferred to, and the beneficiary account has an obscure name."

Once again Simon concurred, and Harry explained, "Of course, customer confidentiality doesn't allow the receiving bank to disclose enough details of the account holder for you to follow up … unless it becomes a criminal investigation."

"Which it damned soon will be!" Sir George snapped.

"Hang on George!" David Casson interjected. "Let's stop and consider for a moment. Don't forget Roger's in Spain. If we or the police instigate proceedings against him, it could take months, with all the cost involved. There's no guarantee that we'd get a penny back at the end of it."

"So, you're suggesting we write off the eighteen grand and let the thieving tyke get away with it?" Sir George reposted. "This isn't a few quid filched from petty cash; this is serious theft!"

"You're right George, but I'm inclined to agree with David," said Lady Lauderham. "And my impression, from reading Mr. Simmonds report, is that he feels we are to some extent culpable through our own negligence."

Sir George stared pointedly at Harry. "Oh does he?"

"I wouldn't go as far as negligence," Harry said, adding firmly, "But allowing the person who produces unaudited figures to sign cheques and authorise transfers *is* inviting trouble."

"But surely they need another signature," Jeremy Radford countered.

"Which your treasurer seems to have acquired," Harry replied.

"That's right," Simon confirmed. "The second signature on all the transfer forms was the late Mr. Debenham's, even though one or two of the transfers were made after he died."

"So Roger forged his signature?" Jeremy suggested.

"Not necessarily," Harry explained. "I understand that before Mr. Debenham's illness, bank transactions were almost always authorised by him and the treasurer. It's possible that Mr. Smailwood may have persuaded him to sign several blank transfer forms … to 'save time'. It's not uncommon when the people needed to authorise transactions are not readily available, and controls are, to put it bluntly, not what they should be."

"Point taken," David Casson replied.

"It's undoubtedly the line the bank would take," Harry added. "Simon tells me the signatures look genuine, so it would be down to you to pursue a charge of fraud or theft against your treasurer."

Jeremy drained his wine glass ostentatiously with a look towards the half empty bottle beside Simon. "So, what you're suggesting is that we either sue Roger or write the money off?"

"I'm in no position to suggest anything," Harry answered. "I'm here simply to present you with the facts, as I find them. The decision is entirely yours."

"But your view is the same as mine; that we shouldn't hold out much hope?" David Casson asked.

Harry nodded. "There's a real possibility of throwing good money after bad."

"There are other considerations," Lady Diana said solemnly. "We won't be able to keep this to ourselves if we pursue an action against Roger. It would become public knowledge, with all the adverse publicity and loss of confidence that would entail. I imagine some would resign their membership; perhaps enough to make the FOSLS no longer viable. It could undo all we've achieved over the past twelve years."

Without waiting for Simon's invitation, Jeremy reached out and helped himself to more wine. "I must say it's against all my instincts to let him get away with it!" he muttered. Holding up the bottle, he asked, "Anyone else?" They all shook their heads.

"I agree," said Sir George.

"I'm of the same opinion, but we may have no alternative," said David Casson. "And we now have to tell the ladies organising the pre-school group that we can't support them after all."

Lady Lauderham held up a hand. "Not necessarily. I don't believe, in all conscience, we can do that. They're committed too far."

"What else can we do?" Sir George replied."We don't have sufficient funds."

Lady Lauderham uncrossed her legs and leaned forward. "I'm willing to make good the lost money," she said, lifting a hand to silence the murmur of surprise. "Subject, of course, to the adoption of the controls suggested in Mr. Simmond's report. So, I suggest we allow him to elucidate."

Harry looked at Simon, whose expression had not fully recovered from the surprise of Lady Diana's generosity. "My suggestions are simple and straightforward," he began. "Firstly, whoever produces the financial statements *should not* authorise payments or transfers of funds. In other words, he shouldn't be an authorising signatory."

Heads nodded in assent, as Harry continued with his recommendations, each designed to ensure that all future financial transactions were transparent and under the committee's control. To murmurs of approval, he concluded, "And finally, I would urge you to have your annual accounts independently audited by a person or organisation qualified to do so."

"Does anyone have any questions or reservations concerning these suggestions?" Lady Lauderham asked. There were none.

"Good!" she exclaimed. "I realise it's irregular, but in the circumstances I suggest we don't minute this meeting."

"How do you intend to account for the money you have so generously offered?" Harry asked.

"The same way it disappeared; as obscurely as possible!" her ladyship replied flatly. "Are we all agreed?"

Again no one demurred.

"Thank you for your work and valuable advice, Mr. Simmonds," she said. "Most generously given, I might add."

"Thank you Harry," said Simon.

"Yes indeed!" Sir George added, as Harry tidied his papers and stood up to leave.

Jeremy Radford held out his hand. "Thank you. May I call you Harry?"

"Of course. I'm happy if I've been of some help."

"You're not leaving, are you, Harry?" David Casson asked.

"I assumed we'd finished, or at least my contribution was," Harry replied.

"You've been extremely helpful, and in the most diplomatic manner, given us the kick up the backside we needed. But we haven't yet come to a conclusion about how we deal with your recommendations, or the cost."

"That's right," said Lady Diana. "I think David is referring to the financial statements you recommend should be available for our quarterly meetings, and the audit of our annual accounts."

Harry settled back onto the settee. "I'm not suggesting you need to go to the expense of a large corporation."

"Does that mean you're volunteering?" Sir George asked.

"No, Sir George. I was about to suggest you use local auditors; from somewhere like Dorchester or Wimbourne. They would be perfectly adequate … and a lot cheaper."

Sir George nodded. "Well, what about the financial statements? Would you be willing to produce those for the time being?"

Her ladyship looked enquiringly at Harry. "I think that's an excellent idea. Could we persuade you?"

Taken out of his stride, Harry looked at Simon, who grinned and spread his hands. "It's entirely up to you, Harry," he said.

"I'm flattered," Harry replied hesitantly. "But I'm not a church-goer."

"So what? Roger was in church every Sunday!" Sir George retorted pointedly.

"Perhaps you'd like a little time to think about it," Simon suggested.

Lady Lauderham tapped her copy of Harry's report with her pen. "I think I speak for everyone in expressing our gratitude, and in endorsing Simon's judgment of your ability and integrity."

Harry felt a flush to his cheeks, as the men nodded and murmured their agreement. "I'd be glad to help, until you can appoint someone on a permanent basis. It will give me a chance to contribute a little something to the community."

"That's what we're all about, Harry," Simon replied. "It's not just about donating cash."

Her Ladyship drained her glass and pushed her spectacles back onto the bridge of her nose. "There are one or two other items to discuss. If you're not in a rush to get away, Harry. It might give you an idea of how we work?"

"No, I'm in no hurry, Lady Diana."

"Please call me Diana."

It had all happened so quickly that Harry was still bemused on the following Saturday, when he picked up Rachel for their 'expedition to darkest Dorset', as she had dubbed it. Before they left, he quizzed Simon about what he had told the FOSL's committee members about him before the meeting. Simon had simply smiled and replied, "Only the truth."

Apparently Harry's report and recommendations; proposals he considered blindingly obvious, had somehow impressed the eminent worthies with whom he now found himself on first name terms. Moreover, he had surprised himself by overriding his normal reticence, to accept their invitation so readily.

However, he had little time or inclination to dwell on such things, because Rachel presented him with a small suitcase and a dress carrier, to be placed in the boot of his car. His inability to conceal his surprise prompted the comment, "I thought we were intending to make a weekend of it."

"Yes; of course," he replied unconvincingly.

"So where's your bag?" she asked.

"I … er … I thought we were doing day trips," he answered lamely.

Their departure was delayed by a return to May Cottage, to hurriedly throw his toilet bag and a couple of changes of clothes into a holdall. He was grateful that Marjorie was not around, saving him the need to attempt an innocent explanation; not that she would have believed it, anyway.

At Rachel's suggestion, they headed towards Bridport, with the intention of making their way eastward along the coast. Happily, the sun finally forced its way from behind the clouds in time for a stop for coffee at West Bay. Despite a chilly breeze, they enjoyed a brief stroll along the quay. Rachel tucked her arm through his as they walked, enjoying the sea air and watching the comings and goings in the harbour.

To Harry, it was a simple, almost forgotten, pleasure; one he had last enjoyed with Sally.

Making the steep climb from the bay, and passing the cliff top golf course, they followed the coastal route, while out on the ocean, the sun played hide and seek with the clouds, casting shimmering mirrors of twinkling light over shifting shades of blue. On the landward side, nature answered the challenge by flaunting her spring finery in vivid greens; presaging the glory of approaching summer.

With his spirits lifted, Harry was in the mood to indulge Rachel's whim of climbing to what she took to be a ruined castle on the hill overlooking Abbotsbury. In spite of the gusting breeze, a good deal stronger and chillier higher up, the climb to what turned out to be a mediaeval chapel, was worth the effort. Rachel, in jeans and a puffy jacket, and with her hair tucked incongruously under a tweed flat cap, nestled against him in the lee of the sturdy chapel walls. Gazing seaward, their eyes followed the extraordinary lance of shingle known as Chesil Beach, as it swept mile upon mile, parallel to the coast, towards hazy Portland. Below them Abbotsbury lay nestled around its church, but for the traffic, for all the world like an illustration from a child's storybook.

Weymouth provided them with the diverting spectacle of *Brits on holiday*. Although it was early in the year and hardly sunbathing weather, the beach and promenade were well populated by hardy souls; many optimistically dressed for a Mediterranean heatwave. The array of garish clothing suggested many of them did not own a mirror.

Harry never ceased to be fascinated by the ability of his fellow countrymen and women, to devour anything fried or grilled, at any time of day. What also intrigued him was their apparent inability to enjoy any form of relaxation without the stimulus of alcohol.

His jaundiced observations were a source of amusement to Rachel, who, having discarded the cap, strolled beside him with her fingers intertwined with his; her golden tresses constantly teased and tormented by the breeze.

At her insistence, '*as appropriate for the seaside*' as she put it, lunch was fish and chips eaten from polystyrene containers. They sauntered along the blustery promenade, passing a colourful clock tower that would not have been out of place in a Disney cartoon, while *Mad King George*, with a seagull perched irreverently on his head, stared down from his plinth with a curiously startled expression.

Harry drew the line at Rachel's playful appeal for 'the child's special'; chicken nuggets and chips served in a plastic sand-castle bucket, with matching spade. However, he had to concede to half an hour of the questionable entertainment of Punch and Judy; something he had never '*got*' even as a child. He was unwise enough to mention it to her, and to his acute embarrassment, she joined in boisterously with the children's calls and shrieks.

The harbour was more to Harry's taste, but the price of looking on enviously at the leisurely passage of vessels, large and small, was to be dragged onto fairground rides afterwards. In the face of Rachel's irrepressible mischief, he found it impossible to maintain his reluctance, and had to admit that he was thoroughly enjoying himself.

The clifftop above Durdle Door was the limit of their '*first day's march*'. By late afternoon the breeze had eased, and they sat in the sun, looking down at the wide curve of sand sweeping round to the majestic limestone arch. Rachel was all for making their way down to the beach, but Harry felt they ought to start looking for somewhere to stay.

They drove inland towards nowhere in particular, and it was Rachel who eventually spotted a sign directing them to a small hotel, adorned with flower-filled hanging baskets, and set in its own well kept gardens.

Harry's mobile rang as they approached the awning covered entrance. While Rachel went in to enquire if they had a vacant room, he retrieved the phone from his coat pocket on the back seat; only to find he had missed the call. It was not a number he immediately recognised, so he ignored it and parked the car beneath some trees.

When he entered the hotel, Rachel was standing at a small reception counter, speaking to the elderly man behind it. Turning to Harry, she asked impishly, "Do you fancy a four poster?"

Caught off guard, he stuttered, "Yeh … why not?"

Rachel returned her attention to the elderly man. "OK. Yes; we'll have that one, please."

Harry heard little more of their conversation, because the thought which had been loitering in the shadows of his mind since she had handed him her overnight bag, had finally slipped its shackles. Her words in the car on the way home from Guy's party echoed in his mind: '*It wouldn't have been an ordeal to share a bed with you.*'

Typically, his euphoria was tempered by apprehension, as he contemplated how long it had been since he last shared a bed with a woman. During the past twenty-five years, there had only been one. Now, here he was with a confident and outgoing woman, with none of his inhibitions and hang-ups; moreover, one who was making all the running.

"Harry!"

The sound of Rachel's raised voice startled him from his reverie. "Sorry; what was it?" he asked.

She raised an eyebrow. "I said: do we want an alarm call? Breakfast is between eight and nine-thirty."

"I don't know. It depends; do we?"

His remark had been made seriously, but she smiled knowingly and picked up the key. "Come on; let's get our bags from the car."

Rachel's face was bathed in a soft, amber glow, as she smiled at him across the flickering candle. She was simply dressed in what he supposed people referred to as 'a little black number', gold earrings and the necklace she had worn to Guy's party. A portrait of loveliness. Her eyes sparkled in the candle light. "More coffee?" she asked.

"No thanks. I enjoyed the meal; the wine was very acceptable and the company delightful."

"Thank you kind sir," she replied. "Are you sure you wouldn't like a brandy?"

"No thanks."

"I can see it's no use trying to get you drunk," she chuckled.

"Oh, it's not that difficult," he replied quietly. "Until quite recently, it would have been difficult to stop me."

"It must have been tough for you."

"My son, Adam, would tell you it was a lot worse for him."

"Are you still in love with your wife?" she asked quietly.

"*Ex*-wife," Harry said flatly. "I suppose so ... in a way. We were married for twenty-two years. I think part of the problem has been staying in touch, because of the kids. Perhaps if it had been a clean break, I might have come to terms with it easier ... and quicker. Maybe I'd have been a better father."

"You're being very hard on yourself," she said.

"You wouldn't say that if you'd seen me the nights I used to come home pissed as a rat!" he retorted. "I guess I was on the road to becoming an alcoholic."

"But you're not!" she replied firmly. "You've got it all back together, and now you've got another chance at life!"

"I hope so," he said, and reached across the table to touch her perfectly manicured fingers. "Look Rachel, not wanting a brandy has got nothing to do with being frightened of getting drunk. A couple of glasses of wine tonight were all I wanted. I can stop when I want to. It's been a wonderful day; the best day I've had in ages. I've spent it with a beautiful woman, who put up with me and made me feel like a man ... not a failed husband and a lousy father. Alcohol can't improve on that."

Rachel entwined her fingers with his. "I've had a lovely day too. You've humoured me and made me laugh. And despite your talent for putting yourself down, you're fun to be with ... and not at all bad looking in candlelight."

Without needing to look, Harry knew there would be an impish grin on her face. "It's probably the poor light, but this is my good side."

Her laugh echoed in the dining room; now deserted but for the two of them. "You are an idiot!" she exclaimed.

Two waitresses appeared, and started setting the tables for breakfast. Rachel folded her napkin and placed it on the table. "I think they're trying to tell us something," she giggled. "We'd better clear off and let them get on with it."

Harry stood up and eased her chair back as she rose to her feet; tall, elegant and desirable.

"It's rather a nice little hotel, isn't it?" she said, running her hand along the polished handrail, as they climbed the wide curving staircase.

"Yes, it is," Harry answered, grateful for the distraction. "It was very clever of you to find it."

"Do you think Guy would approve?" she chuckled.

"To hell with Guy!" he replied, and unlocked the door to their room.

She had left a bedside light on, which illuminated the bed in a harsh, eerie glow, and drew the eye to it, as if to an exhibit in a macabre museum. It was what Harry believed was called a tester, and stood on a raised platform at one end of the spacious room. The simple, unadorned design suggested its origins were not that far back in time. It was also high, and in spite of Rachel's long legs, her feet barely reached the floor when she sat on it and pulled off her shoes.

Harry could not remember feeling so awkward since his teens, and reluctantly averted his gaze from her exposed limbs and the twinkling blue eyes looking up at him.

"I feel I should have brought a nightcap and nightshirt," he said, in a lame attempt at humour.

"Well, it seems very comfortable," she said, and as she bounced, the bed creaked softly. Their eyes met and they grinned at each other like errant children.

"Look; we don't have to … " he began uncertainly.

"I know," she replied and stood up, presenting her back to him and lifting her hair from her neck. "Now shut up and unzip me."

With trembling fingers, Harry obliged.

Easter Sunday dawned dull and overcast, and while they were admiring the almost perfectly symmetrical bowl of Lulworth Cove, it started to rain. Rachel gave Harry an accusing look that said, 'So what was all the hurry for?'

One of the least surprising things he had already learned about her was that she was not '*a morning person*'; at least not in the sense that he understood the word. It had been anything but easy to overcome her reluctance to leave the comfort and warmth of the bed in time for the nine-thirty breakfast curfew.

As a consequence they had only covered the short distance from the hotel to Lulworth by late morning. The ominous blue-grey clouds, bloated and billowing up over the sea, gave warning that the rain was likely to persist for the rest of the day.

"Oh, bloody hell!" Rachel exclaimed, as the intermittent raindrops intensified into a downpour. Caught unawares, they scuttled for cover. She had been in a mischievously petulant mood since he had pulled the bed covers from her, leaving her the choice to lie there and shiver or seek the relative warmth of the bathroom.

Having reached the sanctuary of the car, she turned to him, wiping her hair with a handful of tissues. "What now, Oh Great Leader?"

Aware that she was doing her best to annoy him, Harry chose not to react. "Any suggestions?"

She grinned mischievously. "Yes; you can wipe that smug look off your face, for a start!"

"What do you mean?" he asked, although he knew perfectly well what she meant.

"Given a choice, I'd take a nap!" she said. "In case you've forgotten, I didn't get to sleep until very late!"

Harry grinned sheepishly, feeling his cheeks burn.

She chuckled and pressed a finger against the tip of his nose. "But who's complaining?"

With the rain bouncing off the bonnet and streaming down the windows, the sensible option was to get away from the coast. Harry waited until the drumming on the roof eased to a patter and the wipers were able to clear the windscreen, before he headed inland towards Wool.

Roadside boards announced the attractions of Monkey World and mediaeval jousting at Lulworth Castle, neither of which promised much shelter from the elements. Harry assumed that most of the exhibits at the Bovington Tank Museum would be under cover and would engage his interest for the afternoon, but he suspected they would hold little fascination for Rachel.

He drove on until, much to her amusement, various 'Puddles' began to vie with 'Dorchester' on the road signs, with an occasional 'Piddle' thrown in for good measure. "It's no wonder they have names like that, with this kind of weather!" she exclaimed.

They enjoyed an entertaining diversion to the Tolpuddle Martyrs Museum, before moving on through the rain-washed countryside towards Bere Regis. Having had a substantial, and for Harry, late breakfast, neither of them felt hungry, so they settled for coffee and biscuits at a small cafe, crowded with refugees from the weather. They sat by the window, watching the rain spattering the tables and chairs outside.

"Any idea what you'd like to do now?" Harry asked.

"Not really," Rachel replied wistfully.

"Would you like to head home?"

"Is that what you want?"

"No," he answered. "I thought you might be getting bored."

Rachel shook her head. "No, I'm fine. I just wish this bloody rain would stop!"

"I suppose we could head towards Bournemouth and find a hotel," he suggested. She raised her eyebrows, and glanced at her watch pointedly. "That's not what I meant!" he said awkwardly; and louder than he had intended. Lowering his voice, he added, "I was going to say, it would save us looking around later. We could get a drink or something, and if the weather improves, go for a stroll and maybe see if there's a show on somewhere this evening."

"Good idea, Oh Great One!" she replied.

"Oh God, are we back on that?" he groaned and rolled his eyes.

They eventually checked in to a modern, glass and chrome edifice near the sea front in Bournemouth. The rain stopped later in the day, but neither of them was aware of it. They did not leave the hotel until early evening, when they went in search of a restaurant, with Harry reflecting that, in the twenty-five years he had known Sally, *they* had never once taken a bath together.

Rachel was back in mischief mode, and he did not doubt that he was in for an evening of being teased. But he could not have cared less. The night sky was star spangled; the sea was sighing and chuckling seductively against the shore ... and she looked terrific.

The following morning they woke to a sea mist that enveloped the shore in its pallid, all-pervading embrace, reducing everything to wraithlike shadows.

The hotel had a more indulgent regime on serving breakfast, so Harry made no attempt to flush Rachel from beneath the bed covers. While he waited for her to come to, he made himself a cup of coffee and settled back to watch TV with the sound off.

By mid-morning the mist had lifted, and after a leisurely breakfast, they headed in the direction of Blandford Forum. Rachel needed to be back at Canary Wharf the next morning, so she did not want another late night. However, refreshed by her lie-in, she was in high spirits.

"Good God; this *'Tarrant'* guy put himself about didn't he?" she exclaimed, referring to the sign posts on which the name of every other village seemed to include that word. "Tarrant Crawford, Tarrant Rushton, Tarrant Monkton," she recited.

"It might not be a *he*," Harry replied. "It could be an *it*. I read somewhere that rural place names are often obscure and derived from local features and ancient languages."

At her request, Harry detoured to Shaftesbury. The quaint cottages lining the steep slope of Gold Hill put him in mind of a row of nervous, elderly ladies, huddled together in fear of pitching headlong down the precipitous cobbles. It might have been a scene from a bygone age, were it not for the cameras, hideous shorts and baseball caps.

After a pleasant stroll around the historic town, and tea and scones at *King Alfred's Kitchen*, they made their way homeward; in Harry's case reluctantly. But he felt happier and more content than he had for a long while.

During the journey, Rachel flipped through the pages of a tourist brochure she had picked up in Shaftesbury. "That's something we missed!" she exclaimed suddenly.

"What's that?"

"The Cerne Abbas Giant."

"Oh him," Harry chuckled. "I've heard he's a big lad."

"Very impressive," she replied.

"Perhaps we can pay him a visit another time," Harry suggested tentatively.

"Oh, I think we should," she giggled.

Daylight was fading beneath an overcast sky, when Harry drew up beside Rachel's Range Rover, outside Church House. The front of the house was in darkness, but the glow in the fanlight above the door, revealed that Simon was at home.

Rachel leaned across and kissed him gently. "Thank you Harry; it was fun. I've had a lovely time."

"So have I!" he replied emphatically. "It's just a shame about the iffy weather."

"Never mind; we made the most of it, didn't we?"

"We certainly did," he answered, and released the boot catch, before unclipping his seat belt.

Rachel put her hand on his arm. "Harry, darling ... how can I say this?" she began cautiously. "Don't take this the wrong way. I've really enjoyed our weekend. It's been fun being with you. I like you very much, and I'd love to do this again ... or anything you like. But if you're looking for a settled relationship ... I'm sorry."

"Don't be sorry; I understand what you're saying," he replied. "I wasn't expecting exclusive rights, if that's what you're concerned about. I'm not ready for a serious relationship anyway."

"I'm not talking about 'exclusive rights'," she said firmly. "I'm just not ready to make a commitment at the moment; not even to someone like you. It's nothing to do with my marriage; that's history. Despite how you may feel now, I think you will be looking for a permanent relationship … sooner rather than later. But I can't offer you that."

"I quite understand Rachel; I really do. You're a wonderful girl, and you've done me a power of good this weekend. Don't worry; I'm happy with things the way they are."

"Thank you Harry," she said quietly. "Are you coming in to say hello to Simon?"

"Yes, of course," he replied.

After a few days of Rachel's vibrant company, the quiet and stillness of May Cottage seemed even more palpable.

Harry had not expected his relationship with her to be anything more than casual. Despite the pleasures of the past three days, he did not delude himself that it meant anything more to her than an amusing diversion. Nevertheless his ego had been bruised by the fact that she considered it necessary to discourage any false hopes she suspected him of harbouring; no matter how careful she had been to spare his feelings.

The hope that one day Sally would come back to him was now no more than a fragile flame guttering in the icy blast of reality. The possibility that he might live the rest of his life alone invoked a despondency that no amount of 'brief encounters' could overcome; even with someone like Rachel.

He envied Guy. He had no such problems or concerns. Women who would not give him a second glance seemed to be attracted to Guy like moths to a lamp. During the time Harry had known him, there had been several; each of them attractive and desirable, but none had managed to commit him to a permanent relationship. Harry could not help feeling that Emma might succeed where the others had failed. But that was probably the secret of Guy's success. Women seemed to be attracted by the risk and uncertainty of relationships with men who were impulsive and unpredictable.

With a sigh of resignation, he went into his study to check the messages on his answering machine. There were two. The first was from Marjorie, apologising for the fact that she would not be able to '*make it*' for a day or two. Her croaky voice made an explanation unnecessary, and when he called back and spoke to her husband, Phil, he learned that she had been laid low over the Easter weekend. He sent her his best wishes for a speedy recovery, and made a mental note to send her some flowers ... or perhaps, better still, a bottle of Baileys; her favourite tipple.

The second message was from Guy explaining that he had called on Saturday, but had been unable to reach him. It was probably the call he had missed outside the hotel. Guy wanted him to call back as soon as possible. It was undoubtedly about the proposed meeting, but he decided it could wait one more day.

When Harry looked out of the kitchen window, he was surprised to see that Alfie had already made a start on the garden. While he had been away, the leylandii had been sheered back level with the fence. He went outside, and even by the limited light reflected from the kitchen window, the results were noticeable; albeit somewhat alarming as far as the lawn was concerned.

Alfie had obviously used his contacts to borrow a scarifier and an aerator. As a result, the lawn was an arid expanse resembling the aftermath of twin assaults by locusts and giant earthworms. However, he could see one or two tulips. Spring had arrived, and with luck, everything would bloom and flourish again.

If only he could be as optimistic about his life.

# MAY

## *Into the Sunlight*

May made its entrance cloaked in morning mist, which soon dispersed as the sun's gathering strength lifted the blanket of low cloud, melting it into fluffy white pillows, scattered across a deepening blue counterpane. A cool breeze ensured the temperature remained far from tropical, but the clearing sky promised a fine day for Garstone's May Day Parade. Harry had come to realise how important these occasions were to rural communities, and hoped the weather would be equally kind when Nethercombe Ley held its May Fayre later in the month.

However, such considerations were not foremost in his thoughts. Anticipating the pleasure of his daughter's company for a few days pushed other matters to the back of his mind, keeping an almost permanent smile on his face and a spring in his step. It was something not lost on Marjorie, who was noticeably amused by his boyish exuberance.

She had her own reason for celebration. Her son's tour of duty in Afghanistan was coming to an end, and she looked forward to his homecoming with a mixture of emotions; foremost of which was relief. In spite of her own joy, she indulged Harry's barely concealed excitement and offered thoughtful suggestions to his planned arrangements, while making her own contribution by airing bedding and attending to considerations that rarely intrude on the male thought process. She even quizzed him about Debbie's likes and dislikes regarding food.

Debbie texted to confirm that she and Paul would be arriving the day before her birthday, and intended to stay over the weekend for '*the fete*', as she called it. Harry's eager anticipation was only slightly muted by the disappointment of realising that he would not have her all to himself, and 'the friend' she was bringing was clearly not female. However, it was high time he faced the fact that she was a young woman and no longer his 'little girl'.

Another consideration was Adam. Although he had spoken to Sally about the possibility of including him in Debbie's birthday celebrations, Harry had reservations about their son's enthusiasm. Sally had managed to get Adam to the phone, but he had conceded nothing more than a promise to think about coming. Harry felt he could not expect much more. Even so, their damaged relationship hung over him like a cloud and troubled his conscience.

It had quickly become apparent that turning over the flower beds and, what seemed a disconcertingly large vegetable patch, required more strength and man-hours than Alfie could manage on his own. The idea of an attractive garden was appealing, but the hard graft ahead of them had taken 'some of the gilt off the gingerbread', as Harry's father would say.

However, working under Alfie's supervision, Harry had soon noticed positive results. The grass seed and top-soil they had put down were displaying ambitions of becoming a lawn, and the bordering flower-beds were now tidy and weed free. The apple trees had been pruned back alarmingly, but Alfie had assured him that opening them up, would do them the world of good.

Despite the dark, threatening clouds on the horizon, Harry took a mug of coffee to the bench at the end of the garden, to savour the remaining moments of morning sunshine and enjoy the opera of birdsong in the hawthorn hedge. He watched in fascination, as the gathering storm clouds advanced menacingly, and with the retreating sunlight, created a kaleidoscope of changing light and shadow on the hills.

Harry's thoughts turned to the previous weekend. Despite his misgivings, he had enjoyed Nick and Sue Holding's anniversary celebrations. Sally had turned up alone; her excuse being that Jonathan was unwell. However, it was more than possible that she had chosen to spare him the pain of seeing her with her new husband on such an emotive occasion. He was genuinely happy for his old friends, but celebrating twenty-five years of their marriage and witnessing their joy and happiness had been a bitter-sweet experience. When they raised their glasses to the happy couple, Sally's new wedding ring had sparkled in the sunlight, making it impossible to dispel thoughts of what might have been.

He had learned that Debbie had received her own invitation, offering her the opportunity to bring a 'partner', but she had kept it to herself, so that she could accompany him 'without any argument or fuss', as she had put it. How well mother and daughter knew him.

He was beginning to doubt the wisdom of signing the contract with ACCORS; a decision made against his better judgement. Although, he tried to convince himself that he had done it to please Guy, he had to admit that it had as much to do with increasing his chances of seeing more of a certain Aussie redhead.

It was not something to feel proud of. Harbouring a secret yen for his friend's partner was not a sign of maturity, especially in someone his age. He exonerated himself with the excuse that he had neither the intention nor the nerve to take it any further. Knowing she would give him pretty short shrift if he tried was a powerful enough deterrent to him even contemplating it.

Heavy spots of rain interrupted his daydream, and he hurriedly made his way back to the house, just reaching the sanctuary of the lobby, before the heavens opened. A deep rumble reverberated around the hills, which were now obscured by teeming rain, driven like a billowing curtain on vicious gusts of squalling wind. He stood in the doorway, awed by its sibilant roar and fascinated by the bloated raindrops that spattered on the patio, and made the garden flowers and shrubs bob and sway like puppets.

Not so long ago, he would have had neither the time nor the inclination to appreciate the power and beauty of a storm.

By evening, the stormy showers had passed, and the rain-washed roofs and foliage glistened in golden sunlight. On his way to the post box, Harry was greeted by Ted Flowers, who was dragging a wheelie-bin from the alley beside the shop. Ted's drawn features and the shadows beneath his eyes suggested he was far from well.

"Hello Ted; how are you?" Harry asked.

"Oh, not too bad. I keep telling Peg it's nothing to worry about. But you know what women are like."

Harry was less than convinced, but replied, "I'm glad to hear it."

Ted plucked the torn remnant of an election poster from the hedge beside the shop and dropped it into the bin. Although polling day had come and gone, one or two campaign posters for the County and Parish Council elections remained on fences and trees around the green. In the interests of fairness and, no doubt, self preservation, Bob Andrews had wisely banned all political literature from *The Black Bull*. Likewise, Simon had refused to allow anything beyond basic notices of election meetings on the notice board inside the lychgate.

"So, Gerald Spenser-Smith made it onto the Parish Council," Harry said.

Ted nodded. "Yeh; 'e certainly put himself about the most. I should think 'e got the votes of *The Black Bull* crowd sewn up."

Harry nodded in agreement, and Ted chuckled. "Mind you, 'e got a rough ride in the Memorial Hall last week, when they 'ad the election debate … least ways, that's what they called it."

"Why; what happened?"

"My Lord! You missed a right ding-dong! The sparks were flyin' over the plannin' application for the new 'ouses at Longacre Farm, I can tell yuh!"

"Are they still going ahead with that?" Harry asked. "I thought planning permission had been refused."

"It was, but the developers are appealin' against it. They're looking t'build about fifty new 'ouses there. Most of the villagers are against it; what with all the mess and disruption it'll cause … especially in Mill Lane. They're intendin' to widen that from where the cottages end. They reckon they'll 'ave t'widen the bridge over Mill Brook, too."

"So what was the argument about?"

"Well, a lot of 'em what live up around the 'igh road and on the Manor Estate are for it. The developers are promisin' some low cost starter 'omes … leastways thass what they say. That's gone down well with a lot of people up there. There's nowhere round 'ere the youngsters can afford. One woman was sayin' 'er son's been lookin' for years."

"I can believe that," said Harry.

"It came down to pretty much a split between them and the village," Ted added. "The villagers don't wan' it. It'll mean muck and 'assle and a load a'noise, what with the lorries goin' back an' forth through the village. Spenser-Smith didn't 'alf take some flak. 'E reckoned we don't need the 'ouses … not there anyhow. 'E got called a rich toff; one o' them 'nimbeys' what don't want riff-raff livin' near 'em. Some of the language was ripe, I can tell yuh."

"But he lives in The Meadowcroft; that's not all that close to Longacre Farm," Harry said. "I wouldn't have thought it would affect him that much."

"I know, but by then everybody's 'ackles were up. One or two of 'em from the Manor Estate said they don't like the way the villagers look down their noses at 'em … don't like their kids bein' accused of causing trouble and the like."

"Are you saying there's been a rift in Nethercombe?" Harry asked.

"Always 'as been to some extent," Ted replied. "Ever since the new 'ouses on the old Manor Farm got built."

"Really? I hadn't noticed," Harry said in surprise

"It's nothin' more than a bit of us-and-them most of the time. Things blow up now and again. You've probably noticed the villagers use *The Black Bull*, an' *The Kings 'ead* is the estate pub. It's mostly cause of where they are. But thass not all of it."

"I hope there's no trouble at the May Fayre," Harry said.

Ted chuckled. "No; I shouldn't think so. Might get the odd drunk … that's the worst it usually gets. No need to worry; these things blow over as soon as they start. Everybody'll be too busy 'aving a good time."

Harry felt relieved. "Good. My daughter, Debbie, is coming to stay. It's her twenty-first birthday on Thursday."

"She's a lovely girl; clever too. You must be dead proud of 'er."

"Yes, I am. I still can't believe she's twenty-one though."

"I expect you'll be a granddad before too long," Ted chuckled, and turned towards the alley beside the shop. "Well, I suppose I'd better go and flatten the cardboard boxes. The dustmen'll get stroppy and won't take 'em unless I do."

"Me; a granddad," Harry said to himself. "Good God; I suppose he's right. I hadn't thought of that." He smiled as another thought struck him. 'I wonder if Sally's thought of it. How would she feel about being a grannie?'

He had no time to dwell on the idea, because a bright red Land Rover appeared from Manor Hill and drew up outside *The Black Bull*. Its horn tooted, and the tinted window slid down to reveal Rachel's smiling face.

His pulse quickened as he crossed the green to greet her.

"Hello sailor!" she called. "Looking for a good time?"

"What are you doing here on a Tuesday?"

"Oh thanks; I'm pleased to see you too!"

"I didn't mean it like that," he replied hurriedly. "Of course I'm pleased to see you. It's just unusual for you to be here during the week."

"I've got quite a bit of accrued leave. I'm off to New York for a couple of weeks on Sunday night, so I thought I'd take a few days off for the May Fayre."

"New York?"

"Don't look so worried; New York's a big place. I have no intention of going anywhere near Karl. He'll more than likely be flying anyway. My company's taking over an American investment bank, and a team of us are going over to do some preparatory 'due diligence' work."

"I'm not worried. It's none of my business anyway," Harry replied.

She smiled. "Are you free for dinner, or do you have other plans?"

"No; I don't have any plans."

"OK; how about if I go and freshen up and meet you back here; in say … an hour or so?"

"Sounds good to me."

Predictably, the capricious British weather refused to cooperate with the preparations for the May Fayre. Frequent downpours, borne on unseasonal gusty winds, turned the ground muddy and made erecting the marquees and stalls a hazardous and frustrating process.

Flags and streamers hung limp and sodden, as Harry skirted the village green on his way to pick up Debbie and *her friend* from the station in Dorchester. Some of the bunting had blown down in the recreation ground during the night. It was dangling in the mud and floating in pools of water. He knew it was no more than could be expected from an English summer, but he still found it dispiriting.

Paul was something of a surprise, which Harry found difficult to disguise. The young man greeted him politely and affably when they were introduced, but remained quiet in the back of the car during the journey home. He said little, except in response to Debbie, who sat beside her father, chatting animatedly about her exams and university life.

The heavy market-day traffic in Dorchester, a brief but violent thunderstorm and a series of exasperating road works, made the journey slow and frustrating. By the time they arrived at May Cottage, Debbie was 'desperate for the loo', as she put it, and snatching the keys from Harry, dashed into the house.

Thankfully, the storm had passed, allowing Paul and Harry to unload the bags in sunshine warm enough to cause wisps of vapour to rise from the flagstone path and porch step.

Harry was closing the boot lid when Paul deliberately held his gaze, and in his gentle Canadian drawl, asked, "Do we have a problem, Mr. Simmonds?"

"I don't think so," Harry replied awkwardly.

Paul smiled perceptively. "I guess Debbie didn't tell you. Is my colour a problem ... in my relationship with your daughter?"

Harry's instinct was to avoid a direct answer, but looking into the young man's eyes, he felt he owed him the truth. "No; Debbie didn't tell me. I must admit, you were a bit of a surprise."

"I kinda thought so."

"I'm sure Debbie didn't feel it was worth mentioning," Harry said.

"I love Debbie ... very much," Paul said quietly.

"Then you and I don't have a problem, Paul. In fact, we have something in common."

Paul's smile was genuine and unguarded. "Thank you, Mr. Simmonds."

"What for?" Harry replied. "Debbie's old enough to make her own decisions about her relationships. In my opinion, she's got pretty good judgement. By the way, it's Harry."

There was a message from Sally on the answering machine, letting him know that Jonathan would drop Adam off on his way to Exeter the following morning. It helped to resolve the delicate question of sleeping arrangements. Only two guest bedrooms had a bed and were not cluttered by odd pieces of furniture and packing cases; some still untouched from the move. So Harry was spared the embarrassment of broaching the subject, and simply left it to Debbie.

He was not overly surprised when she instructed Paul to take their bags up to the room with the double bed, leaving the single bedded room for Adam. Harry intended to give up his own bed to his mother and father the following night and set up the camp bed in the least cluttered of the other spare rooms. It was not an attractive proposition, but it would not hurt for one night.

Paul mounted the stairs a little self-consciously with their bags, but Debbie displayed no sign of embarrassment or awkwardness as she followed her father into the sitting room.

"I hope Paul hasn't come as too much of a shock, dad," she said quietly.

"It may surprise you, but I have met black people before," he replied frivolously. "In fact I know some of them well. One of my old business partners, Daniel, is Nigerian, if you remember."

Debbie smiled indulgently. "That's not what I mean, and you know it. I didn't want to say anything until you met Paul. I wanted you to make up your mind about him … in person … as a person."

"What made you think I wouldn't?" Harry answered. "As a matter of fact I have. For what it's worth, I like what I've seen so far. I can assure you I have no issue with the colour of Paul's skin; not that it matters a jot what I or anyone else thinks, if you and he are happy together."

"Thanks dad."

"You're welcome. How long have you known him?"

"Just over three months. We met at a party."

"Has your mum met him?"

"Yes; we went for a meal with her and Jonathan the day before yesterday. He got on well with them. He's met Grandma Grace too. She thinks he's very good looking."

"Oh, does she?" Harry chuckled. "You'd better watch out then. It sounds like your grandmother is developing a roving eye in her old age."

"Dad; you're hopeless!" she giggled, and hugged him.

"Right; time for something to drink and then lunch," Harry said, and called up the stairs. "Tea or coffee, Paul?"

Paul's head appeared round the bedroom doorframe. "Coffee please … with sugar, if you have it. No problem if you don't; but I have a sweet tooth."

"I have a Marjorie, so I'm sure there must be some sugar somewhere," Harry replied. Debbie giggled, and in response to Paul's puzzled expression, Harry explained, "You'll meet her tomorrow."

After a light lunch, Harry settled in his favourite armchair with the local newspapers, while Debbie showed Paul around the village. Having overcome his initial awkwardness, Paul had begun to relax and tell Harry about his home in Vancouver, where his father was a surgeon and his mother a dentist. He had spoken affectionately of his two sisters; the elder of whom was a lawyer and the younger in high school. He was halfway through a post graduate degree in applied economics.

The short period of quiet contemplation, while Debbie and Paul were out, gave Harry the chance to examine his conscience as candidly as he could. He asked himself if it really did trouble him that his daughter was in a relationship with someone who was black. More to the point, would he be happier if her partner was white, but cared less for her than Paul obviously did? It was comforting to reach the conclusion that he could honestly answer 'no'. Debbie's happiness was all that was important. And she *was* happy; demonstrably so. He could take comfort and pleasure from the fact she was in a relationship with a caring young man from a solid family background, who clearly thought the world of her. Beyond that, nothing else mattered.

If he could bear to be completely honest with himself; the real problem was coming to terms with the fact that his 'little girl' was now a young woman; and he, no longer the most important man in her life.

Paul was effusive with his praise for Nethercombe Ley, when he and Debbie returned. "It's a beautiful place!" he exclaimed. "We took a look at the church and met the preacher. He's a big guy ... and real nice."

Harry smiled with pleasure. "Yes, isn't he? Simon's a good friend."

"There was a beautiful horse outside the churchyard," Debbie enthused. "The girl riding it runs the stables we drove past that day we had lunch in Garstone; do you remember?"

"Yes, I do. That's Laura."

Debbie's eyes twinkled. "I know; she invited me for a hack whenever I'm down here. Not this weekend, of course."

"That was kind of her," said Harry. "She'll be busy with the pony rides at the May Fayre on Saturday. What about you, Paul? Do you ride?"

"No; it seems an awful long way to fall."

"A man after my own heart. They don't have brakes either," Harry laughed.

Debbie held out a paper bag. "We called in at the shop to say hello to Mr. and Mrs. Flowers. I bought you a prezzie … your favourites."

Harry was delighted to discover the bag contained sherbet lemons. "Thanks; I didn't realise they had them!" He popped one into his mouth and offered them to Paul, knowing Debbie did not like them.

Paul declined politely and Debbie's expression became serious. "Mr. Flowers doesn't look at all well. Is he alright? I didn't like to say anything."

"I don't really know," Harry replied. "He's been having trouble with his stomach, but he's adamant there's nothing wrong with him."

"He looks real sick," said Paul, "Maybe he ought to get it checked out."

Harry grimaced. "That's what everyone keeps telling him, but he won't listen."

He put down his newspaper. "Now, what do you want to do for dinner tonight? Would you like to try the local pub? I've made a booking at *The Golden Lantern* for tomorrow, if that's OK."

"That's great!" Debbie trilled. "And the pub tonight will be fine. OK with you, Paul?"

Paul's dark eyes gazed at her fondly. "Of course; whatever you want is fine with me."

'You'll do young man,' Harry thought. 'You'll do.'

*The Black Bull* was unexpectedly busy for a Wednesday. The bar-room door was open and the regulars at the bar boisterous and noisy. Harry was about to suggest it might be better to eat in the restaurant, which was quiet and half empty, but Simon had seen them arrive and his large frame filled the entrance lobby.

"Hello Debbie … Paul! Hi Harry; what a pleasure. Rachel and Laura are here. You're very welcome to join us, unless you were planning on a quieter evening, of course?"

Harry looked at Debbie and Paul enquiringly, but Debbie's expression answered the question, even before she replied, "Thank you; we'd love to, wouldn't we Paul?"

Paul smiled indulgently, "Sure."

Simon stood aside to let them pass, and heads turned as they entered; one or two clearly curious at the sight of Paul with Debbie. Stella, '*the cougar*', gave him a long appraising look, which made no secret of her approval.

Rachel and Laura appeared from behind the noisy throng with welcoming smiles, but before greetings could be exchanged, Gerald Spenser-Smith stepped forward, his face smiling and flushed. "Hello there! It's Harry, isn't it? And who are these young people?"

"This is my daughter, Debbie, and her partner, Paul," Harry explained, slightly taken aback by Gerald's '*hail fellow well met*' exuberance.

"Welcome to Nethercombe Ley Debbie and Paul!" said Gerald expansively. "Is this your first visit?"

"It is for Paul," Debbie replied. "I've been here before."

"It's beautiful," said Paul courteously.

"Yes; it's a delightful place to live, isn't it Harry?"

"It certainly is," Harry replied, making the mistake of glancing at Rachel, whose impish grin and mischievously twinkling eyes made him all but lose his composure. "By the way; congratulations on your election to the Parish Council!"

"Thank you, Harry; that's very kind." Turning his attention back to Debbie and Paul, Gerald asked, "Now, what can I get you to drink? I've just been elected to Garstone and Nethercombe Ley Parish Council, and this is the first chance I've had to thank my fellow parishioners for placing their trust in me."

"And get pissed, eh Gerry?" Rachel chuckled.

"Yes it is! And yes, I've had a few, Rachel," Gerald replied indulgently. "But I'm among friends, so where's the harm?"

Rachel patted his shoulder. "None at all Gerry. You've earned it, darling."
Turning to Harry, she said, "Now, are you going to introduce me to your
lovely daughter and her handsome guy?"

What Harry had assumed would be a quiet evening turned out to
be nothing of the kind. Things became even livelier after Simon raised
his glass to Debbie, and revealed that it was the eve of her twenty-first
birthday. The arrival of Harry's neighbours, Alan and Jill Anderson,
added even more merriment to what was already a party atmosphere. It
delighted Harry to see that Debbie was clearly enjoying every minute of
it. She appeared to get on well with everyone; especially Laura, with
whom there seemed a special rapport. Paul, being somewhat reserved,
endured it all good naturedly; his genial indulgence all the more generous
in view of the fact that he did not drink.

Although her normal ebullient self, Rachel took care not to
embarrass Harry by drawing attention to the more intimate nature of
their relationship, for which she earned his unspoken gratitude. Simon
contributed in his own inimitable way; entering into the spirit of the
occasion with his gentle wit and sympathetic tolerance of its more
boisterous moments.

Debbie was blissfully happy when they arrived home shortly before
midnight. Harry and Paul watched with amused affection as she flopped
onto the settee and gazed at them with heavy-lidded eyes. "What a great
bunch of guys!" she exclaimed. "Is that pub cool or what?"

"It's not like that every night," Harry chuckled. "In fact, that's the
liveliest I've known it mid-week."

"Why haven't you invited Rachel tomorrow night?" she asked.

Caught off guard, he answered cautiously. "Well, for a start, I didn't
know she was going to be here. She normally only comes down at
weekends; and secondly … well, I assumed it was going to be a family
thing, with Grandma and Gramps."

"And you didn't want us to know about you and her?" she suggested
playfully.

Harry was momentarily lost for words. "No. Not at all. There's
nothing … I mean …"

Debbie giggled. "Laura let slip about you and Rachel going away for Easter. She thought I knew."

Paul tried to intervene tactfully. "I guess it's your dad's business. Maybe we ought not to pry."

"Thanks Paul," Harry replied, feeling his cheeks burn. "I haven't said anything, because there's nothing much to say. It's nothing serious. We have a drink or a meal together occasionally, when she's staying with Simon. She came to Guy Wolstencroft's fiftieth birthday party with me. And yes, we did a little tour along the coast at Easter. Is that a problem?"

"Dad no, of course not!" Debbie exclaimed. In the process of trying to get up too quickly from the settee, she toppled backwards, giggling childishly. "I'm happy for you! I really am."

Her giggle was infectious, and Harry smiled indulgently. "I'll invite her, if you like."

"I already did," Debbie replied. "But she said the same as you; it's a family dinner and perhaps it *wasn't appropriate*."

"I'll call her in the morning, if it makes you happy."

She gave him her 'I can twist my daddy round my little finger' pout. "And Laura and Simon?"

Harry shook his head in mock disbelief. "And Laura … and Simon, if that's what you want. I'd better call *The Golden Lantern*, too; and warn them to expect half of Dorset!"

A shadow of disappointment fell across Debbie's face as she stood beside Harry, listening to his telephone conversation.

"OK dad. Don't worry; I'm sure Debbie will understand. It can't be helped. Give my love to mum. Tell her to take care and get well soon. I'll hand you over to Debbie now. Bye dad."

He passed the phone, with a whispered, "Grandma's not well."

Debbie managed a wan smile, as she took it. "Hi Gramps … thank you."

139

Harry left her and turned his attention to Paul, who was at the stove preparing his speciality; 'Scrambled Eggs MacKenzie'.

"Problem?" he asked, interpreting Harry's expression.

"Debbie's grandparents won't be joining us," Harry replied. "My mother seems to have trapped a nerve in her neck. She's in a lot of pain. She's in bed with a splitting headache at the moment."

"Oh my; that's too bad," Paul sighed. "Debbie will be so disappointed."

Debbie was; but bore her disappointment bravely. She was clutching the iPad Harry had given her, and although still in her dressing gown, wore the gold bracelet she had received from Paul, and bizarrely, the expensive shoes her mother had bought her.

"Poor grandma," she said wistfully "It sounds as if she's in a lot of pain."

"They're both upset at missing your birthday," Harry said. "Let's see how Grandma is tomorrow. If she's feeling up to it, we'll drive up there. She and Gramps can wish you happy birthday and give you your present. We can have dinner with them some other time … when Grandma's back on her feet."

Debbie kissed him on the forehead. "Thanks dad."

"Breakfast's ready; come and get it birthday girl!" Paul called.

They had just finished eating when the doorbell rang. Harry recognised Marjorie's voice when Debbie answered it. He found her opening the card Marjorie had given her, when he went into the hall.

"Hello Marjorie; why didn't you let yourself in?" he asked.

"I knew you had company," she replied, peeling off her coat.

He scolded her affectionately. "Just let yourself in. I've told you; it doesn't matter if there's anyone else here."

"What a lovely card; thank you!" Debbie exclaimed.

Paul appeared in the kitchen doorway, and Harry quipped, "Paul; come and meet the reason you've been having sugar in your coffee."

It was pleasing, but no surprise to Harry, that Debbie and Marjorie seemed to get on well. Debbie insisted Marjorie have coffee with them and admire her birthday cards, before allowing her to start work. He could still hear their chatter afterwards, as he dealt with his mail in his study.

When the doorbell rang a second time, he expected it to be Adam, but it was Ellen Hardy with a card and a present for Debbie. They had met briefly in January, and he had heard Debbie chatting to her and Rob over the garden fence the previous day. The unexpected gift was typical of their kindness.

Ellen shyly refused the invitation to come in, excusing herself with, "I can't stop; I've got lots to do today. Have a lovely day my dear," she called, as she left.

Debbie removed the wrapping to reveal a Parker pen in a presentation box. "Oh!" she sighed. "Oh, dad; I don't know what to say!"

"I think your *thank you* was all Ellen was expecting," Harry answered gently. "She's a very kind and generous lady; as I have cause to know."

Debbie's mobile phone, noisily demanding her attention, distracted her from giving way to tears. "Hi mum!"

Adam arrived around mid-morning. Harry had been longing to see him, but had not allowed himself to hope his feelings would be returned.

He was topping up the windscreen washer bottle in his car and eyeing a threatening bank of purple cloud, when a silver Mercedes drew up in the lane outside the house. Taking a deep breath to quell the butterflies in his stomach, he called to Debbie; "Adam's here!" and went to greet him.

Adam seemed thinner than when Harry had last seen him. For reasons known only to himself, his eyes were hidden behind a pair of narrow framed sunglasses, of the type beloved by *ZZ-Top* devotees. He also sported what he no doubt imagined was fashionable stubble, but which, in Harry eyes, gave him a slightly mangy, ill-kempt look.

"Hello Adam," Harry said tentatively.

"Hi dad," Adam replied affably, but without any show of affection. The boot lid sprang open and he reached in for his bag.

Jonathan remained in the car. Harry had to walk round it to speak to him. His swarthy good looks and dark, wavy hair, made him look younger than his forty-two years, and Harry had to admit that he could understand why Sally had fallen for him. He had met Jonathan briefly before, but even after more than two years, he still had to force himself to be civil to the man he held responsible for all his pain and heartache.

"Thanks for bringing Adam," Harry said, as pleasantly as he could manage.

Jonathan's nervous smile revealed that he was equally uncomfortable in Harry's presence. "No problem. I was coming this way, and it is a bit off the beaten track, isn't it?"

"I suppose so," Harry replied. "Anyway, it's much appreciated."

They were both spared further embarrassment by Debbie's exclamation as she appeared in the gateway. "Adam! Haven't seen you for ages! What have you been up to?"

"Hi Debs! Happy birthday!" Adam replied, dropping his bag to receive her welcoming hug.

"Well; I'd better be off," Jonathan declared awkwardly. Poking his head out of the open window, he called, "Happy birthday Debbie!"

"Thanks Jonathan," she replied with a wave.

"'Bye Adam! See you Harry," Jonathan said and started the engine.

*'Not for a long time, I hope,'* Harry thought, as he watched the sleek limousine pull away.

Thankfully, Adam was not as sullen and uncommunicative as Harry had feared, but neither was he the cheerful, uninhibited youth of those halcyon days before the family breakup. Unsurprisingly, he was most comfortable with Debbie, although he and Paul seemed to get on amicably.

With Harry, he was polite and amiable, although their conversation tended to consist in the main of questions and answers; with Harry asking almost all the questions. Harry received little by way of enquiry about his own wellbeing, other than an initial, "How's it going, dad?"

As Harry suspected, Rachel took more than a little persuading to join them for dinner, when he called her. "It's very kind of you to ask me," she said. "But it's a family occasion. I only met Debbie yesterday. I'd be out of place."

"No you wouldn't! Look Rachel; I'll be honest with you," Harry confided. "First of all, both of us would honestly love you to come. You'd be doing me a favour, as well. My parents were due to join us, but mother is unwell and there'll only be the four of us. As you know, my son and I have had our problems. We're OK, but I'd appreciate a little moral support to help things along, especially after all the fun of last night. Debbie thoroughly enjoyed it. I'd hate her birthday dinner to turn out to be a damp squib after that. I'm afraid it might be, if it's just me with three youngsters. You've got the personality to perk things up."

"Flatterer!" she exclaimed playfully. "So you want *me* to be the cabaret. Should I wear a red nose or something?"

"No! I told you; Debbie wants you to come. I believe she invited you last night. She hit it off with Laura too. She'd like her and Simon to come, as well. She knows what a good friend Simon has been to me."

"Really?" Rachel asked in surprise.

"I know it sounds odd, but that's what she wants. I'd be hugely grateful," Harry pleaded.

"OK smooth tongue, you can count on me. I don't know what plans Simon has for tonight, but I'll ask him. Would you like me to sound out Laura, as well?"

"Please; if you would."

"I'll speak to them and call you back."

"Thanks Rachel; what a little star you are!"

"I know; and I like to twinkle now and again. Speak to you later, Harry."

Debbie looked up expectantly as he returned to the sitting room.

"Rachel's coming," he said, "but I don't know about Laura and Simon yet. Rachel's going to ask them."

"Thanks dad!"

"Who's Rachel?" Adam asked.

"She's dad's *friend*," Debbie replied, with a hint of mischief. "She's the vicar's sister."

Interpreting Adam's expression, Paul interjected, "If you're thinking buck teeth and thick eye-glasses, you can forget it where this lady is concerned."

Debbie giggled. "She's very tall and blond … quite something. We had dinner with her and Simon last night … and Laura. Simon's a vicar and Laura owns a riding school near here."

"Sounds like I missed out," said Adam.

"It was great! The pub's really cool." Debbie trilled.

Harry need not have worried. Rachel worked her magic, and managed to persuade Simon and Laura to join them for dinner, in spite of their reservations about hardly knowing Debbie. Even so, Simon felt it necessary to call Harry for reassurance that they would not be 'gate crashing', as he put it.

It was Laura who turned out to be 'Miss Popularity' with the youngsters. Her bubbly personality seemed more in tune with their wavelength, despite the fact that she was several years older than them. She was much more knowledgeable about popular culture than *the oldies*, as Harry started to think of Rachel, Simon and himself.

Each of them wore a baffled expression as the conversation turned to *The X Factor, Big Brother* and singers and bands they had never heard of. It drew the amused observation from Rachel: "You only needed Laura. Si and I are surplus to requirements."

"No you're not!" Harry replied. "I'd be sitting here counting the bamboo stems on the wallpaper without you two!"

"Sorry dad!" Debbie exclaimed. "We didn't mean to blank you."

"You're not," Harry chuckled. "It was just a joke … only just I'll admit. You carry on. Just don't spin the 'lazy susan' too fast when the food arrives … and I intend using a fork!"

Debbie's eyes twinkled. She reached into her bag, and handed him a brightly wrapped package.

"What's this? It's your birthday not mine!" Intrigued, Harry undid the wrapping, and removing the lid from the cardboard box, he burst out laughing.

"There you are; no more cramp!" Debbie giggled.

Harry held up a device he had never seen before. It consisted of two plastic chop sticks joined at the top to form an 'm' shaped spring, which allowed the user to eat with them without the difficulties encountered by people as inept as him.

In response to the curious expressions around the table, Adam explained. "It's a family joke. Dad's like, never got the hang of using chop sticks, right. He gets cramp in his hand."

"Not anymore! Not with my *cheat sticks*!" Harry exclaimed. He twirled them around his finger tips, arousing the curiosity and amusement of the waitresses and the couple at the next table.

Debbie turned to Laura. "Dad told me you're doing pony rides at the May Fayre. I suppose you'll be pretty busy."

"I hope so," Laura replied. "It's all for charity, so we'll be hoping to raise a lot of money."

"I guess the horses will be glad when it's over," Adam suggested mischievously.

Laura threw him a disarming smile. "We run two strings of ponies, so we can rest them regularly. It'll be harder on Haylie, Nicky and me. We'll be on our feet all day, leading them."

"If you need some help, for comfort or refreshment breaks, I'll pitch in for while," Rachel said.

"Um … I'd be happy to, as well," Debbie offered hesitantly.

Laura's face lit up with her attractive smile. "Thanks, I think I'll take both of you up on that."

"Are you like, going to have a pony ride, Debs?" Adam asked facetiously.

She pulled a face at him. "I might."

"We cater for everyone!" Laura said; and giving Adam a challenging smile, she added, "We'll pick out a nice one for you, if you like."

Having his bluff called, made Adam blush. He grinned bashfully. "No, I'll leave it to Debs, right. She like, knows what she's doing."

"So you ride, Debbie?" Rachel asked in surprise.

"Yes, but I haven't had much chance since I've been at university."

Rachel turned her gaze on Harry. "You didn't tell me!"

Startled by her unexpected accusation, a mouthful of beer almost went down the wrong way. "I never had any reason to!" he spluttered.

"Debbie's coming for a hack the next time she's here," Laura explained.

"How well do you ride?" Rachel enquired.

"I'm not bad; at least I wasn't when I rode regularly."

"You were good!" Harry insisted. "You won cups and rosettes at the local shows!"

"You're welcome to ride my horse, whenever you're here," Rachel offered. "Monty can be a lazy tyke at times, but he's a sweetie really. I'm sure you'll have no trouble handling him. Just arrange it with Laura."

"You met Monty the other day," Laura explained.

Debbie's eyes widened. "You mean that beautiful chestnut? Is he yours, Rachel?"

"Yes, he is, and he can do with all the exercise he can get!"

"Oh my God! Thank you!" Debbie exclaimed.

Harry turned to Paul. "I have a feeling I'll being seeing a lot more of you from now on," he chuckled. "You and I will have to play golf or find something else to amuse ourselves, while Debbie's giving all her attention to Monty."

"I'm afraid I don't play golf," Paul replied sheepishly.

"Very wise!" said Simon. "I'm told it spoils a good walk. Do you play Adam?"

"No way!" Adam exclaimed. "I can like, never get the ball through the windmill!"

The food arrived, as the conversation dissolved into laughter.

Harry called his parents before they set off the following morning. His father felt there was little improvement in his mother's condition, but she insisted she was well enough for a visit from her grandchildren.

Paul suggested that four people, one a stranger, might be a little too taxing for her. Perhaps it might be better if he did not go with them. Harry could not help wondering how much of his reasoning was based on the fear that he might come as an unwelcome surprise at such a time. After some arguing, Debbie agreed.

Before they left, she cut a wedge from the remains of the birthday cake she had brought from *The Golden Lantern*. She wrapped it carefully in foil to take to Grandma and Gramps, and gathered up her birthday cards and presents to show them.

On the way, they left Paul at a friend's house in Old Basing, which in the event was a wise decision. Grandma Marian was far from well. Although looking drawn and gaunt, she was delighted to see 'both her grandchildren together for the first time in ages', as she made a point of emphasising. Harry kept the visit relatively short, and it was an indication of how unwell she felt that she did not protest too strongly.

They collected Paul on the way back, and with most of the afternoon remaining, Harry chose a route via the chain-link ferry across the entrance to Poole Harbour, at Sandbanks.

The blustery shower that blew in moments before they reached it had vented its wrath by the time they parked the car on the flat deck and left it to climb a steep metal stairway leading to a viewing deck. The sun forced its way between the wind-torn cloud to light the blue-green sea in dancing lights, as the ferry set off, chugging and clanking its way across the narrow channel. The breeze immediately began to torment Debbie's hair, wrapping it in strands around her face and snatching her voice away on a sudden gust, as she turned her head to speak to Paul.

The crossing took only a few minutes, and they were soon passing through the village of Studland, which, Harry remembered, gives its name to the bay adjacent to Swanage. The idea occurred to him that it might be an opportunity to drop in and pay a visit to a certain redhead. But as she and Guy were to be his guests at the May Fayre the following day, he forced himself to resist the temptation. Instead, he took the road towards Corfe Castle.

Spotting an ice cream van parked beside several cars in a wide lay-by, Debbie exclaimed, "Anybody want one?"

"How about I stand for ice cream?" Paul suggested.

Unsurprisingly no-one refused, and Harry pulled into what turned out to be a viewing area, affording panoramic vistas across the Isle of Purbeck Golf Course and the fields and heathland that swept down to the distant splendour of Poole Harbour. Harry and Adam stood by the car, enjoying the view and the sun on their faces, while Paul and Debbie went to the ice cream van.

"Have you played that course dad?" Adam asked.

"No, but I'd very much like to," Harry replied wistfully.

Adam looked thoughtful as he leaned back against the bonnet of the car. "I don't know much about golf right, but it looks tough with all that gorse and stuff."

"I can't see a windmill though," Harry mused, and they both burst out laughing.

"What's so funny?" Debbie asked, as she and Paul returned, carefully clutching large, overfilled cones.

"A golfer's joke!" said Harry.

"Adam doesn't play golf," Debbie replied quizzically.

"That's the joke," said Adam, which set father and son chuckling again.

For a while, they stood quietly savouring the ice cream; captivated by the beauty of the shimmering greens and the russet and gold of the heath, beyond which the wide, misty-blue bay nestled below a pale, cloudless sky.

Harry brought them home beneath the towering ruins of Corfe Castle, and over the river at Wareham, enjoying their exclamations of surprise and delight at the variety and beauty of his newly adopted county.

It had been a thoroughly enjoyable day; the highlight of which for Harry was the feeling that he had begun to renew some semblance of a relationship with his son.

To everyone's relief, the morning of the May Fayre dawned fine and dry. The rain and wind that had blighted the preparations all week had finally relented the previous afternoon, leaving an almost cloudless, azure sky, which the weather forecasters promised would last the whole weekend.

A thin, low mist blanketed the meadows, as Harry looked out from the bathroom window, but he was certain the strengthening power of the sun would soon burn it away. Hopefully it would quickly generate enough warmth to dry the rec and village green enough to prevent them being churned into muddy morasses.

A stroll to the shop revealed the extent of the effort and industry that had gone into repairing the damage caused by the storms of the previous few days. To add to his general feeling of wellbeing, Guy called on his mobile phone to confirm that he and Emma would be arriving later in the morning.

Several vans and a lorry were parked around the green, which was surrounded by orange cones to deter opportunists from avoiding the official car parks. More cones lined the lanes leading to the centre of the village and all the way up one side of Manor Hill.

The village green was a hive of activity. Three men were erecting a multicoloured maypole in the centre; others were placing wooden benches and tables in front of two striped tents, and erecting a low dais opposite *The Black Bull*, where the May Queen was traditionally crowned and the Morris Dancers and country dancers 'did their thing'.

Perhaps the only damper on Harry's high spirits was learning that

Ted was ill again. The anxiety on Peggy's face and her tearful reply to Harry's enquiry after his health, betrayed her disbelief in Ted's constant denial that there was anything seriously wrong with him.

Although Harry felt genuine concern for Ted, and did his best to reassure her, he was aware that dealing with someone else's grief was not one of his strong points. Guiltily, he felt relieved when Mrs. Sillitoe and another woman came into the shop and took over the task of trying to comfort Peggy.

The Morris Dancers began the day's proceedings around ten-thirty, by which time the centre of the village was becoming crowded. The tables and chairs on the green were soon fully occupied by people enjoying a late breakfast burger or a morning 'cuppa' purchased from the adjacent tents. Some required something stronger, even at that early hour, occupying the tables outside *The Black Bull* or standing on the forecourt, glass in hand.

Debbie swayed her hips and clapped her hands in time to the accordion music, while Paul and Harry were more restrained in their participation. As Adam was only just getting out of bed when they had left, they did not expect him to put in an appearance for some time.

By the time Harry's mobile phone rang and he heard Emma's cheerful voice, the Maypole Dancers, of all ages, from children to pensioners, had taken their places; arrayed in colourful costumes and headgear.

Emma explained that they were on their way and expected to arrive within the next thirty minutes. Harry repeated the directions he had given them, which would bring them in through Garstone Green. It was a much longer route, but would avoid the congestion around the rec and the need to negotiate Manor Hill and the centre of the village, which were by now all but impassable.

"I'll meet you at my place. Look out for a magnolia by the gateway. There's plenty of room for you to park on the driveway. See you there!" he called.

There was time to catch the Maypole Dancers before he needed to return home, and to watch a gaggle of small children being shepherded onto the dais by their parents, for the fancy dress competition. There were prizes for several age groups. The under fives were lined up first, and made their way, one-by-one, across the stage before Lady Diana and her panel of judges. Some had to be coaxed and took slow, reluctant steps; others moved with self-conscious haste. However, *Little Bo-Peep* looked poised and confident, as she accepted applause from the onlookers. She beamed from beneath her blue poke bonnet, clutching her crook and the fluffy toy lamb tucked under her arm.

The Maypole Dancers had just begun their second stint when it was time to leave Debbie and Paul and make his way back to the house. On the way Harry found himself smiling to people he did not know and humming the lively tune emanating from the speakers in the trees around the village green. It was a day for fun and pleasure; the sun was shining and all was well in the world.

At least it was, until he found a scruffy, mud spattered Peugeot parked across his driveway, with a twisted traffic cone jammed beneath it. His immediate reaction was that someone must have ignored the parking restrictions and left it there before going into the village. Then he saw a figure he recognised standing at his sitting room window; Steve Edmunds!

Without pausing to close the front door behind him, he strode into the sitting room, and found Adam and Steve with two other unkempt individuals. Steve greeted him with a cocky, "Hi Mr. S! Long time no see!"

"Not long enough!" Harry growled and snatched the glass from his hand. It held a large measure of what he recognised as his favourite, and expensive single malt.

Steve looked startled. "Oh, charmin'!"

"Dad!" Adam exclaimed in surprise, but ignoring him, Harry turned to the thin, sallow faced youth lounging on the settee. "Get your feet off that table!"

The youth looked sullenly at Harry and then at Adam.

"Do it, Rosco," Adam said. In response, Rosco slowly and insolently lifted his grubby trainers from the coffee table.

"What the hell's with you?" Adam exclaimed. "These are my friends, right!"

"Then get some new ones!" Harry retorted. "I'm talking real friends: preferably ones who respect other people's property and don't help themselves to whatever they fancy … ones that don't con you into poker games!"

"Hang on!" Steve protested.

But Harry's blood was up; he could feel it pulsing at his temples. "No, you hang on! Just because Adam fell for it, don't think I was born yesterday. I know your game!"

"No wonder your misses left yuh!"

Until then the thick-set individual standing behind Steve Edmunds had remained silent. He was shaven headed and had a snake tattooed around one of his bare, muscular arms. His black, sleeveless T-shirt was stretched tight across his protruding belly and emblazoned with a silver eagle.

Harry turned towards him in surprise. "Who the hell are you?"

"Who wants to know?"

"I do! It's my house!"

"I'm DP."

"DP what?"

"Just DP."

Harry was uncomfortably aware that this character could be more trouble than the other two, but with his anger and temper aroused, he was in no frame of mind to take any more nonsense in his own sitting room.

"Well, DP," he began slowly and as menacingly as he could manage. "You can keep your opinions about things that are none of your business to yourself!"

Adam broke the brief silence. "Come on guys, let's split."

"Hang on a minute, Adam!" Steve protested. "Your old man's just made a serious accusation. I want an apology!"

"You'll be lucky!" Harry growled. "Now, get out of my house!"

"Come on Guys," said Adam in disgust. Beckoning them from the room, he glared at Harry. "Thanks dad ... for nothing!"

Steve gave Harry what he obviously imagined was a hostile stare, but unable to match the malevolent glare he received in return, he lowered his gaze and followed Adam into the hall. DP walked past with a slow, deliberate swagger; his hands in the pockets of his jeans. As he did so, his elbow brushed against the vase on the small table beside Harry's fireside chair, toppling it into the hearth. It smashed, scattering flowers, water and shards of glass.

"Whoops!" DP leered and strutted slowly out of the room.

Rosco had taken his time to get up off the settee. The state of his dark-rimmed, sunken eyes and sallow complexion suggested he was on some kind of drug.

'I hope to God he's not been taking it in this house,' Harry thought.

Rosco prodded Harry's chest with a nicotine stained finger. "You wanna watch yourself!"

"Get out ... *idiot*!" Harry growled, suddenly feeling weary as the tension and adrenaline drained from him.

He heard car doors slam, followed by the roar of an engine and the squeal of tyres, as whoever was driving gunned the motor and turned the car around in the gateway. As it sped off, Harry sat on the arm of a chair, looking down at the shattered vase. It was the one Grace had given him as a house warming present. The splintered glass and crumpled flowers seemed to symbolize his broken dreams of rebuilding bridges with Adam.

"Who did I think I was kidding?" he murmured.

He had just finished clearing up the mess when Guy's Volvo turned in at the gate. The lilting music he could hear from the village green no longer had its uplifting effect, but Harry greeted his friends as cheerfully as he could.

Guy was dressed elegantly, as always. He wore a pale blue cashmere sweater over a lemon polo shirt and light grey slacks. Emma looked cool and chic in a flowered summer dress, worn beneath a white linen jacket.

She offered her cheek in greeting, which Harry kissed self-consciously, enjoying the smoothness of her skin and a waft of her perfume. He could not help but laugh as Guy offered his cheek.

"Nice place you've got here, mate," Guy said. "But a bugger to get to."

"It's lovely!" Emma exclaimed, gazing around her. "It's got so much character!"

"It's a quicker and more direct route through Larksmead," Harry explained. "But you'd never have made it past the rec where all the main activities and car parks are. Now; do you fancy a coffee before we join the merrymaking?"

"I hope I'm not being cheeky, but could we have a quick look round before we go?" Emma asked.

"Of course. Let's put the kettle on first, then we'll do the tour."

The May Queen was being crowned when they reached the village green. Harry recognised her as Jessica, the youngest of James Lloyd's four daughters, whom he saw most mornings crossing the green on her way to catch the school bus. He could not help thinking, not without a tinge of guilt, that the *Cinderella* dress she wore, with its extravagant frills and puffy sleeves, did far less for her than the school uniform.

Emma particularly enjoyed the fancy dress competition, which by then had reached the adult male category. Predictably, some amusing and bizarre costumes were on show; the winner being a contestant outlandishly and sparsely dressed as Lady Gaga.

They passed the rest of the morning slowly making their way up Manor Hill to the rec, where a small steam fair and most of the stalls and marquees were situated. On the way, they passed several stalls selling craftwork, while encountering a balloon seller, stilt walkers and a woman dressed as Charlie Chaplin cranking a barrel organ. As they progressed, the music constantly changed and was frequently overridden by announcements echoing from the show ground tannoy. The impressive crowds led Harry to reflect on the beneficial effects of extensive publicity and glorious, sunny weather.

When they reached the rec ... or 'showground', as it was known for one week each year, he was not surprised to find Debbie leading a little girl on small piebald pony around a fenced paddock. She was following Laura and two other girls, who each led two ponies and their riders.

"Where's Paul?" Harry called. In response, Debbie pointed towards a queue, made up of mostly of children, at the head of which a large sign proclaimed "Pony Rides". The rest of the notice was obscured by Paul's head as he towered above the youngsters, laughing and chatting with them, while he issued tickets and collected the money.

Behind him, Rachel and another woman were sorting through safety helmets and readying other ponies, which stood tethered to the fence, patiently resigned to their monotonous toil. Rachel looked up and waved a greeting as they approached. Harry smiled and nodded with amusement towards Paul.

"It's amazing what a guy will let himself get talked into when he's in love," Rachel exclaimed.

"He would have to be to let himself in for that!" Harry replied.

There was no sign of Adam and 'the goons', which he reluctantly considered was probably just as well.

The pony rides were suspended for an hour at lunchtime. Simon joined them, and they were able to eat together and enjoy the gourmet delights of pizza, kebabs and any other cholesterol-laden fast-food that took their fancy.

Emma and Laura discovered they had a mutual acquaintance, and were soon chatting animatedly, while Guy, being Guy, made it his business to keep Rachel amused with anecdotes and shaggy-dog stories from his seemingly inexhaustible collection. With Debbie and Paul engaged in conversation with Simon, Harry was left to his own company, and looked around, occasionally nodding or raising a hand in greeting to friends and neighbours as they passed; all the while keeping an eye out for Adam.

He did not mind being left to his thoughts. It was a bright sunny day and the showground was well populated and noisy. As Ted had predicted, *villagers* and *high roaders* were too busy enjoying themselves to bother with any *us and them* nonsense. There were also plenty of outside visitors, to help make the day a success.

"God, please don't let Adam and those other three cause any trouble here!" he muttered under his breath.

It was a little while before any of his companions noticed him standing alone, apparently 'in a world of his own'.

"A penny for them!" he heard Rachel call.

"I was just looking around; taking it all in," he said.

"I think Harry's trying to avoid giving the impression he's with undesirables like us," Guy quipped.

"You were all busy chatting," Harry explained.

"Sorry Harry! We didn't mean to leave you out," Laura exclaimed.

"You didn't. I was quite happy watching everything that's going on."

"Adam and I were always told off if we interrupted other people's conversations," Debbie explained impishly. "Dad thinks it's bad manners."

"He's a gentleman," Emma replied.

Harry felt his cheeks flush. He could not make up his mind if she was serious or poking fun of him.

The afternoon passed in a cacophony of loud music; distorted announcements echoing from the tannoy system and the whir of generators. The dull roar of the crowd was constantly pierced by bursts of laughter, shrieks and excited calls, and occasionally, the wail of a distressed child. The all-pervading smell of fried onions hanging in the air, mixed with the acrid fumes of steam engines and the pungent odour of diesel exhausts, epitomised a uniquely British occasion.

Harry was pleased to notice that, amid the newer, more sophisticated attractions, some old favourites, such as the coconut shy, the rat in the drainpipe and the horticultural displays still survived.

The traditional steam fair in one corner of the rec was particularly busy, offering the bygone delights of gaudily painted chairoplanes, waltzers and a carousel, which Rachel insisted they try. For a while, Harry was transported back to the carefree pleasures of youth.

The evening sun hovered like a fireball above the distant hills, tinting the canvas walls of the marquees and stalls in shades of pink, while casting grotesque, elongated shadows across the recreation ground.

Guy and Emma had already left to attend the annual dinner-dance of a businessmen's association that Guy was involved with. Harry was still mulling over his confrontation with Adam's so-called friends, as he lifted the pint of *Palmer's Best* from the tray Phil Alders had carefully carried to where he stood with Marjorie, Debbie and Paul.

Still troubled by the incident in his sitting room that morning, Harry murmured, "I swear I'll swing for Steve Bloody Edmunds, one of these days!"

"Forget it, mate!" Phil said soothingly. "Lads are a pain in the backside at that age!"

"Yours aren't," Harry replied. "They're serving their community and their country."

"They haven't always been," Marjorie interjected. "They're no angels, even now; believe me."

They were distracted by the sound of raised voices and horses whinnying. It seemed to come from the field behind the beer tent, where Laura's ponies were tethered, waiting to be led back to the stables. Recognising Adam's voice, Harry looked up sharply, spilling his beer in his haste to put it down on an adjacent metal table.

"What the hell are they up to now?" he growled, as he made off in the direction of the commotion.

Debbie attempted to follow him, but he stretched out an arm to restrain her. "No; stay put until I've found out what the hell's going on!"

As he made his way around the large marquee, between the crowds chattering and laughing outside the entrance, he heard Laura's voice. "I won't tell you again; get away from them!"

It was met by the slurred reply, "No 'arm done, babe. They look thirsty."

"Well, they're not! Giving alcohol to a horse is totally irresponsible. Can't you see you're distressing them?"

"You're not distressed are you; you old 'aybag?" Rosco persisted.

At the sound of a braying laugh and Adam's shout of "Quit it Rosco!" Harry quickened his pace.

Laura's voice was shrill. "Get away from them!"

Rosco's slurred voice retorted, "Who d'yuh think you're shovin'? Just, watch it bug eyes! You're askin' for a smack!"

At the sound of Laura's shriek, followed by a ragged cheer from the onlookers, Harry broke into a run. Rounding the side of the marquee, he froze as he stared past the laughing group beside the fence. Laura was doubled over, with one hand tucked under her armpit and her face contorted in pain.

"What the hell?" Harry yelled in alarm, but his concern was tempered, when he noticed the reason for everyone's amusement. Rosco's legs appeared to be made of rubber; his expression one of utter disbelief, as he tottered and swayed. Beer spilled from the plastic glass that fell from his hand, as he staggered to the fence and grasped the top rail, before subsiding to his knees. Four livid weals bore testament to the blow that had landed on the side of his face.

Before Harry could react, he saw Simon leap over the fence and drape a comforting arm around Laura's shoulders. In spite of her pain, her concern was for her horses. The one nearest to her was rolling its eyes and tugging at the rope tethering it to the fence rail. Beyond it, Adam was struggling to hold onto the halters of two others, as they jostled and side-stepped in agitation.

The smirk on DP's face made no secret of the fact that he was finding the whole thing amusing. Beside him, Steve Edmunds seemed rooted to the spot; his eyes staring and his mouth open in amazement. "She bloody well stuck one on him!" he mumbled.

Harry felt an almost uncontrollable urge to 'stick one' on Steve, as he forced his way along the fence rail.

"You evil little bastard!" he growled.

Steve's face paled as he read the malice in Harry's eyes; his usual arrogance and bluster appearing to drain from him. "It's nothing to do with me!" he exclaimed. "I told Rosco ..."

"I'm willing to bet you put him up to it!" Harry growled. "I know you!"

"No I didn't ... I tried to stop him, didn't I Adam?"

Adam held onto the still nervous, fidgeting ponies and stared back wordlessly.

Harry could feel his pulse throbbing at his temples. "Just bugger off and don't ever come back!" he said icily. Gesturing towards Rosco who was being treated by a St. Johns Ambulance medic, he growled malevolently, "And take that scumbag and this grinning moron with you! If I ever set eyes on you again, I won't be responsible for my actions!"

"Whose gonna make us go ... you?" DP leered.

"He'll have plenty of help, sunshine!" Phil interjected menacingly at Harry's shoulder. He was supported by the growls of one or two others at the fence, and Harry heard Rachel's voice call, "Clear off; you've caused enough trouble!"

Harry turned his head as a shout of "Go on, sling yer 'ook!" came from someone behind him.

DP turned away with an arrogant shrug. "Come on Steve; let's get out of this shite 'ole. This bunch of carrot crunchers can keep it! I'll bring the car round. You and Adam bring Rosco over."

Steve was clearly only too happy to get away. "OK. Come on Adam."

Adam did not move. His attention was on Laura, who insisted on quietening and reassuring her ponies, before consenting to have her damaged hand examined.

"Are you coming Adam, or what?"

"No," Adam replied quietly.

"Suit yourself."

Rosco was back on his feet; seemingly sobered by the experience. The right side of his face was dark and swollen, with the marks of Laura's knuckles still prominent. He glanced across at her, as if still unable to believe what had happened, and gestured obscenely with one upraised finger. "F*** you! If I'd known you was gonna try that, I'd a'decked you first; you bitch!"

It drew a ripple of derisive laughter from several onlookers and the taunt: "Yeh, yeh … course you would!"

If Rosco imagined his troubles were over, he quickly realised his mistake, as a shadow fell across him. The warning he received was no less menacing for the quiet manner in which it was delivered. "Don't let this dog-collar fool you. If I hear you threaten this young lady, or speak to her like that again, I'll be the one doing the decking!"

Rosco's eyes betrayed the cold hand of fear that vied with his bewildered expression; both suggesting that he felt he was experiencing a living nightmare. Wordlessly, and without looking back, he trudged across the field after Steve Edmunds, to the clamour of more jeers and cat-calls.

Angry and embarrassed, Harry's immediate instinct was to turn on Adam. "This is your fault; bringing them here! What the hell …?"

"Don't blame Adam, Harry!" Laura exclaimed. "He tried to stop that stupid idiot. Snoopy would have bolted if it wasn't for him!"

Several others added their voices in corroboration, and Harry's anger subsided. But having seen the expression on his father's face, Adam vaulted the fence, and disappeared into the crowd around the marquee.

"Adam; wait!" Harry called, but Adam was quickly swallowed up by the milling crowd making its way to towards the stage at the far end of the rec. Harry tried to follow, but lost him in the melee, as people responded to the booming tannoy, announcing the imminent commencement of the evening concert. For a moment, Harry stood still, helplessly scanning the crowds; desperately hoping to catch a glimpse of his son, and cursing himself for his impetuous reaction. Why hadn't he waited to calm down before reacting so impulsively?

Debbie came to him and slipped her arm through his. "Any sign of him dad?"

Harry shook his head resignedly, "No; he could be anywhere."

A glance at the kitchen clock revealed that it was almost two o'clock. The monotonous, dull thump of drums and bass notes from the rec had long since ceased, and Debbie and Paul had gone to bed over an hour ago. Debbie had wanted to stay up until Adam came back … if he came back. But she had been struggling to keep her eyes open. Harry had eventually persuaded her that there was no point in all of them losing sleep.

Aided by Paul and Debbie, Harry had spent some time looking for Adam, but once it had become obvious that he had left the rec, Harry had persuaded them to give up. The band on stage had been doing its best to deafen everyone within a three mile radius, and while Debbie and Paul enjoyed '*the music*', Harry had returned to May Cottage to check if Adam was there. But there had been no sign of him.

Darkness had fallen by the time Harry had returned to the rec for one final, fruitless search, where he had found Rachel waiting for him. She had dismissed his apologies for 'ruining her evening', and had done her best to ease his troubled mind. After a supper of burgers and beer, they had left, without waiting for the closing fireworks.

*The Black Bull* had still been doing a brisk trade, when he had walked her back to Church House. Revellers had been enjoying the balmy, summer night on the village green, amongst them, a group of scantily clad young women creating a racket in the new play area. Leaving little to the imagination, they had soared recklessly on the swings, screeching and braying, to attract the attention of a group of raucous and equally inebriated lads sprawled across the benches outside the pub.

Harry had reluctantly heeded Rachel's advice to ignore their obscene calls to her, as they had passed them, smiling in accord with an elderly couple, who had grimaced in revulsion at the sight of a young girl on her hands and knees, throwing up in nearby shrubbery. The old chap had gestured towards her, with the comment, "Don't it make you proud to be British?"

* * *

Harry started at the sound of a key turning in the front door lock and the throb of a car engine. Realising he had been dozing, he sat up quickly, his chair scraping the stone floor, as he stumbled to his feet.

Marjorie appeared in the doorway, with Phil behind her, supporting Adam, who was having difficulty staying upright.

"I guessed you'd be up, but I didn't want to wake anybody else by ringing the bell," she whispered. "He's a bit the worse for drink," she added needlessly. "We were in *The King's Head* earlier. He came in with the other three. They were all the worse for wear."

Harry sighed with relief. "Thanks Marjorie. Thank you so much!" Looking past her, he caught Adam's glassy-eyed gaze.

"There he is Marjie ... my ever-loving daddy!" Adam exclaimed with a lop-sided smile. His speech was slurred and his eyes unfocussed. "Bet you're proud of me, dad? I'm taking after you! Pissed as a rat ... a real chip off the old block!"

Adam drooped against Phil, who gently lowered him onto a stair. "There you go sunshine; easy does it!"

"I'll tell you now, because I expect you'll hear about it eventually," Marjorie began. "They got thrown out of *The King's Head*. The landlord refused to serve them, so they started causing trouble; taking the mickey out of him and some of the others ... you know ... mimicking the way people talk round here."

"Oh God!" Harry sighed. "It never rains."

"He's in a bit of a state," Phil added. "He was throwin' up when I found 'im. We 'eard a racket opposite us, and when I went out, I found 'im by the bins outside the Memorial 'All. The other three drove off when our neighbours came out to see what all the noise was about. None of 'em is in a fit state t'drive. One of 'em can 'ardly stand. I just 'ope they don't 'it anybody."

"Thanks Phil ... both of you. I can't tell you how grateful I am," Harry said. Glancing up, he saw Debbie at the head of the stairs; concern etched on her face.

"Adam, are you alright?" she asked.

In reply, Adam slumped against the balusters with a muted groan.

"He's alright. He's not hurt," Marjorie said soothingly.

"Yes, you go back to sleep," Harry said, stooping to lift Adam to his feet. "Come on; let's get you to bed too."

"I'll give you a hand," said Phil.

As they gingerly eased him to his feet, the pungent stench of vomit stung Harry's nostrils. "What a mess!" he murmured. "What a bloody mess!"

# JUNE

## *From the Ashes*

After the excitement and traumas of the previous day, Debbie and Paul were content to spend the first day of June quietly at May Cottage; Debbie reminiscing and scrolling delightedly through pictures she had taken of Laura's ponies. Adam remained in bed all day with the curtains closed, wanting nothing but water, and unable to communicate in anything other than monosyllabic grunts. Harry had removed his stained shirt and jeans, and sponged him down, when he and Phil had put him to bed.

At lunchtime, Harry took a stroll to Church House, where he knew Laura could usually be found after the Sunday morning service. Rachel appeared from behind the churchyard on Monty as he arrived.

"Have you heard from Adam?" she asked.

Harry grinned ruefully. "Marjorie and Phil brought him home last night … enough said!"

Rachel nodded her understanding and did not pursue the matter further.

Simon and Laura greeted him warmly, although Monty treated him with disdain; snorting in apparent disgust when no apple or carrot was forthcoming, and tossing his head as Harry cautiously patted his neck.

Laura's wrist was supported by a sling and her hand heavily bandaged, but thankfully no bones were broken. Harry's attempt to apologise for the incident was met with a generosity of spirit typical of her and Simon, and a denial that there was anything to apologise for.

Harry spent a pleasant half an hour or so with them, while Rachel rode Monty back to his stable. He met her on her way back for a drink in *The Black Bull,* before she left for an evening flight to New York.

When Harry crossed the village green on his way home, Peggy was sticking a notice to one of the glass panes of the shop door. It read: *Temporary Restricted Opening Hours.*

Anticipating the question, she gestured towards it. "Ted's got to go into hospital to 'ave some tests done on Tuesday. He's listened to the doctor at last. They want to keep 'im in for a few days. 'I'm stayin' with 'is sister in Dorchester. It's more convenient for visitin'. Lisa's lookin' after the shop while we're away. They're sending somebody temp'ry to do the Post Office counter."

"I'm sure they'll sort him out once they find out what's wrong," Harry said reassuringly, despite his concerns.

Ted had been losing weight for some time, and his cheerful, irreverent banter had become less prevalent. There had been no sign of him behind the Post Office counter for several days, and Peggy's gaunt and worried look told its own story. She spread her hands in a gesture of resignation, "'Es not too well today. I've left 'im in bed. The sooner they take a look at 'im the better, in my book."

The following morning, Harry drove Debbie and Paul to Dorchester to catch their train. Adam was still too fragile to travel. He did manage to get up before they left, but he was deathly pale, and hid his eyes behind those absurd sunglasses.

As Harry waved goodbye to his daughter at the station, he tried not to dwell on how much he would miss her. Her affection and vibrant personality had been a reminder of half forgotten pleasures; although, as always, the occasional gesture or mannerism had been an aching reminder of her mother.

He had grown fond of Paul; finding the young man's gentle tolerance and undisguised devotion to Debbie endearing. Harry's apology for the embarrassing incident with Adam and his so-called friends had been received with a genial, "These things happen."

On the way home, Harry found himself with time to dwell on the past few days. As he had never been in *The King's Head*, it occurred to him that he ought to redress that omission and call in on the way home to offer the landlord an apology. He also made up his mind to take Phil and Marjorie for a meal one evening, to thank them for their help and support.

What was it Alfie had called Marjorie? '*A little diamond*'. How right he was!

His thoughts turned to Emma. She rarely seemed to be *out* of his thoughts these days; that hair; those eyes; the way she tilted her head … and the way his pulse quickened when he was near her.

"Get a grip for God's sake!" he said out loud. "You're going on fifty; not fifteen!"

It had been interesting to observe how well Emma and Guy got on with Laura and Simon. The two girls seemed to have found an instant rapport, which appeared easier and more relaxed than Laura's friendship with Rachel. Debbie got on well with both of them. It had been pleasing to observe how confident she was with the ponies, and the obvious pleasure it gave her to be around horses again.

Harry's mood improved steadily with the weather. The next day, he made another trip to Dorchester to send a much-recovered Adam on his way home. Encouragingly, colour had returned to Adam's cheeks; and he had discarded the sunglasses. He appeared genuinely contrite; his apology, as they left the house, seemingly sincere.

"Cheers, dad. Sorry for the aggro. I like, didn't mean to screw up your weekend."

"You're welcome here any time," Harry replied. "*Without* those muppets you call friends!"

"Yeh … well," Adam muttered, as if unwilling to commit himself.

Picking up his bag, he peered round the kitchen door. "Chow Marjie!"

"Her name is *Marjorie*!" Harry snapped, but Marjorie appeared from the lobby with an expression of amusement on her face. She looked at Harry and shook her head to indicate that she was not at all troubled.

"Safe journey," she replied. "Take care … and think about what I said!"

"Yeh, right," Adam replied hastily.

"What was it she told you to think about?" Harry asked, closing the front door behind them.

"Oh, nothing. Nothing for you to worry about, dad."

When Harry reached the village green on his way to collect his newspaper later that morning, he found Gerald Spenser-Smith holding forth amid a small group gathered around the broken swings in the newly installed play area.

"Just look at this!" he exclaimed. "You can't do a bloody thing without mindless vandals wrecking it!"

"Who did it?" Harry asked.

"Those yobs from the estate; I'll bet my life on it! Just look at the bloody mess!"

Empty beer and cider cans were scattered around the upturned benches, and one of the chains linking the corner posts of the war memorial was broken.

Harry gestured towards the cottages surrounding the green. "Didn't anyone hear them?"

"Mrs. Haddington and the people at the shop did. I expect a lot more did too, but no-one seems to want to get involved."

Gerald pointed over Harry's shoulder towards the small cul-de-sac, known as The Glebe, which led behind the shrubbery at the far end of green to what was once the village school. "Only Jimmy Lloyd over there came out to them. All he got was foul-mouthed abuse and the usual threats of course. He called the *Old Bill*, but typically they couldn't spare anybody to come and sort it out."

"Too busy giving out speeding tickets, I expect," a voice suggested sourly.

"I only live a few hundred yards away," Harry said. "I heard raised voices, but I assumed it was people leaving the pub."

Gerald shook his head. "No; this happened in the early hours of the morning. We didn't hear anything in The Meadowcroft either. I suppose that's a bit too far away."

Peggy Flowers appeared at the edge of the group. "It was that Moffat lad and 'is cronies," she said. "I saw them from our window. He's on bail, waitin' for 'is court case. Ted couldn't go down; 'e was up all night with 'is stomach."

"What's the lout done?" Gerald asked.

Peggy's brow creased. "I heard 'e robbed a grocer's … somewhere in Wiltshire, it was. Apparently 'im and one or two others threatened the owner and grabbed a load a'money from the till. They know it was 'im from the security cameras."

"Sounds like a nice lad," said Harry sardonically.

"They're a bad lot!" Peggy exclaimed. "His older brother's doin' time for robbin' a petrol station, *and* sellin' drugs. Kevin was always in trouble at school. 'E leads the others astray too. They used to get up to all sorts of trouble in the rec … caused a load of damage too. The people living round there set up a warden scheme in the end. It got better after that, especially after Kevin got put in a young offenders prison."

"Well he's obviously up to his old tricks," Gerald muttered.

Peggy nodded in reply.

"Just look what they done 'ere!" All heads turned to an elderly man who was standing beside the war memorial.

"What is it Tommy?" Peggy asked.

Tommy moved forward on arthritic legs, and lifted his walking stick to point. "Look at this!"

Swirls of blue paint covered the names carved on the plinth, above which, crude swastikas had been sprayed on two faces of the stone cross.

"Oh my God!" Peggy exclaimed, amid growls and murmurs of anger.

Tommy's eyes brimmed with tears, as he gazed in dismay at the disfigured memorial. "Is this all the thanks Charlie and the rest of 'em gets?" he shouted, his voice quaking with emotion.

Peggy gestured towards one of the names. "Charles W. Armor was Tommy's brother. 'E was killed in the Normandy landin's."

Mrs. Chowdri patted Tommy's arm. "No; that's not the way is it, Tommy," she said quietly. "Decent people appreciate what they did."

"It's not right!" Tommy muttered. "It's not right!"

"Don't worry; we'll get it cleaned up, Tommy," Gerald exclaimed. "I'm going to create merry hell to make sure those young bastards get what they deserve!" Turning away, he strode off purposefully across the green.

"You know, Harry," Peggy confided. "I know Mr. Smith means well and all that, but ... well, the police did come out eventually ... from Dorchester. They 'ad a look round and asked me to tell them what I saw. They 'ad a word with Mr. Lloyd, and a few others, as well. I heard Mr. Lloyd talking to one of the policemen. It 'ad somethin' to do with settin' up a Neighbourhood Watch, I think."

His preliminary meetings with the various committees of ACCORS South West had left Harry with few illusions about what lay in store. His initial problem was how to produce a coherent draft report from his copious notes and the organisation's two, thick volumes of processes and procedures.

Although Guy had warned him, he had still been surprised by the labyrinthine management structure, which had evolved over the brief life of the organisation. Managers and staff alike seemed to accept it without question or comment. He already sensed resentment from some quarters, and knew he would meet resistance to any changes he proposed from those with a vested interest in maintaining the status quo. Nick Stenning, the Project Liaison Controller, would be foremost in that resistance.

However, of more immediate interest was the distracting view from his study window. Ribbons of black cloud, their underbellies bloodstained by the setting sun, hovered in ranks, low against the pale sky. He was torn between tilting the louvers of the blind to hide it and taking his camera into the garden to capture its beauty. In the end he did neither, and went into the kitchen to make coffee.

Standing at the kitchen window, Harry was captivated by the burnished gold of the hills, and the gleaming halo crowning their summits, as day reluctantly surrendered to the softer blush of twilight. No matter how hard he tried, he could not concentrate his mind on ACCORS. His thoughts continually drifted to other considerations; among which, the setback to his hopes of a reconciliation with Adam figured prominently.

The danger was that having slipped back under Steve Edmunds' unsavoury influence, Adam would drift into his old ways. There was no way of telling what effect the incident with Laura would have on the situation. She had not stopped apologising. Making a joke of it by telling her it was a left hook Henry Cooper would have been proud of, seemed to have done little to relieve her embarrassment. Neither had the fact that Rachel considered it 'a hoot', and had taken to calling her 'Rocky'. Explaining that 'the little runt had it coming', and that she happened to be at the head of the queue, had similarly failed to relieve her feelings of guilt.

Nothing Harry said could convince her that it was *he* who should apologise, for allowing the situation to arise. Simon had tactfully persuaded him to let the matter lie, suggesting it was the best way to allow Laura to put it behind her.

There was no point in trying to do any more work; he was no longer in the right frame of mind. What he needed was a walk … and some fresh air.

The evening was pleasantly mild when Harry left the house. A gentle breeze was teasing the boughs of the magnolia, as he went out into the lane and turned towards the village green. Emerging from The Pound, he was fascinated by the curious illusion created by the dusky purple twighlight, which made the dark silhouette of the church spire appear to hover above the roofs of the cottages in Church Lane. The lights of *The Black Bull*, brighter and harsher than the comforting glow in the other windows, picked out nearby trees and foliage in spectral relief. He thought he could detect a hint of smoke from the embers of an unseen bonfire.

*Neighbourhood Watch* posters were already prominent around the green, and as yet, there had been no repetition of the vandalism. All was quiet, except for the occasional raised voice or burst of laughter from the pub. Harry made his way to one of the benches beside the desecrated war memorial, and sat down to meditate. But, instead of concentrating his mind on unravelling the maze of ACCORS procedures, he found his thoughts continually straying to waves of titian hair and a pair of enchanting green eyes.

It did no good to remind himself that she was his friend's partner, and more than ten years younger than him. Nor did it help to reflect that she was an attractive, vivacious young woman, who probably regarded him as nothing more than an acquaintance. He found it difficult to ignore the seed of forlorn hope that defiantly refused to be crushed beneath the heel of inescapable reality.

It was not as if he could draw consolation from the fact that Guy was older than him, and in his opinion, not at all good looking. It did not seem to matter. The thought brought to mind something once explained to him by a female colleague. "Men fall in love with their eyes," she had declared. "But women do it with their ears." Harry chuckled to himself at the mischievous thought that, were it the other way round, Guy's prominent ears would be ideally suited for the purpose. Nevertheless, whatever he might lack in looks, Guy seemed to more than make up for with his raffish and extrovert personality.

At least Emma had not told him he was '*sweet*'; that 'honeyed kiss-of-death' that women use to gently deter unwelcome advances ... at least, not yet.

The smell of smoke seemed stronger, and sniffing the air, he thought he sensed movement out of the corner of his eye. Turning his head, he saw a shadow pass in front of the dim security light in the narrow service alley beside the shop. At first he took it to be a cat, but the silhouette that suddenly appeared above the wooden gate was unmistakably human. As the figure dropped to the ground, another appeared, scaling the gate to drop with a stifled grunt, before running off into the shadows of Mill Lane.

Before Harry could react to what he took to be a burglary, he noticed a flicker of light reflected in the shop window; faint at first, but gradually becoming brighter. As it struck him that it was a reflection from behind the glass, the word '*Fire*' formed in his mind, followed by the realisation that whoever he had just seen, must have started it!

With his heart racing, he ran towards the shop. Even before he reached it, he could see a dull, flickering glow through the window. Something appeared to be burning beyond the open doorway leading to the store rooms at the rear, with a haze of smoke hanging above it. Harry tried the main door, which, as he expected, was locked. Pulling out his mobile phone, he dialled the emergency services.

By the time he had put his phone away, people were emerging from *The Black Bull* and the houses around the green. "The Fire Brigade's on its way!" he called, as several of them converged on the shop. It was a relief to recognise Gerald Spenser-Smith among them.

"What the hell's going on?" Gerald exclaimed.

Harry pointed to the shop. "There's a fire. I think it's been started deliberately! I came out for a breath of air and saw them running away."

"Who?"

"I don't know; it was too dark. But they were probably young, because they climbed that gate pretty easily."

"I'll bet it's them vandals back again!" came an exclamation from somewhere behind them.

The fire was spreading to the shop, and belatedly, almost comically, the burglar alarm started to honk like an asthmatic goose; it's red light strobing pathetically in the reflected flicker of the flames.

A group of onlookers, including a child, was edging towards the shop window, trying to peer in; seemingly unaware of the danger.

"Get back!" Harry shouted. "Get that lad away from there!"

"Who d'you think you are?" one of them challenged belligerently.

"If that glass goes, that fire will erupt out of there!" Harry retorted. His warning was reinforced by Gerry's commanding bellow. "He's right! Come on; get back! Well away … all of you!"

It took several minutes to usher the gathering crowd back onto the green, by which time acrid smoke had begun to seep from the entrance doorway and one or two points around the shop window frame. It was then that Harry saw the face at the upstairs window.

"Jesus!" he exclaimed, pointing upward. "It's Lisa!"

"Who is it?"

The sound of Simon's voice was reassuring, but Harry's heart was racing. "It's Lisa!" he shouted, and pointed up at the window. "It looks like she's in trouble! My guess is she can't get downstairs because of the fire!"

Even through the dusty pane, he could see terror on the pale face behind the glass. Lisa's hands were desperately fumbling at the window catch; her mouth open in an inaudible cry. By now, everyone in the gathering crowd was craning their neck and pointing; their voices and calls an incoherent babble. Someone was stupid enough to yell "Jump!"

It seemed to Harry an age since he had dialled 999, although it could not be more than a few minutes. Even so, he was praying for the reassuring sound of sirens to settle his own rising panic. Lisa was not the brightest bulb in the chandelier, and he doubted her ability to think lucidly, even without the terror that must now be gripping her.

"The bloody windows are stuck!" Gerald exclaimed. "Look, she can't get them open!"

"I'm sure Ted's got a ladder at the back!" Simon exclaimed, patting Harry on the arm.

Swallowing hard to calm his fear, Harry ran with Simon towards the service alley, their footsteps echoing in the confined space.

"Where they goin'?" a voice called.

"It's that bossy bugger what was yellin' at us?" added a second. "Thinks 'es a bloody 'ero! Leave it mate! The Fire Brigade's comin'!"

Harry tugged at the locked gate, sobbing with frustration, as he yanked at it in futile desperation.

"Look out!" Simon called, and launched his broad shoulder against the gate. The frame bulged and cracked promisingly, but maddeningly it held. Undeterred, Simon threw himself against the gate once more, splintering the wood around the lock. Finally, it gave way to a lunging kick from the heel of Simon's boot, which smashed it back against the wall dividing the yard beyond it from the cottage next door. They both rushed forward; Simon leading the way.

A thin haze of acrid smoke hung in the yard, unpleasant and irritating to the throat.

"Over here!" Harry called. Covering his mouth and nose with a handkerchief, he pointed to the aluminium ladder resting on the low, sloping roof of a storage shed. Simon had already wound what looked like a clerical stole around his face, and leapt onto a metal keg to pull at the ladder. "It's tied!" he exclaimed. "I can't undo the knots!"

Casting around for something with a sharp edge, Harry became aware of flames flickering from a smashed window, below which lay shreds of cardboard and sacking. 'So that's the way the evil devils started it!' he thought, and steeled himself to get close enough to the burning window frame to snatch a shard of broken glass.

At the sound of footsteps, Harry turned to find Gerald standing beside the broken gate. "How's Lisa doing?" he asked.

"She's got a little window open, but she can't shift the other ones. She says there's smoke coming up the stairs. She's practically hysterical!"

"Wouldn't you be?" Harry retorted. He could hear the sound of a distant siren, but his training as a fire marshall at Bennett's had made him keenly aware of how quickly fire could spread. He intended taking no chances.

"Look; ask Lisa if she can get to the room above here ... *safely*!" he emphasised.

"It's OK. *The Old Bill* has just got here," Gerald replied.

"Just f***ing do it!" Harry yelled, his nerves jangling. Gerry fled back into the alley.

The sound of more splintering wood caught his attention. Simon had used brute strength to rip one end of the ladder free, and jumping off the keg, swung it in an arc, tearing the other end loose, before lowering it to the ground, trailing shards of rope, timber and roofing felt.

Gerry reappeared. "She can. She says the fire hasn't reached upstairs yet ... but the rooms are getting smokey. The hallway at the bottom of the stairs is on fire though!"

Harry pointed upwards. "Tell her to get towels, blankets, anything! Tell her to soak them and put a towel over her mouth and nose. Then get into this room up here. Tell her to shut the door and stuff the rest round it at the bottom. Tell her to get down as low as she can!"

More sirens sounded from the direction of Manor Hill, and the reassuring sight of a police officer appeared; radio in hand. "What's going on, here?" she asked.

"There's a girl trapped up there," Simon replied, propping the ladder against the wall.

"Leave that to the Fire Service, sir!" she ordered. "You're not trained for rescue. Please go and stand clear."

Before Harry or Simon could answer, her radio squawked. The gist of the message, delivered by the metallic, disembodied voice, was chilling. "Can't get through ... cars parked ..."

Gerry appeared once more, puffing like a leaky bellows. "They can't get the bloody fire engines down Manor Hill!" he exclaimed. "Some idiots have parked opposite each other. There's not enough room to get through. They're still trying to find the owners!"

A window opened above them and Lisa's ashen, tear-streaked face appeared. "Get me out! Please!" she screamed. "The stairs're on fire! I can 'ear it!" Her plea ended with a fit of coughing.

Harry swallowed hard. "Right, let's get this ladder up!" but Simon was already extending it, with a screech of metal which suggested it had not been used for some time.

"Alright Lisa!" he shouted. "Hang on! We're coming!"

"You can't do that, sir!" a male voice commanded. Turning his head, Harry could see that another police officer had joined his colleague.

Harry gave them both an icy glare. "If you're going to start on about *Risk Assessments* … and *Health and bloody Safety* …"

The female police officer was unmoved. "Please go and stand clear, sir! You're not trained for this!"

"So bloody well arrest me!" Harry snarled, with no more than a glance at her. Simon steadied the ladder, and he began to climb; slowly and shakily, his legs like jelly. He could hear the police officer reporting below him, but neither she nor her colleague made any attempt to interfere.

Lisa, sobbing and shaking uncontrollably, wrapped her arms around his shoulders the moment his head rose above the windowsill. "It's alright Lisa," he said, as soothingly as he could manage.

Even from outside, he could feel the heat and see smoke creeping under the door. Lisa had followed his instructions as well as she could manage, but the blanket had merely been laid at the foot of the door and smoke was seeping in around it.

Having got this far, it now occurred to him that the major problem was the window frame. It was clearly not wide enough for Lisa to get through. He would need to break the central mullion. To get enough purchase for that, he would have to climb in!

"Oh, bloody hell!" he groaned; but despite his own stomach churning fear, he could not leave this petrified girl to her fate.

Simon called comfortingly to Lisa, reassuring her that she would be safe in a few minutes. All the while, the insistent howl of sirens continued; maddeningly close, but *so* far away.

Up there on the ladder the smoke haze was thinner and somewhat dissipated by the breeze, although Harry knew that would change the moment the bedroom door succumbed to the heat and flames. In a voice both hoarse and unsteady, he called to Simon. "I'll have to climb in and chuck the mattress down. Can you find me something heavy enough to smash the window frame?"

His arms and legs were trembling and his calf muscles ached with tension, but extricating himself from Lisa's embrace, he eased himself up another rung of the ladder. Noticing that the blanket at the door was beginning to smoulder, he realised he had only a few moments to get her out. Only then could he look out for himself. In his heart he knew he had little chance of managing it, but Lisa's uncontrolled sobbing and the terror in her eyes demanded that he must hang on … and try to ignore his own rising panic.

With *The Lord's Prayer* on his lips, he grabbed the window frame, and began hauling himself over the sill.

"Alright; you can come down now! Leave this to us!"

The voice was both commanding and reassuring. Turning his head to look down, Harry caught a glimpse of a yellow helmet, before he and Lisa were suddenly lit by the eerie glare of a powerful lamp.

"Don't leave me!" she screeched.

Over, her shoulder, Harry saw the door begin to blacken and smoulder. "I won't leave you, Lisa," he said quietly.

"Come down!" the voice insisted.

"I can't!" he yelled back. "She won't let go! She's terrified!"

He felt the ladder flex and a heavy tread on the rungs below, and almost burst into tears with relief, as another ladder thumped against the wall beside him.

The howl of sirens increased in volume, a sign that the fire engines had successfully negotiated Manor Hill. A fire officer inched his way past onto the other ladder, and Harry heard the sound of splintering wood and glass, as he slowly made his way down, his legs shaking and barely able to support him. He reached the ground trembling and nauseous, as the tension and adrenaline ebbed from his system. The fire officers brought Lisa down, slowly and carefully, to a waiting paramedic, who draped a blanket round her shoulders. Her face was ashen and streaked with the grubby tracks of tears, but as she passed Harry, she managed a wan smile.

Simon reached out to steady him, and with the police officer, took him along the narrow alley towards the snaking hoses and organised mayhem around the village green. A Dorset Fire and Rescue Service van and two fire engines had finally made it down Manor Hill, together with two police cars and an ambulance. The strobing flashes of their garish lights were multiplied by reflections from the windows of the shop and nearby cottages, which, amid the haze of smoke and the eerie glare of the arc lights, created a sinister, almost alien spectacle.

Flames were licking around the shop window frame, and a pall of smoke hung over the building; acrid and irritating to the eyes and throat. Three police officers were shepherding the crowd further back onto the grass, away from the disciplined organisation of the fire officers.

A paramedic draped a blanket around Harry's shoulders and tried to lead him towards the ambulance.

"I'm OK!" Harry protested, and pointed towards *The Black Bull*. "What I need is over there, not in a bloody ambulance!"

The police officer smiled indulgently. "Best let them check you out, sir," she said.

To Harry's surprise, and then embarrassment, a ripple of applause broke out from the green. "Good old Harry!" someone called.

"Bloody idiot!" Harry muttered shakily.

"Come on Harry," Simon chuckled, "They're proud of you!"

"For what?" Harry replied. "You and I both know we would never have got her out of there in time!"

Simon squeezed his shoulder. "But you tried," he said. "You were her Samaritan, Harry. You did what you could."

"Shall I tell you something?" Harry replied ruefully. "Do you know what I was doing when the firemen arrived? I was saying my prayers! How hypocritical is that?"

"It would seem they were heard," Simon said quietly.

"I don't need to ask what you were up to last night," said Marjorie, hanging up her coat in the lobby. "It's all over the village ... our hero!"

"Hero, my foot!" Harry replied, eliciting a giggle in response.

"They're saying it's those yobs again," she added. Taking a beaker from the mug tree, she helped herself from the cafetiere. Harry grinned; it was a sign of how relaxed their relationship had become.

"So, what happened?" she asked, settling herself on a chair facing him.

Harry recounted the events of the previous evening as briefly as her constant interruptions for more detail would allow. "They took Lisa off to hospital, but I think she's alright ... at least physically," he said.

"Oh, she's back home," Marjorie replied. "Phil saw her this morning. He said she seems perfectly alright. She's milking it for all she's worth; telling everybody you saved her."

"That's nonsense!" Harry protested. "The firemen did the rescuing. Simon did as much, if not more than me. I would never have got her through that window in a month of Sundays!"

Marjorie chuckled, "I can imagine. But like it or not, you're both local heroes."

"It's *not* as far as I'm concerned," he said flatly. "I don't know what she was doing there anyway."

"She was supposed to be keeping an eye on things for Peggy and Ted," Marjorie explained. "Although, from what I can gather, she'd had a couple of her mates round there earlier on."

Harry frowned. "Didn't she hear anything? It looked like whoever it was broke a window at the back and stuffed cardboard and God knows what else in; then set fire to it."

Marjorie wrinkled her nose. "I expect she'd been drinking. She says she was asleep. She woke up to go to the loo, and smelt burning."

"She's damned lucky!" Harry exclaimed. "I for one thought the place was empty; with Peggy and Ted being away!"

He stood up and poured himself more coffee. "I can't get rid of the taste of smoke and this gritty feeling in my throat. When I finally got home ... after talking to the police, the fire brigade and Uncle Tom

Cobleigh and all, I smelt like I'd been set alight myself. I had a bath last night and a shower this morning, but I can still smell it!"

"It's in the air," she replied, "especially round by the shop … or what used to be the shop."

"Is it that bad?"

She nodded. "I went round to have a look before I came here. The walls are all black; the downstairs is gutted and the upstairs at the front's all charred. Part of the roof is, as well. It caught the thatch of Mrs. Sillitoe's next door, but not that badly, as far as I could tell."

"I wonder if Peggy and Ted know," Harry mused.

"I expect the police or somebody will have told them," said Marjorie. "It's not going to help their peace of mind, what with all Ted's going through." Getting to her feet, she sighed, "Well, this won't do; I'd better get on."

"I'd better get back to my desk," Harry replied.

"Why don't you get some fresh air?" she suggested. "Go down to the coast or something. Let the sea air blow the smoke and cobwebs away."

"I've got work to do," he said, although the idea was very appealing.

It was an idea too appealing to ignore. When the following day dawned bright and almost cloudless, Harry made up his mind to *bunk off*, as they used to say in his school days; straight after breakfast.

In the event, it was mid-morning before he managed to get away. The delays began with a telephone call from a reporter on the *Dorset Echo*, followed by a visit from his neighbour Alan, in his capacity as joint editor of *The Valley Voice*.

Alan had heard most of the story already, but wanted it 'straight from the horse's mouth' as he put it. He had also brought a camera for what he called 'a mug shot'. His irreverent sense of humour was much in evidence during the half hour or so of what could only loosely be described as an interview.

The third reason for delay was a touching, but somewhat embarrassing, visit from Lisa and her parents. They arrived bearing gifts of a dwarf apple tree and, what Harry always called, *an Ali Baba Pot* of strawberry plants. In spite of the shaven head, tattoos and an earring, Lisa's father was softly spoken and mild mannered. Her mother, lank haired and overweight like her daughter, said little. She occupied herself gazing around Harry's sitting room, as if she were browsing in the furnishings department of *John Lewis*.

Thankfully, Lisa did not throw her arms around him, as she had the previous night, but she was effusive in her gratitude. She and her parents brushed aside his protestations that he had done little.

"I dunno what I'd a done if you 'adn't bin there," Lisa insisted.

Feeling self-conscious, all Harry could think of to say was, "I've got a daughter about your age, Lisa."

"So you know 'ow me an' the missus feels," Lisa's father interjected. "We're grateful ... more grateful than we can tell you, Mr. Simmonds. I don't care who it was got 'er out o'there. God knows what she'd a done if it 'ad'n a'bin fer you an' the vicar!"

"Lisa was scared out of 'er wits," Lisa's mother added. Lisa nodded her agreement enthusiastically.

Their touching gratitude left Harry lost for words. He could fully understand how they felt; the way he would, had it been Debbie or Adam. He spread his arms in a helpless gesture towards the gifts. "You really shouldn't have, but I do appreciate it. Thank you. Please call me Harry."

"I'm Frank ... Frank Jennings," and motioning to his wife, "This is Geraldine ... Gerry." By way of an aside, he grinned and added, "If you ever needs a plumber ..."

"As a matter of fact I do," Harry laughed.

The Jennings left soon afterwards, but not before Frank and Harry had agreed a date to have his central heating 'looked at'.

❖

Finally on his way, Harry revelled in the glory of Dorset bathed in summer sunshine. Instinctively, he headed towards the Purbeck coast and all its attractions; not the least of which was Emma. He chose a route across the army firing range, through Wool towards Wareham, where he headed south past the hamlets of Stoborough and Norden, until he reached the impossibly quaint village of Corfe Castle, with its mediaeval ruin looming stark and imposing above the picturesque, stone cottages.

Progress was slow behind a queue of traffic winding its way towards the crest of the hill to the weathered stone facade of the *Bankes Arms Hotel*. The sight of holidaymakers crowding the narrow pavements and sitting on the steps of the stone cross at the centre of Corfe Castle's tiny square, made the idea of stopping to look around appealing. However, there were no available parking spaces outside *The Greyhound Inn*, and he was loath to follow the signs directing vehicles to what appeared to be a narrow, congested road behind the church, so he drove on.

'Some other time,' he thought, and glancing in his rear-view mirror, he could see people dotting the steep, grassy castle mound, like grazing sheep. He decided to continue on towards Harmans Cross, taking boyish delight in the shriek of a whistle and a plume of dirty-white steam billowing above the parapet of a stone bridge.

"A steam train," Harry chuckled. "I've got to try that some time."

The green, sunlit headland seemed to envelope the bay in a protective embrace, as Harry approached Swanage, passing turnings to a place with the delightfully eccentric name of Langton Matravers. Ignoring a large car park as he entered the town, he carried on towards the seafront, until suddenly, there on the horizon, was the heart-lifting vista of the sea; sparkling blue-green in the sunlight.

Signs on the approach to the promenade warned of parking limitations and restricted access, so he turned right at some traffic lights and found himself approaching the railway station. Its quaint, yesteryear character and the '*Puffing Billy*' beside the platform, brought a smile of enchantment to his face, transporting him back his childhood and the idyllic world of *The Famous Five*.

Swanage was more crowded and smaller than he had expected, but in his opinion, all the more appealing because of it. Reaching the end of what he took to be the main thoroughfare, he followed the narrow winding streets running parallel to the sea, until he came to a busy open area by a stone quay. People were enjoying the sunshine; queuing at the refreshment kiosk or enjoying an early lunch in the al fresco sea-food restaurant.

The bay continued on to a pier, beyond which, what appeared to be a bell tower rose, as if marooned, on the shoreline. Harry followed the signs to a hillside car park, which presented a panoramic view of the entire bay; all the way round to the gleaming white rocks poised in the sea at the tip of the far headland.

Walking down the steep grassy slope to the shore, he was intrigued by a stone circle with two ionic pillars that resembled the remains of a miniature Greek theatre. The warmth of the sun, the cry of the wheeling gulls and the tang of seaweed on the breeze were simple pleasures he too rarely savoured. He strolled slowly around the bay, passing *The Heritage Museum* and a block of holiday apartments adorned with wrought iron verandas overlooking the sea. It brought to mind the bygone splendour of Edwardian England. Further on, a restaurant projected over the walkway, and beyond it, the buildings retreated to the far side of the promenade, as it widened to sweep round behind the beach towards the cliffs at the far end of the bay.

As traditional as the promenade kiosks and Punch and Judy, the brightly painted shelter beside the Mowlem Theatre was populated by elderly trippers, taking the opportunity to enjoy an ice cream or a packed lunch out of the breeze that had sprung up with the incoming tide. The column close to the shelter drew Harry's attention. He discovered it commemorated a victory by King Alfred's navy over the marauding Danes, but as the action had taken place when the double-headed battle-axe was the ultimate in weapon technology, the significance of the cannon balls crowning the monument eluded him.

A glass fronted arcade with flashing lights and slot-machines faced the sea on the other side of the road, and beside it, he could see the brightly painted canopies of children's funfair rides, in what he took to be raised gardens overlooking the promenade. Apart from that, Swanage seemed to have avoided the surfeit of garish tat and tawdry 'attractions' that scar so many resorts.

Resisting the charm of the sunlit shore, Harry decided to explore the town. Peering into shop windows, he did his best to convince himself that his objective was not really to find Emma. He followed the road as it curved round to the narrow, sloping High Street, and had almost given up the search, when suddenly there it was: *Purbeck Style*. With his heart fluttering, and as nervous as a schoolboy, he passed by slowly on the other side of the street, hoping to catch a glimpse of her beyond the extravagantly posed mannequins in the window. But to no avail. She did not appear to be in the shop.

Perhaps it was just as well. What had he expected … or intended? He had no idea what he would have done if she had been there, or what he would have said if he had plucked up the courage to go in; other than to mutter that he 'just happened to be passing'.

Swallowing his disappointment, he started to make his way back towards the sea, with the intention of finding somewhere to have a cup of coffee. Afterwards, he might take a walk along the promenade. He stopped to browse through a box of second hand books outside a charity shop.

"Well, well Mr. Simmonds; what brings you to sunny Swanage?"

He froze, his heart missing a beat at the sound of the familiar voice. "Hello Emma … I … well, I suppose I'm skiving off work."

"Good for you! It's the perfect day for it," she giggled. Holding up a carrier bag, she added, "I was just coming back from the supermarket; we're out of milk and coffee. I thought it was you I could see up ahead."

He would have loved to tell her how fresh and lovely she looked in the crisp summer dress, but what he said was, "Things got a bit hectic the other day, so I thought I'd have a day at the coast … and found myself here."

He knew it sounded lame, but she smiled and nodded sympathetically. "So, can you stick around for lunch, or have you got somewhere else to go?"

"No I've got all day … lunch would be great!" the words tumbled out in his euphoria.

"I can't leave Paula on her own. But Becky will be in around one-thirty. Can you hang on 'til then?"

"Yes; of course!" Harry could feel his heart thumping. "Shall I meet you here, or would you rather meet somewhere else?"

"I don't mind, but there are some nice places in town. Why don't I meet you by the Alfred Monument; next to the Mowlem; at say … a quarter-to-two?"

"That's fine!" He had tried to keep his voice calm, but suspected his reply had sounded desperately eager.

"OK; catch you later."

Harry watched her cross the road, entranced by the way the sunlight gleaming in her hair, created highlights of burnished copper. He felt his cheeks flush as she turned to smile and wave, before disappearing into the shop.

He was a hopeless case! But what the heck! He was going to spend a delightful hour or so in her company. All he had to do was avoid making a bloody fool of himself; which he realised was easier said than done!

To kill time, he bought a newspaper and sat outside a cafe with a cup of coffee, looking out over the sea. Afterwards he strolled to the railway station to indulge his boyish fondness for steam trains and browse in the gift shop, where a poster offering the experience of driving a steam locomotive caught his attention, as well as his imagination.

He arrived at the curious monument with more than fifteen minutes to spare, and spent the time gazing at the sea, letting the sigh of the breaking waves, the mournful squeal of the gulls and the tang of ozone pervade his senses.

His attention was drawn to two toddlers in floppy sunhats on the beach below, earnestly shovelling sand into plastic buckets, with that innocent solemnity characteristic of the very young. The years fell away, to fill his mind with images of Debbie and Adam on idyllic holidays; long past.

He remained lost in nostalgia, until he heard footsteps close behind him, and there she was; her eyes masked by a large pair of fashion sunglasses, and her hair pinned behind one ear by a clip adorned with a flower. She smiled a greeting. To Harry, the freckles sprinkled across the bridge of her nose, more pronounced and noticeable in the bright sunlight, made her even more attractive.

"How hungry are you?" she asked, pushing her sunglasses up onto her head, to reveal those mesmeric eyes.

"Not especially, but I could eat something," he replied. "I'm happy to go along with whatever you normally do."

"I usually have a sandwich in the kitchen at the shop, but that would be a waste of a day like this, wouldn't it?"

"It certainly would! Any suggestions?"

"Guy managed to get tickets for The Bournemouth Symphony Orchestra at *The Lighthouse* tonight. He'll want to catch a meal beforehand, so I'd prefer something fairly light. Will pizza be OK?" Noticing Harry's quizzical look, she added, "*The Lighthouse* is an arts centre in Poole."

Harry grinned. "Oh I see; I did wonder how they'd manage to get the piano up all those steps." Her laughter, in response to his feeble joke, was gratifying. "If you're going to eat later, don't worry about me," he said.

"No; I need something to tide me over 'til then," she insisted.

"OK; pizza's fine," he replied.

It was amusing and gratifying to notice heads turn as she led him to a small pizzeria glorying in the name *L'Isola della Pizza*. They were greeted by a grey haired chap, with traces of cockney in his Italian accent. "Ah; Signorina Reynolds!" he exclaimed. "It's good to see you again." With a welcoming nod to Harry, he showed them to a table under a parasol in the small garden at the rear, waiting attentively, while they settled themselves and ordered their drinks; sparkling water for Emma and a small beer for Harry.

"I take it you're a regular here?" Harry surmised.

She nodded. "I come here with my girls once or twice a month. We don't open every day in the off-season."

"How many of you are there?"

"Paula's full time; Becky and Pam do part-time through the summer, and Louise comes in once a week to keep my books up to date and do my VAT return."

"How are you finding things in the current situation?" he asked.

"Not too bad really. Things could be better. Luckily some people seem to be adopting a *'to hell with it'* attitude when they're on holiday, especially if the weather's bad and they need to cheer themselves up. I'm trying to keep my prices steady, but it's not easy when costs are going up all the time. But you being an accountant, I don't need to explain it, do I?"

Harry smiled diffidently. "I just do the numbers. I don't have to grapple with the problems of keeping customers happy."

"Guy says you're very good at what you do," she said quietly.

"He always was a flatterer," Harry replied, bringing a knowing smile to her lips.

The arrival of a waiter with their drinks reminded them that they had not looked at the menu. Being familiar with it, Emma needed only a cursory glance. Harry was happy to opt for her choice.

When the waiter had left, she turned her bewitching gaze on him, "So; tell me about Harry Simmonds."

"What do you want to know?" he replied, feeling his cheeks flush.

"Well, for a start, I've been meaning to ask you; is Harry short for Henry ... or Harold, maybe?"

"Henry," he said. "But my first name is Alexander; the same as my dad."

"Is that a family tradition?"

"Sort of. My grandfather and great grandfather were Alexanders, but my grandparents had a difference of opinion. My grandmother bucked the trend and dug her heels in. For some reason, she insisted on calling their eldest son Francis. She relented when my dad came along. I'm an only child. My grandfather was terminally ill when I was born, so for his sake, my parents named me Alexander; although my mum liked the name Harry. It's what she and everyone has always called me." With a chuckle, he added, "She wouldn't have dreamt of putting 'Harry' on my birth certificate. It had to be Alexander Henry."

Emma chuckled. "I agree with your mum. You're definitely a Harry."

"I feel more like a right Charlie these days," he countered, eliciting another delightful giggle.

Her smile faded and she looked at him thoughtfully. "You seem to be managing pretty well. You have a lovely house, and you've made some good friends. Nethercombe Ley is delightful."

"Yes; I suppose I should count myself lucky," he replied.

"Guy was stunned when he found out you were divorced."

Harry grinned ruefully. "Everybody was. Nobody more than me! I never saw it coming, until it was too late."

"I think that's the way it is, pretty often," she said thoughtfully. "Life has a way of kicking you in the teeth when you least expect it."

Harry nodded. "I suppose the hardest part was getting used to being on my own, after twenty odd years with a wife and two kids around all the time."

"Your daughter's a credit to you. Debbie's a great girl."

"Thank you. As a matter of fact, she said nice things about you too."

Emma laughed. "Well, there you go ... and there's Rachel. I shouldn't think life's dull with her around."

"No; it isn't," he laughed. "So, to conclude my potted biography, I like to call myself a management consultant, but all I am is a glorified accountant, really. You already know about my kids and my marriage, so that's about it. That's all there is. Now; how about you?"

She gave him an enigmatic smile. "Well; I was christened Emma Louise Reynolds, in Melbourne, Victoria ... ah ... a *bit* more than thirty years ago. My dad died when I was thirteen. He was killed in a forest fire"

"A forest fire?" Harry repeated in surprise.

"Yes; we get a lot of them in Victoria. My dad was a Park Ranger. My mum's over here, living with me at the moment. She came over about three months ago, but she's going home in two weeks time; she misses her grandchildren. My sister lives just outside Melbourne with her husband and three kids. My brother and his partner live about an hour's drive north of Sydney. They've just had a baby ... a little girl. I came here from *Oz* eleven years ago with my partner, Richie. We met at uni. We were only going to stay for a year at most, but he started a business with a mate; servicing dishwashers and washing machines and things. It was a goer for a while. Then things got tough and he wanted to go back. I didn't; I had a good job managing a boutique ... and a pretty good social life."

"Did he go back?"

"Not straight away. But we'd sort of grown apart, so we went our separate ways."

It seemed an opportune moment to ask one of the questions on Harry's mind. "How did you meet Guy?"

She paused before answering, as if she suspected the other question was, 'What on earth do you see in him?'

"He came into the shop one day, looking for a sweater. We only had a few for men, but it took him ages to make up his mind. He brought it back the next day to exchange it. He'd had second thoughts ... or so he said. I'd been on my own for a while, after breaking up with someone I'd been with for a few years. Guy was charming, witty and funny ... and he asked me out to dinner."

She sipped at her water before continuing. "I came to Swanage to open a new shop for my boss; to get it started and up and running. I fell in love with Dorset. Then I wound up buying the business from her. She was going through a messy divorce at the time. She was having this pretty torrid 'thing' with a rich Italian. Her husband found out, of course ... she wasn't all that discrete. She lives in Genoa now."

She had not mentioned being married. Harry wanted to ask why, but decided it would be indiscrete to do so. All he could think of to say was, "So you got hooked on Dorset?"

"Yes; I love it; don't you?"

He nodded. "It certainly grows on you."

She took another sip of water. "I've got a place on the outskirts of Wareham. Not as grand as yours. It's not very big. It's on a small, new development. I saw the houses being built, and managed to get a mortgage."

"I'd hardly call May Cottage grand," he protested.

"Oh Harry, it's lovely! I'd love a house like that."

He avoided eye contact, lest he betray the thought: *'You only have to say the word!'*

Her long, slender fingers toyed with the opal ring, and she said tentatively. "I don't want to speak out of turn, but I gather you're worried about your son."

Harry sighed. "Yes; there was an unsavoury incident at the May Fayre after you left. Adam's pal Steve turned up and brought a couple of Neanderthals with him."

"I know; Laura told me."

"Oh; I didn't realise."

"Yes; Laura came to the shop last week; we *did lunch,* as they say. She told me what happened."

Harry sighed. "So you know how upset she is. It's my damned fault."

"Harry; it's not! Laura knows how concerned you are about your son. She's worried that she's only made things worse."

"Of course she hasn't! Adam has this *so-called* friend, Steve Edmunds! He egged the others on … making sure he kept his own head down, of course. I only wish I'd belted him while Laura was sorting Rosco out!"

Losing the struggle to keep a straight face, Emma giggled. "I'm sorry; it's not funny, I know. But I wish I'd been there to see it. Fancy Laura, of all people, losing it like that! She's still embarrassed about it. Adam told her not to worry about any comeback from Rosco, though. Apparently, he's been busted for drugs and shoplifting more than once, so he won't be going anywhere near the police. He made the others swear not to say anything about it. I guess it won't do his street cred any favours, if it gets around that he got beaten up by a girl."

It was Harry's turn to laugh. "Watching him stagger around was the funniest thing I've seen for ages. But I didn't know Adam had spoken to Laura about it."

The arrival of the pizzas brought a hiatus to the conversation, while the waiter fussed over the side salad and checked they had everything they needed.

For Harry, enjoying lunch in the sunshine with a vivacious redhead was about as good as it gets.

After Harry had walked Emma back to her shop, the rest of the afternoon was inevitably something of an anticlimax. However, a stroll along the seafront, watching the waves roll languidly onto the sand, and feeling the warmth of the summer sun on his face, gave Harry a feeling of contentment. It evoked the thought: 'Emma's right; Dorset is lovely'.

The red and white striped Punch and Judy booth, now closed up and deserted, reminded him of the Easter weekend with Rachel, and her exuberant participation in the 'entertainment'; a word he had always considered questionable where puppet shows were concerned. Somehow, he could not imagine Emma doing the same.

She must realise he was attracted to her. He did not believe his feeble excuse for being in Swanage had fooled her for a moment. What was she thinking? She probably saw him as a lonely, middle-aged divorcee, licking his wounds; and like a stray cat, grateful for a few moments of attention. And what did she mean by 'Rachel being fun'? Was it a gentle hint that he should be grateful for what he had; perhaps a warning not to entertain any foolish hopes where she herself was concerned?

Was he that pathetic? The unwelcome thought tarnished some of the pleasure of being with her.

What a damned fool he was!

The line was poor, and there was a faint echo, but Harry could tell that Debbie sounded deflated.

"I've got my results, dad," she said flatly.

"And?"

"I don't know how you're going to take this."

"I'm sure you did your best, and that's all you …"

"I got a *first*!" she shrieked.

"What?"

"A *first* … I got a *first*!"

He could picture her dancing round the room in exhilaration, the way she used to as a little girl.

"You clever, clever girl! I'm *so* proud of you!" he bellowed, forgetting he was holding a mug of coffee. Raising his arms in triumph, he spilt it over the kitchen table, soaking his newspaper and unopened mail. But what did he care? He thought his heart would burst with pride.

"What did your mum say?"

"She doesn't know yet! I rang you first."

It brought a lump to his throat. She knew what it meant to him. "You're a very clever girl, and you deserve it … for all your hard work. Your mum will be over the moon! We're both so *very* proud of you."

"Thanks. I love you dad!"

"I love you too, Debbie. Now enjoy it!"

"I will. I'm going to call mum and Adam now; then Grandma Marian and Gramps … and Grandma Grace. I'll call you again later. Bye dad."

He couldn't help it. There was no one else there, so he let the tears flow, and found himself laughing and crying at the same time. 'I must let Marjorie know … and Simon and Laura,' he thought, as he mopped up the spilt coffee and cleaned the table top and floor beneath it. 'I must call Nick and Sue Holding, too; after all Sue is Debbie's godmother. I know she'll be pleased!'

Gabbling in excitement, he cracked his head on the edge of the table, as he rose up from his knees. Though half stunned, he ignored the pain and grabbed for the phone, as it rang for a second time.

"Hi Sally … isn't it great!"

192

As expected, Nick and Sue were thrilled with the news. True to form, Marjorie, Simon and Laura expressed heartfelt delight for Debbie … and for Harry.

He enjoyed a telephone conversation with his excited parents and another longer one with Debbie around lunchtime, after which he shamelessly waylaid anyone in Nethercombe Ley who had met her, however briefly, to share his joy. Had he been in any frame of mind to think coherently, he might have anticipated the card addressed to Debbie, in Ellen's handwriting, that he found on his doormat when he returned home. He wished he could share the news with Peggy and Ted. He felt certain they would be pleased to know of Debbie's success.

Hearing Alan and Jill Anderson in their garden, shortly after they arrived home from work, Harry sauntered outside, and on the pretext of inspecting his lawn, feigned surprise to see them. He doubted his amateurish performance had fooled them, but they seemed genuinely pleased for him. Although Alan's expression registered amusement at Harry's barely contained excitement, he refrained from his usual quips and comments, generously allowing Harry to bask in parental pride. A measure of Alan's generosity of spirit was demonstrated when he suggested they pay a visit to *The Black Bull* after dinner, for '*a celebratory toast to your gifted offspring*', as he phrased it.

It was pleasing to find the Spenser-Smiths and several other regulars clustered around the bar when they arrived. To spare Harry embarrassment, Alan immediately announced the reason for their presence. In response, Harry received even more expressions of pleasure, and requests to pass on congratulations to Debbie. As the icing on his cake of joy, Bob Andrews generously provided a celebratory round of drinks 'On the house'.

Only later, when he was running his bath, did it occur to Harry that he had not told Guy and Emma. Should he? His earlier euphoria had now settled down to a glow of contentment. Perhaps it was a bit too late to call them. Although Guy had known Debbie as a little girl, and Emma had met her at The May Fayre, they might not consider it important enough to be called after ten o'clock at night.

In the end pride overcame doubt. He called Guy's mobile, deeming it more appropriate than calling Emma. His call was redirected to voicemail, and he said hesitantly "Hi; sorry to call so late … It's Harry. I just thought you might like to know … er … my daughter Debbie's got her results. She got a first. See you soon; bye."

Luxuriating in a long soak, with the warm inner glow from a glass of Scotland's finest gift to civilisation, he found himself reflecting on his own reaction to Debbie's achievement. Would he have given way to his emotions so demonstratively and unashamedly in front of his neighbours a year ago? He doubted it. But then again, would he have received so much encouragement to do so? His previous neighbours and colleagues at Eldon Management Services would have offered congratulations, but none would have understood his pride and elation the way his new friends and neighbours had; or have been so generous and kind-hearted in sharing it with him.

The phone on his bedside table rang, as he was pulling back the duvet to get into bed. The scotch; the relaxing bath and the excitement of the day were beginning to take their toll. "Hello?" he said wearily.

"Harry! It's Emma. Guy just checked his voicemail. What fantastic news!"

# JULY

## *Pride and Pleasure*

It was difficult to settle back into a normal routine after the excitement of Debbie's success. It felt a little like '*After the Lord Mayor's Show*'. Later that week, when Harry drove to Reading, for a celebratory lunch with her and Paul, he learned that she had already received cards of congratulation from Simon and Laura, Guy and Emma and Marjorie and Phil. She was moved almost to tears when Harry handed her even more from the Hardys and the Andersons, and passed on congratulations from *The Black Bull* regulars. She giggled delightedly when Harry showed her *The Valley Voice*, in which Alan had generously included a small piece headed: *A First for Nethercombe Resident's Student Daughter*.

Harry's parents were spending their annual week in Devon with Aunt Caroline, and as promised, he called in on his way home, to make sure everything was secure and 'ship shape', as his dad would say. They were particularly concerned about letters and circulars sticking out from the letterbox, which might give away their absence. The stillness and quiet seemed strange, as did the fact that he had let himself in. He was usually greeted by his mother as soon as he drew up outside the house.

He found himself reflecting on how odd it was that, whenever he 'came home', he felt a little like a child again. It was silly, and nothing to do with his parents. He assumed it had something to do with the house. The wallpaper and curtains were different from when he had lived there; the three piece suite in the lounge had changed, and a flat screen TV had replaced the old *chunky monster* which had once stood in the corner. But the feel … the atmosphere of the place had not changed since the days when model aeroplanes and football posters had adorned his bedroom.

Apart from the models and posters, the room remained almost as he had left it to start a new life with Sally, in that pokey little flat over a chemist's shop. What wonderful days they were. The joy; the excitement of living together; of being in their own world. Then the frightening exhilaration when that helpless little one had blessed their lives; the little one who was now the accomplished young woman, who had achieved what no one in the family had ever done before.

But perhaps he should have known his happiness and contentment could not last. Fate is a cruel mistress, who takes perverse pleasure in destroying happiness and wrecking cherished dreams.

When he arrived back at May Cottage, Harry wandered into the garden, to savour the golden glow of the late evening sun. Although he and Alfie had made a start on turning over the vegetable garden, as he optimistically referred to it, progress had been painfully slow. But having finished decorating the spare bedrooms, it was something to occupy him and take his mind off the frustration of his dealings with ACCORS.

Later that evening, he looked through the paperwork he had received in readiness for the meeting of the *Friends of Saint Luke's*. The most worrying item on the agenda was entitled '*The future of the village shop and post office.*'

One thing Harry had already learned about village life was that the local grape vine was a very effective instrument. It was already public knowledge, and a cause for local gossip and concern, that so far, there had been no response from Royal Mail to the Parish Council's enquiry about the future of the post office. He had also heard that the site was owned by an investment company, who were reluctant to confirm that they intended to rebuild the premises as a shop.

He supposed that was the way life is; nothing lasts.

There were more people than Harry had anticipated at Church House when he arrived for the quarterly meeting of The Friends of St. Luke's. Among them were several faces he did not recognise. He had exchanged pleasantries with James Lloyd in *The Black Bull* on several occasions, and one of the ladies was vaguely familiar from his excursions to the village shop. The way Jeremy Radford's arm was draped along the backrest of the settee, led Harry to assume that the slim, elegantly dressed woman beside him was Mrs. Radford. He did not recognise the two men occupying the settee facing them, or the white haired man standing by the window, deep in conversation with Sir George Woodleigh. He had the distinguished, but slightly rumpled look of an academic.

The village shop and the desecration of the war memorial were the main topics of conversation while everyone waited for the meeting to begin. Harry opted for water from the choices on offer, anticipating a long meeting and numerous questions on the finances of the organisation, which would require a clear head and moist vocal chords.

David Casson arrived wearing an open-necked shirt, in contrast to his more formal attire at the previous meeting. Lady Lauderham was the last to arrive; her ample figure crammed into a pair of dark, corduroy slacks and a purple blouse. A red pashmina, embellished with tassels and swirls of silver and gold-thread was draped around her shoulders, and her spectacles hung suspended from a silver cord around her neck, to rest on her generous bosom.

Harry could hear the Radfords discussing the fire and his role in the rescue, and retreated to a seat in a corner. The whole village knew about it, and with heads turning towards him, he kept his eyes glued to the agenda, feeling a flush to his cheeks.

With a gold pen in one hand and a glass of white wine in the other, Lady Diana opened the meeting. "Apologies to anyone inconvenienced by the rescheduling of this meeting at such short notice. Can we take the minutes of the previous meeting as read? Everyone agreed? Jolly good! Let's crack on then."

The first few items on the agenda, mundane, administrative matters carried over from previous meetings, did not spark Harry's interest. However, he could not help noticing that the white haired chap, addressed as 'Professor', seemed annoyingly pedantic and preoccupied with the minutiae of the items under discussion.

The young woman sitting next to Harry, whom Simon had introduced as Anna, seemed a little overawed in the company of such *worthies*. But when they came to the item described on the agenda as *Pre-School Day Centre,* it became apparent that it was she who would bring the project to fruition and manage it. She outlined her plans and the progress made to date quietly, but lucidly; answering the questions put to her, hesitantly at first, but without the need to consult the thick folder on her lap. Harry could not help wondering what her reaction would be if she realised how perilously close to disaster it had come.

When it came to the village shop and post office, there was so little information available, they were unable to discuss anything more than interim arrangements and suggestions for contingency plans, should the loss be permanent.

Harry refocused his mind, when Lady Lauderham announced, "As you know, our treasurer, Roger Smailwood, is now enjoying well-earned retirement in sunny Spain. What some of you may *not* know is that Mr. Simmonds has been keeping an expert eye on our finances in the meantime." She gestured to Harry and heads turned towards him.

"Mr. Simmonds has made some very pertinent and useful suggestions regarding our financial systems and controls," she continued. "I've summarised them on the sheet attached to the agenda."

"These proposals all look very sensible. I'm surprised we're not doing much of it already." The observation came from a small and balding man, neatly dressed in tan trousers and a navy-blue blazer, who was sitting on the settee facing the Radfords. "Are we appointing a successor to Roger, or is it envisaged that Mr. Simmonds will continue in the role?" he asked.

"I think the general consensus is that we're very happy with what Mr. Simmonds is doing, Toby," Lady Diana replied.

The Professor smiled at Harry ingratiatingly. "May I enquire about your qualifications, Mr. Simmonds?"

"Of course," Harry answered. Feeling mischievous, he decided to be equally pedantic. "I'm a member of *The Institute of Chartered Accountants in England and Wales* … I have been for a little over twenty-five years. I've held a practising certificate for eleven years or more. I'm also a *Certified Management Accountant*. I have other business management qualifications, as well; proof of which I am happy to supply … and I'm a member of a recognised association of business consultants."

"No university degree?"

"No Professor. No university degree."

"Good God Philip!" Sir George exclaimed. "What do you expect? Isn't that enough? It's a hell of a lot more than Roger had!"

The Professor smiled defensively, and amid general amusement, he replied, "It was merely an enquiry. There was no implied criticism, I can assure you Mr. Simmonds."

"That's OK," Harry replied, unable to disguise his own amusement. "I'd be happy to supply proof of my qualifications, if you require it."

"That won't be necessary," Sir George interjected, adding pointedly, "Will it Philip?"

The Professor smiled. "Indeed it won't."

"The committee has already enjoyed the benefit of Mr. Simmonds' advice and observations," Lady Diana explained. "As long as he's willing to continue, I can't see why we need to 'fix what ain't broke'. Anyone disagree?"

There was a murmur of approval.

"May I point out that this is not on the agenda?" the Professor suggested.

"I would have thought *Proposals for Financial Controls* covers that," Sir George interceded. "If not, we can deal with it under *Other Business*. What's the problem?"

"How do you feel about it, Harry?" David Casson asked.

"I'm quite happy to carry on until you're ready to appoint someone else," Harry replied.

To Harry's relief, the meeting adopted his recommendations without much further discussion and almost no requirement for clarification; not even from the Professor. However, there was another surprise awaiting him. Under *Other Business,* was an item entitled *Christmas Decorations,* which turned out not to be concerned with decorating the church or the church hall, as he had expected, but a proposal to erect a Christmas tree in the centre of the village.

The proposer was the woman sitting beside the Radfords, who was introduced as Carol Maitland. Her clear complexion and unlined features seemed to belie her greying hair. She rose to her feet nervously, and began hesitantly, "I was wondering if anyone would agree. I thought perhaps a Christmas tree ... on the village green ... and perhaps some fairy lights might make Christmas ... well a bit more festive and jolly."

"Yes; I like that!" Lady Diana exclaimed. One or two other voices concurred.

"Can we afford it?" Mrs. Radford asked.

"It would depend, Jane," David Casson replied. Smiling at Harry, he added, "We would need our treasurer's advice on that."

"I think Gerry Spenser-Smith has been thinking along similar lines," James Lloyd suggested. "He's just taken the Chair of the Parish Council Sports and Recreation Committee. I gather he's intending to approach us about setting up a joint team to run things like this."

"I presume he's after a financial contribution," David replied. "Grants to Parish Councils are bound to get pared back now that local government is having to make savings."

There was a murmur of resigned agreement.

"It's still a good idea though, isn't it?" her Ladyship suggested.

"It depends on the cost," said Sir George. "But there's no harm in talking to the Parish Council; especially if it saves us having to stump up all the money ourselves. In the meantime perhaps we ought to nominate one or two of us to work with Gerry and his Sports and

Recreation bods. If it does come to anything, it'll save us having to call another meeting just for that."

Lady Diana beamed encouragingly. "Good idea George! Now; any volunteers?"

Expressions like, "Can't spare the time" were murmured, but Jane Radford raised her hand to offer her services.

"I think Simon should be included," Jeremy suggested.

Lady Lauderham's voice cut through the general hum of conversation. "OK; Jane and Simon ... who else?"

To Harry's surprise, Sir George looked directly at him. "What about Harry? We ought to have our treasurer there. We need him to look after *our* financial interests."

Harry was momentarily taken aback, but he had to admit, he felt flattered.

Lady Diana gave him no opportunity to refuse. "Right; Jane, Simon and Harry ... anyone else?"

"I'm not sure if I'm allowed to do so, but might I propose the lady whose idea it was?" said Harry, sensing a kindred soul, too unassuming to propose herself. Carol's smile convinced him he was right.

"Good idea!" said Jeremy.

"Right," said Diana, gesturing with her, now empty, glass. "Jane, Simon, Carol and Harry! Everyone agreed?"

Harry stayed to help clear up when everyone else had left, taking the opportunity to ask, "Were you in on that '*Carry On Treasurer*' business, Simon?"

An enigmatic smile was the only answer he received. Being involved in organising the Christmas lights would be another pleasant diversion to occupy his mind.

Seated in the Great Hall of Reading University, facing the battery of gleaming organ pipes and gowned dignitaries, and with the light streaming through the tall, arched windows, the roller-coaster of Harry's emotions soared, as the Dean called, "Deborah Jane Simmonds."

With his heart racing, he watched his daughter climb the steps to the podium, while the flash of Sally's camera flared, flouting the prohibition with several other parents, to capture the brief graduation ceremony. Debbie smiled radiantly, as she turned towards them, before making her way back to her seat.

'Deborah Jane Simmonds, Bachelor of Science'; Harry almost said it out loud. To further confuse the maelstrom of his feelings, he felt Sally squeeze his hand. As their eyes met, it was no surprise to find hers were moist. It was the way they used to be, as they shared a fleeting moment of parental pride and joy in their daughter's achievement. Harry swallowed hard, torn between pleasure and pain. Shaking his head wistfully he croaked, "It seems like only yesterday."

Sally dabbed at her eyes with a tissue. "I was thinking the same thing."

With Harry's emotions threatening to overwhelm him, Ellen's words echoed in his mind. '*You can't never go back.*'

Outside in the sunshine, they were joined by Grace and Adam, who had watched the ceremony on a screen in the overflow marquee. Debbie's joy and the hugs and kisses helped to restore Harry's equilibrium, as he held his daughter at arm's length, to simply enjoy the sight of her; radiant in cap and gown. "We're so proud of you!" he said.

She rewarded him with a broad smile. "Thanks dad. Thank's everybody … for all your support and encouragement!"

After Sally's emotional embrace, Grace and Adam added their congratulations, before giving way, like the families of other graduates, to flurries of exuberant hugs, shrieks and bellows of excitement between their offspring. Harry looked on enviously, as they gave expression to the bonds of friendship forged during the years of shared experience; friendships which, in many cases, would endure for a lifetime.

Glancing at his watch, Harry ushered his little group towards the photographer, for the formal portraits. Debbie insisted on one of her with both her parents and Adam. Even as they posed, the thought came to Harry that, as Adam showed no inclination to follow in his sister's footsteps, it would probably be the last photograph ever taken of them all together.

It was then that Paul appeared, to add his congratulations. Harry had no doubt that he had deliberately waited to allow Debbie to enjoy the first euphoric moments of celebration with her family. It was typically considerate of the young man, and endeared him to Harry even more. The final surprise brought a delighted squeal from Debbie, when she spotted Grandma Marian and Gramps coming towards them.

"I thought you couldn't come!" she exclaimed, as she ran to them.

"Why didn't you tell me you'd changed your mind?" Harry exclaimed. "You could have watched in the marquee with Grace and Adam."

"We only made up our minds at the last minute," his father replied. Nodding towards grandmother and granddaughter, who were locked in an embrace, he added, "We just had to come. I knew your mother would regret it if we didn't."

"It's a shame you missed the ceremony," Harry replied.

His father shrugged resignedly. "Well, never mind; we're here now. I expect you've got lots of pictures for us to see." Smiling at Sally, he added, "Well, who'd have thought it, eh Sally? Our little Deborah with a university degree. You must be a very proud mother."

"I certainly am," Sally replied, uncomfortably aware that she was the reason her former mother-in-law had decided to stay away.

Debbie kissed her grandfather's cheek. "Thanks for coming Gramps."

Gramps hugged her. "What a clever little girl you are!" he croaked, his voice thick with emotion. As if to steady himself, he peered over Debbie's shoulder and grinned self-consciously. "Hello, Grace; it's been a long time. How are you keeping?"

She replied with a warm smile. "I'm very well, thank you Alex. It *has* been a long time … too long."

"Absolutely!" he replied, and releasing Debbie, he embarrassed his grandson by ruffling his hair. "Well, young man; how are you? We don't see much of you these days."

"Yeh; I'm good Gramps. Sorry I like, haven't been around much. But I'm back now, so I'll get over to see you and Grandma a bit more."

"No need to be sorry. As long as you're alright. We're always pleased to see you, but you're young; you've got your own life to live. Don't worry about Grandma and me. You know where we are when you need us."

"Have you met Paul?" Harry gestured towards the young man who had remained unobtrusively to one side.

With characteristic charm, Gramps offered his hand. "I'm afraid I haven't had the pleasure. I'm very pleased to meet you Paul."

"Glad to know you, Mr. Simmonds," Paul replied. "This must be a very special moment for you and Debbie's Grandma."

"It most certainly is, but it does make me wonder where the years have gone."

"Paul; this is my Grandma Marian," Debbie said, leading her forward.

Paul seemed a little wary; no doubt from having heard anecdotes of Grandma's forthright and, at times narrow-minded, opinions. But if she had any qualms about his relationship with her granddaughter, she showed no trace of it. She greeted him graciously, with a genuine smile. She even managed to inject a light hearted touch. With Paul standing well over six feet, and she a little below average height, she had to look up as she took his proffered hand. "My word, I'll get a crick in my neck if I talk to you for very long!"

Debbie's snort of laughter seemed to Harry to be as much from relief as amusement. Nevertheless, it dispelled any hint of tension, and banished the apprehension from Paul's face.

Although she was polite and courteous to Grace and Sally, neither Debbie nor Harry was able to persuade his mother to join them for lunch. Her excuse, without being specific, was: "We've got a lot to do, haven't we Alex?" The expression that flickered across her husband's face, suggested it was news to him.

As they were about to take their leave, Adam held out his hand for

Sally's camera. "Hang on a minute Grandma! Let's get a shot of you and Gramps with Debbie!"

Harry had no doubt that when a copy was printed for them, it would be mounted in a special frame and take pride of place among the family portraits in their lounge.

Sally sighed heavily as she watched them leave. "I know it's my fault, but it's such a shame for Debbie."

"There's no reason to blame yourself," Harry said. "It's mum's problem. I wish she could see that all she's doing is cutting her nose off to spite her face."

"I can understand though," Grace interjected. "After all, you are her son."

"And I'm nearly forty-seven years old; not fourteen!"

"It makes no difference to a mother; especially with a son.

Despite the absence of Grandma and Gramps, the celebration lunch was light-hearted and enjoyable; the atmosphere of joy and celebration all around them in the restaurant helping Debbie to overcome her initial disappointment. The gold watch she wore, a joint congratulatory gift from Sally and Harry, clearly meant a great deal to her.

After the meal, Debbie and Paul followed Grace and Adam to the car park, while Sally and Harry paid the bill.

"I don't suppose you'd consider having Adam to live with you for a while, would you?" she asked hesitantly.

Although taken by surprise, Harry's instinctive reply was, "Of course! Do you think he'd come?"

"I think he probably would," she said. "I'm sure he'd at least consider it. He and Jonathan haven't exactly been seeing eye-to-eye recently. It's not all Adam's fault. Jonathan has been under a lot of stress since his move to the Windsor office. Apparently there are problems with an important client. He's been finding it difficult to relax at home; especially with Adam there all the time. Adam hasn't exactly been overdoing it looking for a job. To put it mildly, there's tension between them."

"Is he still hanging around with Steve Edmunds?" Harry asked.

"No; at least, I don't think so. He went out with one or two of his other old school friends the other evening. The flare up came because Jonathan's been pushing him to put more effort into looking for a job … pointing out job ads in the local paper. All it seems to do is get Adam's back up. They ended up having a row last week, with Adam telling him to mind his own business. Jonathan naturally reminded him that he was living in his house. That only made matters worse. Adam then went on about him breaking up our family, and it being just as much my house. It all got pretty heated … with yours truly in the middle, trying to keep the peace."

"It sounds like splitting them up would do them both good," said Harry. "If we can persuade Adam, I'd be happy to have him. He'll get the same hassle from me that he's getting from Jonathan though."

"I know, but I would appreciate it. To be truthful, it's got to the point where it's causing arguments between Jonathan and me."

"So how do you want to go about it?"

"I'll talk to him," she said. "We'll have to be careful. If he thinks I'm trying to get rid of him, we could be back where we started. He'd probably disappear again. I'm not trying to push him out, but he and Jonathan need to get away from each other for a while."

"OK, I'll wait to hear from you."

"Thanks Harry; I do appreciate it." Her frown was replaced with a smile. "How are things with you? I've been hearing about your partner … Rachel, isn't it? And Adam seems to be quite taken with a girl called Laura. I understand she was at Debbie's birthday dinner. "

Harry was momentarily taken aback. "Is he really?"

Sally giggled. "Yes. He hasn't said so directly, but he's mentioned her several times. Apparently she's 'well fit', as he put it."

Sally's giggle and his son's turn of phrase made Harry smile. "She's also a lot older than him … around thirty I'd say. She's our vicar's girlfriend. She's got a riding school and stables locally. But yes, I'd have to agree with him; she certainly is 'well fit'. She's got a mean left hook too!"

"So I heard!" Sally replied with a chuckle.

"I didn't realise Adam was keen on her though," Harry mused. "She gets on well with Debbie too. But as for Rachel and me, it's not serious. She's not my 'partner'. But she is a lot of fun, and we get on well."

Sally patted his arm. "I'm glad. You deserve it." Reaching into her bag, she handed him an envelope. "Happy birthday for next week."

Harry pulled back the bedroom curtains and looked out at the dull, grey sky and dispiriting rain, which, although not heavy, gave every impression that it had nothing better to do than hang around for the rest of the day.

It was not a particularly inspiring start to his forty-seventh birthday, but then again, neither was the thought that he could see fifty steaming over the horizon. He did not feel old; especially when he was with Rachel, but the greying temples and creases around his eyes that confronted him in the mirror each morning, were sobering evidence that the face he was shaving was gradually metamorphosising into his father.

He went down to the kitchen and made coffee, before sitting at the table to open the birthday cards he had been given at Debbie's graduation lunch.

Sally had written '*Happy Birthday. Hope you have a lovely day,*' in her card. The one from Grace read: '*Wishing you all kinds of nice things*'.

Debbie had included Paul in her card, which bore the legend '*Happy Birthday to the Best Dad in the World*', with her added sentiment, '*With love and thanks for always being there for me*'.

The card from Adam was something of a surprise. Harry had not received any form of acknowledgement of his birthday from him the previous year. This one was typically Adam, with a golfing theme, and a dubious pun on the word 'bogey'. Nevertheless, it made Harry laugh;

more from the pleasure of having received it than from the crude and artless joke.

His parents' card had arrived in the post the previous day. It lay on his desk beside their gift of a pair of silver cuff links. He hardly ever wore such things, except with a dress shirt, but they were beautifully made and obviously chosen with care. He made a mental note to root out one of his double-cuff shirts, and wear them the next time he visited them.

At her graduation lunch, Debbie had declared her intention to visit him on his birthday, but aware that there were graduation parties arranged with her fellow students, he had managed to persuade her against it. His trump card had been the lie that he would be having a meal at the pub with Rachel, Simon and Laura.

None of them had any idea that it was his birthday, and he was content to leave it that way. These days, he was more comfortable celebrating other people's birthdays than being the focus of attention himself. However, he had to admit that, at that moment, sitting alone at the breakfast table, he would not have minded just a little fuss.

Sally had always been 'a birthday person'. She loved surprises as much as their children. The annual ritual of choosing her present, hiding it away and planning her birthday treat had been something he used to relish, as well as teasing her with obscure clues.

He had not bothered much about his own birthday for several years. Once the children had grown up, and Sally had embarked on her new career, she had been less concerned about his low key attitude to it. His birthday celebrations had consisted of little more than a cake; until the demands of her job had given her no time for even that. All he could remember about his birthday last year was that he had been drunk for most of it.

He presumed there would be cards in the post from family and friends, and probably calls from Debbie and his parents. Apart from that, there would be nothing more to look forward to, and he could forget about it for another year.

He took his birthday cards into the study before Marjorie arrived, to keep them out of sight. He knew her well enough to realise it would embarrass her to find out by seeing them lying about or lined up on the mantelpiece in the sitting room. He did not want her to feel obliged to rush out to buy one; especially now they no longer had the village shop. He would need to watch out for the postman, to make sure he spirited any cards away before she spotted them.

He decided that he really ought to get down to work, but there was time for breakfast. Now what did he fancy for his birthday treat? A fry up, with sausages and fried bread? Or croissants with apricot jam? The drawback being that he did not have either. Perhaps scrambled egg? In the end he settled for cornflakes. He had put yesterday's newspaper in the recycling bag, so he found himself reading the packet.

The absurdity made him laugh out loud. 'Happy birthday Harry!'

Debbie called before he had finished his 'feast' of cereal and toast. Seeing her name appear in the small screen on the handset brought a smile to his lips.

"Am I addressing Miss Deborah Simmonds, Bachelor of Science?" he enquired loftily.

He received a delighted giggle in reply, followed by her rendition of, "Happy birthday to you … happy birthday to you … Happy birthday, dear daddy … Happy birthday to you!"

Her animated chatter lifted his spirits; although he felt an element of guilt, as she ended her call with, "Have a lovely time this evening. Say hi to everyone for me! Love you dad! See you soon. Bye!"

He had just settled at his desk, when his parents called. Thankfully, neither of them sang to him, but his mother was cheerful and obviously anxious for reassurance that their present had been well received.

"Thanks mum; the cuff links are great," he said, adding the lie, "They're just what I need. I think I've lost my old pair."

"They're solid silver … and hallmarked," she exclaimed, clearly delighted by his response. "Mr. Davey at the jeweller's said they were engraved by hand."

"They're smashing mum; really stylish," he replied; this time truthfully.

"Is everything alright?" she asked, as she always did. "You obviously haven't started celebrating yet."

Her pointed allusion was a salutary eye-opener to the fact that his condition must have been noticeable last year, even early in the morning. His parents had almost certainly been more aware of his drinking than he had realised.

"No mum; I'm not celebrating at all this year."

"That's a shame; there's no harm in it; as long as it's in moderation."

"No-one here knows it's my birthday. I'm not bothered. Debbie called and I've had lots of cards. I'll make do with that."

"Alright. I'll hand you over to your dad. Look after yourself."

The brief conversation with his father was more straightforward and light-hearted, and without any reference to the previous year. Being a man of few words, he would never let Harry know how worried he really had been. But what Harry did know instinctively was that, whatever happened, his dad would always be there for him.

Marjorie and an email from Sally arrived simultaneously. He opened up the first of the attachments, and filled the screen with a heart-lifting portrait of Debbie in her graduation regalia, clutching her certificate, and beaming with delight.

Pleased that Marjorie was, at last, willing to let herself in, Harry made sure his cards were out of sight and that no other 'incriminating evidence' was visible, before he opened his study door. "Hi Marjorie; come and have a look at this!"

Her face lit up as she appeared in the doorway. "Oh; isn't that lovely! You must be so proud of her!"

Unwilling to miss the opportunity to milk the praise and compliments he knew her generous nature would elicit, he was about to open up another picture, when he became aware of the young man in the hall behind her.

"This is Gary," she said. "I hope you don't mind him coming. He's home on leave. He's looking for something to keep him occupied, so I brought him with me the other day. He gave Alfie a hand in the garden … while you were at Debbie's graduation. I didn't think you'd mind. If it's alright with you, he'd like to do a bit more today."

"Mind? I most certainly don't. But it's raining isn't it?"

"It stopped just before we came out."

Harry held out his hand. "Hello Gary; I can't tell you how grateful I am. I appreciate all the help I can get in that wilderness out there. It's a lot better now, but you should have seen it before Alfie got to work on it. I'm sure he appreciates your help as much as I do."

Gary's grip was firm, and his smile open and friendly. He stood a foot or so taller than Marjorie, from whom he had inherited the colour of his dark, close-cropped hair and hazel eyes. As one would expect from a soldier just returned from a tour of duty, his frame, beneath the close fitting t-shirt, was well honed and lacking any hint of surplus flesh. Untypically, he bore no visible tattoos, which Harry suspected had more to do with concern about his mother's reaction than reluctance to follow fashion.

"My pleasure, Mr. Simmonds," he replied. "I'm glad to have something to do. There's not much going on around here at the moment."

"I told him; he should have been here *last* month!" Marjorie snorted. Noticing that her son's eyes were drawn to the screen, she explained, "That's Debbie, Mr. Simmonds' daughter. Isn't she a pretty girl … as well as clever?"

Gary nodded.

"She's the first Simmonds to achieve a university degree; at least in our branch of the family," Harry said proudly.

"I don't think anybody in our family's ever got one, have they mum?" Gary asked.

"I shouldn't think so," she replied.

Gary turned towards the kitchen. "Well; if it's OK with you Mr. Simmonds, I'll carry on turning over the veg garden."

"It certainly is! Whatever you say is fine by me, Gary. I take it you know where everything is."

He did not doubt he would have a battle on his hands with Marjorie over paying the young man for his work, but it was one that he was determined to win.

The doorbell interrupted Harry's concentration and he looked at his watch; gone half past two. Immersed in the affairs of ACCORS, he had lost all track of time. Marjorie had brought him a mug of coffee before she and Gary left, but that had been more than two hours ago. He was thirsty and his stomach was reminding him that lunch was overdue.

Opening the front door, he was surprised to find Simon and Laura squeezed into his porch. Behind them, he could see a heavy drizzle drifting like a grey curtain on the wind; 'wet rain' as his mother bizarrely referred to it.

"Hello, you two."

"Harry; we're very cross with you!" said Simon, without smiling.

"Why? What on earth have I done?" he asked in surprise, and stood aside, gesturing for them to come in.

Laura pushed her glasses back on the bridge of her nose with a long purple-varnished nail. "I had a call a little while ago from Debbie. She asked me for a favour. Would I buy us all a drink this evening … when we have our meal; to wish you happy birthday from her and Adam. She promised to send me the money to cover it."

Harry swallowed hard. "Oh, I see."

"Why on earth didn't you tell us it was your birthday?" Simon asked quietly.

"I don't know if Debbie told you, Laura. She wanted … or, more to the point, felt obliged to spend my birthday with me. But there are graduation parties going on in Reading. She ought to be letting her hair down at those, instead of trekking all the way down here to waste her time on me. She's earned it after all her hard work. I apologise for implicating you. It was all I could think of to persuade her."

"Oh, Harry!" Laura sighed. "What *are* we going to do with you?"

"Accept my apology, I hope," he replied sheepishly. "I didn't mean to put you on the spot. I thought it was harmless. What did she say when you told her?"

Laura smiled. "I told her I'd be happy to, and she could settle up with me the next time I saw her."

"Bless you for that. She'd only have fretted and given me grief."

Simon laughed. "If you're worried about being given grief, wait 'til Rachel gets here. She's furious with you!"

"What do you mean; '*Wait 'til Rachel gets here?*'"

"I called her," Laura interjected, "To see if she knew. She was just going to a meeting, otherwise she would have called you and 'let you have it' as she put it. She's going to try to leave early. She'll get here as soon as she can."

"Good grief!" Harry exclaimed. "Why on earth is Rachel going to all that trouble?"

"I would imagine it's because she wants to," Simon replied. "And you still haven't answered my question. Why didn't you tell us today was your birthday?"

"I don't bother much these days. I didn't want anyone to feel they had to make a fuss."

Simon put his hand on Harry's shoulder. "Harry, we're your friends. We don't feel we *have* to make a fuss of you; it's something we want to do. Celebrating another year of the precious life God has given you is a pleasure, not a duty."

Laura delved into her capacious shoulder bag and pulled out a large envelope inscribed with his name, in her neat, looping handwriting. "Happy Birthday, Harry."

"Yes; Happy birthday," Simon repeated.

"Thank you." Harry opened the envelope and read '*To a dear friend. Many happy returns of the day. Love from Simon and Laura.*'

"I don't know what to say. All I can think of is, why don't you take your raincoats off and join me for a late lunch?"

"Thanks; but I've already eaten," Simon replied.

"Me too," said Laura.

"Well how about a cup of tea … or coffee, if you prefer?"

"That would be very nice," said Simon.

"We didn't know what to get you, so in the circumstances, we thought treating you to dinner tonight would be appropriate," Laura giggled, struggling to draw her arms from the sleeves of her coat. "It doesn't have to be *The Black Bull*; it can be *The Golden Lantern, Chez Antoine* … or anywhere you like."

A glance at Simon left Harry in no doubt that neither of them was in the mood to brook a refusal. He smiled in delighted resignation. "*The Black Bull* is fine; thank you."

Thankfully, Rachel's wrath turned out to be affectionate exasperation, when her Range Rover turned in at Harry's gate, scattering gravel and startling the Anderson's ginger cat, who had been dozing in the evening sunshine beneath the magnolia.

Unsure of her mood, he opened the front door tentatively, wondering how she would deliver her opening salvo. "Oh, it's you," he said, for want of anything better to say.

"Yes it's me. Who were you expecting?"

He thought flippancy might be worth a try. "I don't know. I thought it might be someone trying to sell me something."

"I may have to deal with you severely!" she exclaimed, taking an overnight case and a dress carrier from her car. Harry grinned, realising her frown and stern expression were pretence.

"Really?"

"Yes. What did you think you were playing at; trying to keep your birthday a secret from everybody?"

"Like I told Laura and Simon, I don't bother much at my age."

"We'll, we do! Birthdays are meant to be celebrated. Just remember that in future!"

"Yes, ma'am!"

Pushing her sunglasses up over her fringe, she put her bag down in the hall, before curling an arm around his neck and pressing her lips to his. "Happy birthday, Harry darling," she said breathlessly, when she tore her mouth away.

"If you are a sales rep, I ought to tell you I don't usually buy anything at the door," he quipped. "But I like your technique, so I'll take everything you've got!"

"I'll bet you will!" she giggled. "But there's no time. I need to freshen up and change. Si and Laura will be waiting for us."

She opened her case and took out a brightly wrapped package and a silver envelope. "You can make do with that for now," she chuckled. "You'll have to wait until later for the rest of my sales pitch."

Harry felt a tingle at the nape of his neck. "Are you staying overnight, then?"

"That was my intention; unless you have any objection."

"I might be daft, but I'm not bloody stupid!" he chortled.

She picked up her bags and started to climb the stairs, watching his reaction, as he tore open the envelope and read the card. It bore a picture of a pair of long johns, a corset and various other items of vintage male and female clothing being tossed from bushes onto a golf green, with the legend: '*Old Golfers are Always ready to Play A Round*'. She had written, '*Happy Birthday Tiger*'.

Satisfied with his appreciative chuckle, she asked, "It's OK to use the bathroom, I presume. You weren't about to use it were you?"

"No, I've shaved and showered. I only need to change."

The gift was an unmistakeably expensive cordless, electric shaver.

"I hope it's alright. I remember you saying your old one was on its last legs," she called.

"Thank you; it's fantastic!"

She leaned over the banister rail, as she reached the landing. "I'll have to be away very early in the morning, I'm afraid." Interpreting his amused expression, she added, "I can get up early, if I have to!"

'*Happy birthday from Guy and me have a triff nite. Sorry to miss it.*' Harry was reading Emma's text message, when the lights in the bar suddenly dimmed. Carla appeared in the doorway, her features bathed in the flickering glow from the candles on the cake she was carrying.

A chorus of 'ahs' from the Spenser-Smiths and the small knot of regulars clustered around the bar preceded the ritual refrain: "Happy birthday to you …"

'For someone who professes not to care about his birthday, you're doing a pretty fair job of loving this, you old hypocrite,' he thought, as he blew out the candles to a ripple of applause.

The lights came up and he stood to raise his glass to everyone, before adding, "You'd better give them all a piece, Carla … and a drink on me, to help wash it down!"

It was received with delighted calls of thanks and raised glasses in response.

"It's *your* birthday; people should be buying *you* drinks!" Rachel protested. "Let me do it!"

Harry shook his head. "I've had a very drinkable Merlot on my kids; an excellent meal, courtesy of Laura and Simon; and I guess I have you to thank for the cake, as well as my posh new shaver. So I haven't done too badly, have I? Anyway, it's *my* birthday and I'll do as I like!"

The unmistakeable 'pop' of a cork, accompanied by more delighted gasps and exclamations, suddenly distracted his attention.

"And I suppose you've arranged this too!" he said, as Bob Andrews came towards them carrying a tray laden with four champagne flutes and a 'smoking' bottle of champagne nestling in an ice bucket.

Rachel's eyes widened. "No! It's nothing to do with me!"

"It's from Emma and Guy," Laura explained. "I called Emma, because I doubted she and Guy knew. They send their love, but they can't make it tonight. They're off to Sardinia for ten days early in the morning. So I'm doing the same for them as I am for Debbie."

"Good grief!" Harry exclaimed. "I hope you haven't told many more people, Laura! You'll wind up broke at this rate!"

From the most unpromising of beginnings, it had turned out to be the most enjoyable birthday Harry could remember in a long time. With the moonlight spilling across the bed and a gentle breeze stirring the curtains through the open window, he lay back on the pillow in a warm glow of contentment, with his fingers locked behind his head.

'Debbie's right; *The Black Bull* is a cool pub, and …'

That was all the coherent thought he could manage, because, at that moment, Rachel's naked silhouette was momentarily illuminated with a silvery gleam, as she flitted past the window and slid under the duvet beside him.

True to her word, Rachel proved she could get up early … if she wanted to. Harry poached a couple of eggs and made toast and coffee, and she left the house shortly after six-thirty.

Relishing the lingering trace of her perfume and feeling unapologetically smug, he took out his new shaver and plugged it in to charge the battery; reading the operating instructions, instead of skimming through the explanatory diagrams, as he usually did. The idea of choosing one of the settings that left a fashionable stubble amused him. He could imagine his mother's reaction and the ribbing he would get in *The Black Bull.*

He looked out of the kitchen window at the emerald green expanse that was now his lawn. The grass was still thin, and there were bare patches if you looked closely, but Alfie had assured him that: "Give it time, and nature and a bit more seed and top soil will take care of that." It would not be too long before it would need cutting.

A few months ago, he would not have believed that the miserable, moss and weed strewn patch could be transformed in such a short time. The shrubs and borders were tidy and plants he had bought and planted, under the guidance of Alfie and the Hardys, were blooming. On sunny days, the garden was alive with butterflies and bees; drawn to the tall, swaying foxgloves and hollyhocks. The clematis, so savagely cut back on Alfie's instructions, had recovered to reclaim dominance of the trellis dividing the flower garden from the fruit and vegetable patch, where Gary's strength and energy were proving so invaluable.

Marjorie's objection to Harry paying her son had been anticipated, but Gary's had not. It had taken a good deal of patience and all Harry's persuasive powers to overcome their combined resistance.

The greenhouse needed a little refurbishment before it would be properly usable, but they had planted one or two rows of beans, lettuce and a few other late cropping veg. The flourishing fruit bushes promised a good crop, but Alfie had warned him not to expect much from the apple trees this year. "But I reckon you'll be makin' your own cider next year," he added with a chuckle.

A small herd of cows was grazing in the field beyond his boundary hedge; the first he had seen there since he moved in. For some inexplicable reason, it pleased him. "'E be gedd'n a real country boy," Harry chuckled to himself.

He was surprised to receive Sally's phone call so soon, with the news that Adam had agreed to spend some time at Nethercombe Ley.

"That was quick," he observed.

"Yes, he didn't take a great deal of persuading really," she explained. "But he made the point that he was 'only doing it on a trial basis'."

"I'd better be on my mettle then; so he gives me high marks," Harry replied.

Sally chuckled. "I wouldn't read too much into that. I think it's a bit of face saving. There seems to be a truce between him and Jonathan at the moment, although it's a bit grudging and sullen. I think they would both welcome the break. Funnily enough, I think Adam enjoyed it the last time he came down to you … apart from the incident at the village fete."

"Has Rosco recovered from the trauma?" Harry chortled.

"I don't know and I don't care!" she said flatly. "That repulsive slug can go to hell, for all I care. As far as I know, Adam hasn't seen him or Steve for some time. He's been going out with another of his old school friends; a boy called Ollie."

"That sounds promising," Harry said.

"Yes, it is. He actually went for a job interview the other day, in a warehouse," Sally sighed. "He didn't get it, unfortunately."

"Never mind; it's a start," Harry said. "And if he's going to live here, it makes no difference anyway. When's he coming?"

"Next weekend, if that's OK with you. He's going to a concert at *The O2 Arena* with Debbie and some of her friends on the Saturday. I think he's staying overnight at her place afterwards."

"No problem. Does he want me to pick him up from there?"

"I think he'd appreciate it. I assume they'll be back late, so it might be easier to do it on Sunday."

"That makes sense. Tell him I'll be there around lunch time. I doubt if any of them will have surfaced before then. I'd better let Marjorie know … or '*Marjie*' as he insisted on calling her."

"Did he? Why?"

"Heaven only knows. I suspect he was trying to wind her up. If he was, it didn't work. She's got two grown up sons, so I would guess very little fazes her where male adolescents are concerned."

"I do appreciate this, Harry. I feel guilty for asking, and I really don't want to push him out, but I can't think of an alternative at the moment."

"There's no need to feel guilty, Sally. He's my responsibility too. Perhaps it's another chance for me to connect with him."

"I'm sure you will. He's not a bad kid really, is he? He's just confused. I think he's just found it all so hard to come to terms with."

'*It hasn't exactly been a picnic for me!*' was Harry's initial reaction, but instead he replied, "No he's not a bad lad, and I didn't help matters before. Let's see if I can make up for it this time."

"Thanks Harry."

"You're welcome. Take care Sally."

"Bye, Harry."

He sat down at the kitchen table, shaking his head in bemusement. What *kind* of a fool goes out of his way to help the ex wife, who *dumped him,* ease the tension in her new marriage? *His kind* was the answer. Despite the anguish and heartache she had caused him, he could not bring himself to spite her deliberately. All those years together meant too much.

Careful not to spill any wine from his generously filled glass, Harry placed it on the occasional table beside him. He chose a canapé from the plate proffered by Cheryl Spenser-Smith and settled himself comfortably in the well upholstered armchair.

"Unless there's anything else I can get anyone, I'll leave you to it then," she said, and placed the still half-full plate on a drum table beside her husband.

"Thanks, darling. I think we have all we need for now," Gerald called over his shoulder, as she closed the door quietly behind her.

"Right," he said, leaning forward on his chair. We have apologies from Reverend Cornish and Pat Buckler, who can't be with us tonight. But there are six of us, so I think I'm safe in declaring that we have a quorum."

The room was smaller than the sitting room at May Cottage, although elegantly furnished, with flowered brocade drapes at the tall windows and several pieces of highly polished furniture, which, to Harry's untrained eye, looked antique and valuable. The large fireplace of honey-coloured brick was an impressive feature, on which a brass carriage clock and an array of porcelain figurines were displayed beneath a portrait of Cheryl. Although it appeared to have been painted some twenty years earlier, she had not lost her looks in the intervening years.

"I suggest we begin with the introductions." Gerry took it for granted that he would chair the meeting. "Shall I start with the Parish Council bods?" He waved his arm towards the two men sitting on a leather chesterfield. "Maurice and Robert sit on the Sports and Recreation Committee with me."

Both smiled deferentially at their introduction. Maurice's balding dome, bushy eyebrows and the fringe of gingery hair over his ears, reminded Harry of the sketches of Mr. Pickwick in his school book. Robert was younger. He was tall and angular, with a full head of unruly brown hair. His expression was open and friendly, and Harry sensed a kindred sense of humour.

"Maurice's speciality is rules and regulations," Gerry explained. "He's a solicitor. He does quite a bit of work for Wiltshire County Council, so he knows the ways and workings of local government. Robert is our sporting man; he's a teacher and a qualified soccer referee. He sports his whistle at matches in the local leagues most weekends."

Both men smiled and nodded in acknowledgement.

"And for the Friends of St. Luke's; you all know Jane, don't you?" Maurice and Robert nodded in affirmation. "Her contacts in the world of catering and events planning will be invaluable. Harry … our local hero … is a numbers man I believe."

Harry blushed and smiled diffidently in response to the murmurs of acknowledgement.

Gerald continued. "Simon tells me you're a management consultant too, so your organisational talents, along with Pat's, will come in very handy."

Turning his charm on Carol Maitland, Gerry exclaimed, "And you are a leading light of the local WI, I understand, Carol."

"I don't know about leading light, but I have been involved for over twenty years," she replied.

"Any plans for a calendar from the Beldene Valley branch?" Robert asked mischievously.

It brought a chuckle in response. "I'm afraid not. We don't know anyone with a wide-angle lens," Carol replied impishly.

The laughter was a pleasant way to start the first meeting of the Nethercombe Ley Social Events Committee, before it got down to more serious business.

During the journey home from Reading, Harry had attempted to have a serious conversation with Adam about his lifestyle, and more importantly, his future. He had *broken the ice* by apologising for reacting so impetuously over the incident with the ponies. Now they had arrived at May Cottage, Harry thought it advisable to make a few things clear to his son, in an attempt to avoid future conflict.

"Right; we've cleared the air," he began. "So I don't want to get too heavy, but there are a few house rules; is that understood?"

Adam put down his can of Coke and nodded.

"OK. Number one: you treat my friends and neighbours with respect; number two: Steve Edmunds and those other two muppets never set foot in this house; number three: any mess you make, you clear up yourself; Marjorie is not a servant. And four: you make an effort to find some form of employment. I don't care what it is … as long as it's legal. I know it's a bit off the beaten track here, so I don't expect you to manage that overnight. But I *do* expect you to make an effort to keep yourself occupied. Have I made myself clear?"

"Yeh, right."

"And stay out of trouble."

"OK dad."

"It may not sound like it, but I'm glad you're here," Harry said, feeling awkward after his uncharacteristic lecture. "For my part, I'll try and make living with me a bit more bearable this time. If there's anything you need, let me know … within reason," he added with a grin.

"OK dad; I'm cool."

"I take it you haven't got around to taking your driving test?"

Adam shook his head. "No; I couldn't afford to keep up the lessons. I like, haven't thought about it much."

"It might be a good idea to start again," Harry suggested. "Especially, as we're out in the sticks here. I'm quite happy to pay for them."

"No thanks dad; I owe you big time already."

"Who's counting?" Harry said. "I don't begrudge the money if it's going to help you sort yourself out. Consider it the rest of your eighteenth birthday present, if you like. I was never happy about just sending you money."

"No sweat. The money came in handy."

"Good. I'm sorry I missed your birthday party ... my own fault, I know. I fully understand why you didn't want me there, but I would've liked to do more than just open my wallet."

"I'd have like been in the crud big time, if you hadn't done that a few months ago," Adam said quietly.

"You're my son," Harry replied. "Whatever's happened between us; whatever you think of me, I'll always be there if you need me ... whether I think you're right or wrong. That's way it is ... the way it always *will* be."

It seemed to embarrass Adam. He avoided eye contact, merely nodding in reply.

"Your mother said something about you doing some work experience with her company."

"Yeh; right. She's been giving me verbals about getting a job. They like, need guys to help at a travelling exhibition they're doing at the end of August. It's only for a couple of weeks or so, right. She kind of volunteered me."

Harry laughed. "That sounds like your mother. I assume it involves more than making the tea?"

"Yeh; they want me to help put the stand up, right ... and take it down again every day." The gleam in Adam's eyes was promising reassurance that he had not lost his sense of humour.

"Will you be moving back in with her while that's going on?"

"I guess so; mum's doing the exhibitions too. She'll like, give me a lift every day."

223

"OK. Welcome t'Nethercombe Ley," Harry enunciated in his best attempt at a comic West Country accent. He had not meant it to allude to the incident in *The Kings Head*, but he could see from his son's self-conscious grin that the connection had been made.

Adam's eye fell on *The Echo*, and the pictures of Harry and Simon below the headline: *Village Heroes Rescue Girl from Shop Blaze*. He raised his eyebrows in surprise. "I didn't know about this. Mum and Debs haven't said anything!"

"That's because they don't know."

"Why not?"

"Because it's not true."

"So, what happened then? Why is it in the paper?"

Harry sighed resignedly. "Because it's a better story than what really happened, I suppose! If you must know, the people who run the shop were away, and the girl who works for them was looking after things. She got trapped upstairs when the fire started. Simon and I tried to get her out, but it was the Fire Brigade who actually rescued her."

"Like, how'd it start?"

"Some yobs started it. We think to get their own back on Peggy. It was probably the crowd that smashed up the swings on the village green. She identified them to the police."

"It says here the girl reckons she would have like, died if it hadn't been for you."

"That's nonsense. Lisa's not all that bright … a sweet girl … but no Einstein. She's no light-weight either."

"She looks well solid, from this picture."

"If you meet her, you'll see for yourself. There's no way I could have got her through that window, let alone carried her down a ladder!"

Adam chuckled. "It would've been great to see you try!"

Harry grinned in response. "Be careful what you say; her dad will be here working on the central heating system over the next week or so. Lisa's thoroughly enjoyed being in the spotlight. All that nonsense she's been spouting is just to make it sound more dramatic, I would imagine. I'm just hoping it's all blown over by now."

"How's Laura?" Adam asked. "Like … how's her hand, I mean?" he added hastily.

"Oh it's as good as new. It wasn't broken, only badly bruised. I think her next fight's with one of the Klitschko brothers."

Adam grinned and tapped his fingers rhythmically on his knee. "I suppose I ought to like go and say sorry to her for what happened," he said tentatively.

"I thought you already had."

Adam's cheeks flushed. "Oh, did she tell you? No; I like … well, didn't really apologise properly. She was in a lot of pain, right. I just told her not to worry."

"Was that before or after you stormed off?"

"I didn't storm off. When I split, I just like … walked. I was well hacked off. When I got to the shops, the guys were outside the takeaway. We went to *The Stag and Hounds*, right; the big pub by the roundabout."

"Look," Harry said quietly. "Why don't we try and put all that behind us and start again. Laura's fine! She doesn't blame you or me; though God knows why. But if you feel you want to apologise to her, go ahead. You might want to thank Marjorie and Phil too, for bringing you home."

Adam nodded. "Yeh, right, OK."

"Fair enough. I know I probably over-reacted, but I saw red when I came back and found Steve Edmunds here. You know what I think of him. To find him knocking back my scotch, as well … and with that doped up 'slug', as your mother calls him, with his stinking feet on the furniture!"

"OK dad. I get it!"

"And which rock did that thug DP crawl out from under?"

"He's Rosco's friend, right. Sorry about the vase; I'll pay for a new one. … when I get some money."

"I'll lend it to you," Harry chuckled, but added more seriously. "Forget the vase; it's not important. You're what's important. I know I haven't been much of a father for the past few years, but you're worth a hell of a lot more than wasting your time on that bunch of deadbeats.

You're decent and intelligent. You can make something of your life. Don't make the mistake I did. You won't find the answer to anything in the bottom of a glass. Don't be *'A chip off the old block'* … that's what you said, wasn't it?"

Adam looked puzzled. "Did I? When?"

"The night Phil and Marjorie brought you home."

"I don't remember; I was like, wasted."

Harry grinned. "Tell me about it; I cleared up after you."

"Sorry."

"Forget it. I guess it's what parent's are for. I remember Gramps cleaning up after me, when I got home after Paul Davies and I had sneaked a bottle of vodka into a youth club dance."

Adam's eyebrows rose. "Yeh? What did Grandma say?"

"She went on without taking a breath for what seemed like hours. The worst thing was she, and everything else, was spinning round me all the time. Gramps calmed her down and took control."

"How old were you?"

"About sixteen. For some reason that escapes me now, we thought it would make us more attractive to girls."

Adam chuckled. "Did it?"

"Only to ones who were turned on by boys throwing up over their shoes!"

Adam's laugh was gratifying. Being able to make him laugh was progress in Harry's estimation. He sighed. "I just wish you could see Steve Edmunds for what he is. As for those other two …"

"Yeh, right. I know I'm a big disappointment to you and mum," Adam said bitterly. "Sorry; I'm not clever like Debs, but I'm not stupid. I know mum wanted me out of the house."

"Adam stop it! Don't say things you know aren't true! Your mother loves you … we both do. Don't forget, she was the one who came and got you out of that rat-hole you were living in. She didn't want you out of the house, but she could see it was doing you no good being constantly at odds with Jonathan. I was the one who suggested you came here for a while."

It was a lie, but 'needs must', Harry thought. "It was for your sake …
and mine! I'd like the chance to make up for everything I failed to be
when your mum left. But don't talk such utter nonsense about being a
disappointment to us; you're not! Debbie went to university because it
was right for her! It was what she wanted. It doesn't mean we care less
about you, or think less of you because you didn't. You haven't found
what's right for you yet. But when you do; whatever it is, we'll be just as
happy for you … and just as proud of you!"

Adam managed a reluctant smile. "Is it OK if I take a shower?"

"Of course; this is your home now. There's no need to ask."

Harry watched Adam carry his bags up the stairs. 'Talk about a chip
off the old block,' he thought. 'We're both experts at cocking things up
and putting our foot in it. And we both fall for women who are out of
reach.'

# AUGUST

## *Sunlight and Sorrow*

Harry switched off the phone and slammed his palm on the table. "That bloody woman!" he exclaimed, telling himself that if he had realised that getting involved with the Social Events Committee would mean having to deal with someone as tiresome and opinionated as Pat Buckler, he would have refused outright.

Adam appeared from the hallway, bleary-eyed from sleep. "Who was that?" he asked, with barely concealed amusement.

"Some pain in the neck on the Social Events Committee!"

"It sounded like she was giving you grief."

"Oh, she could lecture on it," Harry replied. "And talk about pc! She could interpret a sneeze as anti-feminism!"

Adam's chuckle brought a rueful smile to Harry's lips. Pat Buckler was a cross he had to bear; one he suspected the other committee members had inflicted on him by some *fancy footwork*.

She had breezed into the second meeting with a pile of files and papers under her arm, and the air of the commander of an occupying army. She had all but taken over as chair of the meeting, interrupting Gerry with constant comments or 'helpful suggestions', as she had described them. She also had the annoying habit of talking over people before they had finished speaking; often in an infuriatingly patronising manner.

She was neat and slim, and in Harry's estimation, in her forties, with short, dark hair that looked regularly coiffured. Dressed in a white blouse and a severe, grey business suit, of the type favoured by female politicians and solicitors, she had smiled ingratiatingly, as she gazed intently at whoever she was speaking to, or as Harry would have it, '*talking at*'.

Noticing her wedding ring, Harry felt thankful he was not Mr. Buckler. He had met people like her before, although few he could remember being more annoying.

She worked in local government; someone had said as a Housing Officer. In addition to the Parish Council, she sat on the committees of various local charities and welfare organisations, epitomising what he thought of as the '*irritating face*' of the public sector; dogmatic, opinionated and with no discernible sense of humour.

This had been the second call Harry had received from her since the meeting; hectoring and cajoling him over cost estimates for the village Christmas decorations. For the second time, he had explained that, until the Health and Safety risk assessment had been completed and the overall plan drawn up and itemised, he could not supply adequate information to obtain quotes from electrical contractors or for the other installations and safety equipment that would be required.

"Ballpark figures, Harry!" she had insisted. "Get the people to come and have a look! Get an idea of the cost!"

He had replied through gritted teeth, barely able to control his anger. "I've told you, Pat; I *have* spoken to several contractors. One has already had a look around the village green. But until we know what we are *allowed* to do, or the extent of the illuminations we *can* put up, they can't quote for it."

"But a rough idea!"

"They can't give us one ... or at least anything meaningful!" he had snapped, struggling to contain his exasperation. "Constantly hassling them won't help. It could be hundreds ... or thousands. It depends on what we want and how long it's likely to take them. The labour cost is the biggest chunk!"

"I really think you should be more assertive," she had persisted. "Time is running out."

"For Christ's sake, we're only just into August!" he had exclaimed. "It won't take months to put a few lights up!"

"Please don't use that aggressive tone and blasphemous language with me!" she had retorted. "I'm not prepared to put up with confrontational behaviour. I simply want to achieve what you and I have been charged with, and I intend to do so; despite your hostility!"

*'Well, try giving your bloody tongue a rest and do something about it yourself!'* he had thought, but taking a deep breath, he had answered, "I'm sorry if I sounded aggressive. I didn't intend to be. I'm in regular contact with contractors and suppliers based on the information I'm getting from Maurice and Jane. They're waiting for the Council to give the green light. As soon as I have something concrete, I can get quotes very quickly. Then I'll be able to cost the project as a whole."

"Very well, but I must warn you; if I'm subjected to any more language of that kind, I shall make it known to the committee." She had ended the call abruptly.

"I don't think the committee would give a toss if I strangled you," he had growled to himself. "In fact they would probably give me a character reference."

"Who's the dude with Alfie?" Adam asked, gazing out of the kitchen window.

"That's Gary, Marjorie's son. He's in the army; The Royal Corps of Signals. He's just finished a tour in Afghanistan. He's based at Blandford at the moment, so he manages to get home quite easily. He likes to get out there with Alfie. He says it relaxes him."

"It takes all sorts, I suppose," Adam mused.

"Yes; Gary's the sort who likes to keep active," Harry replied pointedly. "Look; I have to go into Dorchester for a couple of hours, so try not to get under Marjorie's feet when she gets back."

"Where is she?" Adam asked.

"She's gone to visit her mother. She's in sheltered housing near Winterbourne Abbas. She's quite frail these days. As she's not been well, Marjorie wanted to check on her and see if there's anything she needs."

"I suppose you're off to do whatever the '*old dragon*' on the phone ordered you to," Adam quipped.

"No; I've got an appointment with someone called Daphne Darling at the FOSL's bank."

"The what bank?"

"Friends of Saint Luke's. It's the local church's charitable organisation. I have a meeting with their bankers."

"Fossils ... Daphne Darling? Is there anything that sounds normal round here?" Adam asked in amusement.

"Think yourself lucky," Harry replied mischievously. "Instead of Adam James, you were nearly christened Adam Stephen Simmonds ... until I pointed out to your mother what the initials on your school name-tabs would look like!"

"I guess she would think that was right-on these days," Adam replied ruefully.

Harry decided that his initial thought: 'I'm not sure about your mother, but I'll bet Marjorie would', was best left unspoken.

Once or twice, since Adam had moved in, Harry had sensed a *frosty atmosphere* pervading between the two of them. More worryingly, Alfie had quietly made him aware of an altercation he had overheard from the garden.

As far as Alfie had been able to make out, it had started when Marjorie had complained to Adam about his untidiness and having to pick up discarded clothes and crockery before she could hoover the carpets. She had obviously taken exception to Adam's reply, because Alfie had heard her '*lay into him*', as Alfie had put it, about 'growing up' and 'acting his age'. She had made it patently clear that she was not prepared to tolerate sarcastic and, what she had uncharacteristically referred to as, '*smart-arsed*' remarks.

Harry had tried to broach the subject with them individually. But Adam had been evasive, and his offer to take his son to task had been flatly refused by Marjorie. "It's nothing for you to worry about," she had replied.

Any comfort Harry had taken from Marjorie's reassurance was swept away two days later. He returned home from having coffee with Simon at Church House, expecting to find her in a light-hearted mood about her forthcoming holiday. Instead, he found her raw-eyed and distressed.

"What on earth's the matter?" he asked.

She wiped away a tear. "I'm sorry Harry; it's no good. I can't go on like this."

"What do you mean? What's happened?"

"Now's not the time. I've got to get off. We've got to get to Gatwick for our flight at half-past five. Phil likes to give himself plenty of time, and I've got to finish packing and sort out a dozen other things before we go."

"Well, have a lovely time," Harry replied lamely.

Marjorie toyed with her wedding ring, unwilling to meet his gaze. "It might be a good idea if you start looking for someone else while I'm away," she said, her voice quaking with emotion.

Harry felt the blood drain from his head, as a seed of suspicion began to take root in his mind. "What?" he exclaimed. "Why?"

"Don't worry; I won't leave you in the lurch. But I think it's best if you find somebody else … I'm sorry, Harry."

"Marjorie! What's happened? Tell me!" he pleaded. "What the hell's he done?"

Tears brimmed and overflowed, and she brushed them from her cheek. "Let's just say things have been said … things that shouldn't have been said."

"What things? What the hell did he say?" Harry asked, feeling panic grip him.

"It's not all Adam's fault. I said things I had no right to say … and after all, he is your son. I know what it means to you having him here."

"Marjorie; sit down. Let's have a cup of coffee and talk this over," he pleaded.

"I haven't got time, Harry," she declared, picking up her bag from a chair. "I'm sorry. I've done the kitchen and bedrooms, as best I can. That's all I can manage today. I must get off."

"Marjorie!" Harry exclaimed helplessly, as she turned and hurried into the hall. "Marjorie; wait! Talk to me! Tell me what's happened!"

"It's for the best," she called and closed the front door behind her.

Harry stood in the hall, stunned and helpless. "I'll swing for him!" he almost sobbed. Looking up at the staircase, he yelled, "Adam! Get down here ... now!"

There was no reply, so he stormed up the stairs, with the blood throbbing at his temples. There was no sign of Adam.

"I can wait!" Harry growled. "You might think you can slink off, but I can wait! When you get home, you're going to be sorry you were born."

As Harry drained his coffee mug, Guy's head appeared around the door of the ACCORS meeting room. He was deeply tanned from his recent holiday, and Harry was amused to notice that his bald pate was peeling.

"How's it going?" Guy asked.

"I'll let you know as soon as I do," Harry quipped, eliciting a giggle from the woman sitting across the table from him. "Tess is explaining some of the procedures to me."

Guy grinned. "Oh I see. Sorry to interrupt. There's something I'd like to have a word with you about. It won't take long. I've got a meeting in ten minutes, but how are you fixed for lunch?"

"Lunch will be fine. I don't need to take up much more of Tess's time. I was intending to go home afterwards and write up what we've got through this morning."

Guy looked at his watch. "Shall I pop back, in say ... an hour or so?"

"Fine; see you then."

Tess waited for the door to close before she asked, "How long have you known Guy?"

"We worked together for eight years," Harry replied.

Her question set him wondering if Guy's *magic touch* was having its customary effect, and if she was fishing for a way to get to know him better. Harry guessed she was in her late forties; well rounded in all the right places; possibly a tad overweight, but not unattractive. During the hour or so he had spent with her, she had proved herself to be intelligent and perceptive. However, knowing Guy as he did, Harry suspected that, even without Emma for competition, her chances would be slim. His guess was that she may be a little '*long in the tooth*' for Guy's taste.

Stifling a grin, he turned his mind back to business. "Now, where do the terms of reference of the Services Management Directive end and those of the Services Co-ordinating Team begin?"

"Good question; it depends," Tess replied with a playful grin.

"On what?"

"On who you speak to and what the circumstances are. There's no fixed policy."

"I see," Harry sighed resignedly.

Tess's giggle was infectious. "Sorry you asked?"

Harry smiled. "I don't have a choice; it's what I'm here for."

Although Tess was helpful and co-operative, Harry felt nowhere near achieving a complete picture of the convoluted operating procedures of ACCORS.

Guy's eventual return was an appropriate and welcome place to stop. "Thanks Tess; you've been very helpful," Harry said.

"I'm not sure I have," she replied, gathering up her papers. "But if you need me again, you know where I am."

"I think you've made an impression there," Guy commented mischievously, as Tess closed the door behind her.

"Harry laughed. "She was asking about you."

Guy assumed an air of innocence. "I'm spoken for. Anyway, Em just called. Would you mind if she joined us for lunch? She's taken the day off to have her central heating boiler serviced, but she had to wait most of the morning for the bloke to arrive. She's a bit cheesed off and at a loose end. I've got a meeting in Dorchester this afternoon, so I thought we might have lunch over in her neck of the woods."

"Of course I don't mind," Harry replied. "How about *The Old Granary?*"

Now that his relationship with Adam had taken another downturn and he faced the prospect of losing Marjorie, an hour or two in Emma's company would be a beacon of light in the gathering gloom.

Guy looked doubtful. "We might not get in. It gets pretty busy at this time of year. But I'll call Em and get her to meet us there."

The quay in Wareham was crowded when Harry arrived. Holidaymakers were milling beside the river, and cars were idling between the two ranks of parked vehicles, while their drivers waited for a space to become available. Guy appeared to have arrived at an opportune moment, because Harry could see his car at the far end, facing the river.

There was a rap on the window and he turned his head to find Guy beside him. "You might have more luck in town," Guy suggested, pointing back along the way Harry had come. "There's more parking behind here; near the church. Take a right and right again. Em's in the restaurant, seeing if she can get us a table."

Harry had to cross the bridge to find room to turn round in the holiday traffic, and it took another twenty-five minutes before he made it back to Guy and Emma.

"We thought you'd stood us up," Guy quipped.

"Sorry. What little parking there was by the church was all taken. I had to go nearly all the way out of town. Even then, I had to wait for a vacant space."

Emma smiled a greeting. "No worries; you're here now."

Unlike Guy, her face was only lightly tanned, although the freckles across her nose were prominent. Harry supposed that, being an *Aussie*, she was well aware of the harm that prolonged exposure to strong sunlight could do to somcone of her colouring. She was dressed in figure-hugging jeans and a pale blue, sleeveless top that drew the eye to the golden tan of her shoulders and arms. The only jewellery she wore was her distinctive fashion watch and the gold rings that dangled from her earlobes. Her sunglasses were perched on her hair, which was drawn back in a beaded band and fell to her shoulders in a loose, wavy tail. Harry had to force himself to stop gazing at her.

"No luck in *The Old Granary*, I'm afraid," said Guy. "The place is heaving."

"We'll have to wait a while, if we want to eat there." Emma added. "They can't fit us in for at least another thirty minutes."

Guy grimaced. "That's no good to me; I've got to be in Dorchester in an hour and a half."

"Where else can we try?" Harry asked.

"Everywhere looks pretty full," said Guy, gesturing towards the fully occupied tables outside *The Quay Inn*. "When I got here, *The Red Lion* and *The Black Bear* looked just as busy. I think I'll have to settle for a sandwich."

"That'll do for me," Harry replied.

Emma gestured towards the river. "Those people look like they're going. Why don't you two grab that bench, while I get us a sarnie from the bakery? Any particular likes or dislikes Harry?"

"No; anything will do."

The two men settled themselves on the bench facing the river. On the opposite bank, holidaymakers were enjoying picnics or just watching the ducks paddle hopefully below the diners on the open terrace of the restaurant. Beyond them, swans were gliding serenely across the dark, glistening water, effortlessly avoiding the puttering progress of an occasional pleasure boat. The vessels moored beyond the arches of the bridge, shone in the golden glow of summer, their pristine brass and varnished woodwork gleaming in the sunlight. What a contrast, Harry thought, to the sorry looking craft he had seen huddled beneath their rime-coated covers on that crisp winter day, six months earlier. The weeks and months seemed to have flown past. His life had changed in so many ways. Now, sitting with his face lifted to the sun, it was almost possible to forget the unhappiness and despair that had once all but consumed him, and which he had tried, but failed, to dispel in bouts of alcoholic stupor.

Guy's voice brought him from his reverie. "What I wanted to ask you is; have you come to any conclusions about Nick Stenning's department yet?"

"From what I've seen so far, a great deal of what his team does seems to duplicate work done by others," Harry replied.

"Absolutely!" Guy concurred. "But I wanted to talk to you outside the office, before you submit your interim report to the board. As the saying goes; 'Walls have ears'; and that's certainly true at ACCORS. Nick's a pretty shrewd political animal … keeps his ear to the ground. I happen to know he's been fishing to find out what people have been telling you. I'm willing to bet he's been grilling his own people about what they've been asked and what they said to you."

"He was present at both meetings I had with his staff," Harry replied. "He insisted on it. They seemed nervous and cautious about what they told me. I got the impression that was his intention."

Guy chuckled. "I'm not surprised. He'll try his damnedest to nullify any changes you recommend. He's got the ear of the Chairman too. He makes sure he stays on the right side of 'Bertie Boy'."

"I take you mean Sir Bertram Chilcott," Harry said. "I believe he's on the Board of one of the NHS trusts, as well. Isn't that a conflict of interest?"

"Probably," Guy answered flatly. "But it wasn't seen as an impediment to him chairing ACCORS. Sir Bertram has his finger in a tasty selection of pies."

Harry blew out his cheeks. "So what you're saying is; I'm wasting my time, and that whatever I put in my report will be kicked into touch."

Guy pursed his lips. "Not necessarily. My advice, if you want it, is to keep your cards close to your chest before you submit your report. It'll save you a lot of hassle and make it more difficult to stymie your recommendations beforehand."

"How the hell do you put up with that, day after day?" Harry exclaimed.

Guy shrugged. "You get used to it. I suppose I've learned to live with it."

"Rather you than me," Harry sighed. "But thanks for the advice. I had already arrived at a similar conclusion. I learned a long time ago not to comment too early on anything I hear or see."

"Very wise," said Guy. Looking over his shoulder, he exclaimed, "Here's Em with the tucker! By the way, that's not distant thunder you can hear; it's my stomach."

Harry laughed, and turned his head, to concentrate his attention on Emma, as she approached, clutching a carrier-bag bearing the logo: *Nellie Crumb Bakery.*

"So; what have you got planned for this afternoon?" Emma asked, as she and Harry watched Guy pull out from the car park and head towards the town centre.

Harry was about to reply that he intended to write up some notes on his meeting with Tess, but somewhere in his tangled thoughts and emotions, a glimmer of perception surfaced. "Nothing really," he replied. "It's a lovely afternoon; I quite fancy a wander around Corfe Castle."

"Oh, right," Emma exclaimed. "I was hoping to catch a ride home, but it's not far. I walked here, so I guess I can walk back."

"It's a bit of a trek to where I've parked, but I'd be happy to give you a lift," he said. Screwing up every ounce of courage, he added, "Do you have to go straight home?"

Her compelling gaze met his, in what he interpreted as a knowing look, and his nerve deserted him. Looking away towards the river, he muttered, "I suppose you've got to get back to the shop."

"No; as a matter of fact, I've decided to take the whole day off," she said quietly.

In the momentary hiatus, Harry inspected his toecaps. Emma broke the awkward silence. "It's such a lovely day, and I owe you for lunch in Swanage, so how about I treat you to a cream tea in Corfe? There's a nice tea room there, with a garden, right under the castle walls."

Harry's heart missed a beat. Even though he suspected she had made the offer to spare his blushes, he could not let the opportunity pass. "You don't owe me at all; it was my pleasure, but a cream tea would be very nice."

"While we're having tea, you can tell me all about your heroics," she said.

Caught unawares, Harry was nonplussed. "What are you talking about?"

"Why didn't you tell me about the fire?" she asked impishly.

Harry shrugged, unsure if she really was interested or merely teasing him. "There's nothing much to tell."

"That's not what Laura told me. She reckons you and Simon are village heroes."

"In my case, village idiot is more like it!" Harry replied defensively.

Emma beamed at him in a way that Reggie, his late father-in-law, would have described as '*enough to make the tail of one's shirt curl*'.

Awkwardness and doubt had been banished from Harry's mind by the time he found himself strolling past *The Fox Inn* beside Emma, with the ruined castle keep silhouetted against an azure sky above the grey, stone roofs of the cottages.

Corfe's tiny museum managed to be both quaint and informative, and provided the added appeal of making it necessary for them to stand close together to look at the exhibits. The petrified dinosaur footprints were a magnet for children, but it was the photographs of bygone rural life that captured Harry's imagination. Somehow they seemed to epitomise the timelessness of villages like Nethercombe Ley.

They learned that the Church of St. Edward the Martyr is dedicated to a canonised Saxon king, murdered by his step-mother and half-brother, and rival for the throne. Harry's speculation about what '*the step-mother from hell*' would have been like as a mother-in-law brought him the satisfaction of a delightful chortle from Emma.

"Who else but you, would think of that!" she exclaimed.

As they emerged from the church into the glare of bright sunlight, a shrill whistle announced the presence of a steam locomotive somewhere beyond *The Bankes Arms Hotel*.

"I'm going to try that before long," Harry said, half to himself. It brought an enigmatic smile to Emma's face, suggesting that she recognised the little boy that lurked within him; as it does in most men.

For the rest of the afternoon, they wandered through the village, doing touristy things. They licked ice cream cones while admiring the model of the castle in its heyday; they visited the castle ruins and made their way up the steep grassy mound to the keep, where they could gaze out and admire the breathtaking panorama of Dorset, spread out below them in all its verdant glory; they browsed in the National Trust shop, where Harry persuaded Emma to let him buy her a comical china duck, dressed in scarf and wellies, which caught her eye.

Despite the crowds, Harry was captivated by Corfe Castle's charm; although with Emma, he would have been happy anywhere. If she *was* with him under sufferance, she betrayed no impression of it, and made the afternoon a delight, with her effervescent personality and mischievous sense of humour.

When they had tea, in the shadow of the ruined castle walls, Emma discovered that the family at the table behind her were fellow *Aussies*. While she chatted with them, in that comfortable, unselfconscious way that seems to come naturally to Australians, Harry took the opportunity to watch her with quiet fascination.

Was he falling in love with her? The sudden thought alarmed him. He had never allowed himself to explore that forbidden territory before.

'For God's sake, Harry; get a grip!' he thought.

At Emma's request, they stopped at a local farm shop on the way back to Wareham. "Guy and I love their lamb," she enthused.

Harry had to agree that all the meat looked very appetising. He bought some thickly sliced bacon and Wiltshire smoked ham.

It was late afternoon when they arrived outside Emma's house, where a bright yellow Volkswagen Beetle stood on the hard-standing in front of the garage door. Noticing his amused interest, Emma said, "That's my Fritz. Guy calls him The Flying Kraut Banana."

"Guten Tag Fritz," Harry quipped.

"Fancy a coffee?" she asked, unclipping her seat belt.

He watched her as she searched in her bag for her keys. He had to refuse. Things were getting out of hand. At least they were as far as he was concerned.

Opening her front door, she called, "Come and have a look at my little house. It's not as grand as May Cottage, but it's all mine and I'm quite proud of it."

It took the wind out of his sales. If he refused, he risked offending her; at least that was the excuse he offered himself.

"You make May Cottage sound like Buckingham Palace," he said. "I'm sure your house is equally impressive, and less draughty."

The house was small, but stylishly decorated and furnished. The lounge-diner was no larger than his study; with french windows which led to a narrow patio and a small, well tended lawn bordered by flower beds. Flashing him a smile of gratitude, Emma placed her new china duck in pride of place on the tiled windowsill at the far end of her narrow kitchen.

"While the coffee's brewing, come and have a look at the rest of my mansion," she said. "It won't take a minute."

A lobby ran beside the kitchen, with doors which led to a toilet, a storage cupboard and the garage. At the end of the lobby, a glass panelled door gave access to the garden. Upstairs consisted of a bathroom and two bedrooms, only one of which was large enough to accommodate a double bed and built in furniture. The decor was feminine, without being overly frilly or fussy. Nothing suggested Guy's influence, but Harry felt a tinge of jealousy, at the thought that he undoubtedly slept there on occasions. The single bed was made up in the other bedroom, but now that Emma's mother had returned home to Melbourne, there was no evidence of occupancy.

The evening sun was dipping behind the rooftops when Harry forced himself to leave. After an hour or so in Emma's cosy lounge, it had taken a great deal of will power to force himself to go; especially when she mentioned that Guy was playing golf that evening. He tried to convince himself that it was his reluctance take advantage of her good nature that had stopped him inviting her out to dinner, but he knew the real reason. He lacked the *'bottle'*.

Reluctantly, he took his leave, and with a final wave, glanced in the rear-view mirror, to catch a parting glimpse of her, as she watered the hanging basket beside her front door.

He regretted his decision the moment he left her house, and all the way home, chided himself for his timidity.

Harry could not remember whether Marjorie was due home from holiday that day or the next, but he called her anyway. He tried her mobile first, but there was no answer. The answering machine on the landline, invited him, in Phil's carefully modulated tones, to, *'Leave … a message … after the tone'*.

"Marjorie; it's Harry. Please call me when you get back. Better still meet me … here or anywhere you like. I've spoken to Adam, so I know …" A click, followed by a persistent hum, suggested that the machine had cut him off. He presumed the memory was full.

"Oh great; that's all I bloody need!" he exclaimed.

Tilting his chair back, he gazed through the rain-flecked window at the hills, whose summits were now almost obscured by a misty curtain of low cloud.

His confrontation with Adam had not followed the course he had expected, although it had begun according to plan. Harry had laid into him, almost from the moment Adam had opened the front door.

"What the hell's been going on?"

Adam had been taken aback and had replied apprehensively, "Like ... how?"

"Don't bloody-well '*like how*' me. I don't know what the hell you've done, but I've had Marjorie in tears! She's had enough! She told me to find someone else!"

Adam's eyes had widened. "No way! OK, we like, had a fight, right. She like, did all the talking!"

"What happened?" Harry had barked.

"She started giving me verbals, right ... about leaving stuff around and like, not putting my clothes in the laundry basket!"

"*Right*!" Harry had retorted, mimicking Adam sarcastically. "And I suppose you gave her plenty of lip."

Adam had blanched and lowered his eyes. "Yeh; I guess I did. I didn't mean to, but she like, started tearing me off about growing up and considering other people. Stuff like that. I guess I like, told her to back off."

"Oh, I guess you did!" Harry had sneered. "But then, the truth isn't always welcome is it?"

Adam's eyes had blazed with anger for a second, but he had leaned against the door jamb and replied quietly. "I never meant that to happen, right. But she kept on about what you'd been through ... how I'd like, made things worse and stuff. I guess I kinda lost it. I said stuff like, she was wasn't my mother ... or even family. I was really hacked off, right. I guess I like, said whatever came into my head!"

"Which was?" Harry had snapped.

"Well, I was like, 'You're here to clean', right. I said stuff about her sticking her nose in my family's business."

"That must have made you feel quite a man!" Harry had snarled, and gesturing towards the kitchen table, he had snapped, "Do you see that? *Your* clothes ... laundered and pressed. The clothes *you* leave strewn about without any thought for her, or the fact that she's not paid to do it! But she's just here to clean and clear up after you! That's all isn't it?"

"Dad; I'm sorry. I never meant it. I was like …" But unable to express himself, and close to tears, Adam had thrown up his hands helplessly.

Harry had felt the anger drain from him. "There's no point in saying sorry to me. It's Marjorie who's been hurt; badly enough to want to get the hell out of here. At this moment, I know exactly how she feels."

A look akin to panic had flitted across Adam's face. "I didn't know she'd taken it like that. She went ballistic. I like, couldn't get a word in. I just took off. I thought she'd have calmed down by now, right."

"Well, she *like,* hasn't," Harry had said quietly and deliberately; suddenly feeling weary and defeated. "She's told me to look for somebody else."

"I'll talk to her dad. I'll tell her I didn't *mean* it!"

Harry had smiled sardonically. "There's no point. She's on holiday. She and Phil have gone to his brother's place in Greece. It's probably too late to change her mind, anyway."

"Oh yeh; I forgot," Adam had mumbled. "But I'll call her when she gets back, right. I'll tell her not to leave. I'll split … for good."

"Don't be a bloody idiot Adam! She's probably doing this because she thinks that if she stays, it'll make things worse between you and me. If you tell her that, it will confirm what she already believes. Do you think she'd be able to come here and face me, thinking she'd driven you out?"

Adam's contrition had seemed genuine, if wasted. "Dad; I'm sorry. I'm gutted. I really am."

Harry had heaved another sigh of resignation. "I know. *You're* sorry. *I'm* sorry … *everybody's* sorry. Being sorry seems to be in fashion these days. Just take these clothes up and start packing your bag and whatever else you think you're going to need for the next couple of weeks. I'll drive you to your mother's place, tomorrow. For God's sake don't say anything about this to her. If she finds out, your life really will be hell, I can promise you."

"OK. But I am like, gonna move out and get out of your hair, dad; as soon as I can, right"

"Don't be stupid, Adam!" Harry had sighed. "What's the point? The damage has been done. Anyway, where would you go; back to your mother?"

"I dunno; I'll like, find somewhere."

"How, and with what?"

"I've got a job."

Adam's reply had taken Harry by surprise. "You haven't said anything. Where?"

"At Kirkland's, the furnishing store, right … on the Motts End trading estate. Marjorie told me they were like, advertising for sales guys in the showroom. Her cousin's the assistant manager."

"It seems Marjorie does have her uses beyond just cleaning then?" Harry had commented acidly. "And he gave you a job?"

"Yeh." Adam had sounded defensive. "Not in the showroom. They like, need somebody in the warehouse; starting at the end of next month. It's only temporary, for a month or two. It's as-and-when after that."

"Well it's something, anyway," Harry had replied.

"While I look for something permanent," Adam had added quietly.

"Even if you *could* find a flat or something around here, I very much doubt what you'll earn would even cover your rent, let alone luxuries … like food, and heat," Harry had replied. "We'll just have to try to sort things out when you get back in a couple of weeks."

Harry finished his coffee and put the mug into the dishwasher. It was almost full, so he set it going before Marjorie saw it and realised that he and Adam had not run it for the past couple of days. That was *if* Marjorie came. He was certain she had returned from holiday; either yesterday or the day before. Under normal circumstances she was due that afternoon.

She had not replied to his truncated message on her answering machine, but on the plus side, neither had she or Phil called to warn him not to expect her. He felt nervous; desperately wanting her to call, but at the same time terrified she would confirm that there was nothing he could do or say to change her mind.

The whole sorry mess had seemed to be a sobering experience for Adam. He had done his best to stay out of Harry's way since their confrontation, and had remained taciturn throughout the journey to his mother's house the previous day. Harry had been content to leave things that way, and let him brood.

Thankfully for both of them, Sally and Jonathan had been at work. Adam had a key to let himself in, and Harry had left straight away. He had no wish to enter the house Sally shared with her new husband. As silly and adolescent as it may be, that was how he felt, and he saw no point in pretending otherwise.

The startling ring of the telephone on the worktop brought his thoughts back to Marjorie. He picked it up with trepidation, assuming it was her; but a number he did not recognise was displayed on the screen.

"Hello; Harry Simmonds," he said tentatively.

"Harry!" The distress was apparent in his mother's voice, even from a single word spoken from a hundred miles away.

"Hello mum; what's up?" he said.

"Harry; It's your dad. He's had a stroke."

Harry's stomach churned. "A stroke?"

"That's what they say it was."

"Oh God! How is he?" he asked anxiously.

"He was unconscious when they brought him in. The doctors are with him now."

"Where are you, mum?"

"I'm at 'The Royal Berks'. Someone just brought me a cup of tea and let me phone you."

"Is anyone there with you?" he asked.

"No; I came here in a taxi. Fran, next door, said she'd make sure everything's locked up."

"What happened?"

"Well, it was peculiar. One minute he was standing in the kitchen asking me if I wanted him to pick some runner beans, and the next thing I knew he started mumbling. Then he started staggering and slumped across the sink. I couldn't make out what he was saying; he kept slurring and mumbling. Then he fell down. He went down with a terrible bump. I didn't know what to do. Oh, Harry!" She broke down and began sobbing.

"Don't worry mum, he'll be alright. He's as tough as old boots," Harry said as soothingly as his own anxiety would allow, although his heart was racing and he felt momentarily nauseous. "I'm leaving straight away, mum. I'll be with you as soon as I can."

"Don't go mad! I don't want you in here as well!" she sniffed.

"Is there anyone I can talk to?" he asked. "A doctor or a nurse?"

"No, they're down by the nurses' station. This is a normal phone I'm on, not a mobile one."

"Look, Debbie's only a few minutes away. I'll call her and get her to come and stay with you until I get there."

"You'll do no such thing!" she snapped. "I don't want her scared out of her wits, poor love. I'll be *perfectly* alright until you get here."

"Are you sure mum?"

"Yes, of course."

"OK. I'm on my way."

With his heart racing, he scribbled a hasty note to Marjorie and left it on the kitchen table. She had his mobile number, so there was no need to leave details of where he could be contacted. Now, what else did he need to do before he left? His mind was in turmoil and for a moment he found himself incapable of rational thought. All that concerned him was his father, lying helpless in a hospital bed and his mother, alone and no doubt terrified.

The wipers swept back and forth across the windscreen, and the tyres hissed over the rain drenched surface of the M3, but Harry kept his foot down on the accelerator as hard he dared. His headlights did little to improve visibility, barely penetrating the misty spray swirling behind the blur of glowing tail lights. However, cars were still passing him, driven with little heed to the conditions; brake lights flaring as they approached more carefully driven vehicles.

He absorbed little of *Test Match Special*, while he tried to come to terms with the situation. How badly would his father be incapacitated; and for how long? How would his mother cope? Would he need to '*up sticks*' and move in with them? It was something his love for them would allow him to do without question, although leaving May Cottage would be a wrench.

As usual the traffic in Reading's congested thoroughfares was heavy and slow moving. Finding a space in the hospital car park proved impossible, and he eventually left the car in a nearby street, hardly caring if it was legally parked. Only then did it occur to him that he had no idea where to find his father. However, a kindly chap, of about his father's age, deciphered his babbled enquiry at Reception, and directed him to the Acute Stroke Unit.

He arrived out of breath and trembling with anxiety. A young nurse with an unidentifiable accent, checked his identity, and led him along a corridor. She apologised for being unable to answer any of the questions that tumbled from his lips.

His questions were answered when the nurse opened the door to a small room. His mother was sitting, head bowed, her face buried in a handful of tissues, with a female doctor on one side of her and an older woman on the other. They all looked up as the door opened.

"Mum?" Harry croaked.

As his mother lifted her head, he saw her anguished expression and the tears streaming down her cheeks. Her eyes were dull and raw with grief.

"Oh Harry … Harry! He's gone!" she wailed. She tried to stand, but her legs would not support her, and she slumped back onto the seat.

The doctor stood up. "I'm so sorry," she said quietly. "Your father suffered a series of strokes. I'm afraid we couldn't save him. He died a short while ago."

The room seemed to spin. Harry knelt at his mother's feet, cradling her head and stroking her hair, while she clung to him, weeping with shuddering sobs.

"Would you like us to leave you alone for a while?" the doctor asked.

"Yes please," Harry replied, feeling the hot tears spill from own his eyes.

"When you feel ready, let one of the nurses know. I'll answer any questions you have." The doctor gestured towards the other woman. "Miriam is a member of our Bereavement Team; she'll be on hand to give you any help you need."

The door closed, leaving mother and son to give way to their grief in private. Although shocked and distressed, Harry's immediate concern was for his mother. He held her close to him, occasionally wiping his own tear streaked face with a one of her tissues, while she sobbed helplessly.

Surely it was a mistake; how could it be true? His father couldn't possibly be dead!

Later that afternoon, the doctor; who Harry learned was a consultant, explained that his father had never recovered consciousness. A series of serious strokes had resulted in a fatal heart attack. She suspected that there had been at least one minor stroke previously. Harry was unaware of it and equally certain that his mother knew nothing about it either. His father may have failed to recognise it as a problem; possibly having adopted his standard response to ill health by trying to ignore it.

Harry and his mother were allowed a few moments for a final parting with the gentle man, who appeared to be merely sleeping and might open his eyes at any moment, demanding to know what all the fuss was about. His mother gently stroked her husband's hair and bestowed a final kiss on his forehead, before, with a half sobbed, "Oh, Alex!" she turned to Harry and buried her face in his shoulder.

Choking back his own anguish, Harry squeezed his father's lifeless hand and whispered shakily, "Bye dad." Then with a comforting arm around his mother's shoulder, he led her away.

Harry called his mother's doctor before they left the hospital, for something to calm her and help her to sleep. They collected the prescription from the surgery on the way home, but she adamantly refused to take it. "I don't want to be drugged!" she asserted. "There's nothing wrong with me, and there's too much to do!"

"You won't be drugged. It's only to help you sleep, mum," he replied. "We can't do anything until we get the Death Certificate and register it. I'll take care of that."

"But we need to let people know!" she insisted.

"I know, but we don't have to do everything this minute," Harry replied soothingly. "Just sit down and I'll make us a cup of tea."

But she followed him into the kitchen, fidgeting with the cups and saucers and checking the tap after he had turned it off. Her hands were trembling, and Harry put his arm around her, as she began to sob once again. Overcome by her distress, and his loss, he let his own tears flow.

Later, he managed to settle her in front of the TV, to provide at least some small distraction, while he went into the hall to make a start on the telephone calls. He dreaded calling Uncle Frank, although he appreciated that, being his dad's brother, he ought to be the first to know. Frank would expect it.

He began hesitantly. "Uncle Frank; it's Harry. I'm afraid I have some really sad news."

For once, his garrulous uncle was lost for words, and Harry's explanation of the circumstances was met with silence for a few moments. Then Harry heard a long, rasping sigh and the exclamation, "Oh, dear God!"

After the initial shock, Uncle Frank's first thoughts were for Harry's mother. "Poor Marian; how is she lad? She must be heartbroken."

There was a brief muffled exchange in the background, when Frank responded to a question from Aunt Jenny, who was herself in poor health and confined to a wheelchair. Uncle Frank had recovered some of his composure when he resumed the conversation, with an uninterrupted flow of questions and suggestions, interspersed with advice and a long message of condolence for Marian.

Harry appreciated that it was all meant sincerely and that his uncle was having to come to terms with the loss of a much loved younger brother, but he was nevertheless relieved when the call ended, some twenty minutes later.

His next call was to Sally, who was shocked and full of concern for him and his mother.

"I was wondering if you'd tell Adam," Harry said. "I think it would be better for him to hear it face-to-face than from a phone call."

"Of course," Sally replied. "I agree entirely. If there's anything I can do, you know you only have to ask."

"Thanks Sally; I appreciate it."

"Can I let my mum know?" she asked.

"Yes, please do."

"Have you told Debbie?"

"No; not yet. I can't leave mum. Despite what she says, I don't think she's up to being left alone."

"Of course not," Sally replied. "Do you want me to go and tell her?"

"Thanks Sally. I really appreciate the offer, but it's a long way for you to drive. I'm a lot closer, and I expect Adam will need comforting. I'll leave it until the morning. Mum's neighbour, Fran, has offered to keep her company for an hour or two, tomorrow."

"OK, if you're sure. But call me if there's anything I can do."

"I will. Thanks."

"Give my love to Marian, and look after yourself Harry."

"I will. Bye Sally."

"Bye Harry; take care."

When he looked up, his mother was watching him from the doorway to the lounge.

"That was Sally," he explained. "I called her to ask if she'd tell Adam. She sends her love."

"I don't envy her that," his mother said flatly. "Have you called Frank?"

"Yes, I have."

"I'll bet he was shocked."

"Yes, he was. It knocked him sideways. He and Aunt Jenny send their love and condolences."

"What about Debbie?" she asked.

"I want to go and see her," he replied. "I don't want to tell her over the phone."

"No, you're right," she nodded. "While you're gone I'd better phone Judith and Caroline."

"I'll go in the morning," Harry said. "Fran has offered to come in and stay with you."

"I'll be alright on my own. I'm not a baby!" she exclaimed.

"I know, but I'm not leaving you. We both have too much going on in our heads at the moment!"

"I think I'll phone Judith; it'll give me something to do. I can't sit around here with you wrapping me in cotton wool," she said.

"OK mum. If you feel up to it. You phone your sisters. Go and sit down and I'll bring you the phone. Do you fancy another cuppa?"

"No! I'll have tea coming out of my ears at this rate!" she snapped. But her expression softened immediately. "I'm sorry, darling. I didn't mean to be ungrateful. It's just … well."

"I know mum … I know," he murmured, and gave her the handset.

Harry's opportunity to visit Debbie came later that evening, when Aunt Judith and Uncle Ed appeared on the doorstep.

"We just came over to give you both a bit of support, if that's alright," said Uncle Ed.

Aunt Judy wrapped an arm around her sister and tearfully led her into the lounge. Uncle Ed followed Harry into the kitchen. "My word, this is a shocker, Harry!"

"Yes," Harry replied lamely.

"I can't quite make out what happened from what Judy's told me."

Harry related the circumstances as he knew them, and they made their way into the lounge, with yet more tea.

With his mother in good hands for the next hour or two, Harry decided to bite the bullet and drive back to Reading to give Debbie the bad news. Thankfully the rain had stopped. He assumed the rush hour traffic would have thinned, but to avoid a wasted journey, he thought it best to check that Debbie was at home before setting out. He used his mobile, deliberately choosing to call the land line at the house Debbie shared with her fellow students. He sighed with relief when he recognised the answering voice.

"Hello Paul. It's Harry; Debbie's dad. Is she there?"

"Hi Harry. Sure; she's watching TV. Hold on, I'll go get her."

"No! Paul wait! ..." Harry exclaimed. "... Are you still there?"

"Yeh, I'm still here."

"Paul; the thing is; I need to come over to speak to Debbie. I have some very sad news for her. She'll be very distressed when I tell her. Do you think you could arrange for some privacy for us?"

"Sure," Paul replied in his easy drawl. "There's only Malinta here apart from Debbie and me. She's in her room. I'll talk with her, and we'll stay out of your way."

"Don't tell Debbie about this call or that I'm coming over, will you?"

"Of course not," Paul replied quietly. "If she asks, I'll say it was one of my friends calling."

"Thanks Paul, I appreciate it. But I didn't intend to exclude you. Debbie will need you."

"OK; whatever you think is best. I'll be here for her."

"I know, Paul; I'm counting on it."

Debbie's face lit up with a broad smile as Paul led Harry into the tiny living room, where she was sitting on a small settee with her knees drawn up under her.

"Hello dad! What a lovely surprise; what brings you here?" she said, before intuition allowed her to see behind his forced smile. "What's up? Is it Adam?"

"No love, it's nothing to do with Adam," he replied. Sitting down beside her, he took her hands between his. "I'm afraid it's Gramps."

"Oh my God! What's happened? Is he alright?"

"He's had a series of serious strokes … I'm afraid …"

"No!" she wailed, her eyes, brimming with tears; pleading with him not to say it.

"I'm afraid so my love. He died this afternoon. He didn't suffer; he was unconscious. I'm sure he never really knew anything about it."

Harry took her in his arms and gently rocked her, the way he used to when she was upset as a little girl. Trembling and weeping, she clung to him, pressing her tear streaked face against his. He found it impossible to restrain his own tears, and looking up, his eyes met Paul's compassionate gaze.

"I'm so sorry!" Paul said quietly.

It was some time before Debbie stopped sobbing and brought her emotions under a semblance of control. She clung to Harry, burying her face in his neck and uttering occasional heaving sobs. "Poor Grandma," she wailed. "What will she do?"

"Leave that to me. I'll look after Grandma," he said soothingly.

"We all will," she answered, her voice trembling with emotion. "What happened to Gramps?"

Harry explained as gently and carefully as he could, giving her no more information than he thought she could cope with at that moment. Paul appeared with a tray bearing mugs of tea. "I thought this might help," he said.

"Thanks Paul; you're a star," Harry replied gratefully, adding with a rueful grin, "I see you've learned at bit about the English and our cure-all for every situation."

Paul smiled diffidently, and made to leave the room, but Harry held up a hand. "There's no need to go Paul, unless you want to."

"Thanks; but I think it's best I give you and Debbie a little time alone."

It took a while before Debbie could compose herself sufficiently to speak without her words being punctuated by sudden bursts of tears. Harry patiently avoided interrupting the flow of, at times, incoherent thoughts she articulated, as she grieved for her adored Gramps, with whom she had shared that special, almost mystical, bond between the young and their grandparents.

Images swam into Harry's mind; of the love radiating in his father's expression, as he had patiently indulged a laughing, chattering little girl in endless games of catch, hide-and-seek, dolls' tea parties, and whatever else her fertile, infant imagination had demanded; of Gramps sitting under the cherry tree in the garden, with Debbie on one knee and Adam on the other. The pride in his father's expression, as he had posed with Debbie after her graduation, would remain indelibly etched in Harry's memory; as he suspected it would in Debbie's.

Harry's apologies for returning so late were brushed aside by Aunt Judith and Uncle Ed. Like his mother, they were more concerned with how Debbie had taken the news, and her emotional state.

"She's taken it badly; as expected," Harry explained. "But she sends you her love, mum. I promised I'd bring her over to see you tomorrow."

"Poor love," his mother murmured. "I'll bake her a chocolate sponge; she loves those."

Aunt Judith sighed. "They were very close weren't they?"

"Yes, they were," Harry replied.

"He absolutely worshipped her!" his mother exclaimed softly.

Uncle Ed stood up. "Come on Judith; we'd better be going and leave these two to get some rest. They've had a long and difficult day." Turning to Harry, he said, "Don't forget; you know where we are if you need us."

"I do, and thanks," Harry answered, suddenly feeling weary.

As he turned into the driveway of May Cottage, Harry felt a sense of relief. It was good to be home, even if it was unlikely to be permanent. He had not succeeded in persuading his mother to consider moving in with him, and he had no intention of leaving her to cope alone, so far away.

Uncle Ed and Aunt Judith had generously volunteered to stay with her until after the funeral, to leave him free to take care of the arrangements and attend to his own affairs. He had rung Simon, who, as always, had been compassionate and understanding. When he had called Marjorie to let her know he would not be home for a day or two, she had assured him that what had happened between her and Adam could be put aside for the time being. She would take care of May Cottage. The note on the kitchen table testified that she had been as good as her word.

*Have been shopping for you. Milk, butter, bacon and eggs in the fridge. Also got you some bread and a few other things I thought might be useful. Let me know if you need anything else before Thursday.*

His mail was sorted into three separate piles beside the note: junk mail in one; what were obviously condolence cards in another, and everything else in the third.

'If only there were one or two Marjories running the country,' Harry thought.

He made a cup of coffee and went into the study to check for messages on the answerphone. The first was from one of his former partners, asking him to call back; the next was Rachel. He had called her the previous day, but she had heard the news from Simon and had already left the message: "Hi Harry, I just called to say I'm so sorry to hear about your father. I feel for you. I'll call again. Hope to see you at the weekend. Bye darling."

Two of the others were from people at ACCORS, The fifth cut-off with no message. The last touched him deeply: "Hi Harry; it's Emma. Laura told me about your dad. I've been there and I know words can't take away the pain. But I just wanted you to know how sorry I am. I'm thinking of you. Guy and I are here for you whenever you need us. Knowing you, I expect you're more concerned about your mum, but make sure you take care of yourself too. All our love; bye."

He went back to the kitchen table and began opening the sympathy cards. The first one he opened was from Marjorie, Phil and Gary; the next from Guy and Emma. There were others from Simon and Laura, Alan and Jill Anderson, Ellen and Rob Hardy, and even Alfie Cox and his wife. Word had obviously spread. It meant a great deal to him that so many of the cards were from his neighbours. Having sorted the *wheat from the chaff* in the third pile, he looked out at his garden, now in full bloom, and at the distant green hills.

The silence and stillness provided the first opportunity to give free rein to his emotions; to begin to come to terms with the dreadful finality of his father's death. He would never see his dad again; never speak to him; share a joke, or have the chance to simply enjoy his company. He was haunted and shamed by the occasions he had regarded visiting his parents as an untimely interruption to his busy life. That was not how he really felt. If he had only known …

He shook his head. But we never do, and we never can. Nor can we ever atone for things we could and should have done when we had the chance. With hardly a conscious thought, he pulled on a sweater and left the house to make his way along the lane towards Hallows Hill.

Cotton-ball clouds studded the cobalt sky, like a fleet of becalmed galleons. All that disturbed the still, summer afternoon was the incessant twitter and chatter of birds in the nearby copse and hedgerows, and the occasional buzz of an inquisitive insect. Harry looked out across the sunlit valley towards Copper Hill; at the straggle of gorse and briar below its domed, treeless summit. For some reason, it brought to mind Guy's balding pate, and set him chuckling to himself.

The peaceful, green meadows, the gold of the unharvested cornfields and the exuberant song of a blackbird in the twisted branches of a gnarled beech, led him to contemplate the insignificance of a life within the infinite span of time.

Someone would have stood here when Nelson's *'Hearts of Oak'* had been holding Napoleon's all-conquering hoards at bay. Harry could picture yeoman farmers and smock-clad labourers toiling in the fields below. He could almost hear their wind-borne calls and laughter. Now, only birdsong and the muted drone of a distant tractor disturbed the silence.

He could imagine terrified villagers, almost seven-hundred years ago, kneeling here in desperate prayer; the only remedy they understood that might offer sanctuary from the ravages of a merciless disease. Who would succumb and who would be spared had been the random judgment of nature, regardless of wealth, privilege, or the number of Hail Marys raised heavenward.

Moving around the edge of the copse, Harry gazed down at Nethercombe Ley, nestled around the time-worn masonry of the Church of St. Luke the Evangelist. His heart lifted at the sight of the cottages and the tight circle of oaks surrounding the village green; the tiled and slated roofs, shimmering in the afternoon sunlight, rising in ranks up the steep slope of Manor Hill towards the Memorial Hall, the green expanse of the rec and the gaudy splash of the Manor Estate.

His eye followed the narrow ribbon of hedgerows flanking the lane that led beyond May Cottage to wind its way towards the cluster of barns and stables at Garstone Farm; and on, between the overhanging trees, to the hamlet of Beaumott Hulme.

There was only the faintest breeze, discernible by the nod of a buttercup or the sway of cow parsley. Except for the unhurried progress of the tractor and the languid meandering of a herd of grazing cows in a distant field, all was quiet and motionless.

Leaving May Cottage and Nethercombe Ley would be a painful wrench, but if his mother refused to move in with him, Harry could see no alternative. He doubted she would manage on her own, and he would not abandon her to cope as best she could. He would have to make the sacrifice and move in with her. Grinning ruefully, he realised he would be an unmarried, forty-seven year old, living at home with his mother.

The family home had seemed strangely quiet and empty during the past few days. With his mind largely occupied elsewhere, he had occasionally wandered into the lounge, half expecting to find his father in his favourite chair, looking up from his newspaper with that kindly, unassuming smile Harry knew so well. A chapter had closed; one filled with that gentle, paternal love he had taken so much for granted, all his life.

And so it was for his mother. She had lost her companion and soul-mate. After more than fifty years, the husband who had courted her, cherished her with a love that had produced a dearly loved son, and shared a lifetime of hopes and aspirations, had been taken from her cruelly and abruptly; leaving her to face an uncertain future without the comfort and reassurance of his affection and devotion.

Harry was dreading the funeral. He found it difficult to cope with other people's grief. Having to support his mother, without Sally to sustain him, would be especially difficult.

Although it was too early for anyone to be able to face the ordeal of disposing of his father's clothes and personal effects, his mother had already decided that she wanted Debbie to have the car. Adam was to have his grandfather's gold retirement watch. She still had no idea of her grandson's problems, but Harry saw no reason to raise an objection.

Debbie had burst into tears when Harry told her. "Grandma should sell it!" she had protested. "She'll need the money!" But Grandma had reassured her that she was well provided for, and that Debbie should regard it as a farewell gift from the grandfather who had loved her so dearly. The touching sentiment had evoked floods of tears from both of them. Harry had no doubt that Debbie would care for it as lovingly as her beloved Gramps had.

He had been pleasantly surprised by Adam's reaction. "But the watch should be yours dad!"

"You look after it for both of us," Harry had replied. "All I ask is; if you should ever think of getting rid of it, give me first offer. Don't sell it to anyone else."

Adam had retorted irately. "What d'you take me for?"

"I'm sorry. That was uncalled for," Harry had replied contritely. However, Adam's anger had abated as swiftly as it arose. "I guess I asked for that," he had said. "But don't worry; dad. Nothing could make me part with it."

Harry walked slowly back to the stile, and before making his way home, turned to let his gaze sweep across the valley. He had always intended to bring his father here, knowing he would be moved by its tranquillity and serenity. But, as with so many other things, it was too late.

His father had looked calm and at peace lying in the Chapel of Rest; as if he would at any moment open his eyes and bestow on Harry one of those affectionate, reassuring smiles that had warmed and illuminated his life. Harry had not intended to go, and his mother had not wanted to. She had been content with her tearful farewell at the hospital. She and Harry would have preferred to comfort themselves with cherished memories, but Uncle Frank, still shaken by his brother's sudden death, had wanted to 'pay his respects' and say a last goodbye.

Frank didn't drive much anymore, so Harry had felt obliged to fetch him from Sittingbourne. He had been moved by the tears glistening in the old man's eyes and coursing down his cheeks, as he had taken a final, quaking leave of the 'little brother' who had meant so much to him.

Harry had been unable to provide an answer to Frank's constant murmur of, "Why him?"

# SEPTEMBER

## *A Bitter Harvest*

Sally and Grace were among the last of the mourners to emerge into the sunshine, while the final bars of *Stranger on the Shore* still wafted from the chapel. They had slipped in at the last moment to take their seats behind the other mourners. Harry had not noticed them until he delivered a brief eulogy to his father, shortly before the curtains closed in a final farewell to the gentle man whose image smiled at him from the order of service.

Debbie was still sobbing helplessly, and Sally took her in a consoling embrace, knowing with a mother's instinct, that it was worth a thousand words of solace. Harry met Adam's tear filled gaze and recognised an empathy he had feared permanently lost. Adam opened his mouth to speak, but could find no words. He just shook his head and lowered his eyes to the ground. Harry squeezed his shoulder and received a wan smile in reply.

Beside them, Harry's mother, watery eyed and drawn, paused from accepting condolences and offering thanks for kind words, to pat Adam's cheek affectionately and glance across at Debbie with a reassuring smile; her own grief momentarily disregarded in her concern for the distress of her grandchildren. She had held up remarkably well over the past week or so, but Harry expected her to give way to her emotions once the ordeal of the final parting was over. He kissed her cheek and she responded by carefully removing a piece of lint from the collar of his jacket; the way she used to when she had inspected him before he left for school.

Harry felt a hand on his arm, and turned to face Uncle Frank. "This is a rum do, Harry. I never thought our Alex would be the first to go."

"I suppose none of us can ever know what's in store," Harry replied.

"But he was no age. I'm on tablets for my blood pressure; I've got arthritis in this shoulder and I've had a new hip. So where's the sense in it all?"

Harry made no attempt to reply to what he took to be a rhetorical question.

"It was his time, Frank," his mother replied resignedly. "Alex always said he'd had a good life and wouldn't change things. So there's no sense in us trying to work out the whys and wherefores. All we can do is carry on the best we can."

Frank nodded. "I suppose you're right, Marian."

Debbie had finally managed to stem her tears. She stood, raw-eyed and pale with Uncle Ed and Aunt Judith, who was patting her hand and offering consolation, which Harry imagined she only half heard. Grace and Aunt Caroline were reading the messages attached to the floral tributes laid out on the grass to one side of the chapel entrance.

Although he knew it was hardly appropriate, Harry could not help thinking how attractive Sally looked in her dark, tailored suit. But somehow, he felt his father would have understood.

The intervention of several members of the bowling club, expressing their sorrow at the loss of a cherished friend and club member, prevented him from walking over to have a word with her. The men all wore dark blazers with the club badge embroidered on the breast pocket, grey flannel trousers and black ties. The immaculately turned out ladies were dressed in suitably sombre colours. Harry listened courteously to their anecdotes, some of which he had heard before. Nevertheless, they were related with warmth and affection for a man they genuinely mourned. One old boy seemed to sum it up for all of them with, "'E were a grand lad, were your dad. Nothin' were too much trouble. They don't make 'em like that anymore!" Eventually, they moved off towards the car park, and Harry had a moment to himself.

He looked up at the almost cloudless sky, his eyes drawn to a red kite gliding effortlessly on the thermals. Beyond the trees bordering the cemetery, he could hear children in the playground of the local primary school. Harry found their excited shrieks and laughter uplifting; a reminder of the renewal of life.

Looking back, he saw his mother turn from a group of her neighbours and look purposefully at Sally, who was standing alone outside the chapel entrance. Sally looked apprehensive as her erstwhile mother-in-law approached, and Harry held his breath; wondering what was about to happen.

"What are you doing there, Sally?" his mother asked.

"I wanted to pay my respects. I hope you don't mind."

"Of course not! Don't stand there on your own. You and Grace *will* come back to the house and have a cup of tea with us, won't you?"

"Well …" Sally said hesitantly, but Grace answered for both of them. "Thank you, Marian; we would love to."

Harry could have hugged his mother, even before she added, "It was good of you to come Sally. Alex was very fond of you. He loved being a grandfather. He used to say you were responsible for two of the nicest things that ever happened to him. That goes for me too, for that matter."

"Thank you," Sally replied, the relief evident in her voice and expression. "He was a lovely man; a real gentleman."

"Yes he was, wasn't he? Quite a charmer when he wanted to be, especially when he was younger. Anyway, come and say hello to Ed and Judith."

Harry watched them walk towards his Aunt and Uncle, feeling tears pricking his eyes; tears of pleasure for their reconciliation; and tears of sorrow that it should have taken such unhappy circumstances to bring it about.

Later, with mostly family mourners remaining; friends and acquaintances having drifted away, Harry shepherded his mother towards the black limousines waiting at the end of the pathway. He braced himself for a flood of tears, as she made a final parting from her soulmate of more than fifty years, but she remained dry-eyed and did not look back.

"Do you want me to take care of arranging a plot for dad's ashes?" Harry suggested.

"No thank you, darling; that won't be necessary."

"I see. Have you already done it?" Harry asked in surprise.

"No; he's not having one. He's going home."

"How do you mean?"

"I'm going to scatter his ashes in Kent, where he was born. I was hoping you'd come with me."

Trying to conceal his surprise, Harry replied, "Of course I will. Is that what he wanted?"

"I think so. In fact I think he would have liked to move back there; especially with all that new building going on all round us. He mentioned it earlier in the year. Of course we didn't know how little time he had left."

Harry grinned, and the irony was obviously not lost on her, because she responded with a self-conscious smile.

As if reading his mind, she said, "There's no point bringing flowers here. He won't see them. He won't *be* here. But he will be *here,*" and she placed a hand over her heart. "Always."

"You're absolutely right, mum," Harry replied. Her eyes brimmed with tears, and he squeezed her hand. "Thanks for being kind to Sally."

"There's no need to thank me for that," she said, recovering her composure. "It's times like this that make you realise what's important. There's no point trying to live in the past or worrying about what you can't do anything about. We've just got to make the best of it."

Harry gave her a brief hug. "All the same, it meant a lot to her and Grace … and to me."

They walked on for a few moments in silence, under the canopy of the trees. Then she said suddenly, "A little bird told me you've got a girlfriend; it's the first I've heard of it."

"She's not my girlfriend, mum. It's nothing serious," he replied hurriedly, feeling like an adolescent under his mother's interrogation.

"From what I hear she's got legs up to her armpits."

Harry laughed out loud at his mother's uncharacteristic turn of phrase, making her chuckle and Uncle Frank and several other family members look at him with what he took to be disapproval.

"Yes, she has got long legs. But like I said, it's not serious. We just have the odd meal or night out together."

"Alright; I suppose you're old enough to look after yourself," she said pointedly. "Just make sure you know what you're getting into. Don't get hurt like that again."

"I won't," he answered; thankful they had reached the waiting limousines.

Harry managed to exchange a few words with Sally when they returned to his mother's house. The showers forecast for the afternoon did not materialise, so they took their tea into the garden to discuss their son and his troubles, in private.

Sally was effusive in expressing her pleasure that Adam was no longer so moody and uncommunicative. "I've noticed he spends a lot less time on his Xbox and watching TV in his room," she enthused. "He told me he's got a job … of sorts. I know it's not what he wants, but it's something. At least he seems to be settling in well with you."

Stifling the thought 'If you only knew the truth', Harry replied, "Yes. It's a start, so let's hope for the best."

"Apart from the spats with Jonathan, he wasn't all that much trouble when he lived with me," Sally mused. "But it used to be hard work getting him to respond or take an interest in anything; especially his future. I can't tell you how relieved I am to know he's pulling himself together at last."

Unwilling to deflate her optimism, Harry refrained from comment, and for a while, he and Sally continued to discuss their concerns for their children, and their pride in them, the way they used to. But their life together now seemed such a long time ago, and for no reason that he could identify, he no longer felt totally at ease when he was alone with her.

The late summer sunshine eventually tempted others into the garden; one of them being Uncle Frank, who interrupted their conversation, to regale them with his stock of anecdotes about his and his late brother's childhood. They had heard the stories many times before, and considered them no less monotonous for yet another airing. Harry could not help it, but he had always found his uncle a little tedious. It made him feel guilty, because at heart, the old boy was a kindly soul. It was just that he tended to repeat the same stories every time they met, and could never resist using a sentence where a single word would suffice. However, Harry could appreciate how severely shocked Frank had been by his younger brother's death. Reminiscing about their boyhood and adolescence obviously helped to ease his grief and sense of loss. So he and Sally listened sympathetically and laughed in all the appropriate places.

Harry's mother came to their rescue by calling everyone into the house to drink a toast to her late husband. Harry was not the only one to raise an eyebrow at her choice of champagne, but as she explained, it was in celebration of her husband's life.

She had resisted Harry's attempts to persuade her to come back with him to May Cottage for a while. He suspected her decision was, in part, because she considered he needed time to himself. Thankfully, Uncle Ed and Aunt Judith were happy to stay with her for a few more days. After that, she was planning to visit Aunt Caroline for a week or two. But she promised to come and see him soon.

Adam still had a few days of work left with Sally's company, so Harry drove home alone. Thankfully, the journey was free of incident and hold-ups. He turned off at Ferndown, resisting the temptation to continue on to Sandbanks, and take the ferry to the Isle of Purbeck, and Swanage.

A few moments with Emma was just what he needed to lift his spirits, but he could think of no plausible excuse. He could hardly claim to be 'just passing through' on today of all days. Turning up straight from his father's funeral would hardly impress her.

He had completely misjudged his mother. He had expected her to be grief-stricken for a long time, if not for the rest of her life. But after the first few days of shock and distress, she had displayed an inner strength he had not anticipated. She had also come to some unexpectedly practical decisions about her future; hinting that she might consider Aunt Caroline's offer to move in with her.

The irony of that made him smile. After all the fruitless attempts he had made to persuade his parents to move, it transpired that his father had been hankering to move back to Kent, and now, his mother was considering moving to Devon. However, knowing her as he did, Harry doubted she would actually do so. The likelihood was that, once things had settled down, the comfort and familiarity of the house she had lived in for so many years would outweigh other considerations.

Thankfully his father's will was uncomplicated and his role as executor would amount to little more than the transfer of the jointly held assets to his mother. Harry made a mental note to speak to her about making a new will, once the dust had settled.

He arrived home tired and depressed, to find he had two voicemail messages. One was from Doug Waghorne, the managing director of a company which had once been a client of Eldon Management Services. Doug wanted him to call back, a soon as he could. The other message was from Simon, inviting him to supper, whenever he felt in need of company.

Harry decided to put off calling Doug for a day or so, and feeling that he had earned it, poured himself a sizeable scotch, before settling down with the *Daily Telegraph* in the sitting room. It did not take long to come to the conclusion that reading about other people's misfortunes and the vacuous posturing of celebrities and politicians was doing nothing to help dispel his melancholy.

He felt the need for fresh air, and leaving the newspaper and the scotch untouched, he wandered in the direction of the village, with no particular destination in mind. As he crossed the green, his thoughts filled with reminiscences of his childhood; of cricket in the garden on summer evenings, when his father had bowled gentle off-breaks for him to drive into the shrubbery; of intricate sandcastles built together on sunlit beaches; of school rugger matches on winter afternoons, with dad amongst the other fathers, muffled against the biting cold, calling encouragement from the touchline. But most of all, he remembered the patience, understanding and comforting reassurance of his father's love.

Passing the chattering children on the swings and the groups seated at the rustic tables outside *The Black Bull*, Harry made his way between the ancient cottages in Church Lane to the churchyard. At the lychgate, he stopped to look over the wall at some weatherworn headstones, whose epitaphs were now all but erased. Despite the lichen and the flaking surface of the stone, he could still make out some of the names and dates. One read; Edwin Meredith Stainsbridge 1729-1812 and below it, the faint trace of the name Elizabeth; probably his wife.

"Not a bad innings for those days," Harry said out loud. It led him to wonder about Edwin and Elizabeth, and their lives in a very different Nethercombe Ley, almost three hundred years ago.

The church door was ajar, and on an impulse, Harry went through the lychgate and along the worn, uneven paving towards the porch. Recognising the musty odour of aged wood and fabric, he peered around the door, surprised by how light and spacious it was inside. The church was deserted, so cautiously and self-consciously, he went in.

His attention was immediately captured by rainbow-coloured beams of the evening sun, which streamed through a corner of a stained glass window, illuminating the lead-framed panes in radiant hues and igniting the cross above altar in a blaze of gleaming gold. Harry walked slowly between the stone pillars of the nave towards the large lectern carved in the shape of an eagle with its wings spread. Sliding into one of the front pews, he gazed up at the stone pulpit at the head of four well-worn steps set in a carved, wooden screen, which masked a rank of organ pipes. Disappointingly, there was no tomb topped by an effigy of a knight in final repose, but there were several ornate memorial plaques, with flower-filled vases, in niches on either side of the nave.

Comforted by the stillness and quiet, Harry watched the dust motes hovering in the tinted sunbeams, and allowed himself the indulgence of a silent, but guilt-ridden, prayer for his father, in whatever hereafter there may be. The guilt was for resorting to prayer, contrary to his religious doubts and indifference, and for so many things he had neglected to say or do before it was too late. Bowing his head, he made no attempt to stem the tears blurring his vision.

It was a few moments before he sensed that he was not alone. Looking up he saw Simon watching him from the doorway to the vestry. Harry smiled weakly, and Simon's expression changed from concern to compassion.

"I hope I'm not intruding. The door was open and it all looked so peaceful," Harry said, hurriedly brushing away his tears.

Simon came towards him. "It's God's house," he said. "He welcomes us all, especially when we need comfort and peace."

Harry shook his head. "I just can't get it into my head that my dad's gone and I'll never see him or have the chance to speak to him again."

Simon squeezed into the pew beside him. "I know; the finality is bewildering. It takes time."

"Have you lost your father?" Harry asked.

"Well, yes and no," Simon replied. "He's still alive, as far as I know. The last I heard, he was living in Cape Town. I haven't seen him since he left my mother more than thirty years ago."

"Is that by choice?" Harry suggested. "Not seeing him I mean."

"It's his choice. He's never made any attempt to contact us. No birthday cards or presents; nothing. I wrote to him when I was ordained, and again shortly before Zoe and I were married, but he never replied to either letter."

"That's sad," Harry sighed. "I don't understand how anyone can just walk away from their family."

"I suppose he had his reasons," said Simon wistfully. "It affected Rachel more than me; she being a little older."

"So what made you choose the church?" Harry asked. "I assumed your father was a clergyman or something."

"My stepfather was an army chaplain. He was a wonderful man. He couldn't have been a better father to Rachel and me if we'd been his own flesh and blood."

Harry grinned self-consciously. "You make me feel guilty for bemoaning my lot. I had a wonderful, carefree childhood, with two loving parents. I didn't even have to share them with a brother or sister."

"That's nothing to feel guilty about. It's something to be grateful for," said Simon.

Harry sighed. "I suppose you're right."

"I'll leave you in peace and contemplation," Simon said gently. "I respect your doubts about religion, but if it you feel it might help, I could suggest some passages that may bring a little comfort."

"Thank you Simon. You've helped me already, but I'll bear that in mind."

Simon stood up. "The choir won't arrive for practice for another hour or more. You won't be disturbed before then. If you leave before they arrive, just close the door behind you, if you will. I'll come over and lock up later. By the way, if you feel up to it, you're very welcome at Church House for supper … when you're ready."

Patting Harry's shoulder, Simon rose to his feet and slipped away quietly.

Pulling up his collar and tucking his chin into his chest, Harry leaned into the wind that roared through the trees above his head, whipping the upper branches into a flailing frenzy and rocking the lower boughs, until they swayed and creaked alarmingly. Twigs and foliage fell swirling and spinning, to be swept across the village green amongst the tumbling leaves. From behind one of the cottages, a swinging gate hinge added its banshee shriek to the unearthly howl.

The canvas covering the charred remains of the shop flapped and snapped in the savage gusts, a poignant reminder of how much it had meant to the community. Walking the extra distance to the church hall annexe for a newspaper and a few essentials was no hardship; at least not in calmer weather, but the loss amounted to more than the contents of its shelves and the inconvenience of no longer having a post office. The shop had been where neighbours met to gossip and exchange pleasantries and local news; welcomed by its hospitable proprietors. Despite the cheerful goodwill of the volunteers who ran the Community Market, it seemed to Harry that Nethercombe Ley was a poorer place without Peggy's guileless good nature and Ted's wry humour.

Although they had both displayed confidence and optimism the last time he had seen them, Ted had lost an alarming amount of weight, leaving Harry with the suspicion that his condition was more serious than they realised, or perhaps would admit.

Having dropped off Rob's newspaper and one or two groceries for Ellen, he was glad to gain the sanctuary of home. It was only when he was settled at the kitchen table with a mug of coffee, that he noticed the date at the head of the newspaper, and felt his throat constrict.

Did Sally remember what today was? Was she thinking of this day, twenty-four years ago, when they had stood side by side before the altar and made their marriage vows? He swallowed hard. Even with celebrations muted by his father's death, it would still have been a day to cherish.

He remembered his nervousness and the elation of turning to see her coming down the aisle towards him, smiling and radiant. A kaleidoscope of images flooded his mind; the thrill of beginning their life together; the joy when their children were born and of watching them grow; the satisfaction of their achievements and the contentment of their life together.

But it had not lasted for Sally. He had no idea how long she had made herself endure the frustration of a marriage that no longer fulfilled her. He had assumed it began when the children grew up, but he was no longer sure. Had she stayed with him, would she have felt no more than the obligation to celebrate another year of marriage, when in her heart there was no real joy?

It did not matter anymore. Although at moments like this, memories of his life with her tugged at his heart-strings, he no longer thought of her as 'his Sally'. Did she ever think of those halcyon days when they had been young and in love? She had loved him then; he had no doubt about that. Did she realise what today was, and did she remember … the way he remembered?

He envied Simon his strength and resilience, when he had enjoyed such a tragically short time before happiness had been so cruelly snatched from him. Harry thought of the petite bride in the photograph above Simon's fireplace, and marvelled at his friend's ability to talk about her with calmness and composure. There must still be pain and anguish beneath that tranquil facade; especially when he had to comfort others in times of sorrow and misfortune.

Harry had experienced that compassion and the strength of Simon's faith, when he had supper at Church House. He had remained in the church for some time after Simon left, with his mind a maelstrom of random thoughts and emotions, until the light had faded and the burnished gleam of the cross had dimmed.

While they ate, Simon had said little, encouraging Harry to talk about whatever came to mind; merely prompting when he had felt it might help to elucidate or help Harry to deal with his confused feelings. Later, over coffee in the sitting room, their conversation had become more general and relaxed; and had inevitably turned to Rachel.

"I've never asked you before, but I hope you don't have any reservations about my relationship with Rachel," Harry had asked cautiously.

"Goodness no; why should I?"

"Well, brothers often feel protective of their sisters, don't they?"

"I wasn't aware Rachel was in need of my protection," Simon had chuckled.

"I understand she's had a pretty tough time in recent years."

Simon had frowned. "Oh you mean her marriage. It grieves me to say it, but I wasn't too surprised it didn't last. I sincerely hoped it would, but Rachel has always been impulsive. The first I knew of it was when she called me on honeymoon in Hawaii."

"What did you make of her husband … Karl isn't it?" Harry had asked tentatively.

"I only met him a few times, when they came over. They usually stayed in London or occasionally with our mother. They only came here for a couple of brief visits. There wasn't much chance to get to know Karl. He was polite and amiable, but seemed a little brash. I got the impression he could be quite volatile. I must confess I had reservations about the combination of that and Rachel's impetuous nature."

"Do you think Rachel will want a divorce eventually?" Harry had asked.

"I don't know. But my guess would be yes. Why do you ask?"

"No reason. It's just that Rachel said there was no chance of them getting back together, so it seems odd that they're still married."

Simon had smiled enigmatically. "Impulsiveness is not Rachel's only trait. She's also capable of ignoring anything she chooses not to contemplate. But I suspect the real reason is that she finds it useful at the moment, as a means of deterring the possibility of making a similar mistake again."

Harry had felt his cheeks burn, and had retorted, "I can assure you I don't have any illusions about that!"

"Harry please!" Simon had held up a hand. "That's not what I meant. Your relationship with Rachel is none of my business. But if you and she were intending to marry, I would feel nothing but joy for both of you."

Harry had grinned ruefully. "I'm not ready for anything permanent, and Rachel warned me from the outset not to expect our relationship to go beyond where it is now. I can't say I blame her. I'm sure Sally wouldn't."

Simon had reached out and patted his arm. "Harry, that's utter nonsense. Rachel's an attractive and desirable woman … yes vicars do know words like that. But you shouldn't assume her reluctance to form a permanent relationship is about you. I happen to know she's very fond of you. She admires you; and if she doesn't want anything more at the moment, it's not because of you or your imagined imperfections. I'm saying this as a friend, Harry; you've got to stop punishing yourself for what's happened with your marriage. Stop deceiving yourself that everything was your fault. From what you've told me of Sally, I'm sure she doesn't feel that way at all."

Simon's forthrightness had made him feel a little awkward, and he had responded, as he often did in such situations, with an attempt at humour. "Anyway; I'm not sure I could cope with having your sister for a wife."

"Perhaps it's you I'd need to feel protective about," Simon had countered, and with the tension eased, their laughter had been spontaneous.

Before he left, Harry had remembered something which had been at the back of his mind for some time. "By the way; does St. Luke's have bells?"

"Yes it does," Simon had answered; his smile revealing that he had understood the reason for the question. "But I'm afraid you won't hear them for months … maybe as long as another year."

"What a shame," Harry had replied. "I love the sound of church bells. I imagine it's disappointing for couples getting married."

Simon had nodded in agreement. "Yes; I've had to disappoint several couples. The bells were removed because of structural faults discovered when the bell loft was inspected last year. We're still waiting for the go-ahead to get the work done."

Encouraged by Simon's gentle counselling, Harry had spoken about his concern for his mother's future and his unfulfilled hope of rebuilding his relationship with Adam. He had even joined Simon in a brief prayer, without feeling guilty or embarrassed.

By the time he had left, Harry had felt more relaxed and at ease in his mind.

Harry found Marjorie sitting at the kitchen table when he arrived home from having two new front tyres fitted on his car; the cost, together with wheel balancing and tracking adjustment, resulting in what he thought of as a 'surgical operation on his wallet'.

It surprised him to see that she was sewing a button on one of Adam's shirts. Beside her on the worktop was a pile of his clothes, freshly ironed and folded.

"What's this? You're not still doing his washing and ironing?" Harry exclaimed incredulously. "After the way he's treated you?"

She grinned and pointed to the impressive bouquet that all but filled the sink. "I think we're managing to sort things out," she said quietly.

Harry could recognise Chrysanthemums, Begonias and Lilies amongst the colourful array of blooms and greenery. "They must have cost him a packet," he said. "I hope they came with a grovelling apology."

She nodded and giggled almost girlishly. "They did. And you can add shuffling in here on his knees."

Harry felt almost heady with relief. "So does that mean we can forget all that nonsense about me finding someone else?"

"I suppose so," she replied. "If that's alright with you."

"Thank God!" was all Harry could manage by way of a reply. "But even so, that's not your job. I've told him he has to do his own laundry … and sew his own damn buttons on!"

Marjorie bit off the end of the cotton and grinned. "I know, but have you seen it after he's done it. You wouldn't know his clothes had been near an iron."

"That's not the point. You do enough around here already … and after the way he's treated you! I've told him enough times about all this 'Marjie' business, too!"

She looked at him in amusement. "I wouldn't worry too much about that; it's just his way. I think we're managing to sort it all out between us, so don't worry. He didn't ask me to do his laundry. Anyway, I'd rather do it than see him going about looking like a tramp."

"I don't know how he does it," Harry sighed. "He seems to be able to blag and charm his way out of everything".

"It's probably hereditary," she said impishly.

Harry chuckled. "You could be right. From what my mother says, he's probably inherited the charm from his grandfather."

Marjorie smiled in amusement. "He's not short of courage, either," she said, and in response to Harry's quizzical look, she continued, "Don't tell him I told you, but while you were away, he came all the way down here ... on the train, to apologise and beg me not to leave."

"Really?"

"Yes; I'm not supposed to say a word about it, so don't let on I told you. He just turned up on my doorstep and begged me to let him apologise for everything he'd said and done to upset me. He *did* as well; in front of Phil and Gary ... and my other son, Sean and Barbara, his wife. He told me there was no need for me to go, because he's going to look for another job and find somewhere else to live. He said he was going 'get out of your hair' as he put it."

Her eyes glistened with tears. "He broke down Harry. He said that everything I said was true ... I'm afraid I've said a lot more than I should at times, but it *was* said in anger. I tried to tell him not to be silly, but he said you and his mother would be better off without him, and he didn't intend being a burden to you anymore."

Harry handed her a tissue to wipe her eyes, while he tried to absorb what she had said.

"I think losing his granddad like that has hit him hard," she sniffed.

"I'm sure it has," Harry said quietly. "Where is he by the way?"

Marjorie nodded towards the window, and looking out, Harry could hardly believe his eyes. Alfie and Rob were chatting over the fence and beyond them Gary was turning over another weed-strewn area bordering the vegetable garden. Behind Gary, Adam was raking the earth and pulling out weeds and dead roots.

"Good grief!" Harry exclaimed. "He must be ill ... delirious I should think!" But his attempt at humour felt hollow. Marjorie's answering smile revealed that his attempt to hide his feelings had failed.

"What brought that on?" Harry asked.

"You'd better ask him," she chuckled. Her smile faded, and she added, "Talk to him Harry; he needs you. You need each other!"

As he went into the garden, Adam's embarrassed grin allowed Harry's mischievous instincts to overcome his emotions. "I see you've had to take on extra labour, Alfie," he quipped.

Alfie chuckled in response, and Harry's attention was drawn to the sheen of perspiration on Adam's forehead and the redness of his face.

Adam grinned sheepishly and leaned on the rake. "I was like, press ganged!" he exclaimed. "Don't let all this fool you, right. Gary and I are digging an escape tunnel!"

Harry had to curb an overwhelming urge to hug his son.

"They bin at it all mornin'," Rob chuckled. "So by my reckonin', they oughta come up under my rhubarb."

"It's about time to knock off now, anyway," said Alfie. "I'm ready for a pint; how about you Rob?"

"That's not a bad idea," Rob replied. "What about you 'Arry? You lads fancy a pint?"

"I've got a couple of calls to make first," Harry answered. "But I'll join you in half an hour or so."

"Sounds like a plan," Gary said. "You up for it Adam?"

Adam hesitated. "Well … I like …"

Harry put his hand on his shoulder. "Go on; you've earned it!" Taking out his wallet, he handed Adam a twenty pound note. "Which reminds me. I went to the cash machine on the way home. Here's the twenty quid I borrowed yesterday."

Adam looked momentarily puzzled, until he realised what his father was doing, and smiled diffidently. "It can wait dad." Making sure no-one could overhear, he added, "Thanks dad, but no. I owe you big time already. I don't know how I'm ever going to repay you."

Gesturing towards the house, Harry replied, "You've made a pretty decent start already!"

Pushing the note into Adam's hand, he said, "I'll see you in *The King's Head* in about half an hour. We'll see what they've got to offer for lunch. But when we get home, you and I are going to have a long heart-to-heart talk."

Harry stood at a window in the sitting room with a wry smile, as he watched the red Mini pull out into the lane. The incongruous pyramid on its roof sported a large red 'L' with the legend *Amie's Driving Academy* on each side.

Although it was some time since Adam had last had a driving lesson, it did not appear to have affected his confidence. He had greeted his instructor with no sign of apprehension or nervousness. The fact that she was an attractive brunette, no doubt made the prospect less stressful, and remembering from his youth how fickle a young male heart can be, Harry wondered mischievously if she might come to rival Laura in Adam's affections.

With Adam's return, life had become livelier … and noisier. But now he had made peace with Marjorie, May Cottage was the better for his presence. In Harry's opinion, even the assault on his ears by the relentless thump of the dirges Adam called music was a price worth paying.

Working in the garden appeared to have a beneficial effect. Adam had lost, what to Harry's eyes, had seemed the scrawny, slightly ill-kempt look of previous months. He appeared to have put on a little weight too. Encouragingly, he needed no persuading to accompany Harry on visits to Grandma Marian.

There had been the occasional mention of someone called Sharon. Harry presumed it was a girl who worked with Sally, but whoever Sharon was, she did not appear to have taken pride of place in his affections. He still hung on Laura's every word and gazed at her with scarcely concealed adoration whenever they met. Harry would not have been surprised if he had taken up riding.

The change in Adam's relationship with Marjorie was unmistakable. She appeared to have won not just his respect, but his affection. Their good natured bantering, which included Gary when he was around, often left Harry and Alfie as bemused onlookers. Adam still retained the irritating habit of calling her *Marjie,* but this did not concern her in the slightest. Brushing aside Harry's protests, she seemed happy to provide coffee on-tap, and cakes and pastries for *'The Three Secateurs'*, as Adam had dubbed Alfie's little band.

The only problem with Marjorie was her opposition to Harry's suggestion that he should increase her wages, to take account of the extra laundry, Adam's ironing and the countless other small and thoughtful things she did for both of them.

Adam had acquired a bike on eBay to get to work. As well as working with Alfie and Gary in the garden, he had taken over Harry's role of running errands for Ellen Hardy to the community market and the small parade of shops on the high road. He could do no wrong in her eyes and regularly went missing, only to be found on the other side of the fence, helping her and Rob, or enjoying a cup of tea and a slice of home-baked cake.

"'Es a lovely boy," Ellen cooed. "I'm so glad you made it up with 'im, Harry."

To Harry's undisguised amusement and surprise, Adam had announced that he intended to celebrate his birthday, at the beginning of October, hill-walking in Cumbria with his friend Ollie, Gary and one of Gary's army pals. Harry would have loved to witness Sally's reaction when she heard the news.

Returning to his study, Harry glanced at the letter from Doug Waghorne which lay on his desk. He remembered the letter-head from several years ago. Eldon Management Services had been contracted to advise on an overhaul of the management structure of a medium sized group of engineering companies, of which Doug had been, and still was, the CEO. As Eldon's project director for the contract, Harry had worked closely with Doug, and a mutual respect and friendship had ensued.

A man who knew his own mind, Doug had tracked Harry down. When Harry, had returned Doug's call, he had learned that Doug saw him as the man to advise them on restructuring the organisation, with a view to expanding into a new area of business. They had met to discuss it over lunch in Leicester, where the group had its headquarters. Doug had put on weight and lost some of his hair since the last time they had met, but he had not changed in any other way. Harry had found the idea of working with him again very tempting; especially as the work would not start until the New Year, by which time his contract with ACCORS would have ended.

The prospect of several months of interesting and challenging work, after the tedium and internal politics of a quango, was appealing. However, Harry was loath to commit to something he knew would consume a great deal of his time, while his mother's needs and future were uncertain,

She had not yet made up her mind where she intended to live, and he had no intention of trying to hurry her into a decision, or leaving her to cope on her own. Sympathising with his problem, Doug had allowed him a little time to make up his mind. But a decision would have to be made … and soon.

Guy watched his ball fly off the tee and arc towards a clump of trees and shrubs, yards to the right of the fairway. The distinctive *clack* of ball on wood told its own story; as did the flurry of leaves that spiralled down lazily to join the yellow-gold carpet of those already strewn beneath the foliage.

"Sorry partner," he sighed.

"Forget it. We're here for a bit of fun; that's all," Harry replied.

It was the eighteenth hole, and as any chance of a respectable score had disappeared by the thirteenth, Harry saw no point in giving way to disappointment. His own ball was nestling in a deep fairway bunker, so he could predict, with some confidence, that they would fail to score on yet another hole.

"I'll take a provisional," Guy declared resignedly. Teeing up a second ball, he promptly hooked it into the brook running parallel to the left-hand side of the fairway.

"Something ending in 'ocks'!" he said bitterly.

"Never mind; we might find your first one," Alan suggested. In Harry's opinion the remark had been made more in sympathy than conviction. Alan could afford to be magnanimous; his ball and that of his partner were clearly visible on the fairway, two hundred yards or so ahead.

Accepting Alan Anderson's invitation to enter his golf club's charity pairs competition had seemed to Harry an ideal way to unwind and relax after the trauma of the previous weeks; even though he had not swung a club for over a year.

Guy played most Saturdays, and had seemed an ideal choice of partner. He certainly looked the part; immaculately turned out in grey slacks and a pale blue sweater over a silver-grey polo shirt, both of which bore his own club's logo. A white flat cap and two-tone black and white golf shoes completed the picture of the 'golfer-about-town'.

However, Guy's golf mirrored his lifestyle; colourful and sometimes erratic. He was capable of producing excellent drives and iron shots amongst the misfires. He could putt like a demon, but his problem throughout the round had been getting his ball near enough to the hole to enable him to do so. Harry's golf had been equally unpredictable and had displayed all the hallmarks of a long lay-off. But a few hours in the fresh air, coupled with Alan's irrepressible humour and his partner Keith's dry wit had provided a much needed pick-me-up.

"So, in my guise of the almighty press, where are we with the Christmas lights and the community market?" Alan asked, as they followed Guy from the tee and made their way to where they estimated his first ball had landed.

Harry sighed, "Well, if we ignore the minefield of health and safety requirements and the intransigence of the banks, they're both coming along nicely."

Alan looked puzzled. "What's the problem with the banks?"

"Basically, getting them to give us a deal that doesn't saddle the operation with crippling charges and restrictions," Harry explained.

"Surely, all you need is a simple current account?" Keith suggested.

"That's just it," Harry replied. "I don't know if Alan has mentioned it, but a bunch of young hooligans set fire to the village shop a few months ago."

Keith's eyebrows rose, and Harry continued. "We believe it was done to get even with Peggy … she and her husband used to run the shop. She identified the yobs who vandalised the swings on the village green and defaced the war memorial."

"So they burnt the bloody shop down?" Keith exclaimed incredulously. "Was anybody hurt?"

"No, thank God!" Alan answered. "But the girl who works for Peggy and Ted was trapped upstairs in the shop. If it hadn't been for Harry and our local vicar …"

"That's neither here nor there!" Harry interjected hurriedly. "Apparently the shop will have to be pulled down, but the organisation that owns the property doesn't seem interested in replacing it. The idea of putting up one or two houses is more appealing; and undoubtedly more lucrative."

Keith replied with an understanding shrug.

"It looks like we could lose the post office for good," Harry added. "That, and the loss of the shop, will be particularly difficult for our elderly inhabitants and inconvenient for a lot of others. We've set up something we're calling a 'Community Market', for want of a better name, in the annexe to the church hall. It's mainly for basics, but it's meant to give people a chance to sell locally grown produce, as well."

Keith nodded. "So you need the services of a friendly bank for that?"

"Yes; the operation is intended to be non-profit making. Any surplus it does make will be used for the benefit of the community as a whole. There's no shortage of volunteers to man it and bring in groceries and newspapers and things, but ideally, we could do with a modest overdraft facility. That would allow us to hold a small stock of basic items. Most banks don't seem interested. The only one that *is* prepared to play ball wants personal guarantees from what they call 'trustees'. The charges they're quoting are ridiculous! At the moment, we're relying on a short-term loan from The Friends of St. Luke's Church and people paying in advance for what they want brought in. It creates paperwork and it's particularly hard on the elderly and the not so well off."

"Do you have any ideas, Keith?" Alan asked. By way of explanation, he added, "Keith is in financial advisory services."

"We're only small beer. I doubt our problem would interest the big boys," said Harry.

"Remind me when we get back to the locker room and I'll give you a contact that might be willing to help," Keith replied. "The person I have in mind, Val Cooke, runs a small business advisory service. I'll have a word with her and tell her to expect a call from you, if you like. She might be able to oil the wheels or put you on to someone who can do something for you."

"Thanks very much," said Harry.

"I can't guarantee anything, but Val's been helpful to several of our clients."

"Any help is much appreciated," Harry replied.

When they caught up with Guy, he was already poking about in the dense shrubbery, and directing a stream of colourful language to where he imagined his wayward ball to be hidden.

"Give it up Guy!" said Harry. "We aren't about to trouble the scorers. If Emma's picking you up after dinner, why don't we call it a day, get showered and changed, and drown our sorrows?"

The frown disappeared from Guy's brow. "That's the best suggestion I've heard all bloody day!" he exclaimed.

Harry gave Jill a peck on the cheek to thank her for the lift, as he got out of the Anderson's car. He had to help Alan, who was in a state that Harry's mother would call 'pickled'. Guy had been little better, when Emma arrived in Fritz to collect him from the golf club.

She had rolled those lovely eyes at Harry, and adopted a pained expression, when Guy had greeted her expansively; batting away his restless hands and turning her face away as he flopped onto the seat beside her and attempted to bestow an inebriated kiss on her lips.

"D'you need a ride home, Harry?" she had asked.

"Thanks; but Jill and Alan are giving me a lift," he had replied, trying not to show his irritation at Guy's ill concealed amorous intentions.

As if sensing it, she had added, "Pity; it means I'll have to cope with Wolstencroft the human octopus on my own … at least until he falls asleep. From experience, that won't be long. I'll be amazed if he makes it out of the car park!"

Guy had grinned and raised his hand in a parting salute, as Emma revved the engine and pulled away.

Harry had carefully paced himself throughout the pre-dinner drinks and the meal, restricting himself to a couple of pints and a glass of wine. He was proud of having managed to control his drinking over the past year, and had no inclination to spoil his record; especially now that Adam was living with him again.

By the time the dinner was over; the speeches made and prizes awarded, half the seventy or so participants had been red faced and boisterous; greeting each winner with banter and raucous comments as they collected their prize.

The award for 'Best Endeavours' had taken Harry and Guy by surprise. Neither had expected to receive anything for coming last, but they had been called forward to receive a bottle of wine each. Being guests, they had received a more restrained and polite reception.

* * *

By the time he arrived home, Harry's jealous annoyance with Guy had been replaced by contentment; until he pushed the '*play messages*' button on his telephone console.

"Hello Harry. It's Pat … Pat Buckler."

"Oh, God no!" he groaned. He was about to stop the message, when it continued, "I've only just heard the news about your sad loss Harry. John and I would like to offer our sincere condolences. I'm sure the Christmas lights have been the last thing on your mind. Regarding our meeting tomorrow, I just wanted to let you know that I've investigated prices with local wholesalers, so you don't need to worry about that. If there's anything else I can do to take the burden of that off you, please don't hesitate to get in touch. My number's on the schedule I've e-mailed to everyone on the committee. Once again, my commiserations. Bye."

"Well I'm blowed!" Harry exclaimed in amazement. "Who'd have thought it! Who would have damned well thought it!"

"This is a comparison of the quotes we've received from electrical contractors so far," Harry explained, handing copies to the committee members assembled in the Spenser-Smith's impressive drawing room. "We asked them to quote separately for supply and installation and the other electrical fittings we'll need; and for installation only. From the enquiries Pat has made with wholesalers, it seems that the supply and install option works out on average six-percent cheaper. That's due to discounts the contactors can get that are not available to us."

"And it's within our budget!" Pat interjected enthusiastically.

"Does this include the Christmas tree?" Carol asked.

"Oh yes!" Pat exclaimed. "It's all included!"

"Well yes; but it only covers the illuminations, of course," Harry explained. "We have to provide the tree. I believe Jane has that in hand. The quotes for illuminations are based on her projection of something twenty to twenty-five feet high."

Jane nodded in response. "I can get a seven-metre Norway Spruce from a chap I've done business with in the West Midlands, for around three-seventy-five. That includes delivery, but not erection, of course."

"Will that be big enough?" Pat asked.

"Seven metres is nearly twenty-three feet; that's roughly the height of a two-storey building," Jane replied, barely concealing her irritation. "That ought to be plenty for the village green."

"Oh, that's big enough alright!" Gerald exclaimed, and received approving nods in response. "Where are we with '*Elf an' Safety*' Maurice?"

"There are one or two issues with siting and shielding the electrical cabling. They want the safety barriers out further from the tree, too; but nothing important. We should get the go ahead by the end of the month."

"And you Carol, are organising the lighting-up ceremony with Robert, and co-ordinating it with Simon." Gerald's statement, although benign, was more of an enquiry about progress.

Carol replied in that vein, with a glance and a smile at Simon. "We thought a carol service would be nice. We're also looking into the possibility of getting a celebrity to switch the lights on. Somebody we can afford, of course. Hopefully, whoever it is will attract a good crowd."

Pat raised her hand, as if holding up traffic. "Wouldn't a local dignitary; like our Member of Parliament, be more appropriate?" Her question was more of a statement.

It prompted a vigorous shake of the head from Gerald. "Not in my book!" he exclaimed. "This is meant to be a bit special; to put Nethercombe on the map! If we can get a celebrity, let's go for it. We won't have any trouble finding a tame politician or what-have-you, if we can't get anybody else!"

Everyone else agreed, and Carol continued. "Robert is getting quotes for posters, and he's been talking to the local press. As you know he's damaged his back. He won't be on his feet again for another week or so. But he's sure that, if we do manage to get a celebrity, we'll almost certainly get the local press and radio interested ... possibly even TV coverage."

"How are we doing for sponsors?" Harry asked. In response to the blank looks from Carol and several others, he continued, "I was just thinking, if we get a celebrity's name on the posters, we might tempt one or two local companies to sponsor us. The coverage could make it worth their while."

"Of course! Why didn't I bloody-well think of that?" Gerald exclaimed.

It drew an instant rebuke from Pat. "Mr. Spenser-Smith! May I remind you that you are chair of this meeting? Please moderate your language!"

Gerald threw her a brief and amused, "Sorry Pat", before bestowing a broad smile on everyone. "Excellent! I think we can leave the details of the carol service to Simon," he added archly.

"Yes," Simon replied. "Assuming we choose a convenient date, we should be alright as far as St. Luke's choir is concerned." With a gentle smile, he added, "Fortunately, there doesn't seem to be much else for me to worry about. Everything seems to be very well in hand."

"It does indeed," Gerald beamed. "Well done team!"

"What's our next project, then?" Maurice asked mischievously.

Gerald held up a fore-finger in reply, as if about to conduct them in song. "You may well ask. Organising the New Year's Eve Ball is taken care of ... for this year. But I understand the Parish Council wouldn't be averse to us taking that off their hands next year. They want to retain control of the May Fayre, of course. It's too much for us to take on, anyway. But they see this committee taking the burden of the smaller events off, what they see as, their overfull plate."

"Not to mention some of the cost!" Jane interjected pointedly.

Gerald chuckled. "Yes; and some of the cost. But ... ," he continued, "I've been thinking. How do you feel about a Saint Valentine's Ball?" Glancing around at the assembly, he added, "Any comments ... for it, or agin it?"

"Oh; yes!" Pat exclaimed enthusiastically.

"Why not?" Harry said. He had meant it as no more than a casual remark, but Carol giggled. "I didn't realise you were such a romantic, Harry," she said impishly.

"Oh, I'm sure there are sides to our Harry we could never imagine!" Gerald exclaimed, with a mischievous grin. "Rescuing maidens in distress is only one of his many facets!"

Harry felt his cheeks flush, but he had to smile. "I'm sorry I spoke. Are you ever going to let me forget that?"

Gerald burst out laughing. "Of course not! You were mean, moody and magnificent on that ladder, Harry. I shall never forget the way you laid into the *Old Bill* when they tried to stop you!"

Harry looked to Simon for support, but could see that his friend was finding it difficult to restrain his amusement. His face was creased by an impish grin.

Losing his own battle to keep a straight face, Harry said, "I was going to offer to buy you all a drink afterwards! But I'm having second thoughts; you rotten lot!"

"That's as good a reason I can think of to wind things up and spare Harry's blushes," Gerald replied. "Unless anyone has anything else to contribute."

*'We plough the fields and scatter the good seed on the land ...'* Harry lifted his voice with the rest of the congregation, in the ageless celebration of another harvest.

He could not fully explain why he was there, even to himself. He did not believe it was because of any deep religious conviction. He suspected it was, in part, a reaction to his father's death. A need for solace and comfort in a shared experience. He would admit that it was also to please Simon, whose compassionate understanding and companionship had sustained him in his struggle to overcome his grief. Another factor was that he now liked to think of himself as part of the village community, for which seasonal celebrations and traditions hold a significance no longer relevant in urban life.

* * *

He had slipped into the church unobtrusively and seated himself behind the rest of the congregation. It had been some moments before Simon had seen him, as he delivered his opening address. His surprise and pleasure had been evident in his smile. Seated several rows ahead of Harry, Laura had noticed Simon's reaction, and turning to follow his gaze, had rewarded Harry with her own welcoming smile.

To his embarrassment, it had attracted the attention of Lady Diana. Her comical mime had suggested she was inviting him to join her and Sir George and Lady Woodleigh in the front pews. It had caused several other heads to turn towards him in curiosity. Feeling embarrassed and self-conscious, Harry had pretended to misunderstand, and replied by raising his hand in greeting, as they had stood to sing '*For the beauty of the earth …*'

During the service, he had taken his cue from the regular worshippers, participating as best he could, and making the unfamiliar responses hesitantly and awkwardly.

\* \* \*

Now, as they sang the final hymn, it was surprising to realise that he found the experience uplifting. He assumed it was largely due to the pleasure of joining everyone in singing familiar, well-loved hymns. But the flowers and corn dollies adorning the pews and niches around the church, together with the laden altar, bedecked and surrounded with what Simon had eloquently described as '*God's earthly bounty*', had induced unexpected feelings of contentment and wellbeing.

The service closed with Simon's blessing, and picking up his coat from the pew beside him, Harry made to leave. As he did so, he heard Laura call to him, and looked back to see her indicating some trestle tables laden with cakes and crockery in a corner, beyond the font.

"Aren't you staying for coffee Harry?" she asked, making her way towards him through the chattering throng beginning to fill the aisle.

"I didn't realise refreshments were included in the price of a ticket," he answered impishly.

She giggled girlishly. "Oh yes; we have cake and a cuppa once a month; and at special times of the year, like now, at our Christmas Carol Service and at Easter. We ladies have set up an informal rota to provide the cakes. I'd avoid the coffee sponge if I were you; I made it."

"It looks delicious," Harry replied gallantly. "I'm very partial to coffee sponge."

"Harry; how lovely to see you!"

He turned at the sound of Simon's voice, and returned the greeting self-consciously, wondering what excuse he could offer for being there. But Simon's expression made it perfectly clear that he had no interest in the reason. He could probably explain it better than Harry, anyway.

The sight of his friend in his *working clothes*, as Simon was apt to describe them, still seemed somewhat incongruous. They made him appear even larger.

"I enjoyed the service," Harry said. "It was so … what's the word; joyous!"

"Thank you Harry. That's the intention. This is our way of celebrating God's gift of the harvest. We ask for His blessing on the offerings you see at the altar, before it all goes to the Salvation Army hostel and a few other local charities."

"That's wonderful. I can add some fruit and vegetables, unless you have enough already."

"We never have enough for the needy," Simon replied. "Your contribution would be very much appreciated."

Their conversation was interrupted by Laura returning with a tray laden with steaming beakers. "Here you are; black coffee for you Harry, and white for you Simon."

They both thanked her, each gingerly claiming a hot mug from the tray.

"Help yourself to cake, Harry," she said. "But don't feel obliged to have any of mine."

"I fully intend to enjoy a piece of your coffee sponge," he replied.

"So do I!" Lady Diana exclaimed over his shoulder. "It looks delicious, doesn't it Harry?"

It was almost three quarters of an hour later when he left the church, refreshed in body and spirit. Contrary to his fears, no-one had seemed disconcerted by or overly curious about his presence there, and he had been welcomed by several people he had never met before.

'It's a bit like a club,' he mused. 'But a friendly one for all that.'

# OCTOBER

## *Making Plans*

Rachel's smile was half mischievous, half quizzical. "So how do you fancy skiing?" she asked.

"Skiing; me?"

"Why not?" she replied, cupping her wine glass between her hands.

"Because I'm forty-seven years old and I've never been near a pair of skis in my life!"

"So what? There's a first time for everything. It's not that difficult to get the hang of it; a bit like riding a bike."

"I broke my arm falling off a bike," Harry quipped. "I stand every chance of breaking my bloody neck on skis!"

Rachel's eyes sparkled and she broke into one of her earthy chuckles. "There's always the après-ski," she said. "Log fires; gluwein, and oh those kuchen!"

"Those what?"

"Cakes to you."

"Now that I *could* manage!"

"Well, why not give it a go?" she coaxed. "You're always saying you're looking for a fresh start, so try something new. I'm sure you'll love it."

"I'll think about it."

"Well, don't take too long. We need to get the flights and the hotel booked soon."

"When are you thinking of going?" Harry asked.

"Early Feb. We always go around that time."

"We?"

"Yes, a group of us go; mostly guys I work with." Interpreting his look, she added, "Don't worry; they're not all male. In the modern world, 'guys' includes 'gels' as well as 'chaps'." She unravelled her endless legs from beneath her, and raised an eyebrow. "Of course," she murmured, "There will be added extras."

Leaning forward to fill her glass from the bottle on the side table, she chuckled with amusement at Harry's awkwardness, and stood up, statuesque and desirable. She looked down at him, holding out her free hand. "Come on; let's see if we can tempt you with a sample of the complimentary extras on Rachel's Exotic Ski Tours."

Harry stood up and took her hand. "I do hope you're not offering inappropriate incentives to influence my decision."

"And what would you call an inappropriate incentive?"

"Oh, a Teasmade; carriage clock or a Parker pen; that's what the TV ads usually offer mugs to get them hooked, isn't it?"

"How about bed?"

"Oh, that's perfectly acceptable ... *and* non taxable," he retorted.

Rachel's shriek of laughter echoed in the hallway as she led him towards the steep staircase.

Harry was dragged from sleep by the sound of Marjorie's voice in the hall. "It's only me!" she called. It had taken him months to persuade her to let herself in, but at that particular moment, it no longer seemed such a good idea.

Rachel was still asleep, her flaxen hair spilling across the pillow. He slipped out of bed, careful not to wake her and dressed quickly, before creeping out of the room and closing the door quietly behind him. He found Marjorie in the lobby, off the kitchen.

"I didn't wake you up, did I?" she asked

"No; I was already awake," he lied.

"I'll get some coffee going in a minute," she said. "You look as if you could do with it. Overslept did you?"

Feeling self-conscious, he left her in the lobby and seated himself at the kitchen table.

"Well, it won't do you any harm. You're usually such an early bird," she called.

"You can leave the bedrooms for today," he said hesitantly.

Marjorie's head appeared around a cupboard door. "If you say so. I was going to strip your bed to make up a load for the washing machine, but I can leave it, if you like."

"I think that would be a good idea," he replied, adding sheepishly, "There's somebody still in it."

Her face lit up playfully. "Oh well; it's a good job you told me, or I might have gone barging in with the hoover."

Harry could not suppress a chuckle, and she responded with a giggle. "Would you like me to clear off and leave it 'til tomorrow?"

"There's no need ... unless you feel uncomfortable."

"Good lord, no!" she exclaimed. "I'll just give downstairs a good going over today. I won't use the hoover until she gets up."

Harry had finished his breakfast and was on his third cup of coffee when Rachel appeared in the kitchen doorway, stretching and yawning, and wearing his towelling bathrobe. Marjorie looked up from polishing the taps and both women eyed each other; neither with any apparent awkwardness.

"Have you two met?" Harry asked, realising that it was the first time Rachel had been at May Cottage when Marjorie was there.

"Only briefly at the May Fayre," Rachel replied.

"I've seen you in the village, and once or twice on your horse," said Marjorie. "I'll make some fresh coffee if you'd like some."

"Please Marjorie." Rachel lowered herself onto a chair opposite Harry, and reached across to take a remnant of toast from his plate.

"Would you like some fresh toast?" Marjorie asked.

293

"That's kind of you Marjorie," Harry interjected quietly, "But Rachel's quite capable of getting her own breakfast, aren't you?"

With her back to Marjorie, Rachel wrinkled her nose and poked out her tongue. "Why yes, of course, dear," she replied.

"Well, while you're doing that, do you mind if I check my e-mails?" he said, rising from the table.

Rachel shook her head. "No, go ahead."

He winked at Marjorie. "You can carry on now that Sleeping Beauty has awakened."

"Ha, bloody-ha!" Rachel retorted, her chair scraping over the tiled floor as she stood up. "I want to call in at the stables and have a word with Laura this morning. Monty's been a bit off colour and more to the point for him, off his feed. She'd like the vet to have a look at him, so I'll just make myself some toast and take a shower. I'll be on my way then."

"OK," Harry called and went out into the hallway, relieved that she was not expecting him to spend the morning with her. For one thing, he did not want to be hassled about the skiing trip. Although his initial instinct was to refuse, he *was* at least prepared to consider it, but without any more coercion … verbal or physical. Nor was he in the mood to be ribbed about his stuffiness and prevarication.

He occasionally found her teasing a little wearing. However, he was honest enough to admit that it was not really her fault. She could sometimes be annoyingly opinionated and disconcertingly outspoken, but in truth, the real problem was that she wasn't Emma.

Ensconced in the privacy of his study, he lowered himself into his new 'executive chair' and put his feet up on the window sill. A spectral mist obscured the foot of the hills, creating the impression that they were floating above the earth. The garden was beginning to look a little sorry for itself after the glory of summer and the fruitfulness of early autumn, but it still gave him pleasure and satisfaction to sit and admire it.

The wonderful job Alfie and his band of helpers had done, with the minimum of assistance from him, made him reflect on all the help and kindness he had received since he moved into May Cottage. He had done his best to reciprocate whenever an opportunity arose, but it would be nice to do something to express his appreciation in a more tangible way. The question was how?

He dismissed his first idea of taking everyone out for a meal, suspecting that Rob and Ellen would not feel comfortable in such surroundings; nor would Alfie. Buying everyone a present seemed a little ostentatious. Some might even feel obliged to buy him one in return.

He tapped a pencil against his teeth absently, as he sought inspiration. It came suddenly. A Christmas party! He smiled broadly as the idea took shape in his mind. If he made sure everyone realised it would be informal, and they could come and leave as they pleased, Alfie and the Hardys might not feel too overawed to accept an invitation.

It seemed the perfect solution, but it wouldn't be a bad idea to get another opinion. Marjorie would probably say there was no need, and Rachel would tell him to do whatever he felt like. So why not bounce it off Emma; and why not now?

He felt his pulse quicken as he selected the number from his contacts directory and heard it ring.

"Hello, 'Purbeck Style'. How can I help you?" The accent was distinctively Dorset.

"Oh; um … is Emma there?"

"Would you hold on a moment please? Who shall I say is calling?"

"It's Harry … Harry Simmonds."

He could hear a muffled conversation in the background, followed by the sound of footsteps. "Hi Harry Simmonds, how's it going?"

The sound of her voice brought a smile to his lips. "Pretty good thanks. How are things with you?"

"OK I guess. The carrier's lost part of my order, but apart from that, no worries."

Harry chuckled boyishly. "Sorry for calling you at work, I know you're busy."

"No; the season's over, so it's not too bad," she answered. "Anyway I'm never too busy to talk to you."

"I've just had an idea, and I wanted to bounce it off somebody sensible while it's still fresh in my mind."

"What kind of an idea?"

"Well, I wanted to do something to say thank you to all the people who have been so kind to me since I moved here. What I came up with was a party; perhaps just before Christmas. What d'you think?"

"Am I invited?"

"Of course."

"Then I think it's a great idea," she giggled.

"No; seriously. What *do* you think? "

"I think it's a wonderful idea," she enthused, adding quietly, "What does Rachel think?"

"I haven't mentioned it to her yet," he replied guiltily. "But I can guess what her reaction will be."

"Which is?"

"She'll tell me to do whatever I want to," Harry continued. "Rachel's a party person, but let's face it, *organising* one isn't her thing."

"Well, for what it's worth, *my* opinion is that it's a very kind and generous gesture. I'm sure it will be appreciated by everyone you invite."

"Thank you; that's what I was hoping for."

"I don't want to tread on anyone's toes," she began hesitantly, "but if you need any help arranging it, you only have to ask."

"I'd be very grateful for all the help I can get!" he exclaimed, hardly able to believe his luck. "You won't be treading on anyone's toes. I can't ask Marjorie to get involved. She does more than enough already."

"OK. You think about the sort of thing you want; and the people you want to invite and we'll talk about it some more."

"That's great! Thanks Emma."

"You're welcome. Sorry Harry, I'm afraid I have to go; Paula's trying to deal with two customers at once, now."

"OK. Thanks again Emma."

"Catch you later, Harry; bye."

Basking in a warm glow of satisfaction, he stretched out his legs and tilted his chair back. A thinly veiled excuse to speak to her had turned out better than he could ever have imagined.

The sound of Rachel's voice in the hall, thanking Marjorie, brought home to him the somewhat unedifying fact that calling one woman, having just climbed out of bed with another, was not something he ought to feel proud of. However, it did wonders for his ego.

It was good to have Adam home again. He had returned from the Lake District the previous evening; in his own words 'well knackered' and frustrated from a long rail journey fraught with delays. He had arrived wanting nothing more than his bed.

He appeared the next morning soon after Harry returned from the short drive to the service station on the high road. He looked pensive. Something was clearly on his mind; something he appeared to be building up to, but was not sure how to broach with his father. Even more significant was the fact that he was up before ten o'clock on a Sunday!

"Coffee?" Harry asked, as Adam settled himself drowsily at the kitchen table.

"No thanks."

"Toast?"

"No; I'm good thanks."

"How was the weather in Cumbria?" Harry asked mischievously.

Adam rolled his eyes in reply.

"I did warn you about the Lakes at this time of year," Harry chuckled.

"Yeh, right. But you didn't tell me it would like, start off fine and wait 'til we were on top of a stonking great hill before chucking it down!"

They both laughed, but Harry could sense that Adam was nervous and unsettled.

"Why the worried look?" he asked.

"I'm not worried," Adam replied quietly. "I was just thinking."

"At this time of the morning?"

Adam grinned sheepishly. "I've been thinking ... about what I want to do, right."

"Good! That sounds promising."

"I'm not sure you're going to like it though, dad."

Harry sat down, trying to interpret Adam's expression. "Is it legal?" he asked flippantly.

"Yes."

"You're not thinking of taking up poker for a living, are you?"

Adam chuckled. "Not really! But if we can be serious for a minute; what I mean is, I like, wouldn't be earning any money."

"Are we talking University?"

"No." Adam paused and took a deep breath. "Voluntary work … in Africa."

Harry was momentarily thrown. "What sort of voluntary work?"

"Well; it's like helping to build schools and amenities, right. I met up with Ollie Chandler again soon after I went to live with mum. He told me about it. You know Ollie; he was the kid at school with wild, wiry hair. You used to say he looked like he'd been electrocuted."

Harry laughed. "Yes, I remember him; nice lad."

"Well, I talked with him about it again last week. He's signed up with PAVT; that's the Pan Africa Volunteers Trust, right. It sends teams of volunteers to African communities to help set up the kind of basic facilities *we* take for granted. The teams are mostly students and guys my age, right. Ollie's going to Ghana. It like … well, got me thinking. It sounds kind of my thing; something I could get into."

Harry took a deep breath. "I see. What made you think I wouldn't like it?"

"Well, when I first got here, you told me to find something useful to do to earn my keep."

"What you've just told me sounds pretty useful to me."

"Yeh, but it doesn't pay anything. All they get is travel and food and stuff, right; nothing else."

"How long would you have to commit to?" Harry asked.

"A year. Students often take a sabbatical to do it."

Harry's heart sank at the thought of losing his son again for such a long time, but he managed to conceal his disappointment. "You're serious about this, and you've thought about it, and what it involves?" he asked deliberately.

"Yes dad. I have thought about it; a lot. I've talked a lot with Ollie too. It's like, something useful I can commit to, while I make up my mind what I want to do with my life."

"Have you told your mother?"

"Yeh; she's cool with it. She told me to speak to you."

"In that case, you'd better contact these people and find out more about it."

"I already have."

"Oh, I see."

"Yeh. I've got a bunch of their stuff upstairs, if you want to see it."

Harry nodded. "Yes, I'd like to. It sounds like a commendable thing to do."

"Thanks dad. But ..."

"But what?"

"Well; you'll like, be on your own again."

"I'm not senile yet. I *can* manage to dress myself *and* go to the loo on my own."

Adam grinned. "You know what I mean. We've just kinda got to know each other again. I don't know if you've noticed, but I've grown up a bit lately. I've been talking to Debs and Marjorie, right. I think I understand now what you've been through."

"Yes, I have noticed," said Harry. "But none of that matters. You're young; you've got *your* life ahead of you. That's what's important."

"Thanks dad," Adam replied, the relief clear on his face. "I wish I'd like, been more help. I should have tried to understand. I thought you didn't care. I like, didn't get why you could just let mum go like that. I think I do now. It was *because* you cared about her, right?"

"That's all water under the bridge," Harry replied awkwardly. "So don't worry about me! I don't have a problem with being on my own. I've got a lot of friends here."

"I know. I've noticed. You seem pretty well respected in Nethercombe."

"I don't know about that," Harry said diffidently. "Everyone's been very kind and welcoming. So there's nothing to worry about. I'll be fine."

"Can I like, ask a personal question?" Adam said cautiously.

"You can ask. I might not choose to answer it."

"About Rachel, right?"

"What about her?"

Adam avoided eye contact. "I was like, wondering. Is she … you…?"

"Is she likely to be your stepmother, you mean?" Harry interjected playfully. "The answer's no, if that's what's worrying you."

"I'm not worried. She's cool; and fun! I was just curious."

"Don't tell her … or *anyone* I've told you; keep it to yourself. She's already married." Noticing the look of surprise on Adam's face, Harry added, "Her husband's an American. They're separated; he lives in New York. But even if she *were* free, there's no chance of us getting together on a permanent basis. She doesn't want that, and neither do I."

"Oh, right."

"Domesticity isn't exactly Rachel's strong point," Harry added with a chuckle. "Can you see her in a pinnie, baking cakes?"

Adam laughed. "No way!" Then, more seriously, he asked, "What about this Aussie chick?"

"Chick?" Harry exclaimed in amusement. "This Aussie *chick* is twice your age! She's Guy Wolstencroft's partner. Do you remember Guy? He was one of my colleagues at Bennetts."

Adam shook his head.

"Well anyway, you can forget about cosy family jaunts down under."

"Right … shame!" Adam replied, grinning broadly.

Harry stood up and patted his shoulder. "I don't know about you, but my stomach's complaining that breakfast is long overdue."

"Yeh, I'm hungry now." Adam arched an eyebrow. "Any chance of a fry up?"

"Good idea!"

Harry stood at the lobby door watching his breath drift in a nebulous cloud on the misty morning air. The patio paving stones were studded with patches of glistening rime and the lawn lay crisp and pale beneath a sugar dusting of hoar frost.

'The first real autumn frost already,' he thought. It did not bode well for the coming winter. In a week or so, the clocks would go back, hastening the inexorable shortening of the precious hours of daylight. To Harry, the dark mornings and dispiriting gloom of early evenings epitomised the heartache of recent bleak and lonely winters. With the loss of his father still a raw and ever present sorrow, he anticipated their approach with increasing dismay.

It was Sally's birthday; her forty-fifth. He imagined she would not thank anyone for reminding her; especially their son, who was most likely to find it amusing to do so. Harry felt guilty for the fact that she had continued to send him a birthday card each year, while he, in his alcohol fuelled depression, had not bothered to reciprocate. Her gesture had been thoughtful and made with the best of intentions, although it had compounded his misery, leading him to cherish false hopes that she might come back to him one day.

He had remembered to send her a card this year, and although a poignant reminder of what they had once shared, the memories no longer invoked despair and longing. Sally had gone forever. He could accept that now, and yearning for that old life no longer haunted him or filled his waking hours. His overriding sense of loss was for his father; and it was a vivacious redhead who stirred his emotions.

With a sigh, he closed the door to shut out the chill, autumn air. Returning to the kitchen, he heard the stairs creak, as his mother cautiously made her way down their steep incline. He knew it was her without looking. Adam usually bounded down, two steps at a time, and there was no way it would be him at seven o'clock in the morning.

How would she cope with her first winter for over fifty years without her life-long companion? She had borne her loss bravely. He did not doubt there were moments when she gave way to despair and grief, but she obviously chose to do so privately and without ostentation; the way she and his father had lived their lives.

So far she had given no indication of when, or if, she intended to go back home to live, although she seemed in no hurry to leave Devon and Aunt Caroline. All he knew was, that whatever she chose to do, he intended to support her, and to use a modern cliché, 'to be there for her'.

"You're an early riser," she said as she padded into the kitchen, swathed in the fluffy, pink dressing gown he and Sally had given her several Christmasses ago.

"It's the country air, mum," he quipped. "Us country folk gets up with the lark."

"You're as daft as your father," she chuckled.

He refilled the kettle to make tea, knowing she preferred it to coffee, while she stood at the window gazing out.

"You've certainly made a difference to the garden," she said quietly.

"I can't claim much credit for it," he confessed. "I have Alfie to thank for that. He's recently retired but wanted to keep busy. He comes in once or twice a week. Marjorie's son, Gary, has done a lot of work out there too, when he's been home on leave. Your grandson has done his share as well."

"I didn't know he was interested in gardening," she said.

"Nor did I; and I suspect, neither did he!" Harry chuckled. "But he's really got stuck in. He's been helping the Hardys with their garden too. They think the world of him."

"Good," she said quietly. "It's a relief to know he's sorting himself out at last."

'She obviously knows more about Adam's recent problems than I realised,' Harry mused. Perhaps it was no more than could be expected. She was no fool. In recent weeks, she had proved herself to be more astute and resourceful than he had given her credit for.

He had returned from Poole the previous evening to find her sitting on the bench at the end of the garden. The hills had been lit with a golden, autumnal glow by the setting sun, and she had been gazing at them, apparently deep in meditation. Since her arrival, she had got to know Marjorie and the Hardys, but Harry sensed she was unsettled and finding it difficult to relax.

"I've made up my mind!" she said suddenly.

"Have you mum? What about?"

"About the house. I'm going to sell up."

"Are you?"

"Yes. There's nothing to stay there for now; only memories. I'll still have *those* wherever I am. Your dad's gone, and trying to carry on living in the past won't bring him back."

"You're right, mum. You've got to do whatever you feel is right for you. You're more than welcome here, you know that."

She turned to face him. "Yes, darling; I do," she said. "It's lovely here; so peaceful. Don't take this the wrong way; it's right for you, but not for me. I'd only get in your way, anyway."

"That's nonsense!" Harry exclaimed. "There's bags of room here, and there'll never be a time when you're in my way!"

"Alright," she replied and brushed her hand over his hair affectionately. "I'm lucky to have you, and I'm grateful for the offer. Don't be offended, but I've decided to move in with Caroline."

"I'm not offended," Harry replied. "I only want what's best for you."

"It's been lovely staying with her. She's enjoyed it too. It's been over seven years since she lost Will, and she's never liked living on her own. She's not like Judith; she's not one for socialising. She hardly ever goes out now. I don't think her car had been out of the garage for months before I arrived. She catches the bus into Brixham, and once in a blue moon she has a trip to Paignton or Totnes. Her neighbours take her to Sainsbury's every week. That's about the limit of it. We've been out and about quite a lot while I've been there … two old biddies. We've joined the National Trust, too. They've got lots of places; and once you've joined, it doesn't cost anything to get in, or park."

Harry gave her a hug. "Go for it mum. But don't forget; you and Aunt Caroline are always welcome."

"Oh, we'll come and visit, don't worry. As long as you understand."

"Yes, of course I understand. It will be good for both of you."

"She needs some work done on her roof; there's a damp patch on the ceiling in one of the bedrooms. She can't afford to get it done, and if I sell the house, I can get that sorted out for her. She'll argue like mad, but we'll cross that bridge when we get to it. I know she'd love a conservatory too; like the one her neighbours have had done. We could sit in there and look out over the fields. I'm going to try to get her to let me do that as well. You wouldn't mind, would you?"

"Why should I mind, mum?"

"Well, it will mean less for you and Debbie and Adam when I'm gone."

"To hell with that!" Harry exclaimed. "I want you to be comfortable and happy; so do Debbie and Adam. Spend the lot … enjoy life! I don't need it and I don't want it! Your grandchildren have already had plenty of help. It's time they made their own way … with a bit of support along the way, I'll grant you. But they won't have any worries. They'll have all this eventually. That's a hell of a lot more help than you and dad ever had."

"I suppose you're right," she sighed, adding with a frown, "Jenny's condition's getting worse. Her doctor's recommended they get her an orthopaedic bed, but they cost a fortune. There's no way they can afford it on their pensions, and they get precious little help from Social Services. I'd love to treat her to one, but I doubt Frank will let me. You know what a stubborn devil he can be."

"It would hurt his pride," Harry said. "Perhaps we could suggest that dad left them something in his will. They won't know the difference."

"That's a good idea; we could try it," she replied. "Now; shall I start breakfast? What about Adam?"

"He won't be up for another hour or so," Harry replied. "He knows exactly how long it takes him to get to work, and he won't haul his backside out of bed a minute before he has to."

A glance at the wall clock confirmed that it was almost one o'clock. The prospect of a break for lunch and the chance to escape ACCORS' overheated and airless meeting room was becoming ever more appealing to Harry. Listening to the Project Liaison Controller, Nick Stenning, as he attempted to justify his department's ineffectiveness as achievement, led Harry to wonder anew why he had allowed Guy to talk him into taking on the contract. His instincts had warned him to shy away from the muddle and confusion Guy had described, but in spite of that, he had decided to take it on. It wasn't because he needed the money, although no-one had raised an eyebrow at the fee he had quoted. No; he had needed to get back to work; to put his experience and professional skills to good use again. However, he would admit that renewing his acquaintance with Guy, and with it, the chance to see more of Emma, had played a part.

Nick Stenning's thin nasal whine was irritating, and his narrow features and close-set eyes suggestive of the evasiveness Harry had experienced in his dealings with him. Nick represented the worst characteristics of the public sector; having proved himself to be manipulative, evasive and a slave to *systems and procedures,* even when they flew in the face of common sense.

Despite his initial misgivings, Harry had set about navigating his way through ACCORS' labyrinthine operations with a rigour and thoroughness honed from twenty-five years of experience and business acumen. He thought he had seen it all, but what he had discovered was a catalogue of waste and inefficiency, the like of which he had never witnessed before. Unbelievably, Nick Stenning was now attempting to portray it as, '*Progress and achievement; moving ACCORS' aims and objectives forward'.*

Nick avoided eye contact with anyone else around the table, keeping them firmly fixed on his copy of Harry's report, as he remarked, "Mr. Simmonds' recommendations obviously reflect the situation ... *as he sees it.* But I'm afraid they fail to address the fundamental problems of logistics and morale we would encounter by disrupting the efforts of our hard working and highly successful teams."

Harry was tempted to reply, *'What you mean is: reorganisation would destroy your cosy little setup and force you to get off your backside and do something!'* Instead, he chose his words carefully. "Reporting on the situation *'as I see it'*, is what I've been contracted to do, Mr. Stenning, and to suggest ways to improve efficiency. That is precisely what I've done."

Sensing the mounting tension, Shirley Cochran, ACCORS' CEO, tapped her pen on the papers in front of her. "I must say your report is very comprehensive and erudite, Mr. Simmonds." Glancing around the table, she added, "I'm sure my fellow directors would agree that your projection of four-and-a-half million pounds of saving in operating costs is most impressive. However, one can't help wondering if it's really achievable. Dare I say, perhaps a little optimistic?"

Nick Stenning opened his mouth, no doubt seeking to seize on this point, but Harry forestalled his intervention, addressing Shirley directly and ignoring Nick's attempt to gain their attention. "I've set out how I arrived at those proposals in the schedule I included," he explained. "I will admit, at this stage, they're still estimates, but I've based my calculations on your budgets and forecasts of operating expenditure. In my opinion, those savings most certainly *are* achievable."

"I see your proposals include what you refer to as *Rationalising Locations,*" Sir Bertram Chilcott observed languidly, running his hands through his thinning, grey hair and adjusting his spectacles to peer more closely at his copy of the report.

Harry paused to consider his answer. He had met 'Bertie Boy', as Guy irreverently referred to him, only once before. Sir Bertram had been conspicuous by his absence at previous meetings. He was slightly built and wore a crisp, pale pink shirt and a red silk tie. The jacket of his finely tailored suit hung over the chair behind him, arranged with immaculate precision. Although chair of ACCORS' Board of Directors, Sir Bertram seemed to prefer leaving the details of running the organisation to Shirley Cochran.

"Yes; that's correct," Harry replied quietly. "As you're aware, your operations are currently divided between three sites: the headquarters here in Poole, a second office in Taunton and another in Exeter. However, the third floor at Taunton is unoccupied, while little more than half the space is utilised at *Swan House* in Exeter. However, there appears to be sufficient room here in Poole to accommodate the entire operation."

"I'm afraid it's not as simple as that," Jeffrey Barber interjected. He appeared to be in his late fifties, or perhaps early sixties, and spoke with traces of a Geordie accent. Harry had never been able to completely clarify the responsibilities that came under his title of 'Facilities Director'. "We need the space for future expansion," he added.

"Of course we do!" Nick Stenning exclaimed. "I was about to…"

"I believe we have lease obligations on these premises," Sir Bertram remarked, ignoring his Project Liaison Controller's anxious attempt to intervene.

"You do indeed," Harry replied. "But my information is that the Taunton lease is relatively short term; less than six months to the next renewal. Incidentally, I've looked at the terms of the lease on Swan House and taken some advice. There doesn't appear to be anything to prevent you sub-letting unneeded space to a third party on a temporary basis; subject to the owner's approval."

"You've certainly done your homework," Shirley Cochran chuckled.

Harry replied with a smile. "It's what you're paying me for."

"But we aren't paying you to disrupt the smooth working of our organisation!" Nick interposed waspishly.

"I fail to see how pointing out potential savings and efficiencies is *disrupting* your organisation," Harry replied.

"But, to suggest cramming us all in here at Poole, with all the upheaval and cost that would entail …"

"The cost of moving would be minimal compared to the rent and overheads on running those buildings!" Harry retorted. "Wouldn't you find it easier to manage your teams if they were all under one roof, rather than scattered over three sites as they are now?"

"*My staff* are where they're *needed!*" Nick snapped. Turning to Sir Bertram with an ingratiating smile, he added, "It's quite obvious Mr. Simmonds hasn't grasped the technicalities of the work we do."

Harry stifled the impulse to respond to the implied insult, and again paused to control his irritation. "I don't need to *grasp the technicalities* of your organisation Mr. Stenning, to observe that people spend a great deal of their time travelling from one location to another; more often than not to attend meetings."

"That's nonsense!" Stenning exclaimed. "Our work requires us to meet on a regular basis to discuss the way forward; to prioritise our objectives and maximise our core competences."

'Straight out of the Corporate Gobbledegook Manual,' Harry thought.

"I don't know where you got the idea that people are wasting time travelling unnecessarily!" Stenning exclaimed with a dismissive sneer.

"It's what I've been told by the managers and staff, actually," Harry replied, enjoying the surprise on Stenning's face. "Many of them share my opinion that having everyone working under one roof would make managing the organisation a lot easier, as well as saving man-hours and travel costs."

"It sounds reasonable," Duncan Bruce remarked. As Director of Corporate Affairs, he was Guy's superior. He still wore his jacket, and despite being overweight and flabby, with jowls that reminded Harry of a bloodhound, he seemed to be the only person in the room not affected by the heat. "It would make sense to bring all the PR and HR people together here as well," he said absently.

Shirley Cochran looked purposefully at Nick Stenning. "You're always saying how stressful you find the long hours and all the travelling."

"I do it because it's necessary!" he retorted petulantly, and with another smile at Sir Bertram, he added, "I'm more than happy to accept the pressure of what I consider a rewarding challenge."

Harry suppressed a wry grin. He could imagine Nick playing the part of the harassed, overworked executive. However, the evidence suggested that he delegated the real work to his managers and spent nearly all his time attending meetings and conferences or travelling to and from them.

The CEO adjusted her spectacles as she addressed Harry. "Your observations on merging our three *Projects Departments* are very interesting," she remarked.

"That's not the word I would use!" Stenning spluttered. "It's … it's preposterous!"

"Where's this in the report?" Sir Bertram enquired, betraying the fact that he had not read it, by flipping the pages back and forth. Shirley leaned towards him, holding out her own copy. "Page twenty-two: *Working Practices and Efficiencies*."

'Or rather '*inefficiencies*,' Harry thought.

"What exactly is being proposed?" Sir Bertram asked in his languid drawl.

"Redundancies!" Stenning exclaimed.

"Really?" Sir Bertram asked casually. "How many are we talking about?"

"Mr. Simmonds doesn't *specify* how many," Nick replied acidly. "He proposes that we merge my department with *Project Planning* and *Project Management*. It would be chaos … absolute chaos! This report appears to be nothing more than an exercise in penny-pinching!"

"I beg to differ," Harry replied flatly. "I'm offering constructive suggestions for consideration. They're proposals that offer potentially significant improvement in efficiency, as well as a reduction in operating costs."

"It would emasculate the whole operation!" Stenning reposted.

"Please Nick," Shirley protested, holding up a hand to silence him. "Let's keep a sense of proportion here. Perhaps this might be an opportune moment to adjourn for lunch. I suggest that we reconvene at … shall we say, two-thirty?"

"I'd rather we made it three o'clock," Sir Bertram drawled. "There's nowhere one can get a decent lunch around here. We'll never make it to *The Coq d'Or* and back by half-two."

"There's fish and chips on the quay," Nick chuckled, and grinned at Sir Bertram ingratiatingly, in the hope that his feeble joke would be appreciated.

"Quite!" Sir Bertram replied, without apparent amusement.

"OK; three it is then," Shirley proclaimed to the room at large. Turning to Harry she asked, "Would you care to join us for lunch Mr. Simmonds?"

"That's kind of you, but I'm afraid I have one or two calls I have to make," Harry lied. "And and I need to find a bank." He wanted ... needed a break from them; fresh air and the chance to clear his mind.

"Oh, that's a shame," Shirley replied with a smile.

"Yes, it is," Nick Stenning interjected. "*The Coq d'Or* has a very nice wine list. I believe you enjoy a glass ... or two, Mr. Simmonds."

For a moment Harry was nonplussed by the remark, which was clearly what Stenning had intended. It was obvious that he was slyly letting Harry know that he had found out about his recent past. Harry dismissed the possibility that he had learned about it from Guy. He had no concerns about Guy's loyalty and discretion.

"A lot of people do," Harry replied casually, determined to deny the slimy little rat the satisfaction of upsetting him.

"Yes, of course," Stenning said condescendingly, adding quietly. "There's no harm in it ... in moderation. It wouldn't do to let it interfere with one's work though."

Harry fixed him with a hostile glare. Stenning looked away quickly, tucking his papers into a large folder. But he had not finished. "By the way," he said casually. "I ran into a former colleague of yours a week or so ago; at a conference in Brighton. Craig Carterton. He asked to be remembered to you."

The penny dropped. 'So *that's* how he knows!' One of the last duties Harry had carried out before he left Eldon Management Services was to fire Craig Carterton. Harry had not enjoyed doing it, because Craig was likeable and affable. But the idiot had thought he could get away with misappropriating a couple of lap-tops and various other office equipment, which, at first, everyone had assumed were either lost or stolen. Not content with that, he had ordered stationery using company accounts, and had thought he could get away with flogging the whole lot on eBay.

Despite the fact that Harry and his partners had spared Craig involvement with the police and hence a criminal record, he had bitterly resented being sacked; claiming he had been harshly treated. By that time, he, like nearly everyone else at Eldon Management Services, had been aware of Harry's heavy drinking and bouts of depression … and the reason for it.

Harry glared at Stenning, who refused to make eye contact. *'Just mention Sally, that's all,'* he thought. *'Just try it!'*

He was brought from his malevolent musing by Shirley's voice, as she followed Duncan Bruce out of the room. "See you at three Mr. Simmonds."

"Yes," Harry replied, snapping the locks shut on his briefcase.

"I'm surprised you're not having lunch with your friend Guy," Stenning remarked as he made his way to the door.

"Are you?" Harry replied curtly. "*I'm* surprised you imagine it's any of your business."

Stenning's answering smile was patronising and smug. "It must have been a godsend; Guy getting you this contract after being out of work for so long."

Harry took a deep breath to calm the fury building inside him. He had no intention of giving Stenning the satisfaction of rising to the bait and seeing him lose his temper!

"You'd better trot along, or the others might go without out you," Harry replied with an icy smile. "It would be *such a shame* if you missed your chance to have lunch with Sir Bertram."

It was gratifying to watch the smile fade from Stenning's face. "What's that supposed to mean?" he asked petulantly.

"Nothing," Harry said quietly. "We're only halfway through my report. I just thought you might need a good meal to sustain you through what's likely to be a long and *challenging* afternoon."

Poole harbour was a cauldron of short, choppy swells, which burst between the moored vessels in curtains of icy spray, and drifted on fitful gusts of a buffeting wind. There were few people braving the elements on the exposed quay, but welcoming the chill after the overheated meeting room at ACCORS, Harry turned up the collar of his heavy coat.

The break for lunch could not have come at a more opportune moment. Although he had come close to losing his temper, Harry took pride in having maintained his professionalism in the face of Nick Stenning's crude provocation. He was too long in the tooth not to recognise the insinuations about his past and his relationship with Guy, as a veiled threat to discredit him. However, Stenning's machinations merely fuelled Harry's contempt for 'the self serving creep'. "OK, Mr. Stenning," he said to himself. "You want to play rough? So be it!"

He had other things on his mind, apart from ACCORS and Nick Stenning. The persistent rain of the past few days had prevented a hike to Hallows Hill, and although he loved having Adam to live with him, peace … and especially quiet were at a premium when his son was around.

Adam had already arranged an interview with PAVT, increasing the likelihood that he would soon be off to Africa. Harry's own research had led him to conclude that it was a respected and well run organisation, so he could think of no reason why Adam should not spend a year with them. It could well be the making of him. Selfishness made Harry resent the prospect of losing him, when they had made such progress in putting their past differences behind them. But it was Adam's choice and his life. Harry had to accept that he had no right to feel resentment. Anyway, there had been more than enough disappointments in recent years; surely he could cope with one more.

Another dilemma was the demon he had let loose by accepting Emma's offer to help him organise his Christmas party. Although it was weeks away, he had lost no time in drawing up a list of people he wanted to invite; mainly to give him an excuse to call her back. As a result, he had found himself alone with her in his sitting room, delightfully, and disturbingly, close on the settee, while they discussed food, decorations and various other things that needed consideration.

It made his scalp tingle to recall watching her as she had made notes on the pad she had brought with her; admiring her slim, elegant fingers with those long, pink-varnished nails, talons as Guy referred to them, curled around the stubby pen. Her glorious hair, piled up and held by a large comb-like clip, had glowed in the beam of pale sunlight streaming through a window, illuminating the ringlets that dangled over her ears. It had reminded him of illustrations on the covers of Bronte novels. Intoxicated by her perfume and the tantalising, curly wisps of hair behind her ears, he had almost given way to a powerful urge to kiss her neck. Suddenly coming to his senses, he had stood up so abruptly that he had startled her. "I ... er ... I think I'd better measure the alcove for the tree," he had stammered.

She had looked up at him with a puzzled expression. "There's plenty of time for that; it's not even November yet. Anyway, I would think anything less than three metres would fit easily."

"I'd better just check though," he had insisted. "I've got a tape measure in the kitchen. I'll just go and get it. Would you like coffee or tea while I'm there?"

She had tilted her head in that appealing way and looked at him in amusement. "No, I'm good thanks. We had one less than half an hour ago."

"Oh ... yes; right. Well I'll just get the tape measure then."

What if he *had* kissed her? Imagining the anger blazing in those green eyes sent an icy chill up his spine. Her humiliating rebuke would no doubt have included a few unflattering, Antipodean epithets.

His momentary panic passed. She would not have stayed so long if she had suspected, nor would she have invited him to sit down beside her and go through her notes. Nevertheless, it was a *wake-up call*, and a reminder of the obvious, if unwelcome, solution. Having accepted her offer to help him with the party, he could not put her off now without offending her; at least that was what he had convinced himself. But after that, he simply had to keep his distance. It was easier said than done, but he knew he had to do it; and above all, avoid being alone with her.

Reaching the Old Lifeboat Station, Harry looked at his watch, and with a shrug, reluctantly started to make his way back to ACCORS and the resumption of his confrontation with Nick Stenning.

"Right Mr. Stenning," he murmured. "Let's see how you enjoy my report on departmental expenditure; especially *your* department. I can't wait to see the Directors' faces, when I present them with my analysis of the huge overspend; especially what you've claimed for first-class rail and air fares … not to mention taxis and hotel bills for conferences."

Adam tossed his bag onto the back seat and lowered himself onto the passenger seat of Harry's BMW.

"How did it go then?" Harry asked.

"Pretty good. They're really cool; they've offered me an induction course. The next one's at the beginning of next month, right. I'll need to do that if I want to be on the same project as Ollie."

"That sounds promising," Harry replied, as he reversed out of the parking bay in the station car park. "With any luck, you'll get the chance to take your driving test before you go."

"Yeh; fingers crossed," Adam replied. "The induction course is meant to like check out my suitability and adaptability, so that I know what I'm committing to, right. To make sure I won't change my mind after a few weeks."

"And you're sure of that after talking to them?"

"Yes dad. Well, as sure as anybody can be."

"Good. And I take it you needn't have worried about having to put details of your little brush with the law on your disclosure form?"

"No; I told them everything. I think the letter from the solicitor helped. I'm pretty sure they'd already checked me out anyway. They don't think there'll be any sweat about my visa."

Harry nodded. "OK. So how long does this induction course last?"

"About a week … the first week in November. I've got stuff in my bag; like, what I'll need to take and what I need to do, right. The worst part is the jabs. If I sign up, I've like, got to have a whole bunch of them.

They have to be done at least eight weeks before I go."

"That's cutting it fine for the beginning of January," said Harry.

"Yeh; it'll be like, eight and a half weeks from the induction course to the fourth of January. That's when we fly out."

"Rather you than me!" Harry chuckled. "I don't mind needles, but like everything, I prefer them in moderation."

"Yeh, right! You should see the list!" Adam exclaimed. "I'll probably look like a sieve afterwards!"

"You'd better call Doc Williams as soon as we get home," Harry suggested. "She might have to order some of the more nasty ones."

"Cheers dad; that makes me feel *so much* better!"

"My pleasure," Harry chuckled. "What happens after the induction … if you decide to commit?"

"We do a prep course in December for a week or ten days; just before Christmas, right. Then we all assemble for like, a final briefing on the second of January. We're off on the fourth."

"How many of you will there be on the project?"

"About nine of us. But there'll be about fifteen of us in the district; with team leaders and stuff like that."

"Whereabouts in Ghana will you be?"

"Somewhere in the east. I can't remember the name of the place, but it's all in the paperwork they gave me."

"OK; so what do you fancy for lunch?" Harry asked. "Pizza?"

"Could we get a curry?"

"Why not; let's find somewhere to park and see what we can find."

As Harry emerged from the copse and clambered over the stile, he could see Copper hill on the other side of the valley, glowing in the amber sunlight of a crisp, October afternoon. Now that the weather had improved, he could enjoy a little time to himself, away from ACCORS and the demands of local committees, to take his favourite hike to the summit of Hallows Hill. The ditches and verges on either side of the lanes leading from Nethercombe Ley were choked with fallen leaves. Chivvied by occasional gusts, they had rustled and skittered around his feet like playful sprites.

In Harry's opinion, autumn was the loveliest of the seasons, with its ethereal mists and panoply of reds, golds and greens. Although heralding the departure of summer's glory, and harbinger of the darkness and cold of winter, autumn's mellow sunlight and aura of quiet melancholy never failed to move him. Reaching the summit of Hallows Hill, he sighed contentedly, and with Keats' evocative words: '*Season of mists and mellow fruitfulness*' slipping into his mind, he looked out at the quiet pastures and sombre barren fields, now slumbering in a cloak of russets and browns.

Above him, a feathery, white vapour trail was spreading across the pale blue sky, slowly dissolving, like his forlorn hope that Adam might change his mind. But it was Adam's life, and he would have to resign himself to being alone again. Contrary to his expectations, time did not seem to make living alone any easier. In fact the longer it went on, the more difficult it was to cope with.

A call from Emma, with a few suggestions for the party, had lifted his spirits, although it had also served as an unwelcome reminder to keep his feelings in check. The party preparations had to be the last time he allowed himself to be alone with her. No more feeble excuses to visit Swanage or Wareham; for her sake as much as his. She had been tolerant and understanding so far, but he realised there would come a time when he would exhaust her patience. There was also Guy to consider. It was no way to treat a friend. Sooner or later, Guy would become aware of his infatuation with her; if he wasn't already.

Since inviting him to join her on the skiing trip, Rachel's enthusiasm for visits to Nethercombe ... and him seemed to be cooling. After intimating that she would '*come down*' for the weekend to celebrate her birthday, she had cried off at the last minute, claiming pressure of work. She had called to apologise, and promised to 'make it up to him' another time, but the seed of suspicion had been sown. Her birthday present and card still lay on Harry's hall table, and he had hastily called Bob Andrews at *The Black Bull* to cancel the cake and champagne he had ordered for the evening.

Simon's only comment had been to express his disappointment, but Harry sensed that he too suspected another reason for his sister's change of mind.

Harry was aware that he had no cause to feel aggrieved. Rachel had warned him from the outset not to expect too much. He enjoyed her company and the intimacy of their relationship, but he had to admit that his feelings for her were not as strong as they had been for Sally ... or were for Emma.

Selling his mother's house was also proving to be a drain on his time and energy; a task made no easier by her residence with Aunt Caroline in Devon, and her reluctance to trust the estate agent with a key. Her nervousness about having '*strangers*' in her house, while she was not there, had meant that the burden of meeting prospective buyers had fallen on Harry. So far he had made the lengthy journey three times; each to no avail. On one occasion, he and the estate agent had waited for over an hour for a couple who did not even bother to show up. Even though there were no offers so far, Harry had rejected the suggestion that they might reduce the asking price. It was too early in the proceedings, and he took perverse pleasure in reminding the agent of his initial sales pitch: '*We'll have no problem getting that price for a house of this quality, Mr. Simmonds!*'

He had felt tired and dejected recently; something Sally used to call '*a downer*'. Perhaps he needed a holiday. If he discounted the Easter weekend with Rachel, he had not had one for nearly four years. But he found the idea of going on holiday on his own less than appealing. Nor did he fancy *hurtling down an icy mountain with a plank strapped to each foot*. The only person he would know was Rachel, who would be amongst her colleagues.

The one high point in recent weeks had been Debbie's announcement of her job with the Environment Agency. She was understandably excited at the prospect of starting her new career at the beginning of December. Grandma Marian and Aunt Caroline had been delighted to learn she would be based in Exeter; '*Just up the road*', as she had put it. They were fondly anticipating regular visits from her.

It pleased Harry to think that Exeter was not that far from Nethercombe Ley either, and now that Debbie enjoyed the convenience of Gramp's car, he dared to hope that he would see more of her and Paul.

Coming to terms with the loss of his father was still a struggle, and looking out across harvested fields dotted with hay bales and basking in the golden sunlight, he was filled with remorse and regret for not having brought him here. He, more than anyone, would have appreciated its peace and tranquillity and understood the uplifting part it played in Harry's struggle to adjust to the changes in his life.

Harry sighed. He would never have believed a few years ago that his contented, comfortable life would be turned upside down in so short a time, and that so much of what he cherished would be taken from him. It was frightening to recall the bouts of dark depression and how often he had relied on alcohol to blur the pain and anguish.

Thankfully, those '*bad old days*' were now almost a distant memory. He had come a long way; an achievement he acknowledged would not have been possible without the companionship and support of his new friends and neighbours.

He could face the future with a clear head, and a little of the optimism and determination decidedly lacking during the previous two years.

"So what do I do if they call?" Harry asked, glancing dubiously at the basket on the hall table.

Marjorie and Adam had filled it with a variety of sweets and chocolate bars, and had tied balloons decorated with witches and bats to float above it.

"Oh they'll call alright," Marjorie said. "Halloween is quite a big thing in Nethercombe. They'll see the pumpkin on the gate post, so they know they'll be welcome."

"I didn't think there were many kids in Nethercombe … apart from on the estate," he said.

"There are more than you think," she replied. "And the kids from the estate will come, don't worry. They always know where the best treats are!"

Adam looked at his father with a pained expression. "All you have to do is wait 'til they say 'trick or treat', right? And like, let them choose from the basket or the plate with the cup cakes. That's simple enough, even for you isn't it?"

"Am I really expected be lectured by somebody looking like that?" Harry chuckled.

Marjorie had made up Adam's face in pale green to look like a zombie, with crudely stitched wounds drawn in eye liner on his forehead and cheeks. She had even dabbed lipstick at the corners of his mouth to represent dribbling blood. He had gelled his hair to stick up in spikes around a bloodied rubber axe fixed on a wire, giving it the appearance of being embedded in his skull. His black t-shirt with a white skeleton motif completed the incongruous picture.

Harry could hardly look at him without bursting into laughter.

"And like, be really terrified if the little ones are dressed up to look scary, right!" Adam added.

"OK; *right!* I did have kids of my own!" Harry reposted. "I was just wondering what happened to the youngest one!"

"Yeh; right. So how come you don't know anything about trick or treating?"

"Your mother took care of all that," Harry replied. "I was usually at work."

"Well I'm off then," said Marjorie, tugging on her coat.

Harry caught his reflexion in the hall mirror and winced at the sight of his hair slicked back against his skull, the white face-paint and the thick black eye shadow. In his opinion, he looked more like a startled panda than Count Dracula.

"OK. Marjorie. As always, thanks. Have a happy Halloween, or whatever the saying is."

"And to you!" she giggled. "Don't forget to wear the cloak and put the fangs in your mouth!"

"Chow Marjie!" Adam called from the kitchen "See you later!"

"Are you sure you're not coming to the do at the pub, Harry?" she asked.

"No, I think I'll dish out the goodies and then have an early night."

"Alright; but Halloween is a good night at *The Kings Head.* The fancy dress costumes are always good for a laugh, and the barbecue in the rec is worth going for on its own."

"Sorry to be a wet blanket," he said.

"Don't be silly; of course you're not!" she replied, opening the front door.

The overcast sky was already turning mid afternoon into early evening when she stepped into the porch, shuddering as she glanced at the repulsive rubber tarantula tied to the knocker. Like the angel-hair cobwebs draped across the magnolia, it was Adam's handiwork.

Harry pushed the fangs into his mouth and gave her what he hoped was a scary smile. "Goodbye my dear!" he croaked.

He was not sure whether her laughter was due to his pathetic attempt at a Vincent Price imitation, or the way he gagged as the awful odour of the plastic fangs filled his nostrils.

By seven o'clock, the time Marjorie had advised him the younger trick-or-treaters would have finished their rounds, the basket was still pretty full. All but two of the cup cakes were still sitting untouched on the plate.

The doorbell had only been rung three times; once by the Chowdri girls, with their mother, Padmana; another by a boy of about ten, accompanied by his little sister and both parents; and finally by two adolescent boys, who appeared bored with the whole process. Harry had dropped a handful of sweets into a bag they held out lethargically in front of them.

"Well that was well worth all the effort, wasn't it?" he said sourly, as Adam made ready to leave for *The King's Head*. "I'm so glad I let you and Marjorie talk me into it."

"Never mind dad; it's like your first year, right. I'm sure word will get around for next year."

"Ain't gonna be no next year!" Harry retorted. "I intend turning out all the lights and going to bed as soon as it gets dark!"

Adam chuckled. "Way to go dad! That's getting into the spirit of it! Come on Daddy Dracula; put your cloak on and come with me!"

"No; I think I've had enough excitement for one evening," Harry replied. "You go and enjoy yourself."

\* \* \*

He was dozing in his armchair when the insistent *ding-dong; ding-dong; ding-dong* of the doorbell dragged him back to consciousness. He rose as quickly as his befuddled mind would allow and made his way to the front door.

The startled expressions on the faces of the four girls in his porch reminded him of his hurried attempt to remove the greasepaint Marjorie had applied to his face. He had only succeeded in smearing it, and decided to leave it until he showered before getting into bed.

"Bloody hell! That's cool; it's like, real scary!" one of the girls exclaimed, but before he could reply, another asked, "Can I use your loo?"

"Be my guest," Harry replied. She swept past him as he gestured towards the door.

"Would the rest of you like to come in and wait?" he asked. "It looks cold out there."

He moved aside to let them into the hall, and noticing his black and white streaked face in the mirror, he grinned sheepishly. "I was just wiping this stuff off. I look like an anaemic badger!"

It brought gratifying laughter from the girls, and the comment, "It's very effective ... very unusual."

They were dressed in a variety of costumes. He recognized one, beneath the stars and glitter of her makeup, as Jess Lloyd; the May Queen. She was dressed as a wizard, complete with cape and spangled conical hat. Another girl wore a black wig and a long cloak over what appeared to be a black body stocking, through which her skimpy underwear and several tattoos were visible. The third was a witch with a tall black hat, stick-on warts and a false, hooked nose. All he noticed of the girl who had rushed to the toilet was a good deal of leather with zips and buckles prominent.

"I'm afraid I can only offer you sweets and these cakes," he said self-consciously. "We were catering for little ones mostly."

"No probs," The witch replied. "Lynn was desperate for a pee. Old misery-guts over the road told us to clear off. We saw the pumpkin on your gatepost."

"Can I have a cake?" the girl in the body stocking asked.

"Of course; take what you like, all of you," Harry answered, trying to keep his eyes from straying from her face to what was disconcertingly visible when the cloak parted as she moved.

"Your daughter's just graduated from university hasn't she?" Jess asked, taking a KitKat from the basket.

"Yes," Harry replied, adding, "Take a handful."

"Where was she?" Jess asked. "I'll be looking at universities next year."

"She was at Reading. She graduated in meteorology and climatology." He managed to stop himself mentioning that she had achieved a first. "What are you intending to do?" he asked.

"Medicine," she replied. "I want to be a paediatrician."

"Excellent," he said. "But I'm not sure Reading will be much good to you; unless you want to treat baby animals."

She gave him a smile that revealed her even, white teeth. The fourth girl appeared from the toilet with an audible sigh of relief. "That's better; thanks!" she said.

"You're welcome," Harry chuckled. "Have you all finished trick-or-treating for the evening?"

"We're going to try the pubs now," the witch replied, and rattled a plastic bucket with *St. Anne's* painted on it. Harry had not noticed it while she had been standing behind Jess. "We're trying to raise some money for Saint Anne's Hospice," she explained.

Harry pulled out a handful of change from his pocket. "OK, let's see what I've got here."

There were several pound coins and some silver, and he dropped it all into the bucket.

"Cool; thanks!" Jess exclaimed; the sentiment echoed by the others.

"My pleasure," he said. "It's for a good cause. Good luck with the pubs."

As they turned towards the door, with another chorus of 'Thank yous', he asked, "Anyone want more cake or sweets?"

"Thanks; I'd love a cake," the girl in leather replied. "Thanks for letting me use your loo. You're a nice man." Taking his face between her hands, she planted a kiss on his forehead. "And I love your makeup; it's really cute."

Harry chuckled to himself, as he waved them goodbye and returned their call of 'Happy Halloween', before closing the door.

"Adam would have enjoyed that visit," he said quietly. "That body stocking would have had his eyes popping out like organ stops."

\* \* \*

He had been about to climb the stairs to bed, when Adam arrived home; relatively sober and, more surprisingly, before midnight. The half empty basket and the two remaining cup cakes drew an immediate comment. "I see you've like, had a lot more callers, dad."

"Only four," Harry replied, aware that Adam was looking at him wide eyed.

"Dad! What have you been up to?" Adam asked with a broad grin.

"Nothing; why?"

"Have you seen yourself?"

Harry moved to the mirror, and took in the ghostly pallor of his face, marked with pale black streaks and smudges ... and the outline of the girl's lips in blue lipstick on his forehead.

Enjoying Adam's bemused expression, he chortled, "I've been told I'm cute. I'm getting to quite like this trick or treating."

# NOVEMBER

## *Through the Mist*

Harry collected up his papers and followed Guy out of ACCORS' Board Room, skirting a small group in the corridor ostentatiously engaged in discussion outside one of the meeting rooms. Heads nodded sagely, brows were solemnly furrowed and faces bore expressions of earnest concentration. How many times had he seen it? The ambitious, the hopeful and the hangers on, grasping the opportunity to demonstrate their 'dedication and commitment'.

As the lift doors closed, Guy looked at Harry purposefully. "You do realise you could get yourself at least another three months on your contract, don't you? Perhaps more."

"Possibly," Harry replied, "But to what purpose? It's pretty obvious that Nick Stenning's talked the directors out of adopting my suggestion to merge departments. Even Shirley Cochran seems to have cooled to the idea."

Guy nodded. "Maybe. But you've put the cat amongst the pigeons with your reports."

"Why wasn't Stenning at this meeting?" Harry asked.

"I don't know," Guy replied. "He seems to have succeeded in heading off the possibility of getting his department swallowed up by *Project Management*, but the word is, he's been getting it in the ear about his operating costs. Apparently the budgets of some quangos; especially the smaller ones like us, are coming under scrutiny from the Ministries. It's got Bertie Boy rattled. Your report has been a bit of a bombshell. He's let Nick know, in no uncertain terms, that he's got to cut back … *drastically!*"

"I should think so!" said Harry. "Stenning's travel costs are ridiculous."

Remembering that Guy had attended the meeting to deputise for his boss, Duncan Bruce, who was on sick leave, Harry asked, "By the way, how's Duncan?"

"Coming along," Guy replied. "Gallstones apparently. He should be back in harness soon."

The lift doors opened and Guy led Harry out across the deserted foyer. "I still think you should consider extending your contract," he urged. "Everyone knows we're a mess and your recommendations are no great surprise."

"What's the point?" Harry exclaimed in exasperation. "No-one seems able to make up their mind about anything!"

"It's prevarication they're after!" Guy exclaimed. "The opportunity to tell the Ministry you're taking a look at one or two other areas will suit them down to the ground and take the pressure off for a while."

"What *other areas*? I've looked at everything already! The problems … and the solutions are staring everybody in the face!" Harry retorted.

"You could suggest looking at alternative solutions," Guy insisted.

"I actually thought the CEO was on board at one point," Harry mused.

"Oh, she is!" Guy replied. "Shirley's well aware of the problems, but she can't get the go-ahead from Bertie Boy to do what's needed."

Harry shrugged resignedly. "I can't say I'm surprised," he sighed. "Sir Bertram hasn't shown much interest; none that I've noticed, anyway."

"Sir Bertram likes a quiet life," Guy chuckled. "I'm willing to bet he's going along with this because he's being leaned on from above to cut costs."

"If that's the case, why is he taking so little interest?" Harry asked.

Guy replied with a wry grin. "Like I said, I don't doubt prevarication is what he and one or two others are after. They hope that going along with this will drag things out, until it blows over and gets forgotten."

"Like government enquiries?" Harry suggested sardonically.

"Precisely!" Guy exclaimed. "They're hoping some panic or cock-up elsewhere will push this onto the back burner. That's why I'm sure you'd have no difficulty in stringing out your contract. That way it looks as if they're doing something, while delaying things as long as possible."

"My God!" Harry exclaimed. "What a waste! Any business run like this place wouldn't last six months! And you're saying Shirley Cochran can't do anything about it on her own?"

"Afraid not," Guy sighed. "She'd love to get to grips with things. Come to think of it, I don't think she'd mind getting to grips with you either!"

"You what?" Harry exclaimed.

Guy laughed. "Oh, come on; don't pretend you didn't notice. She was hanging on your every word."

Harry felt his cheeks flush. "You're barmy! Anyway, she's not my type."

"Sorry, I forgot; leggy blondes are your preference, aren't they?"

As the entrance doors slid open, Harry punched Guy's shoulder playfully. "Any plans for New Year's Eve?" he asked.

Guy stroked his chin thoughtfully. "Not that I know of."

"Well, according to Marjorie, Nethercombe holds a New Year's Eve ball in the Memorial Hall. I expect we'll end up there if Rachel decides to spend the New Year at Church House."

"An old fashioned country shindig, eh? It might be fun!" Guy exclaimed.

"It's organised by the Parish Council," Harry explained. "The price of the ticket covers the food and live music. The landlord of *The Kings Head* runs a bar, and I think there are a few fireworks as well. You and Emma are welcome to stay over at 'Simmonds Towers'."

"Why not?"

"OK. I'll see about getting some tickets."

"I'm sure our little bluey would enjoy that."

"Our what?"

"It's Aussie for a copper knob."

Harry laughed. "I'll bet she just loves being called that."

"Oh, she doesn't mind," Guy chuckled. "As long as she doesn't know, that is. Got time for a pie and a pint?"

"I'll take the pie, but I'm driving."

"Alright; make it a pie and a lemonade. It's a nice day, so let's get something on the quay."

Despite the stultifying restrictions of health and safety regulations and the previous day's rain, the bonfire was blazing brightly, albeit almost too far away for even the nearest onlooker to benefit from the heat. The banners of yellow flame and showers of sparks that streamed into the purple night sky had already consumed *Guy Fawkes,* who, looking more like a ragamuffin tramp than a would-be terrorist, had tilted like a drunken sailor, before subsiding slowly into the inferno, with tragi-comic dignity.

His namesake was devouring a large hotdog, while gazing up at the bursting blooms of light that crackled and boomed high above the cheering, whooping crowd.

"Very impressive, Harry!" he exclaimed, between the deafening reports.

"It's not bad is it?" Harry yelled into the turmoil.

Emma's animated features were illuminated in ever changing hues, and Harry saw her lips form the words, "Really lovely!" although the sound was lost in a salvo of detonations.

Beside her, Laura stood with her arm through Simon's; their heads close together as they gazed skyward. A few yards beyond them, Marjorie was waving her arms in exaggerated gestures, her distorted shadow performing a macabre ballet on the canvas wall of the marquee, as she tried to communicate with Phil and the Hardys.

Harry felt a glow of satisfaction at the pleasure of sharing such a simple occasion with those who had honoured him with their friendship, and who, in turn, had found a place in his heart.

The fireworks concluded with a frenzied crescendo of flashes, crashes and eruptions of cascading light, leaving the onlookers with their ears ringing and a haze of sulphurous smoke hanging over the recreation ground. Cheers and a ripple of applause filled the abrupt silence.

Rachel, accompanied by the gaggle of associates she had brought from Canary Wharf, appeared from the marquee, where they had remained throughout the firework display. A picture of elegance, she wore a grey reefer jacket over a ski sweater, jeans and knee-length boots. A long, red scarf was wound around her neck, with a matching woollen hat adorning her blonde tresses.

"Ah; there you are!" she called and made towards Harry and his companions. En route, she stopped to greet Marjorie, prompting Harry to reflect that whatever faults she might possess, they did not include impoliteness.

"We've been here all the time; watching the fireworks," he replied casually.

"You missed a terrific display, Rachel," Laura exclaimed.

"When you've seen one firework display, you've seen 'em all, especially if you've been in New York on the fourth of July," Robin replied, reinforcing Harry's opinion that he was the least likeable of the group that Rachel had introduced to them earlier.

"Oh, we're simple, country folk," Guy replied flippantly. Robin and Rachel ignored his sarcasm, and she began introducing her colleagues to a nearby group of *Black Bull* regulars.

Robin, or the *'condescending little creep'*, as Harry thought of him, was short and flabby, with dark, curly hair, and a noticeable paunch, although he appeared to be not much over thirty. The vulgar, ostentatious wristwatch and heavy signet ring did nothing to mitigate Harry's first impression; nor did his habit of peppering his conversation with 'city jargon' in his *'Dell Boy'* accent

Oliver seemed to be of a similar age, but was slim and well over six-feet tall. He hid his thin, fair hair under a tweed, flat cap and wore a

Burberry trenchcoat over a mustard waistcoat and moleskin trousers. He affected an upper class drawl, although the occasional flattened vowel suggested more humble origins. However, his most noticeable feature was a prominent nose which made him appear hawk-like in profile. He remained aloof and had said little to anyone other than his companions. His interest seemed to be focused on the girl beside him, who had been introduced as Lydia.

Lydia was almost as tall as Rachel, with short cropped hair and classic high cheek bones. She had a pleasant, friendly nature, and the good manners to express her appreciation of the evening's entertainment. Harry guessed she was in her early twenties. She spoke in that eccentric manner, adopted by well educated young women, of elongating vowels, as if their mouths are frozen in a permanent smile; so that 'amazing' becomes '*ameezing*' and 'OK' pronounced '*eekee*'.

But it was Julian who commanded Harry's attention. From the greying temples and creases at the corners of his eyes, Harry guessed he was probably in his fifties, but younger looking than Guy … and noticeably fitter. He was about Harry's height and fashionably tanned, with, again unlike Guy, a head of luxuriant wavy hair. He exuded urbane charm, especially in the company of women.

Rachel's deference towards him suggested he held a senior position in the organisation where she worked, although she had made no reference to their professional relationship. However, it was Julian's manner with her that aroused Harry's suspicion, and he would admit, not a little jealousy. Julian's hand rested in the small of Rachel's back while she introduced her friends, and he looked at her with, what seemed to Harry, a proprietorial smile.

But Harry had no time to dwell on such things, because Robin suddenly asked dismissively, "What's this place called?" Grinning at Oliver and Lydia, he added, "Rachel did tell us, but I can't remember … something bloody weird!"

"It's called Nethercombe Ley," Harry replied flatly; reflecting that, having taken an initial dislike to him, Robin was someone he could bring himself to seriously detest, if he got to know him better.

Robin held up his half empty glass and smiled again at Oliver. "At least the beer's just about drinkable; not far off gnat's piss, but drinkable!" Giving Harry a searching look, he said, "It's Harry isn't it? What do you *do*, Harry?"

Gritting his teeth, Harry kept his reply brief. "I'm an accountant."

"And what does an accountant make?"

"He doesn't make anything. An accountant works with figures."

Robin laughed disdainfully. "I meant what sort of *money* do accountants get?"

"I know what you meant," Harry retorted curtly. "I don't know about other accountants, but I would assume that, like me, they work on the basis that the only people who need to know are them and HM Revenue and Customs."

"Quite right!" said Julian, who had obviously been listening to their exchange. Harry would have welcomed the intervention had he not noticed him give Rachel's rear a gentle pat as he turned towards them. She continued her conversation without reacting.

Robin grinned. "No offence intended my friend. I was just curious."

*'I'm not your bloody friend; not if my life depended on it!'* Harry thought.

"We're off for some liquid refreshment," Guy called.

As he and Simon moved off towards the marquee, Robin's attention shifted to Emma; and more specifically, to her cleavage, as she squatted on her haunches to retrieve a fallen glove.

"That's what I like; tottie throwing itself at my feet," he smirked. "What's your name again darlin'?"

Emma stared back icily. "The same as it was when Rachel introduced us," she replied flatly, and turned away to follow Laura towards the marquee.

Robin grimaced at Julian. "Lairy bitch!" he sneered. "It sounds Australian, so what can you expect!"

Instinctively Harry clenched his fists, feeling his finger nails digging into his palms. "I don't know what you expect where *you* come from, but *we* treat women with respect around here!" he barked.

Rachel turned to face them. "What's going on?" she asked.

Julian intervened, putting an arm round Robin's shoulder. "It's OK Rache. Robin didn't mean anything. He's had a little too much to drink, that's all."

Robin assumed an air of innocence. "Oh dear; I seem to have upset Harry," he sneered. With his face close to Julian's ear, he murmured, "He must be giving her one. I wonder if the old fella knows."

Unfortunately for Robin, his voice carried a little further than he had intended; just far enough for Harry to hear. To his surprise, he found himself whirled round by the lapels of his coat and transfixed by Harry's outraged glare.

"You repulsive, dirty minded little runt!" Harry snarled.

Recognising the fury in those blazing eyes, Robin's astonishment turned to alarm, as he tried to wrest himself free.

Rachel's startled yelp of, "Stop it!" pierced the red mist of Harry's malevolence, giving Julian the opportunity to drag Robin from his grasp. She glared at Harry. "What the hell's come over you?"

"Get him out of my sight!" Harry growled.

Visibly alarmed, Julian needed no second bidding to lead the ashen faced Robin away.

"What brought that on?" Rachel exclaimed.

"Ask him!"

"I'm asking you! I thought it might be nice for you to meet one or two people before we go to Austria."

"You've got to be kidding!" Harry growled. "I wouldn't spend another minute in the company of that little shit!"

Lydia gasped in alarm and looked at Oliver, who, attempting to make an impression, assumed an expression that suggested he regarded Harry as something he would normally scrape off his shoe.

"I suggest you take care what you say!" he drawled haughtily.

Harry shrugged. "I suggest you'd be better off giving that advice to your pal."

Oliver seemed to decide that was as far as he was prepared to go by way of personal involvement. Taking Lydia's hand, he led her away.

"Come on Lydia, let's find Robin and Julian."

"I've seen a side to you tonight, I never suspected!" Rachel declared. "I've told everyone what a lovely guy you are. Robin's had a little too much to drink. I would have thought you, of all people, would understand that!"

"I see; so that's the way it is," Harry replied flatly. "OK, you're right. I've had plenty of experience of being drunk; enough to know that alcohol only brings out the worst of what's already there. And if you want home truths, I don't think you'd tolerate that jumped up barrow-boy for five minutes if he wasn't one of Julian's cronies!"

"Go to hell!" she exclaimed, and turning on her heel, she stormed off after her colleagues.

"I've been there," Harry sighed, suddenly realising that Gerald Spenser-Smith was watching him.

Gerry's eyebrows rose. "Lover's tiff?" he asked mischievously.

"Sod off Gerry," Harry replied with a self-conscious grin.

Gerry chortled. "The missus is nattering with her pals, so why don't we both sod off and grab a beer at *The Kings Head*?"

"I'd love to," Harry answered, "but I've got people staying overnight. They're in the beer tent."

"In that case, I'll stand you a pint in there."

It was warm and humid in the crowded marquee. The throng gathered around the bar suggested it would be some time before they were served, but Harry heard a familiar voice call his name. Looking up he saw Simon, half a head taller than anyone else, at the front of the melee. Simon mouthed "pint?" and Harry nodded, gesturing towards Gerry beside him.

"Simon appears to be getting them in," he said.

"Well, *I* was going to buy you one," Gerry replied. "But I can't say I'm sorry about not having to fight my way through that scrum. By the way, have you heard of *The Dream Dolls*?"

"I think so," Harry replied. "They're a girl band aren't they?"

"So I'm told," Gerry replied. "The reason I mention it is; one of Jimmy Lloyd's girls knows one of them. There's a chance we might be able to get her to switch our Christmas lights on. Apparently she's from

Sturminster Newton. Her parents still live there, so she's sort of local … well, from Dorset, anyway."

There was no sign of Rachel and her entourage. Noticing Harry looking around, Gerry said, "Best make it up with her as soon as possible, old son. Take it from an old hand; the longer they stew, the tougher it gets. They've got memories like elephants. Give 'em time to think about it and they'll dig up things from yonks ago. It all gets dragged out as previous form when they pass sentence."

Harry laughed. "I know; I was married for over twenty years."

Emma and Laura appeared from around the edge of the throng, each carrying a wine glass, closely followed by Guy with a pint in each hand. Simon finally appeared with what looked like orange juice and another pint.

"There you go," said Guy, handing one of the glasses to Harry, while Simon did the same to Gerry.

Simon raised his orange juice. "Here's to a thoroughly enjoyable evening. Cheers everyone!"

They all responded by raising their glasses; Emma adding, "Thanks for inviting us; it's lovely!"

"The jungle drums are saying our Harry's been in fighting mood and threatened to knock some poor devil's block off!" Guy quipped.

"Yes; he was challenging all-comers!" Gerry chortled.

Laura's eyes widened. "What on earth happened, Harry?"

Harry avoided Emma's enquiring look. "Nothing really. One of those hooray-henries got up my nose, that's all. I suppose I should have ignored it."

"Rancid Robin, I presume," said Guy.

Laura frowned. "He really is an unpleasant little man. I'm surprised Rachel puts up with him."

"I have a feeling she doesn't have much choice," said Harry.

It was impossible to put the confrontation out of his mind, but to avoid becoming a damper on a pleasant occasion, Harry did his best to be light-hearted and convivial. It was some time later, when the crowd had thinned and they were tucking into hamburgers and hot dogs, that

Simon looked up and said quietly, "I think Rachel's looking for you, Harry."

Harry turned to see her standing at the entrance to the marquee; her expression unchanging as she noticed him. She mouthed, 'I need to speak to you.' Excusing himself and handing his drink to Simon, Harry went towards her.

"Not here!" she said abruptly, and turned to move away, as he reached her. Harry's heart sank; sensing that this was the moment he had been dreading, but had known to be inevitable.

When she was satisfied they could not be overheard, Rachel stopped. "I know what happened," she said quietly.

"I expect you do," he replied. "Have your friends gone?"

"No; they're in *The Kings Head*. I hoped you might have calmed down ... and perhaps felt like apologising."

Harry's hackles rose. "What the hell for?" he exclaimed. "If we're talking apologies, it ought to be your friend Robin. Not to me but ..."

"Oh; of course!" Rachel interjected acidly. "He was rude about your *precious* Emma, wasn't he?"

Harry deliberately ignored her sarcasm. "Rude? He was downright bloody insulting! Not to mention sneering and sarcastic about Nethercombe and everything and everybody."

"He's had too much to drink!" Rachel exclaimed.

"Don't give me all that guff again!" Harry snapped. "He's obnoxious; drunk or sober!"

Rachel gave a mocking laugh. "Oh, so you're suddenly a character expert! Well, how about putting some thought to your own shortcomings?"

"I have!" Harry replied coldly. "But the difference between your Robin and me is; I know what I am ... and everything I'm not. But I hope I never get to the point where I look down my nose at good, honest people, whose shoelaces I'm not fit to tie!"

"You never had any intention of coming skiing, did you?" she said deliberately. "This has given you the perfect excuse, hasn't it?"

Harry sighed wearily. "Come on Rachel! Are you seriously suggesting

I provoked that just to avoid saying no to the bloody skiing trip? I was going to tell you properly, to your face. I wanted to explain that I just don't fancy being the odd one out. Be honest; you know I would be. The rest of you are competent skiers and you all work together. I'd have to put up with in-jokes I didn't understand and the embarrassment of falling on my backside every five minutes. But in spite of my misgivings, I did try to psych myself up to say yes, purely to please you! It's a good job I didn't, isn't it … for both of us?"

"What do you mean?" she retorted.

"Don't take me for a complete fool Rachel! I'll buy what you said about the original reason for bringing them down here. But things have changed haven't they? My set-to with Robin has served its purpose for you, hasn't it? Do you imagine I'm too stupid to see that?"

"Everything OK Rache?"

Harry looked round at the shadowy figure, who had approached unnoticed; his face pale in the reflected glow of the bonfire.

Rachel answered without turning her head. "Yes Julian, I'm fine."

"Well, if you're finished, it's time we were leaving," he said.

"Yes; we're finished," she replied flatly.

Julian held out his hand to her and looked at Harry meaningfully. Harry deliberately held his gaze, keeping his face expressionless until Julian looked away.

"Safe journey," Harry said bitterly, and turned to make his way back to the marquee.

A deep sense of sorrow swept over him, as he walked back in the darkness. He was not in love with Rachel; he had never felt about her the way he had Sally. Nevertheless, he felt a profound loss. She had become part of his life. Her generous nature and ebullient personality had lifted him from the depths of despair. However, he had always known that sooner or later the novelty of having him as her occasional, weekend lover would wear thin. He had never deluded himself that, when she was at home in London, she remained glued to *The X Factor* or *Strictly Come Dancing*. But he had not envisaged such an acrimonious break.

He had been staring at his feet as he walked, and Simon's voice made him look up sharply in surprise. "Are you alright Harry?"

"I don't know," he answered honestly.

Simon handed him his beer. "I thought you might need this. I know it's none of my business; and you can tell me so, but I take it you and Rachel have quarrelled."

Harry replied with a wry grin. "It's a bit more than that. It's been coming for a while."

Simon put his hand on Harry's shoulder. "As I said, it's none of my business."

"Isn't it?" Harry said. "She is your sister."

"Yes, and she means the world to me. But what I wanted to say was: whatever's happened is between the two of you. I'm still your friend Harry … unless you tell me otherwise."

"Thanks Simon. The last thing I want is to lose your friendship. But I'm afraid I've blown it with Rachel … for good."

"I wouldn't be too sure of that," said Simon quietly.

Harry laughed. "You would if you'd heard her tell me what she thought of me!"

"I can guess," Simon chuckled. "But I've known Rachel a lot longer than you have."

"I didn't expect it to end like this," Harry said wistfully.

Simon patted his shoulder. "Look; if you'd prefer to be alone, I can put Emma and Guy up for tonight."

"Thanks for the offer, but I need cheering up; and who better than Guy?"

Thankfully Guy was in top form, with his armoury of quips, quirky observations and shaggy dog stories. No-one mentioned Harry's conversation with Rachel, and desperate to avoid being a *wet blanket*, he allowed himself to be carried along with the fun; joining in as best he could. At one point he caught Marjorie's eye across the marquee. She smiled, but the flicker of concern in her expression indicated that she was aware of what had happened.

It was approaching midnight when they all strolled home, in

company with the Hardys, parting company with the Spenser-Smiths and Simon and Laura outside *The Black Bull*.

May Cottage was strangely quiet now that Adam was away. Still the silence was a pleasant relief from the tuneless dirges emanating from the kitchen radio when he was at home.

"Coffee, anyone?" Harry asked, as Emma and Guy shed their coats and scarves.

"Rather!" Guy replied.

"I'll make it," Emma suggested, but Harry held up a hand. "No; you're my guests. Go and make yourselves comfortable. Help yourselves to a brandy or whatever you fancy."

"A brandy would be much appreciated," said Guy. He and Emma made their way to the sitting room, while Harry went into the kitchen.

As he filled the kettle, his eye caught the sparkle of the ruby, set in the ring lying on the windowsill. He remembered Rachel slipping it off when she had washed up the wine glasses after lunch the previous Sunday. He had intended to return it to her at the bonfire party, but the enjoyable distraction of having Emma and Guy as house guests had driven it from his mind. Rachel had spotted the ring in a jeweller's window in Wimbourne Minster, and he had bought it when she had tried it on and discovered it fitted the middle finger of her right hand. He made a mental note to call in at Church House and leave it with Simon, although he was prepared for her to send it back.

As he ladled coffee into the cafetiere, he heard footsteps in the hall and the sibilant creak of the kitchen door opening behind him. He knew without looking that it was Emma. She smiled, as he turned to face her, but then her expression became serious. "I don't know exactly what the hassle with that toad, Robin, was all about, but my guess is he made a remark about me. Am I right?"

Harry nodded. "Something like that. He got right up my nose."

"Thanks for standing up for me. I don't want to know what he said, but I can guess the gist of it. The way he looked at me made my flesh creep."

"According to Rachel, he's a nice guy when he's sober," Harry replied.

Emma gave a little shudder. "I'll take her word for it!" she said, and reached out to touch his arm. "I get the impression you and Rachel had words over it. I don't want to pry, but I'd hate to think I've been the cause of any trouble between you."

"It wasn't any fault of yours," Harry assured her. "If it hadn't been that, I would have found another reason to have a go at that obnoxious little swine."

"But if it's come between you and Rachel ..."

Harry sighed wistfully. "It hasn't ... not really. It's been on the cards for some time. I think it gave her the perfect opportunity." Noticing Emma's surprise, he added, "I'm not saying she planned it; I know her well enough to realise she's not like that, but it served its purpose."

"Oh, Harry; I'm so sorry!"

"Don't be sorry," he said. "Neither of us thought it was forever, or intended it to be. She made sure, right from the outset, that I understood it wasn't an exclusive or permanent relationship. As my son would say, 'I was cool with that'. It would appear that Julian has the inside track now."

"I see," she said. "Apparently he's got a swish apartment in the Docklands area." In reply to Harry's quizzical look, she added, "I've been invited there."

"Really?"

Emma grinned impishly. "Don't sound so surprised. I do get the odd improper suggestion occasionally!"

"I didn't mean that!" Harry exclaimed. "What I meant was; he knew you were with Guy."

"That wouldn't bother him. According to him, his wife spends most of her time at their place in Surrey. All very convenient. He told me about the apartment when we were in the beer tent before the fireworks started. He's invited me to dinner the next time I'm in London."

For the second time that night Julian evoked Harry's jealousy, as well as grudging envy. Married or single, he could not envisage having the confidence or courage to brazenly proposition a woman he had only just met ... or even one he already knew, for that matter.

"What did you say?" he asked, and immediately realised he had *put his foot in it* again.

Emma's eyes twinkled. "Wouldn't you like to know?" she giggled.

The sudden click of the kettle cut-off switch came as a welcome distraction. Harry filled the cafetiere wordlessly; the best way to make sure he did not commit another gaffe.

They could hear the sound of snoring as soon as they opened the kitchen door. Reaching the sitting room, they found Guy sound asleep in an armchair; legs outstretched, head thrown back and mouth wide open.

"Now, how could any girl resist that?" Emma chortled.

Remembrance Sunday dawned grey and overcast; and remained that way, with a chill wind chivvying an intermittent, icy drizzle before it. Harry had never attended an Armistice Day ceremony, and decided it was time he did; especially as it was less than a five minute walk to the war memorial.

His decision was also a gesture of solidarity with his neighbours. Alan Anderson had written a witty, but searingly scornful, article in *The Valley Voice*, deriding the Health and Safety zealots for imposing ridiculous new conditions on the ceremony. The *'Clipboard Clowns'*, as Alan had dubbed them, had demanded *'A Risk Assessment Survey'* and the submission of a formal request to close Manor Hill, and the exits from the lanes leading to the village green, to traffic. It had to be submitted *'on the correct form'*, of course. It was suggested that stewards should be appointed *'to control'* the assembly at the war memorial, and someone with first-aid qualifications should be on hand in case of accidents.

The villagers' initial disdain and amused disbelief had quickly turned to anger and to a barrage of protest, led by Gerald Spenser-Smith and the local branch of the Royal British Legion. The ridiculous demands had eventually been moderated to, as Alan had written, *Something as close to common sense as little men with too much power can manage*. However, they still insisted that signs warning of road closures must be in place at least a week beforehand, and that traffic cones had to be placed at the top of Manor Hill and the entrances to Mill Lane and The Pound, an hour before the parade.

Harry left the house before Adam was up, knowing his son would be loath to drag himself out of bed before lunch on such a bleak day. He had not seen Rachel since bonfire night; not that he expected to. He had put her ring in an envelope and left it with Simon, together with a short note thanking her for the happy times they had spent together, and expressing his regret that their relationship had ended that way. As far as he knew, she had not been back to Nethercombe in the meantime.

He still felt pangs of jealousy, but they stemmed mostly from resentment of Julian's condescending self assurance and, what to Harry, seemed unctuous charm with women. Especially galling was the fact that he had tried it on with Emma, and that her reaction had been amusement rather than indignation.

He would never understand women; especially women like Rachel. She would always mystify him. Emma seemed less enigmatic, with her vivacious, outgoing personality. But what did he know? He had *thought* he understood Sally.

How could someone like Emma feel flattered or amused at being propositioned by a smarmy womaniser like Julian? It brought to mind the unsolicited advice of Mike, an old friend from his youth, who used to chide him about his shyness and tell him to be more outgoing. The gospel according to Mike was that women prefer men to be confident and assertive, which Harry's limited experience seemed to confirm. Mike's advice had concluded with something along the lines of: 'The worst they can do is say *no*,' which in Harry's opinion, was all very well, provided '*no*' was the exception rather than the norm. However, the humiliation of rejection appeared to play little part in the lives of the Mikes and Julians of this world.

Thirty minutes before 'the eleventh hour' Harry walked the short distance to the village green, wrapped up against the rawness of the weather in a scarf and heavy coat. When he arrived, he found a large group of people milling around the War Memorial; all wearing poppies; some holding wreaths and sprays of flowers. He was greeted warmly by the Chowdris and the Alders, including Gary, who wore his uniform and campaign medals. An elderly woman handed Harry a photocopied sheet containing the Order of Service, which reminded him uncomfortably of his father's funeral, only two months before.

Harry passed the war memorial almost every day, but never ceased to be moved by all the names covering three sides of the plinth that supported the stone cross. So many ... from such a small village.

Among the names beneath the legend '1939-1945' was 'Miss D.A. Long'; a reminder that selfless sacrifice in time of war is not the sole preserve of the male population. Harry had learned from his enquiries that Dorothy ... Dot Long had been the daughter of the then landlord of *The Black Bull*. Lured away from Nethercombe Ley by the bright city lights before the war, she had been fatally wounded by shrapnel, while manning a searchlight battery.

There were two names under Korea and Malaya. 'Will we never learn and accept the utter futility of war?' Harry reflected. Although no-one remained who had known the young men whose names appeared beneath the words 'The Great War', their memory lived on in the soul of the village.

Harry had little time to brood. He could hear the muffled thump of a bass drum, gradually coming closer. A few moments later, the Farmers Union Brass Band, in blue kepis and green blazers, appeared from Manor Hill. It was closely followed by a group of Cadets and Scouts, led by a youngster bearing a Royal British Legion banner. Behind them marched a small parade of mostly elderly men, displaying their medals and wearing a variety of berets, cap badges and insignia denoting the military units they had once served.

Among the marchers, Harry recognised Alfie Cox and Tommy

Armor, who, despite his arthritis, was marching as best he could and carrying a large wreath of poppies. For a few, like Tommy, pride was tempered by the anguish of reliving the loss of a loved one, with whom they had shared the joys and sorrows of a short life.

As the procession reached *The Black Bull*, Simon and the choir of Saint Luke's appeared at the entrance to Church Lane, wearing white surplices and cassocks beneath dark woollen cloaks. Harry stifled a smile as the sight of Simon reminded him of a monster penguin. He could only guess how many layers of clothing he and the choristers had on under their vestments to keep out the raw winter chill.

Faces appeared at the windows of *The Black Bull*, and as the marchers skirted the village green, a group of dignitaries, including Sir George Woodleigh, Gerald Spenser-Smith and Lady Diana Lauderham, emerged from the entrance, each carrying a wreath. They made their way slowly across the grass; Lady Diana sporting a striking Cossack-style fur hat, a black, woollen coat and leather boots.

Harry watched the elderly men as they approached; arms swinging; heads erect; eyes looking straight ahead. Perhaps not marching with the vigour and precision they once had, but every bit as proudly.

'They feel special again,' Harry thought. Having been blessed with the good fortune never to have experienced war, he could only imagine how the older ones felt. They were no doubt remembering the horror, hardship and terror they had experienced, while taking pride in having served their country in time of need.

As they reached the memorial, the crowd eased back, to give the parade room to form up. Simon and the choir stood to one side, allowing the band to move behind it, leaving the place of honour in front for the ex-servicemen and dignitaries. Alfie looked at Gary and winked. Gary understood; the way only someone who had shared a soldier's experiences could.

Simon stepped forward, hushing the low hum of voices as he cleared his throat. "Welcome to our Service of Remembrance, to honour these members of our community who have given their lives in the service of their country." Slowly and reverently, he recited the names carved on the memorial, after which he paused, and said, "We will now sing the hymn *Abide With Me*."

The band played the introductory bars, before the choir led the other voices as they straggled into the opening lines. *'Abide with me; fast flows the eventide; the darkness deepens; Lord with me abide …'*

Harry looked around him as he sang; moved by the emotive words of a hymn written by a dying man, almost seventy years before the first of those two horrific conflicts which drenched the world in blood.

The village had turned out in force. Harry suspected it was partly a gesture of defiance at the interference of petty bureaucracy. One or two onlookers watched from outside *The Black Bull* and the gardens of the cottages around the green, preferring to remain as spectators, rather than take part.

To one side of him, Harry noticed Laura, wearing a heavy coat with a fur lined hood that framed her face, making it appear almost angelic. Behind her stood Alan and Jill Anderson and Rob and Ellen Hardy. To Harry's surprise, he saw Adam approaching across the green, grinning self consciously as he met his father's gaze.

'Well I never,' Harry thought. 'You live and learn.'

*'… in life, in death, O Lord; abide with me.'*

A brief pause followed the hymn, during which a magpie swooped from a tree to land on top of the stone cross, from where it peered at the assembly, bobbing its head from side to side in curiosity. The wave of an ex-serviceman's arm sent it flapping back to its sanctuary above them.

Simon opened his prayer book, holding down a loose sheet of paper, as a sudden gust tried to snatch it from his grasp. "Let us pray." Heads bowed, as he began: "Lord, we offer our prayers for those who made the ultimate sacrifice …"

Simon's prayer was simple and moving; redolent of the pride and sorrow of a small community in honouring its sons and daughters, who had known it, loved it, and answered their nation's call; never to return.

There was a hum of 'Amen', before Simon glanced at his watch and continued, "Before we bow our heads in silence, let us say the prayer that Jesus taught us. "Our Father, Who art in heaven …"

As the rumble of the Lord's Prayer ended in another 'Amen', Simon consulted his watch once more, and after a few seconds, announced, "We will now take a few moments of silent contemplation to remember the fallen."

In the sudden quiet, the icy breath of early winter teased and tugged at uncovered hair and pursued withered leaves and twigs beneath the almost bare branches of the oaks, which surrounded the silent assembly like mute sentinels.

Harry's thoughts drifted to his father, who had been a boy during the Second World War and whose National Service afterwards had consisted of 'two wasted years counting blankets and dishing out uniforms', as he had once described it. The stillness and poignancy of the moment brought home to Harry how much he missed him.

The silence was suddenly broken by a bray of laughter from *The Black Bull*. It ended abruptly; the result of a sharp reprimand, Harry presumed. It was strange how long two minutes seemed in complete silence.

He did not notice the signal, but a girl stepped forward from the band, holding a bugle at her side. Harry could not suppress a smile of delighted surprise as he recognised her. He had last seen her on Halloween night, dressed in little more than an eye-catching body-stocking. He could not have felt more proud of her if she had been his own daughter, as she lifted her bugle to her lips, and the haunting notes of 'The Last Post' drifted across the village green; all the more poignant for a thin, faltering start. The fading echo of the final, lingering note still hung on the wind, as Sir George Woodleigh cleared his throat and delivered Laurence Binyon's evocative words:

"'They shall not grow old, as we that are left grow old:
Age shall not weary them, nor the years contemn.
At the going down of the sun and in the morning
We will remember them.'"

"We will remember them," came the murmured response, as Tommy Armor lifted the large wreath and made the most touching gesture of an already moving ceremony. Turning to Gary, he beckoned him forward, and together, the old soldier and the young one rested the wreath on the wide step of the memorial; Gary deferentially taking his cue from Tommy, as they came to attention and saluted.

Watching the dignitaries and others lay their wreaths and flowers, Harry noticed Marjorie dab at her eyes with a tissue. How many sleepless nights had she endured, haunted by the nightmarish dread of a visit from a solemn MoD messenger? Phil's weak smile betrayed his struggle with his emotions. He blinked rapidly, before looking away across the green, as the band played the opening bars, and the choir began, 'Oh God Our Help in Ages Past ...'

Simon concluded the ceremony with a final blessing, and as the crowd around the memorial began to disperse, he and the choir followed the band around the green, to the strains of 'Tipperary'.

"Can I buy you that pint now, Harry?" Gerry asked. Turning to Gary he added, "And you, young man ... and your family."

Harry had intended to allow himself only a short time at the memorial, before getting down to work on his final report for ACCORS, but the simple and moving service had heightened his sense of belonging. The lure of a pint of *Jimmy Riddle,* in the company of his friends and neighbours, was too strong a temptation. He even found himself persuading the Alders to join Adam and him for a pub lunch.

It was mid afternoon when they arrived back at May Cottage, with Harry reflecting on his good fortune in having chosen Nethercombe Ley as his home.

Adam and Marjorie were sitting at the kitchen table chatting over cups of hot chocolate when Harry arrived home from his final meeting with the Board of ACCORS.

"How did it go, dad?"

"Very satisfying," Harry replied. "Thank God; it was the last one!"

"Are they going to do anything about your recommendations?"

"I don't know. The way they operate, there's probably more chance of an earthquake in Garstone. But it's their problem. I've done what I was contracted to do. It's up to them now." With a chuckle, he added, "They've paid me though, so it hasn't all been a waste of time."

Marjorie reached down to the bag beside her on the floor and took out an envelope. "Here you are; your New Years Eve tickets."

"Thanks Marjorie. Who do I owe for these?"

"Me," she replied. "But there's no hurry."

"He's just been paid. Get the money now!" Adam urged impishly.

Harry took out his wallet and passed five twenty-pound notes to Marjorie, wondering what to do with Rachel's ticket. Thinking aloud, he looked at Adam. "It's a pity you'll miss the party. But I don't doubt you've got something lined up in London."

"We've been invited to a party by Ollie's sister; she's a nurse at The Chelsea and Westminster, right. And I think PAVT are organising something before we leave, too."

"Apparently we're having a haggis piped in this year," said Marjorie.

"Oh, I'll miss it! I'm gutted!" Adam exclaimed, failing to dodge the skilfully wielded newspaper that wacked him on the side of the head.

"Marjie!" he yelped.

"That's for your sarcasm!" she giggled. "You'd better mind your manners in Africa, or they'll feed you to the lions!"

Harry laughed with them. The way she had won Adam's respect and affection was remarkable and gratifying. Even the epithet, 'Marjie', which had originated as a challenge, had become a term of endearment. He could never have imagined the influence she would have when she had first appeared on his doorstep, almost a year ago.

"Gary's home; and he and I have got a cool little earner lined up," Adam announced.

"Good; doing what?" Harry asked.

Adam winked at Marjorie and affected a lofty air. "We have received a painting commission."

"A painting commission, eh?" Harry chuckled. "What is it, a makeover for the Sistine Chapel?"

Adam grinned. "No; the Memorial Hall."

"I can just see it; art lovers flocking from all over the world!" Harry exclaimed.

"You may scoff," Adam sniffed. "We artists are rarely appreciated during our lifetime. Take Van Gogh for instance."

"Is he the one that cut his own ear off?" Marjorie asked.

"Yeh! Then he shot himself in anger and frustration," Adam replied.

Harry chortled. "I'm not surprised. He wouldn't have been able to see to paint if he couldn't keep his glasses on and his hat kept falling over his eyes!"

Marjorie rolled her eyes. "It's a mad house!" she muttered. "I'm off home in case it's catching."

Betty and Sheila Greenaway were the duty staff at the Community Market, when Harry arrived to pick up his newspaper and some milk and eggs. They lived in one of the cottages in Church Lane. According to Marjorie, they had lived together for many years; ever since Betty's brother, Rex, had abandoned Sheila and their two children and 'run off' with a barmaid from *The King's Head*.

The scandal had fuelled Nethercombe gossip for weeks. But kind-hearted Betty had taken pity on her sister-in-law and given her and her children a home. The two seemed inseparable. Now that Sheila's children had grown up and flown the nest, it was rare to see one without the other. Notorious village gossips, they had a seemingly limitless capacity for recycling tittle-tattle.

They were deep in conversation with Mrs. Chowdri when Harry arrived. He caught the words, "Shouldn't think he's got long."

He took little notice, other than to return their greeting, because his eyes were drawn to a tray of duck eggs. It was Betty's comment, "It's Peggy I feel sorry for," that made him look up sharply. Noticing his curiosity, she asked, "Have you 'eard about poor Ted, Mr. Simmonds?"

"I heard he's had another big operation," Harry replied.

Sheila mouthed the word 'cancer', as if saying it out loud was somehow sacrilegious.

"Oh good grief!" Harry exclaimed, although it came as no surprise.

Betty folded her arms; a gesture seemingly designed to add gravity to her words. "Lisa went to see Peggy at the weekend. Apparently there's not much more they can do."

"They can't do much more," Sheila repeated.

"That's dreadful! How is Peggy?" Harry asked.

"She's puttin' a brave face on it, accordin' to Lisa," Betty replied. "But she must be devastated."

"Devastated," Sheila echoed.

"It's such a shame. They were such a friendly couple," said Mrs. Chowdri. "Always so helpful."

"Yes," said Harry, noting that she was already using the past tense. There seemed little more to say on the subject, but he guessed it would not prevent the Greenaways from doing so.

The arrival of Billy Shepcot, a neighbour of the Greenaways, distracted them. "Back again Billy?" Sheila asked.

"I forgot the spuds," Billy replied. "I got a'do me own chips now the chip shop's gone."

"I know; It was 'andy bein' up there by the bus stop," Sheila exclaimed. "But it's gone the way of everthin' else. It's all change these days."

Billy looked at Harry intently, as if he considered him somehow responsible. "It's bin there since nineteen-forty-six! Ol' Reg Liddiard opened it up with 'is missus when 'e got demobbed. It's one o'they take-it-away places now. All that foreign muck! I dunno!"

Harry made what he hoped were sympathetic noises, before hurriedly collecting his *Daily Telegraph* from the 'reserved' rack. He paid Betty for the other items he needed, and made his exit, leaving Billy and

Sheila to wring the last dregs of remorse from the loss of the fish and chip shop.

Harry left the church hall annexe too engrossed in the lead article on the front page of his newspaper to pay much attention to where he was going. He did not realise anyone was coming up the steps towards him until they almost collided.

"Hello Harry."

He looked up, startled by the familiar voice. "Hello Rachel," he replied nervously.

She was dressed in jodhpurs and riding boots, and the blue hacking jacket she had been wearing when he first met her. Her hair was pulled back with a plait tied in a velvet bow; just as it was then.

"How are you?" she asked.

"I'm fine, thanks. How are things with you?"

"Oh not bad," she said.

As she took her purse out of her pocket, he noticed the ring on her finger. She smiled as she followed his gaze. "Thank you for letting me keep it. I love it. I can assure you it has tremendous sentimental value."

"You earned it, putting up with me," he said.

"Oh Harry, I didn't *put up* with you! We had fun didn't we?"

"Yes," he replied. "*I* certainly did."

"So did I," she said. "I'm sorry for the things I said. I didn't mean to hurt you. I was embarrassed and angry; not just with you … with myself mostly. The whole evening was a disaster. I should never have brought them."

Harry shrugged. "It doesn't matter. But you were right. I overreacted, I suppose. But that's me. I'm old fashioned. I just don't like men talking about women like that."

Rachel touched his sleeve. "I know. Robin was out of order. You're a decent, honourable guy, Harry."

'Go on say it; *and sweet!*' he thought.

"Things just got a bit too rich for us, didn't they?" she said. "But we can still be friends can't we?"

Recognising the time-honoured phrase that brings down the curtain on love affairs, Harry smiled ruefully. But realising she was sincere, he replied honestly, "Yes; of course."

To his surprise, she kissed his cheek as she passed him. "Tell her, Harry," she said softly.

"What?"

"Tell her how you feel! You never know!"

She disappeared through the doorway, without giving him the chance to reply.

For a moment he stood there, with the breeze tugging at his hair and riffling the pages of his newspaper. He had got in wrong again. He had expected her to hold a grudge for a long time, avoiding him or cutting him dead if they met. But she had held out an olive branch at the first opportunity. He shook his head and laughed. Whoever came up with the epithet 'the weaker sex' had no idea!

\* \* \*

There was another surprise awaiting him when he arrived home. Marjorie was dusting the banister rail, and greeted him with an enigmatic smile. "You've got visitors," she said. "They're in the sitting room. I've made them some coffee. I'll bring you a cup in a minute."

The sitting room door was ajar, but as Harry approached, it was opened wide by Simon, who was grinning from ear to ear. "I hope you don't mind us hanging around until you got back," he said.

"Of course not," Harry replied. "Hello Laura; what a pleasant surprise!"

Laura's pretty face lit up with a smile, her bright eyes sparkling behind the shining lenses of her glasses. "Hi Harry," she said, seeming to stifle a giggle.

"We just wanted you to know ..." Simon began, but Laura forestalled him by thrusting out her hand, to display a diamond ring. "Laura has foolishly agreed to marry me."

"How wonderful! Congratulations!" Harry exclaimed with genuine delight, and shook Simon's hand. Realising it was expected, he kissed

Laura's cheek self-consciously, and turned to Marjorie, who had appeared in the doorway with a mug of coffee. "Guess what, Marjorie?"

Her knowing smile gave her away, but she played her part sportingly. "What?"

"Laura and I are going to be married," Simon said.

"Congratulations!" Taking Laura's outstretched hand, Marjorie admired the ring. "Oh, isn't that lovely!" she cooed, and immediately asked the obvious question; one that had not occurred to Harry. "When's the wedding?"

"As soon as possible after Easter," Laura said and giggled nervously. "I'm not sure how I'll cope with being a clergyman's wife."

"There's nothing to worry about," said Marjorie. "You'll be a real asset to your husband."

Laura beamed. "Thank you!"

"Yes, thank you Marjorie," said Simon. "That's what I've been telling her."

Marjorie smiled awkwardly. "Well I'd better carry on," she said and hurried out of the room.

"She's really nice, isn't she?" Laura exclaimed.

"Adam and I think she's a bit special," Harry replied.

"We're thinking of having a small celebratory drink at Church House for family and a few friends at the weekend," said Simon. "It's Laura's birthday on Saturday. We wondered if you'd care to join us? When I say family, that's just Laura's parents, her sister and her sister's husband, plus my mother … and Rachel," he added hesitantly. "She knows we're inviting you and she's quite happy, as long as you are."

"I've just spoken to her," Harry replied. "We seem to have cleared the air."

Laura clasped Harry's hand. "Oh, good. I'm so glad!"

"Yes, but I think you ought to know. Rachel and I are friends again, but not … well quite as we were," Harry said awkwardly. "I'm very honoured to be asked. Thank you."

"We'd like to invite Emma and Guy as well," Laura added. "We think of them as *our* friends now, as well … if you don't mind."

"Of course I don't!" Harry replied. "Why should I? What right have I or anybody else to tell you who you can be friends with? But for what it's worth, I'm delighted."

Laura kissed *his* cheek this time. "Thanks Harry; do you think they'll come?"

"Unless they're committed to something they can't get out of, I think you can bet on it," Harry replied, adding with a mischievous grin, "At least you could if you weren't engaged to a man of the cloth."

Laura and Simon chuckled. "I think we'd better be off," Simon said. "Laura can't wait to tell everyone at the stables. We need to let a few more people know, and invite them on Saturday. I have a meeting with the Bishop this afternoon, as well."

Harry accompanied them to the front door, pausing to allow them to detour to the kitchen to say goodbye to Marjorie. "See you on Saturday ... around seven-thirty," Simon called as they left.

Harry wandered into the kitchen, and found Marjorie in the process of putting things away in a large plastic box on wheels. It had a telescopic towing handle and compartments for a seemingly infinite quantity of cleaning fluids, cloths, sponges and gadgetry. Adam had christened it her '*Tardis*', claiming it was like Doctor Who's police box; bigger inside than out.

"Have you heard about Ted Flowers?" he asked.

"Yes," she sighed. "It doesn't sound very promising, does it?"

Harry shook his head. On a more upbeat note, he said, "That was nicely done with Laura. I think you've done her confidence a power of good."

"It's no more than the truth. She's a lovely girl," she replied. "I don't know much about it; not going to church and that, but from what I can gather, she's just what he needs after that terrible business of losing his first wife. I'm probably speaking out of turn, but you two are a pair."

"What do you mean?" he asked in surprise.

"It might get me the sack, but in for a penny ..."

Harry looked up at the sky through the kitchen window. "Nope; no flying pigs!"

Marjorie managed a weak smile. "You've both been on your own too long. I know there's been Rachel, but ... well, you know what I mean."

"Yes, I know what you mean," Harry replied hesitantly. "But they aren't exactly queuing up at the door."

Marjorie gave him a searching look. "They might, if you weren't so quick to find fault with yourself."

"Those two are well suited though, aren't they?" he said, deliberately changing the subject.

"They seem to be," she replied.

"Any suggestions for an appropriate engagement present?" Harry asked.

Marjorie looked pensive. "It depends on how much you want to spend."

"I don't mind really. I'm not thinking of anything ostentatious, but as they're good friends and very special people, I'd like to get them something nice."

Marjorie pursed her lips. "I'll have a think about it."

Harry wandered back to the lounge to collect the coffee mugs, mulling over Marjorie's words. She was right, of course; he had been on his own too long. But what did she mean about him 'finding fault with himself'? He was not aware of doing so. But he was not blind to his faults and shortcomings, especially when it came to relationships with women. Surely that was being honest?

The truth, however unwelcome, was that Sally had felt the need to start a new life with someone else, and Rachel had grown tired of him for basically the same reasons. So, unless he was prepared to end up a lonely old bachelor, he needed to shake himself up; throw off the straightjacket that confined him.

It brought a rueful smile to his face. "Easier said than done, Harry, old son," he murmured. "I can't see you turning into George Clooney anytime soon."

'*Tell her Harry,*' Rachel had said.

He had obviously given himself away by confronting Robin, although Rachel's reaction implied that she had already been aware of his feelings for Emma. Who else knew? He didn't doubt Emma did. Guy had never said anything to suggest that he suspected, neither had Simon or Laura. Marjorie had probably guessed; she didn't miss much.

Guy's track record suggested his relationship with Emma ought to be well into overtime by now. There had been one or two occasions when she had reacted to Guy's flippancy with annoyance, but nothing more of significance to suggest it had run its course. Harry shook his head. He was clutching at straws!

Emma obviously liked him, but was that enough for *a fool* like him to rush in '*where angels fear to tread*'? He had no illusions about how heavily the odds were stacked against him. However, there was no point feeling that way about her, if he did not have the intention, or more to the point, *the guts,* to do anything about it.

No matter how gently she rejected him, it would still be painful. But there would never be another Emma. If he chickened out now, he would spend the rest of his life wondering if he had let that *million-to-one chance* slip through his fingers.

As Rachel said, 'You never know.'

# DECEMBER

## *Full Circle*

Adam appeared in the study doorway holding two steaming mugs of coffee. Raising his eyebrows at the neat piles of Christmas cards on Harry's desk, he said, "I didn't realise you knew so many people, dad. Getting the cards printed with your picture of Nethercombe in the snow was well cool."

Harry cleared a space for the mugs. "I'm glad you approve. You need to sign some of them."

"Do I?"

"Yes; unless you intend to buy your own. The family cards are in the pile next to the phone. I thought you might like to be included on Marjorie and Phil's, and the ones for Alfie and Rob and Ellen as well. I want to post them in Dorchester when I take you to the station."

Adam drew up a chair beside his father. "Wouldn't it be easier to text everybody or e-mail them?"

"That's hardly in the spirit of Christmas! Apart from Grandma Grace, none of the older family members owns a computer and those who've got a mobile phone can't do much more than take a call on it. Can you imagine what Grandma Marian would make of a text?"

Adam grinned in response. "You bought her a mobile last Christmas didn't you?"

"Yes, but she never remembers to take it with her; and if she does, it's never switched on."

Their laughter reflected the comfortable and easy relationship they now shared, leading Harry to reflect momentarily on the perilous course it had taken in recent years.

"I take it you're buying your own cards for your mother, and Debbie and your grandmothers?"

Adam nodded. "Of course. I can afford it now I've been paid for my sweated labour."

"You call slapping a coat of paint on the Memorial Hall sweated labour?" Harry retorted mischievously.

Adam adopted an air of feigned grievance. "Gary and I worked hard on that, right! It took us like, all weekend!"

"It pains me to say so, but you made a good job of it," Harry replied. Handing Adam a pen, he asked, "By the way, what time is your train?"

"I've got to be at PAVT headquarters at two o'clock. I've booked a ticket for the ten-thirteen to Waterloo."

"OK; in that case we'll need to leave in an hour to make sure we get you to the station on time. Emma's bringing the decorations for the party, so I need to be back here before twelve. I've got to pick up a Christmas tree as well."

Adam's eyebrows rose. "Oo-oo-ooh! Emma's coming!"

"Put a sock in it!" Harry retorted.

Adam chuckled playfully. "I'm sorry to miss the party; I wanna meet this Emma. I guess I'll get the chance one day."

"Not if I can help it!"

Adam grinned, enjoying his father's embarrassment. "According to Phil, she's quite a babe."

"I'm sure Marjorie would be thrilled to know he thinks so," said Harry. "Although I can't imagine Phil calling her a babe!"

"Maybe not. But he says she's quite something. Anyway Marjorie wouldn't care; she can handle Phil."

Harry laughed. "I don't think there's much our Marjorie can't handle; that includes you and me."

Harry folded the step-ladder and stood in the doorway to the sitting room, gazing around it with a glow of satisfaction. A tall Norway spruce, crowned with a gleaming star, stood in the alcove beside the fireplace; its lights, in the form of tiny Dickensian lanterns, twinkling on and off in rhythmic sequence. Emma had dressed it simply and elegantly with delicate ribbon bows and sparkling silver and gold balls. The mantelpiece was stylishly decorated with holly and candles and spirals of ribbon, interspersed with pine cones. She had draped the pictures with sprigs of laurel and holly, and an ornamental candle, held in a base of holly and pine cones, adorned each occasional table.

"Does His Lordship approve?" she called from the kitchen, where she was enjoying a well-earned cup of coffee.

"Yes; thank you Reynolds," he replied loftily, in a mock aristocratic drawl. "In fact it's rather splendid. Jolly well done old girl!"

"You idiot!" she giggled, adding, "Not so much of the *old*, if you please!"

She had also adorned the mirror and picture frames in the hall with greenery. The laurel wreath she had made rested on the hall table, ready to hang from the brass knocker on the front door. Harry picked up the steps, with the thought, 'The girl has class, in addition to her many other attributes.'

Rachel's advice came to him once more. '*Tell her Harry.*' His inclination was to wait until after his party. If, as he feared, it was not what she wanted to hear, it would avoid the embarrassment of trying to pretend it hadn't happened and avoiding each other all evening. But she was here … now; just the two of them. There wouldn't be a better opportunity. 'It's her you want! For once in your life, throw caution to the wind!'

Emma looked up at him, her eyes sparkling, when he went into the kitchen. She was sitting with her elbows resting on the kitchen table; her coffee mug held in both hands.

"You're a very clever girl!" he said. He had not meant to sound so pompous, but distracted by what he was dying to tell her, and how he was going to say it, he had said the first thing that came into his head.

"No worries," she said. "I've got some mistletoe in the car. It was wickedly expensive, but Guy insisted on having it. You're welcome to a sprig, if you want it."

Harry's heart was racing. "I don't think it'll get much use here," he replied hesitantly. Giving way to his natural instinct to disguise his discomfort with a joke, he added, "It might make Marjorie nervous."

Emma chuckled, and looked up at him thoughtfully. "I'm glad you're on good terms with Rachel again."

The sudden remark took him unawares. What did she mean by it? "Yes. We're … ah … friends … but nothing more than that now," he stammered.

"That's a shame," Emma said quietly.

"No; it's fine … for both of us!" Harry exclaimed. "I suppose you could say we ran out of steam."

Emma gave him an understanding nod. "She's still very fond of you, Harry. She doesn't want you to be unhappy."

"I'm fond of her too," Harry replied awkwardly, still puzzled by the drift of the conversation.

Emma put down her cup. "She's not serious about Julian. I can understand why she's attracted to him. He's suave, charming and good looking, but she knows exactly where he's coming from." Interpreting Harry's quizzical expression, she added, "Rachel and I had a little chinwag at Simon and Laura's engagement party."

Harry froze at the thought, 'God! Has Rachel blabbed about what she said outside the church hall?'

Emma chuckled to herself. "She asked if Guy and I were thinking of getting hitched."

Alarm bells rang in Harry's mind. "Really?" he said, trying to sound unconcerned. But Emma's attention had been captured by the front page of *The Valley Voice*, so his hope for a denial went unfulfilled. '*Well, are you?*' He almost blurted it out loud in frustration.

Emma looked up from the lead article. "So you still don't know what's happening about the village shop?"

"No." To give himself a moment to compose himself, Harry took the steps into the lobby and hung them on their brackets, before returning to the kitchen. "Whatever happens, we've probably lost the post office. The smart money's on them building a couple of cottages on the site."

"It's such a shame," she sighed. "It seems like the heart's being torn out of the countryside these days."

"Everything's run by townies now," Harry exclaimed sourly. "They won't be happy until they've bricked and concreted it over completely! They haven't a clue about anything that goes on outside the towns and cities. Ask them where milk comes from and they'll say *Waitrose*."

Emma giggled. "Spoken like a true son of the soil."

"OK; pot calling kettle black," Harry replied with a wry grin. "I was just like them before I came to live here. But I've learned a lot in the past year. I've come to appreciate a lot of things I never understood before."

"I've noticed," Emma said quietly. "You've changed since I first met you."

"Have I?"

"Yes. You seemed a bit lost then; insecure. You're more … well, confident and sure of yourself now."

"Thank you. I hope I am. A lot of people have helped me get my act together; not least you and Guy."

Emma tilted her head and treated him to a heart-stopping smile. "As usual you're being too modest Mr. Simmonds. You're understating your own contribution."

He grinned self-consciously. Her remarks about Rachel and him, and her and Guy getting married had unnerved him, and his resolve crumbled. It was as if she had read his mind and was deliberately pre-empting what she feared he was about to say.

She interrupted his train of thought. "I hear you did a terrific job at ACCORS. According to Guy, they were impressed by your ideas and professionalism. You've really stirred things up, though."

"They damn well need it!" Harry exclaimed. "I still can't believe the state they're in."

"What are you planning to do now?" she asked.

"I've got something lined up with an organisation I've worked with before. Much more straightforward ... and *sane*!"

"That's good. But I really meant you; yourself."

He shrugged his shoulders. "It depends on what life throws at me, I suppose." Unable to curb his impatience, and with his heart in his mouth, he asked, "What about you? *Are* you thinking of getting married?"

Her look was disarming. "I can't say. I haven't been asked yet!"

The mischievous glint in her eyes suggested that she knew Guy would eventually come to his senses and marry her. He would be a fool not to. Harry looked away. "Sorry; it's none of my business," he mumbled.

Emma looked at her watch. "It's time I made a move!" she said, and stood up. "I'll just hang the wreath on the door, then I'll be on my way."

"I can do that," Harry insisted. "Thanks for all you've done Emma. Everything looks wonderful!"

"Glad you like it."

"I certainly do. I can't thank you enough!"

"No worries. It's what friends are for."

Her words resonated in his mind, as he waited for her to pack up her rolls of ribbon and a few unused candles. Returning her wave as she reversed Fritz into the lane, he murmured, "OK, I get the message! We're *friends*! Nothing more!"

Adam's absence was a dispiriting reminder that the days to his departure were rapidly ticking by. The thought was seldom out of Harry's mind now, and with it, the awareness of how much he would miss his son's cheerful companionship. During the past weeks, the house had come to life. Even the din that Adam called music was preferable to the hours of solitude he had endured in recent years.

However, his party was something to look forward to, and with it the chance to catch up with some old friends. He had not managed to get together with his school friend, Paul Davies, all year. It had taken a great deal of reassurance and perseverance to persuade Alfie Cox and the Hardys to come. According to Rob, Ellen had been shopping for a new dress, so that she would not '*Show Harry up*'. Harry found it touching. He had grown fond enough of her and Rob to regard them almost as family.

His immediate concern was the turnout when the Christmas lights were switched on. A lot of effort had gone into planning it and overcoming petty regulations. It would be a shame if it fell flat due to local apathy. It surprised him to realise that he cared so much; something he could never have envisaged when he first moved in.

He chuckled to himself. "I'm becoming a proper Nethercombrian; if that's the right word."

The murmur of the crowd was audible the moment Harry left the house and lengthened his stride to catch up to his neighbours. Ellen, with her arm through Rob's, turned to him with a smile as he reached them. "This is quite something, idnit?" she said.

"It certainly is," Harry replied, delighted at seeing so many cars parked around the village green. Casting his gaze over the crowd spilling across the grass and onto the forecourt of *The Black Bull,* he added, "I didn't realise there were that many people living in Nethercombe."

It was gratifying to see that the occasion had captured the imagination of the whole village. Nearly everyone seemed to have turned out; standing in families and groups, chattering excitedly and milling around expectantly. A queue had formed at a brightly lit kebab van, and Bob Andrews had enterprisingly 'fired up' his barbeque in the car park at the rear of the pub. He was doing a brisk trade in 'burgers and bangers', while on the forecourt, where the facade and the potted fir trees were already festooned with coloured fairy lights, chestnuts roasting over a brazier were proving equally popular.

As they crossed the village green below the strings of, as yet, lifeless coloured bulbs, Harry noticed the logo of a local radio station on the doors of one of the cars. The number of vehicles prompted Rob to speculate, "I'm not so sure all this lot lives in Nethercombe. I reckon a lot of 'em are outsiders!"

"I'm sure you're right, Rob," Harry replied, trying not to make his excitement appear too obvious.

"You must be tickled; seein' as 'ow you 'ad a lot t'do with it," Rob exclaimed.

"A lot of people were involved. I was only one of them," Harry answered diffidently, raising his arm in reply to Marjorie's wave. They made their way to where she stood with Phil, Alfie Cox; and surprisingly, Peggy Flowers.

"Peggy; how lovely to see you! How are you?" Harry exclaimed. "How's Ted?"

"Oh, he 'as good days and bad. He'd a'loved to see this," she replied. "But 'e said to wish everybody all the best and a Merry Christmas."

All heads turned towards Church Lane, where Simon's shaggy mane could be seen, bobbing above the throng. Harry watched as he led a group of dignitaries and St.Luke's choir in procession to a small dais beside the entrance to the pub. Adults and children alike covered their ears, as a rushing sound, like a steam train, followed by a piercing howl from the speakers positioned at each end of the forecourt, revealed that proceedings were about to begin.

Gerald Spenser-Smith's head and shoulders rose above the crowd, as he mounted the makeshift platform and was handed a microphone. The babble of voices hushed, as a metallic click came from the speakers, and Gerry's amplified voice reverberated from the wall of *The Black Bull*. "Is it on? Oh … right. Can you all hear me?"

In reply, he received a spirited, "Yes!" that would not have disgraced a pantomime audience.

"Jolly good! Ladies, gentlemen and children; fellow parishioners. As chair of the Nethercombe Ley Social Events Committee, it's my pleasure and privilege to welcome you all to the first of what we hope will become the *annual tradition* of switching on Nethercombe Ley's Christmas illuminations."

A loud cheer rose into the cool night air.

"But before we do so, I'm sure you'd all like to join me in thanking my little band of festive elves, who have so generously given their time, and put in so much effort to make this possible. So let's hear it for the members of The Nethercombe Ley Social Events Committee!"

Another cheer erupted, accompanied by applause and a few of the whoops and shrieks which have pervaded society through the modern media. Carol Maitland, who was standing a few feet away with her husband, looked towards Harry and smiled bashfully. Phil Alders patted Harry's back, and to his embarrassment, several others turned to him and Carol with smiles and polite applause.

"So, without further ado," Gerald continued, "I'll hand over to Reverend Cornish of St. Luke's and Reverend Cartwright of The Garstone and Nethercombe Ley Methodist Congregation, for a brief blessing."

The babble of voices faded as Simon and Reverend Cartwright mounted the dais. Heads bowed as each gave a short prayer, reminding everyone of the true meaning of Christmas, and exhorting them to offer compassion and charity to those in need and less fortunate than themselves. In conclusion, Simon prayed for divine blessing on the illuminations, as a simple expression of the joy and fellowship of Christmas.

Adding his voice to the drone of 'Amen', Harry's eyes were drawn to the faded, weather-stained canvas still screening the charred remains of the village shop, and his heart went out to Peggy, who had found the courage to celebrate with the community she and her husband had served and loved; knowing that this might be Ted's last Christmas.

A ripple of excitement emanated from the front of the crowd, followed by Gerald's voice booming, "And now! The moment we've all been waiting for! Please welcome … Dorset's very own … Chaline McNeill!"

To more cheers and whoops, a carefully coiffured tangle of blond locks rose into view, as a pretty girl, wearing a fun-fur jacket mounted the dais, smiling broadly and waving in response to the cheers and wolf-whistles.

Alfie looked mystified. "Who's she then?" he asked.

"She's a pop star Alfie," Marjorie explained. "She's one of *The Dream Dolls*."

Phil winked at Harry. "You must know '*Smooth My Style*', Alfie!" he declared impishly. "I'd a'thought you'd got that on your iPod."

"The only pods I got 'ave peas in 'em!" Alfie retorted.

The accompanying laughter was drowned out by a sudden squeal from the speakers, as Chaline began to clap her hands above her head and chant, "Come on baby, smooth my style ... smooth my style ... smooth my style".

Rob and Ellen looked as puzzled as Alfie, as the crowd took up the chant, swaying and clapping as they sang.

"Wass she on about?" Alfie bellowed in Harry's ear.

"Search me!" Harry hollered back.

To Harry and his companions, the chanting seemed to go on interminably. It eventually abated and became one or two isolated voices and the odd whistle and whoop.

Chaline grabbed the microphone. "Yeh! Right! Are you all havin' a good time?"

She received the obligatory answering chorus of, "Ye-e-e-e-h!"

Milking the adoration, she shrieked, "Are you all lookin' forward to Christmas?" invoking another ragged bellow in response.

"Well, right ... yeh! So, shall we switch the lights on?"

"Ye-e-e-h!"

"Ready? ... Five! ... Four!" The excited crowd joined her in the countdown. "Three! ... Two! ... One!" With an exaggerated flourish, Chaline pushed the large, red button mounted on the glitter-sprayed box held up by Gerald.

For a few moments, nothing happened. The groans of disappointment amused Harry, as the thought occurred to him that it was not just young children who were gullible enough to believe a button on a wooden box could generate electricity. The switches were under the supervision of Bob Andrews, who was watching from a window of *The Black Bull*.

Harry's heart missed a beat, when one or two bulbs flickered, before suddenly, to time honoured 'Oohs' and 'Ahs', all but one or two came to life in gleaming multicoloured chains draped between the oaks. A roar of delight rose into the night air, as the tall, shadowy Christmas tree at the corner of the green burst into a blaze of twinkling lights. More lights lit up at the same time in the windows and on the facades of several cottages around the green, generating a mounting wave of applause and shouts of approval.

Harry looked up at the dark, shadowy silhouette of the church spire, as St. Luke's choir led everyone into, *'Oh Come All Ye Faithful'*; certain that he was not the only one with a lump in his throat. Some began to drift away, but it was satisfying to observe that most gathered around the Christmas tree for the carols.

Chaline's stock rose considerably in Harry's estimation, when he noticed her sitting at one of the wooden tables outside *The Black Bull*, cheerfully signing autographs for the swarm of youngsters, and some not so young, surrounding her.

Later, after Father Christmas and his 'Round Table' elves had circled the village green, with *'Jingle Bells'* reverberating deafeningly from their four-wheel-drive 'sleigh', Harry made his way home with Ellen and Rob; relaxed and in high spirits.

He was nervous about his party; although Emma and Marjorie had assured him there was nothing to worry about. If the number of acceptances was any indication, they were right.

Only a handful of the fifty-odd people he had invited were unable to come. He had invited Peggy and Ted Flowers out of affection, even though he realised Ted's deteriorating health would prevent them from accepting. Grace had been full of apologies; she had already accepted an invitation to a family wedding.

Of his colleagues on the Special Events Committee, Pat Buckler and her husband would be in Cologne for the Christmas markets, Robert would be orienteering somewhere in Scotland, and Maurice and his wife would be at sea, on their annual winter cruise. The other committee members had accepted with alacrity.

And there was Rachel. Mindful of her not inconsiderable contribution to ending his loneliness, he had included a note to that effect with her invitation. She had called to thank him personally, and to apologise for the fact that she was committed to attend a function arranged by her employer; otherwise, she assured him, she would have been thrilled to come.

To his surprise, and pleasure, his mother had informed him that she and Aunt Caroline would be arriving with Debbie and Paul.

If only Adam could be there ... and, of course, his father.

For the first time in three years, Harry was experiencing something of the spirit of Christmas, as he gazed around the crowded room. Everyone was in high spirits, and thankfully, there were no 'wallflowers'; something he was taking special care to watch out for.

He had given up trying to coax his mother and Aunt Caroline from the kitchen, where they had taken charge of the oven and microwave. They appeared perfectly content, and, as their pink cheeks and noses suggested, just the slightest bit tipsy. Even Marjorie's offer of help had been rebuffed, and she had been shooed away good naturedly.

He could claim very little credit for the success of the party, which was due almost entirely to the combined effort and organisational skills of Marjorie and Emma. The food had been discussed, decided on and ordered with the minimum of input from him; most of it having arrived earlier in the day in a Waitrose van. They had brought the rest with them, ready prepared. His mother had literally *put the icing on the cake* by bringing home-made mince pies and one of her special yule logs; a favourite of Harry's. His brief had been simply to supply the drinks and 'play the charming host'.

He was not sure about the charm, but he had not stinted on the booze. His guests had brought so much with them, that he probably had enough to throw another party. He had laid out the drinks for everyone to help themselves, but was still doing his duty, wine and champagne in hand, topping up and making sure that the less self-assured were not nursing empty glasses.

To his great satisfaction, so was Emma. She was moving between his guests in a pale green dress that set off her bewitching eyes and glorious hair. She seemed to be sharing a joke with the Hardys, as she topped up Rob's beer. Even though he now knew there was no hope for him, Harry could not take his eyes off her. Looking up suddenly, she caught him watching her. He blushed, but she gave him a warm smile, and although he could not hear above the music and babble of voices, he read her lips; "Is it all OK? Are you happy?"

"Yes; thank you so much!" he called back.

Ellen had obviously gone to a great deal of trouble to 'dress up in her new party frock', as Rob had described it. She had been to the hairdresser, and to Rob's dismay and discomfort, had made him wear a suit and a collar and tie. Harry had kissed her cheek and complimented her on the dress when she arrived. She had replied with a shy smile that clearly registered relief as well as pleasure. She smiled again now and raised her glass, containing what looked as if it might be shandy.

"Lovely party Harry!" Lady Diana exclaimed, holding out her glass. "And delicious champagne. It was so kind of you to invite us." She gestured to her companion, The Right Honourable Denis Allaway, Member of Parliament for somewhere Harry could not remember. "I've been telling Denis about the work you do for the FOSLs."

"It's a pleasure," Harry replied. "I can't claim to do much, but I enjoy it. Being involved in a small way has been good for me. This party is really to express my appreciation for being welcomed and for all the kindness I've received this year."

"Well, it's a jolly nice gesture!" said Denis. "Thanks for letting me come with Diana!"

"You're very welcome," Harry replied.

Casting his eyes around the room, Denis asked, "Who's the redhead? I assumed she was your wife, but Diana tells me you're unattached at the moment."

Harry felt like replying facetiously, 'No I'm semi-detached.' Instead he answered, "That's Emma; my friend's partner. She and Marjorie over there did all the work. I'm just taking the credit under false pretences."

Guy appeared from behind Lady Diana with his glass prominent, and almost empty. "Don't believe a word of it!" he exclaimed. "Harry's a black belt in self deprecation!"

"I'm beginning to realise that, the more I get to know him," Diana chuckled.

Harry felt mischievous. "This is Guy, the partner of the young lady you were just asking about," he said. "Guy, this is Lady Diana Lauderham and The Right Honourable Denis Allaway."

"You're a fortunate man, Guy!" Denis said; not so right honourably Harry thought, in view of the fact he was Diana's escort. The wine and champagne bottles in his hands were now virtually empty, so it was an opportunity to leave them all to it and return to the kitchen for fresh supplies.

Standing in the hallway, he surveyed the lively, noisy throng with satisfaction and pleasure, noting some interesting groups. Predictably, Rob and Ellen were in conversation with Geraldine and Lisa Jennings. Frank Jennings and Sanjay and Padmana Chowdri were chatting animatedly with Alan and Jill Anderson, Phil Alders and Jeremy and Jane Radford.

Gerald Spenser-Smith was leaning on the mantelpiece, with Cheryl beside him. They were chatting with Harry's friends, Geoff and Emily Keats; his old school chum, Paul Davies and Paul's wife, Tracy, whose melodic Welsh lilt could be made out during occasional ebbs in the waves of chatter and laughter.

In the centre of the room, Guy and Paul MacKenzie appeared to be trading travel anecdotes with Diana and Denis Allaway, while on the far side of the room, Simon and Laura had made the acquaintance of John and Emma Ledgerwood and Doug and Maggie Gatward; friends who had remained even-handedly loyal to both Sally and Harry since their divorce.

Harry's equally supportive friends, Nick and Sue Holding, who had celebrated their twenty-fifth wedding anniversary earlier in the year, were showing Sarah Woodleigh and Annabel Casson what Harry guessed were photographs of their grandchild.

Annabel's husband, David, was part of what seemed to Harry the most intriguing and diverse group, which included Carol Maitland and her husband John, Sir George Woodleigh, Gary Alders, Alfie Cox and Debbie.

Emma continued to move between the groups, refilling glasses, while Marjorie made it her business to ensure the 'nuts and nibbles', as she referred to them, were circulating and regularly replenished.

When Harry went into the kitchen, he found his mother transferring hot, golden-brown rolls from an oven tray onto a large serving plate. "It's all just about ready," she announced.

"Yes, you can tell them to come and help themselves," Aunt Caroline exclaimed. A sudden hiccup made her giggle girlishly, and in a surge of affection, Harry put an arm around her shoulders and the other round his mother's waist. Surveying the feast covering the table and almost every work top, he kissed their perspiring foreheads. "Thank you so much for all you've done, both of you; but most of all for coming!" he said. "You've made it extra special!"

Emma appeared in the kitchen doorway with an empty bottle in each hand. "I wish I had a camera!" she exclaimed. "That would make a lovely picture!" Gazing at the food, she added, "Wow, it's some party!"

"You deserve as much credit as anybody," Harry replied. "You're still hard at work. You should be enjoying yourself!"

"Don't be silly. I'm having a great time getting to know everybody!" she replied, dropping the empty bottles into the plastic bin that Marjorie had thoughtfully provided. Taking a bottle of Chablis from the fridge, she asked, "Is there any more Saint Emilion? Sir George … or '*Georgie*', as he wants me to call him, seems to be getting through it at quite a lick."

Harry chuckled. "I think there are a couple of bottles left." Releasing his aunt and mother from his embrace, he said, "I'll just go and have a look in the lobby."

Watching Harry draw the corks from the Chablis and St. Emelion, Emma exclaimed, "You ladies are doing all the hard work! Come and enjoy the party!"

Harry's mother mopped her brow with a tissue. "Don't worry about us, Emma, we're quite happy."

Taking the opened wine bottles from Harry, Emma asked, "Are you ready for them to eat?"

"Yes; tell them to come and help themselves," Aunt Caroline replied. As the door swung to, she exclaimed, "What a lovely girl!"

"Yes," Harry replied. "God knows how I'd have managed without her and Marjorie organising everything."

"That's the sort of girl you should be looking for!" his mother replied emphatically.

"Mum; I've told you …"

But she had not finished. "You're like your father. I thought he was never going to get around to asking me out!"

Aunt Caroline hiccupped again. "I remember!" she giggled.

To Harry's relief, the noise of the electric whisk drowned out his mother's voice, as she whipped cream for the desserts. Aware of her propensity to labour a point, he held up a hand, as the high-pitched whine stopped. "Mum, don't start that again, please! I know you mean well, but Emma's spoken for … and *way* out of my league!"

He stopped abruptly; suddenly aware of the startled expression on her face, as she stared past him towards the door. The increase in the volume of noise from the sitting room had been masked by the whisk when the door had opened. He did not need to look to know who was standing in the doorway.

"I've just thought," Emma said. "It's Harry's party; he ought to the one who invites everybody to tuck in."

"OK," Harry replied, unable to face her. "I'll be out in a minute."

This time the door closed properly, with a distinct 'click'. Recognising his discomfort, his mother reached out and touched his arm. "I'm sorry, darling. I didn't mean to embarrass you."

"I know mum. It's alright, don't worry; forget it," he said. "I'd better go and tell them grub's up. I suggest you two tuck in first, before the hungry hoards descend."

He returned to the sitting room and turned down the music, while Guy tinkled a glass with a pen to gain everyone's attention. Harry avoided eye contact with Emma, although she did not appear to be perturbed by anything she may have overheard.

"When you're ready, please make your way to the kitchen and help yourselves to the food," he said. "There appears to be enough for twice as many people as this, so I hope you all have healthy appetites."

He was not disappointed. An hour later, the kitchen was littered with dirty plates, and everyone was devouring the cakes and puddings; many of them enjoying a second helping. The sound of a spoon tinkling against a glass again brought a hush to conversations. The music was turned down once more, and Debbie came towards him.

Harry's heart swelled with pride, as she took him by the hand and led him to the centre of the room; a vision of loveliness in a bright blue dress; chestnut hair tumbling below her shoulders in waves, and that smile she had inherited from her mother. She waited patiently for the applause to subside, before she began.

"Well dad; everyone is having a lovely time. There are people here much more competent at this sort of thing than me, but it seems I've been chosen to say a few words of thanks on behalf of everyone for this lovely party." Again she waited for the 'Hear; Hears' and clapping to abate.

"Grandma and Aunt Caroline … and Aunty Sue and Uncle Nick … and some of your other old friends have known you longer than I have, but perhaps Grandma, Adam and I are most aware of what you've been through recently."

There were sympathetic murmurs from his older friends.

"So it's wonderful to see you're happy again, and settled in your new home. You've made lots of new friends too, who … who …" She swallowed hard, trying to control her emotions, but her lower lip trembled, and the tears began to flow. Harry took her in his arms and hugged her, stroking her hair.

"Sorry, dad. I wanted to say so much more ... and better than that," she sobbed.

Harry kissed the top of her head. Amid the applause and murmurs of sympathy, he replied, "You said it all my love; all I could ever wish for!"

"I'm alright now," she said abruptly. Wiping away her tears, she lifted her head and pulled away from Harry's embrace, to deliver a halting apology. "I'm so sorry everyone; I ... I didn't do that very well, did I?"

As the cries of contradiction and empathy subsided, Lady Diana patted Debbie's arm. "You did very well, my dear. I think you expressed everyone's sentiments most eloquently!"

Harry shuffled his feet, trying to calm his emotions, while his tearful mother hugged her granddaughter. Marjorie's eyes were welling with tears and Ellen was dabbing at hers with a handkerchief. Harry cleared his throat, and forced a smile to his lips. "Well," he began, "I'm not sure how to follow that!"

It was received with a ripple of amusement.

"As many of you know, Debbie has a degree in meteorology and climatology. You also know how proud of her I am. However, she appears to have been caught out by, what she would no doubt call 'sudden precipitation'."

As the burst of relieved laughter subsided, Harry turned to Debbie and said quietly, "Thank you my love. I don't have the words to express my gratitude for your love and support."

Feeling the flush to his cheeks, he returned his attention to his guests. "Now; let me start by thanking you all for coming. This party is really to express my gratitude for the help and support I've received in recent years; not just from my family and old friends, but from my new friends and neighbours as well. Thank you all for your kindness and friendship; and for helping me to make Nethercombe Ley my home."

Again there was a burst of applause.

"Secondly, let me put the record straight. This party has little to do with my feeble efforts. It was planned and organised, with military precision, by Emma and Marjorie. I just did as I was told!"

"Well, that's a first!" his mother exclaimed impishly, prompting another burst of laughter.

"It was a pleasure Harry," Emma replied; her eyes glistening. "I know Marjorie feels the same."

"Of course it was!" Marjorie declared. "You make it sound like the feeding of the five thousand."

Harry chuckled with everyone else. "I'm sure Simon will correct me if I'm wrong, but I don't think as much preparation went into that as this party!"

To a wave of delighted laughter and more applause, he gestured towards his mother and Aunt Caroline. "The rest was taken care of by these two very special ladies. Thank you both for the hot food and the homemade cakes. It was all delicious."

Aunt Caroline giggled shyly and his mother lowered her eyes and blushed in response to the applause.

"If you'll bear with me …" he continued, "There are two people I wish could have been here today. My dad, of course, who sadly passed away in the summer, and my son, Adam, who's doing his final prep course, before being unleashed on some poor, unsuspecting Ghanaians. He sent me a text an hour ago, expressing these tender, filial sentiments: 'Hope all OK. Save me some profiteroles.'

Over the ripple of amusement, he added, "Finally; there's just one more … very important thing I'd like to say. I'm sure you'd all like to join me in raising your glasses to congratulate Laura and Simon on their recent engagement, and to wish them the joy and happiness they so richly deserve in their future life together."

A blush came to Laura's cheeks and she beamed in response to the raised glasses. Simon slipped an arm around her shoulders, as voices repeated Harry's toast. "Laura and I thank you all for your kind wishes," he said. "Especially you Harry. Thank you for your friendship and generosity, for which so many of us in Nethercombe Ley have reason to be grateful."

"Hear! Hear!" Gerald exclaimed.

Harry smiled diffidently, as the sentiment was repeated around the room. Laura kissed his cheek. "Thank you Harry. It's a *lovely* party."

Catching a familiar waft of perfume, Harry turned to find Emma beside him. "Coffee Harry?" she suggested.

"I'll make it Emma. You've done more than enough," he replied; remembering her asking the same question in Guy's kitchen, what seemed half a lifetime ago.

She wrinkled her nose and pulled a face at him.

"I'll give you a hand," said Marjorie, and fixed Harry with a commanding look. "Stay with your guests and mingle!" she ordered.

"Mingle?" he repeated mischievously, and received a playful slap on the arm.

"I'm glad to see you're keeping him in order!" his mother chuckled, and followed Marjorie and Emma to the kitchen.

Harry returned his attention to Simon and Laura. "Well, I'd better do as I'm told and *mingle* hadn't I?" he chuckled.

The rest of the evening passed far too quickly for Harry. He circulated and chatted with his guests; catching up with the achievements and disappointments of old friends, while introducing them to his fellow 'Nethercombrians'.

Despite his entreaties to concentrate on enjoying themselves, Emma and Marjorie continued to be perfect hostesses; Emma topping up and dispensing drinks, and Marjorie clearing abandoned crockery and glasses. Attempts to dissuade her and his mother and Aunt Caroline from continuously running the dish washer and washing glasses by hand, proved futile. He eventually gave up.

* * *

The Hardys and Alfie were the first to leave; Rob, red faced and uncharacteristically loquacious, as he and Ellen said their goodbyes. "Thanks 'Arry that was smashin'!" he exclaimed.

The sentiment was endorsed by Ellen. "I'm full up," she giggled. "I reckon I shan't need to eat again afore Christmas. We never bin to a posh party like this before."

"No we 'aven't," Rob concurred. "You knows some nice people 'Arry."

"Of course. You and Ellen and Alfie are some of them," Harry replied.

"Thanks very much," Alfie said, as Harry helped him on with his coat. He settled his trilby, slightly askew, on the back of head, with the exclamation, "I've 'ad a really grand time!"

"My pleasure; thanks for coming," said Harry. "Give my regards to your wife. I hope she's better soon. You'll all come next year won't you?"

He had meant it as a joke, but Alfie looked at him intently. "You gonna make this a reg'lar event then?" he asked, swaying slightly.

"Why not?" Harry replied jovially. Wishing them goodnight, he closed the door with a chuckle. "Why not?" he repeated to himself.

"Why not what?" Emma asked, as she passed him on her way to the kitchen.

"Oh, nothing."

"Marjorie and I have been learning some interesting things about you from your mum," she said with an impish grin.

"Oh God!" he groaned.

Unable to stifle her laughter, Emma let it escape with a snort. "I would have loved to see you as a choirboy. I'll bet you were really cute."

"How long do you get for matricide these days?" he asked, losing the struggle to prevent himself laughing.

"Don't say that!" Emma exclaimed. "You're mum's lovely. She's proud of you. She only wants you to be happy!"

"I know; but you need to take some of what she says with a pinch of salt!" he replied pointedly.

She gave him a searching look. "Most mums are pretty clued up on their sons," she answered quietly. "She only has your best interests at heart, Harry; you know that."

It was well past midnight by the time the last of Harry's guests left, leaving only his mother, Paul and Debbie in the sitting room. Aunt Caroline had already gone to bed, having fallen asleep earlier in an armchair.

Harry had arranged a mini-bus to and from the hotel in Dorchester, where most of his old friends were staying. He was looking forward to having lunch with them the following day.

Guy and Emma were staying overnight at Church House, and were the last to leave with Simon and Laura. Before they left, they thanked Harry's exhausted mother, who was stretched out on a settee in the sitting room. Guy shook Harry's hand. "Great party mate! Thanks."

Simon added his thanks. "Wonderful, Harry. Thank you so much."

"You're very welcome," Harry replied and gestured towards Emma. "But you should thank this young lady and Marjorie, not me!"

Emma buttoned her coat. "Nonsense; I was happy to help. Everybody had a great time. As long as you were pleased with it."

"Pleased? As I believe Wayne Rooney would put it, 'I'm over the moon!'" he replied. "I can't thank you enough."

Laura kissed his cheek. "That was a lovely, lovely party Harry. Thank you!"

Harry looked at Guy. "Call in for coffee on the way home tomorrow morning, if you've got time." Turning to Simon and Laura, he added, "You're welcome too; you know that, but I know Sunday is your busy day Simon."

Simon chuckled. "It certainly is."

"Thanks; but I don't think there'll be time," Emma said doubtfully, and kissed Harry's cheek. "But if we don't see you before, have a great Christmas. Don't forget my birthday dinner; the twenty-eighth at *La Terrazza.*"

"Merry Christmas all!" Guy called to the sitting room, and grasped Harry's hand again. "And you mate; have a good one!"

Fearing his emotions might get the better of him, Harry paused to steady himself. "Thanks … all of you; for everything you've done, and for being there for me." Dismissing their denials with a wave of his hand, he continued, "I'm sure I'll see Simon and Laura beforehand; but Guy … Emma; have a lovely Christmas!"

They left with their feet crunching on gravel; calling their parting goodbyes.

Harry's mother appeared from the sitting room, as he closed and locked the front door. "I'm off to bed," she said.

Harry took her in his arms and kissed her forehead. "Goodnight mum. Thanks for all you've done."

"It *was* a nice party, wasn't it?" she replied. "Emma and Marjorie never stopped all evening. Those girls worked like slaves. You ought to send them some flowers or something, to say thank you."

He held her by the shoulders at arm's length. "That's an excellent idea, mum!"

"I do get them occasionally!" she quipped, adding wistfully, "I didn't mean to embarrass you. I didn't realise Emma was there."

"It's alright mum. It doesn't matter."

"I'm right though," she said, mounting the bottom stair. "She's just the girl for you."

Harry grinned awkwardly. 'Tell me about it!' he thought, but what he said was, "Goodnight, mum."

Harry and Debbie spent Christmas quietly in Devon, with his mother and Aunt Caroline. The success of his party; the simple joy of St. Luke's carol service a few days afterwards, and the heart-lifting sight of the Christmas tree and fairy lights whenever he crossed the village green, had lifted his spirits. However, like the rest of his family, he found his ability to enjoy the festive season muted by his father's conspicuous absence.

His mother did her best to cope with the unavoidable reminders of her loss at such an emotive time of year. There were moments when her eyes would suddenly brim with tears, but she and Aunt Caroline produced a Christmas lunch which was epic, even by their standards.

Adam spent Christmas Day and the few days before it, with his mother. Sally brought him to join them on Boxing Day, picking up Debbie for a mother and daughter shopping spree in London the following day.

Harry could cope with these arrangements now. He could meet Sally without the anguish that would once have overwhelmed him. So, it seemed, could his mother, because she greeted Sally warmly and insisted that she stay for lunch.

Sally looked tired, prompting Harry to ask if she was working too hard. She answered with a grimace and a sigh of resignation. "It's all hands to the pump in these tough times." Noticing his interest in her new, sporty Mercedes, she added, "Being worked half to death needs *some* compensation."

"It's very nice," Harry replied. "I don't doubt you've more than earned it."

She reached into the boot and handed him a slim, wooden box bearing the legend *'J Nismes-Delclou'*, which Harry recognised as vintage Armagnac. "Merry Christmas," she chuckled.

All he could manage in reply was, "Oh … thank you!" But before he could apologise for having nothing for her, she said, "It's not really a Christmas present; it's just a little thank you for straightening Adam out."

"I can't claim much credit for that!" Harry replied. "You did *your* share. Marjorie and her family, plus a few others … not least Adam himself, deserve a lot of credit!"

"I'm sure you had something to do with it," she said quietly. "But, anyway, it's a huge relief to have the old Adam back."

"Of course it is! It's been a privilege having me as a guest, hasn't it pater?" Adam exclaimed, as he emerged from the house wearing a paper hat, a plastic moustache from a cracker and a mischievous grin.

"If he wasn't clearing off to torment those poor Africans, I'd send him back to you!" Harry exclaimed, feigning to cuff him round the head.

Sally giggled and patted her son's cheek. "Just make sure you stay out of trouble … and *keep in touch*!"

"I will mum," he replied, hugging her, as her tears darkened the collar of his shirt.

"And take good care of yourself, or I'll come after you and show you up in front of everybody again!"

"Oh God! Not that!" Adam exclaimed, but his eyes were glistening. "I love you mum!"

Sally sniffed, and gave him one last squeeze. "I love you too, darling; even when you worry me out of my wits."

It took everyone a few minutes to recover their composure after the tearful parting, but for Harry it was liberating to realise that he could now meet Sally without the heartache of old. It was the thought of being with Emma in two days time that tugged at his emotions.

To lift their spirits, Aunt Caroline employed a tried and tested remedy. She put the kettle on.

Guy turned the empty brandy balloon between his fingers, as he watched Emma and Laura cross the restaurant. "Why do women go to the loo together?" he asked.

"No idea!" Harry replied. "Perhaps it's ritualistic."

He was aware that he had drunk more than he should; more than he had done for some time, but he was unrepentant. The intoxicating combination of his friends' company, a good Chianti and Emma beside him during the meal had been perfect ingredients for a delightful evening. He had been prepared for her to be a little aloof, perhaps even wary of him, but she had been in sparkling form; clearly enjoying the occasion. She had seated him beside her, and although it was wishful thinking, he fancied she had even been flirting with him at times.

"As a man of the cloth, Simon, what do you think the reason is?" Harry asked.

Simon grinned. "I couldn't hazard a guess. It's not something that cropped up in my theology studies."

The head waiter appeared at Guy's elbow, and placed the bill in front of him. "Dey talk about-a de men," he suggested.

"Thanks Paulo; you're probably right," Guy replied, fishing his spectacles out of his inside pocket.

"What do we owe?" Harry asked.

Guy shook his head. "Nothing; this is on me."

"Oh come on Guy!" Simon protested. "You must let us pay our share!"

"I'm sorry, that's against my religion," said Guy impishly. "Emma wanted to share her birthday bash with you lot; so it's my shout."

"Well, if you're sure. Thank you; that's very generous," Simon replied.

"It certainly is. Thanks Guy," said Harry.

"Anyway, I've got my own reason for celebrating," Guy began. Pulling out a credit card from his wallet, he placed it on the bill. "While the girls are powdering their noses, I'll let you into a little secret."

He smiled self-consciously and lifted his glasses off his nose. "It won't come as any surprise to you Harry, but the writing's on the wall for ACCORS. There's a pretty strong rumour that the government's going to take an axe to it before long. The thing is; I've been offered a job with an NHS trust; '*oop noorth*'...Yorkshire to be precise. It's where my roots are. I'm off at the end of February. So I've decided to take a leaf out of your book, Simon ... I'm going to ask Emma to marry me."

For a moment the words did not fully penetrate Harry's fuddled mind, but when 'the penny dropped', his senses reeled. He only half heard Simon reply, "Good for you, Guy. She's a lovely girl."

"Yes, she is a poppet, isn't she? I thought I'd whisk her off to London. A stockbroker pal of mine has invited us to his New Year's Eve bash; not far from the London Eye. Em's never been on it, and it came to me that it's just the place to pop the question. While I'm at it, I might as well go the whole hog; you know, swish hotel, theatre and all that."

Even as the words, "What about the Nethercombe party?" started to form on his lips, Harry realised how futile and pathetic his reaction was, and bit them back. A parochial bunfight in a village hall could hardly compete with the glamour of London as a place to propose; especially to a girl like Emma.

Struggling to regain his equilibrium, he forced a smile to his lips and held out his hand. "That's great, Guy; just great! About bloody time too!"

Guy laughed. "I knew you'd say something like that!" Gripping

Harry's hand, he put a finger to his lips. "But not a word when the girlies come back."

"Of course not," Simon replied. "Are you planning to go down on one knee?"

"Christ no!" Guy exclaimed. "It might spoil the moment if she has to help me up again." Then, remembering who he was speaking to, he added, "Sorry about the Lord's name, and all that."

Simon laughed. "Not a problem."

Harry's mind was in turmoil. The earlier euphoria had evaporated and he was only vaguely aware of Guy's jocular banter with Paulo, as he paid the bill.

A swarthy young waiter arrived with their coats, as Emma and Laura returned, chattering and giggling. It was remarkable how quickly they had become such good friends, Harry thought, as he got to his feet, careful to avoid tripping over a chair or upsetting something on the table.

"Thank you all for coming; and for your cards and prezzies!" Emma said. "I've really enjoyed my birthday dinner."

"So have we," Simon replied. "Are you quite sure we can't contribute, Guy?"

"Absolutely sure."

Simon shrugged on his coat. "Well thanks again," he said. "Enjoy the remainder of your birthday, Emma."

"Thanks Simon," she replied, offering her cheek for a kiss.

"See you soon, Guy!" Simon said, and turned to Harry and Laura. "I'll get the car and meet you outside."

"OK," Harry replied absently.

"Happy Birthday Em. See you on New Year's Eve!" Laura trilled, hugging her and kissing her cheek.

"Thanks. Yes. We must arrange to do the January sales too!"

"Great! 'Bye Guy! Thanks for a lovely evening!" Laura exclaimed, and planted a kiss on his cheek. With a parting wave to Emma, she left; her heels tap-tapping on the wooden floor, as she trotted after Simon.

Guy patted Emma's shoulder. "While Paulo's getting us a cab, I'm going to the boys' room to powder something." Looking at Harry, he grinned, "You don't want to come with me do you?"

"No thanks," Harry replied, forcing a smile.

"What's that about?" Emma asked, as she slipped her arms into the jacket the waiter held out for her.

"Oh, nothing; just one of Guy's jokes."

"Are you alright?" she asked, eyeing him quizzically.

"Yes; perhaps one or two glasses too many. Apart from that I'm fine. Sorry."

Emma patted his wrist. "There's nothing to be sorry for. We've all had a good time, haven't we?"

"Yes," he answered; desperate to get away. "Look, I'd better go. Simon and Laura will be waiting. Happy birthday."

He turned and walked towards the door, but heard her footsteps behind him, as she followed him out onto the pavement. "Harry wait! What's the hurry? Hang on a minute and say goodbye to Guy!"

His inherent courtesy had momentarily deserted him, but he did not want to go back in there. The last thing he needed now was a 'good old boys' routine with Guy.

"I'm sorry; I wasn't thinking," he said.

"And what about my birthday kiss?" she said playfully. "I got one from everyone else."

Harry felt his chest tighten. The cold, damp night air, reacting with the wine and brandy, was making him feel unsteady. "I'm not really comfortable with that sort of thing," he mumbled.

Emma's eyebrows rose. "Do you find the idea of kissing me that unpleasant?"

He realised she was teasing him, but it still stung. It made him feel foolish and, together with his embarrassment and confusion, conspired to open the floodgates on his misery. "You know damned well I don't!" he retorted, more bitterly than he had intended. "You know how I feel … you've known *all* along!"

Emma's eyes widened. "Have I?"

"Yes, you have! Even I'm not too dumb to realise that! I'm sorry … truly sorry!"

With his emotions finally unshackled, everything poured out in a torrent. "I know it's pathetic, but there's not much we can do about our feelings. You've been great … humouring me and everything. I hope I haven't made you feel … well, too uncomfortable around me. I know what I am; I'm a bloody fool! I wish I was different … like Guy. He's the *luckiest* man in the world! I'm sorry … really sorry!"

Emma looked astonished; apparently lost for words. She opened her mouth, as if to reply, but was distracted by Simon tooting his car horn, as he pulled out from the side road at the end of the block. Seizing the chance, Harry turned away abruptly and started to run unsteadily towards the car. "Bye Emma!" he called. "Happy New Year! You and Guy have a wonderful life!"

He was momentarily aware of something hitting his foot and skittering away in the darkness, just before he reached the car and wrenched the rear door open. He had no idea what it was and cared even less.

"We're not in that much of a hurry," Simon called jovially over his shoulder.

Harry flopped onto the seat behind Laura, panting as he struggled to fasten the seat belt; grateful for the darkness that hid the tears stinging his eyes.

Laura half turned towards him. "Is everything alright, Harry?"

"Yes, I'm fine, thanks." Compounding the lie, he added, "I thought you were trying to hurry me up."

Simon laughed, as the car pulled away from the kerb. "No; I was just letting you know where we were."

The journey home was an ordeal of grappling with his despair, while trying to respond cordially to Simon and Laura. It was Laura who gave him the opportunity for respite. Lost in melancholy, with his head resting against the window, Harry was watching the ghostly silhouettes of trees and hedges glide past, unaware that Laura had spoken to him, until he heard her say in a heavy whisper, "He's not answering. I think he's asleep."

"I expect he is," Simon replied quietly. "He drank rather more than he usually does."

Laura sighed. "Poor Harry! I think he's lonely, especially now he hasn't got Rachel. I wish we could find someone for him."

"That's something he has to do for himself," Simon replied. "He wouldn't thank us for interfering."

Was that how his friends saw him; sad, lonely and pathetic? Next year both couples would be married, and preoccupied with the joys and aspirations of their new relationships, while he, '*Poor Harry*', would look on enviously; like a street urchin with his nose pressed against a sweetshop window.

What was Emma thinking now; now that '*Poor, half-pissed Harry*' had poured his heart out like a pathetic, love-sick schoolboy?

He was dozing when they arrived at May Cottage, and with an exchange of 'Good Nights' and a 'thank you', he let himself in as quietly and carefully as he could, so that he did not wake Adam.

Taking off his coat, he put his keys on the hall table and searched his pockets for his mobile phone, intending to recharge it overnight. He searched a second time, turning out each pocket carefully, but all he found was a packet of mints. Where on earth was his phone? He could remember using it to call his mother before they went into *La Terrazza*, but his mind was a blank after that. It was no use trying to call the restaurant tonight, or phoning Simon to see if it was in the car. It would have to wait until the morning.

He went into the sitting room, closing the door quietly before switching on the lights and opening the drinks cabinet for a much needed nightcap. It would not stop at one, but he did not care. He felt in the mood to get very drunk; something he had not done for a long time. He took out his *Laphroaig Single Malt* and a glass, and was in the process of unscrewing the cap, when he stopped … and heaving a sigh, carefully and deliberately put the glass and the whisky back in the cabinet.

"No you don't! Not this time Harry; not this time!" he said to himself. "That really would be the end."

He sank into the chair beside the lifeless fireplace and kicked off his shoes. He would not find the blessed oblivion of sleep tonight. Or so he thought.

* * *

He woke to find Adam standing over him with an expression of concern etched on his face. "Dad; are you OK?"

Harry yawned and ran his tongue over his parched lips. "Apart from a taste like the bottom of a parrot cage in my mouth, yes," he replied.

Adam's expression relaxed. "I thought …"

"You thought I was pissed!" Harry interjected with a grin. "But I'm not; only a little merry. You ought to be able to tell the difference by now; you've had enough experience of it."

"So, what's up?" Adam asked intuitively.

"Nothing's up," Harry replied. "I've been celebrating with my friends and fell asleep in the chair."

Adam smiled with relief. "How was your little Aussie sheila? Did she enjoy her birthday?"

"She's not *my* Aussie sheila!" Harry said quietly. "In fact she and Guy are getting married."

"*Oh dad!*" Adam groaned and subsided into the chair opposite his father.

"What's '*Oh dad*' all about?" Harry asked defensively.

"Come on dad; don't try it on with me. I've never met her, but from what Marjorie's says …"

"Oh; so you and Marjorie have taken charge of my relationships now have you?"

"No; don't be stupid!" Adam replied. "But from what Marjorie says about her, and the way you talk about her, she sounds … well, like somebody you could be happy with. So don't try smoke-screening. I know you."

Harry grinned ruefully. "I'm not. Whatever I do or say doesn't make a ha'porth of difference now, anyway."

Adam sighed. "Why didn't you like, tell her how you feel about her?"

"I didn't need to; she already knows. But actually, I did tell her; I blurted it out outside the restaurant."

"What did she say?"

Harry laughed bitterly. "I never waited to find out. I literally ran away!"

Adam reached out and grasped his father's hand. "Fancy a coffee?"

"That would be very nice," Harry replied. "By the way, you can drive us down to Devon for Grandma's farewell banquet tomorrow, if you like."

Adam's face broke into a broad smile. "Cool! Thanks dad.

An early call to Church House established that his mobile phone was not in Simon's car. A call from his ex-partner, Brian Luscombe, hoping for a decision on his ideas for a new partnership, delayed Harry's call to the restaurant, but when he managed to get through, he was again disappointed. There was no sign of his phone. Somehow; somewhere it must have fallen out of his pocket.

It was not until they were about to set out for Brixham, that Harry remembered hearing something hit the ground outside *La Terrazza*, leading him to reflect that it was not only his dignity that he had lost there. The chances of ever seeing the phone again were negligible, but fortunately, it was not the latest must-have model. There was nothing more sensitive stored in it than phone numbers; most of which were in the directory of the land line.

Arranging a replacement proved to be a simple process, involving a phone call to the service provider and a visit to the company's outlet in Dorchester. Once the paperwork was sorted out, Harry became the proud, if bewildered, owner of a new *'All-Singing-All-Dancing'* gadget, with several 'hot apps', which, the enthusiastic young lad in the store assured him, would do just about everything short of waking him up with tea and toast each morning.

Adam was impressed, but qualified his admiration with the comment that he and Marjorie would probably bet each other how long it would take Harry to work out how to use it.

Harry countered with, "Right; you're out of the will!"

"What again?"

"If you teach me to use it, you're back in."

Adam winced. "That'll take months. I've only got a few days!"

"Well, it's either that or you have to hope Debbie will throw you a few crumbs when I'm gone!"

"You're a cruel man and a wicked father!"

Their easy banter brought home to Harry how much he would miss the pleasure of their relaxed relationship. Although Adam would be allowed home on leave every four months or so, those short reunions would flash by so swiftly, whereas the year would pass far too slowly.

Weekends with Rachel were already a fading memory, and much of the joy of the past few months would diminish with the loss of first Adam, and then Guy and Emma; especially Emma.

Although he no longer cherished any false hopes about Emma, Guy's announcement had left him feeling empty and dejected. He had not fully made up his mind to commit to the new business partnership, although Brian was very enthusiastic and persuasive. However, he needed to get back to regular work, and a new venture might rekindle his enthusiasm for life.

When they picked up the A3022 outside Paignton, Harry switched on the SatNav. He had missed the turn to Aunt Caroline's house more than once before, but the soothing female voice guided them unerringly to a row of bungalows facing open fields. Seeing his father's car parked outside was momentarily heart-stopping, even though it had belonged to Debbie for several months.

Aunt Judith and Uncle Ed made such a fuss of Adam, he might have been leaving to go to war, and Grandma Marian and Aunt Caroline produced a memorable valedictory dinner. The size of the joint of beef seemed to imply that they did not expect Adam to eat a proper meal again for months. Coming so soon after the overindulgence of Christmas and the richness of Emma's birthday meal, it made Harry reluctant to look in the mirror, and even more disinclined to venture anywhere near the bathroom scales.

Debbie was uncharacteristically subdued, which Harry attributed to her brother's impending departure. But after dinner, when they were all replete and inert in front of the TV, she quietly announced that she and Paul were no longer '*an item*'; at least for the present. She claimed it was a mutual decision, but Harry guessed it was more her wish than Paul's. His hunch was given greater credence when she went on to explain that, 'things had been moving too quickly' and they both 'needed a little time and space.'

Everyone expressed genuine regret. They had all taken to Paul, with his gentle, caring nature and undisguised adoration of Debbie. Harry wondered if he had asked her to marry him, suspecting that the last thing the young man really wanted was 'time or space' away from her. Paul was probably having the same struggle to come to terms with rejection that Harry had experienced.

Debbie was a little more forthcoming during a walk across the fields the following morning, when she and Harry found themselves some distance ahead of '*the ancients*', as Adam affectionately referred to them.

"Adam told me that Emma and Guy are getting married," she said.

"Yes," Harry replied, as nonchalantly as he could manage. "Someone has finally thrown a net over Mr Wolstencroft."

"How do you feel about it?" she asked pointedly.

"I'm happy for them, of course!" Harry replied. "It's about time someone made an honest man of him."

Debbie gave him a searching look, which suggested she was not convinced. As a distraction, he said, "I was wondering if you'd turned down a proposal from Paul."

Her laugh was gentle but without humour. "No! Things were just moving a little too quickly. He wanted us to buy a house and to take me to meet his parents in Vancouver. Paul's a lovely guy. I'm very fond of him, but I'm not sure I'm ready for that kind of commitment yet."

Harry could not help wondering how much her decision had been influenced by his and Sally's parting.

"I want to get established in my job and get a place of my own, without being pressured into anything," she said.

"How did Paul take it?" Harry asked.

"He wasn't happy, but he's accepted it. I didn't want to hurt him, but he *was* taking a lot for granted. I don't think it makes sense to commit to a relationship I'm not absolutely sure about, and until I've seen something of life."

"Learning from your mother's mistakes," Harry murmured, half to himself.

"No! That's not what I meant!" Debbie replied sharply. "And mum doesn't feel it was a mistake! She loved you! She still does, in a way."

"OK," Harry said soothingly. "Let's not make an issue of it. If that's how you feel, you've made the right decision. I'm sure it wasn't an easy one to make."

The glowering sky matched Harry's mood, as he emerged from the copse and clambered over the stile. Hunching his shoulders against fitful gusts of an icy north wind, he made his way to the summit of Hallows Hill.

New Year's Eve. Another year; another cycle in life's capricious odyssey. Was it really a year ago that he had stood here, in the gloom of mid-winter, looking out over the valley for the first time?

It was not only Emma that had won his heart. He had fallen in love with the timeless beauty of Dorset; at times enigmatic, at others coquettish, but always glorious. Dressed in her finery, changing with the seasons and mellowed by the customs and traditions of generations of her sons and daughters, she had enchanted him.

May Cottage and Nethercombe Ley had become more than a refuge; they were home in ways he could never have anticipated a year ago. He had come to regard his neighbours as friends; sharing their pleasures and tribulations, and absorbing the timeless rhythm of rural life. He had found peace and, with a few exceptions, the tranquillity he had needed so badly.

But he could not stay. Dorset had restored his spirit, and healed his pain, but it could not take away the emptiness of living alone. He could not envisage spending the rest of his life without someone to share its joys and sorrows. As much as he loved May Cottage and Nethercombe Ley, he was pragmatic enough to realise he was unlikely to satisfy that need tucked away in a rural backwater.

He lifted his face to the wind that moaned through the bare branches of the copse and harried billowing ramparts of dark cumulus across a sullen, pewter sky. Below him, the fields lay cloaked in the browns and tans of winter, their drab cheerlessness tempered by the green of hedgerows and patches of woodland and pasture. Here and there a lone tree raised skeletal branches heavenward, as if offering a silent prayer for the advent of spring.

It brought to mind that first day, when his spirits had been so low, and he had met Rachel. It was she who had dragged him from his despair and self-pity, although it could never have worked out between them. He would not have been able to cope with her restless unpredictability for too long, and she would never have managed to sustain the patience for an endless battle with his reticence and reserve. Still, it had been a lot of fun; and happily, they were still friends.

The shock of his father's death and the example of his mother's inner strength and resilience had forced him to face the unpalatable truth, that trying to hold on to the past was futile. As Ellen had so succinctly put it: '*You can't never go back!*'

There would always be a quiet corner of his heart that belonged to Sally; how could it be otherwise? But it was time to move on. He had no way of knowing what the coming year would bring, but he was ready to face it.

He looked at his watch. Time to return home for a final few, precious moments with Adam, before he left. Taking a parting look across the valley, Harry was filled with that blissful, haunting melancholy, that nature, even in her dowdiest apparel, can inspire.

He was going to be OK.

Adam's bags were in the hall when Harry opened the front door. He could hear him in the kitchen with Marjorie. She was putting on her coat when Harry went in.

"Don't forget; let us know how you're getting on," she said. "E-mail or text me when you get there."

"Don't worry, I will," Adam replied. "If and when I'm somewhere I can get a connection. Gary and I are *Facebook Friends*, so why don't you and Phil log in and keep up to date?"

"I expect Phil knows how to do it," she replied.

"Great!" Adam exclaimed, and reached into his pocket. "By the way; thanks ... for everything."

"What's this?" she asked in surprise, taking the small, velvet covered box that Adam held out to her.

"It's not much. It's just to say like ... thanks for everything."

A tear tracked its way down Marjorie's cheek, as she opened the box and gazed at the gold earrings. "They're lovely! But you shouldn't have done this!"

Adam kissed her cheek. "Yes I should. Phil and Gary, and especially *you*, have done an awful lot for me. I really appreciate it. So does dad."

"I certainly do!" said Harry.

Marjorie wiped away a tear and gently patted Adam's cheek. "Well, you take good care of yourself" she sniffed, and with a half sobbed, "See you at the party, Harry!" she hurried into the hall.

"Yes," said Harry.

As the front door closed, Adam looked at him questioningly. "I thought you weren't going?"

"I'm not. But I don't feel like explaining or being coerced just at the moment. I'll worry about it some other time."

Adam frowned. "You will be alright, won't you dad?"

"Yes, of course; I'll be fine!" Harry said, adding, "The earrings were a nice gesture."

Adam grinned. "I just wanted to like, show my appreciation for all she's done for me … for both of us, in a way. I took a leaf out of my dad's book, right? A proper 'chip off the old block', this time."

Harry squeezed Adam's shoulder, to which he replied with a self-conscious smile. "I'd better get the rest of my stuff," he said hesitantly, and went upstairs.

Remembering he had not had lunch, Harry filled the kettle and dropped a slice of bread into the toaster. While he waited, he idly turned the pages of the *Daily Echo*. The estate agents' advertisements were a painful reminder of his decision to leave Nethercombe Ley, if and when he could summon the willpower. He had no idea where he intended to go. It would probably depend on what decision he made about Brian Luscombe's partnership proposal.

Steeling himself to leave would need all the determination he could muster. In his heart he longed to stay. But unless he was prepared to risk spending the rest of his life alone, there was no alternative. Sooner, rather than later, he would have to *bite the bullet; start the ball rolling*, before sentimentality had a chance to stifle common sense.

He had no illusions about the wrench it would be to leave May Cottage and the precious friendships he had made. He looked out wistfully at his garden, which gave him so much pleasure and pride. Thanks to the efforts of Alfie, Gary and Adam, and the advice and encouragement of Rob and Ellen, it was a delight; and practical.

He would miss the changing moods of the distant hills and his regular commune with his inner self on Hallows Hill. For a moment, he toyed with the idea of keeping May Cottage as a weekend retreat. But if he became involved in a new business venture, having no-one to come home to, would inevitably result in him throwing himself into it single-mindedly; leaving little time for anything else. So his head overruled his heart and cautioned against the impracticality of maintaining such a large house for, what would inevitably be, no more than occasional visits.

The chime of the doorbell brought him from his reverie. His stomach lurched. This was it … time for Adam to go!

"That'll be Ollie!" Adam called from his bedroom.

"OK. I'll get it!" Harry answered.

The advertising flyer on the doormat proclaimed: 'Vesuvius Pizzas – Create Your Own Mouthwatering Toppings – Unmissable Introductory Offer – Two for the Price of One'.

"Not another take-away!" Harry groaned. "I'm afraid in my case your offer's entirely 'missable'; if it's all the same to you Mr. Vesuvius."

Straightening up, he tossed the flyer onto the hall table, and opened the front door ... to find himself gazing into a pair of beguiling green eyes that sparkled back at him from beneath a mop of titian waves and curls.

"Emma! What are you doing here?"

She tilted her head in that appealing way. "I was under the impression I'd been invited to a party," she said quietly. "That *is* right, isn't it?"

Totally bemused, Harry half-whispered, "Yes."

Emma held up a bottle of champagne, and grinned impishly. "I thought this might get us in the party mood before we go."

"But ... but Guy said you were spending New Year's Eve in London," Harry stammered. Peering round her towards her yellow Beetle, he asked, "Where is he?"

Emma shrugged. "In London, I guess. I told him I'd already made other plans." She sighed dramatically, exclaiming in mock indignation, "I've been trying to call you, but I got no reply from either number! I've texted you too! I even e-mailed you!"

Harry grinned sheepishly. "I lost my mobile; outside *La Terrazza*, I think. I haven't got round to figuring out how to use my new one yet; it's still in the box. I haven't had time to look at my e-mails either. Adam and I have been staying with my mother in Devon for a couple of days. We didn't get home until around mid-day."

"I know," she said. "Marjorie answered the phone when I called ... *yet again* ... this morning. She said you'd be back by lunchtime." Holding his gaze, she added quietly, "She thought you'd be pleased to see me. I hope she was right."

Harry's throat felt dry. "You know damned well I am!" he croaked.

"Well, can I come in?"

"Of course; I'm sorry!" He stood aside, catching a delightful waft of her perfume as she passed him. Following her into the sitting room, he instinctively looked down at her left hand … and held his breath; there was no engagement ring. His momentary elation turned to embarrassment, as he realised she had noticed. "Guy told us he was going to ask you to marry him," he said lamely.

"*Did* he?" she replied softly. "Well, you know Guy. He's a creature of impulse. I'm sure he found the idea of proposing appealing at the time; much more appealing than he'd find the reality of marriage. I guessed he was up to something, when he came out with the idea of a romantic New Year's Eve in London. It wasn't difficult to work it out."

"Did he propose?" Harry asked.

"No!" she chuckled. "I managed to steer him away from that. Getting married is something we'd both have regretted. I can't say I ever saw myself as Mrs.Guy Wolstencroft. You sort of gave the game away, anyway."

"Me? How?"

"I left a happy and slightly tipsy fella at the table in the *La Terrazza*, and came back to find he'd turned into a sad, unhappy grouch I could hardly get a word out of." She giggled mischievously. "Then, you come out with, '*You and Guy have a wonderful life!* '"

"Sad and unhappy doesn't come anywhere near it!" Harry said deliberately.

Brushing his cheek with her fingertips, she murmured, "I hope you really are pleased to see me."

Harry's heart was racing. "More than I could ever tell you!"

Emma treated him to a heart-lifting smile, tilting her head the way he loved. "We left an important conversation unfinished … if you remember," she said, adding quietly, "Guy and I have gone as far as we were ever going to. I've felt it for some time; even before you came into my life. I think Guy sensed it."

"So why do you think he made up his mind to propose to you?"

"Who knows? Guy is Guy. I guess he was in one of his romantic moods. He might have thought it was what I wanted; why I was cooling towards our relationship. Reaching fifty has been a real problem for him. Perhaps that and the thought of moving back north was what put the idea into his head. Despite the devil-may-care act, he's not as self assured as he makes out."

"How did he take it?"

"OK really. We had a long, serious talk … it was well overdue … and we agreed that it was time to go our separate ways. It was all pretty amicable."

"Poor Guy!" Harry sighed. "I can imagine with how he must be feeling."

"He's OK; honestly," she insisted. "Don't worry; he'll be the same old Guy again in no time."

"Does he know where you are?"

Emma grinned conspiratorially. "Yes. He didn't seem all that surprised. Guy can be a bit shrewder than we give him credit for sometimes. I told him what I felt … hoped was happening between you and me."

"What did he say?"

"He accepted it as '*one of those things*'."

Harry took a deep breath. "You knew how I felt all the time, didn't you?"

"I wasn't sure," she chuckled, and placed the champagne on a side table. "You kept blowing hot and cold. I tried to give you as much encouragement as I dared, but I was never quite sure where I stood … And there was Rachel!"

"It was never serious between Rachel and me!" Harry replied emphatically.

She spread her hands. "I didn't know that before bonfire night. I can't imagine she's lost out to another woman too often. So all I could do was wait … and hope. I guess that was why I hung on with Guy. You were growing on me; I was afraid of losing touch with you." She laughed suddenly. "And when you do finally get around to telling me how you feel, you take off like Usain Bolt!"

Harry grinned self-consciously; his pulse pounding. Needing a distraction to steady himself, he picked up the champagne. "I'll just put this in the fridge to cool. Make yourself comfortable."

Reaching the doorway to the hall, he looked back at her; hardly able to believe he was not dreaming. 'You've got you want!' resonated in his mind. 'Your million-to-one chance! Now take it!'

He took a deep breath and looked into her bewitching eyes. "In case there's any remaining doubt in your mind; I've never been so pleased to see anyone in my whole life! And so you're in *no doubt* about where you stand ... I love you Miss Reynolds!"

Her dazzling smile was all the answer he needed. Blushing to the roots of his hair, Harry turned to go out into the hall, but Emma was off the settee and right behind him; grabbing his arm. "No you don't Alexander Henry!" she exclaimed. "You're not running off again! This time I get a kiss ... *and* the chance to say '*I love you*' right back at you!"

Elation and euphoria had driven everything else from Harry's mind, including the fact that they were not alone. Looking up to the head of the stairs, he gestured towards the face grinning back at him like The Cheshire Cat. "This is my son, Adam," he said awkwardly.

It was Emma's turn to blush; her eyes twinkling with suppressed mirth.

"Adam ... this is Emma," Harry said hesitantly.

"Hi Adam!" Emma giggled.

Adam came down the steep staircase two-at-a-time, with his backpack over one shoulder and his hand held out to her. "I'm *so* glad to meet you, Emma!"

"I guess I'd better get my things from the car," she said, gingerly withdrawing her hand from Adam's vigorous pumping. "By the way Harry, I brought some of that bacon you like, from the farm shop. I thought we could have it for breakfast."

"Breakfast?" Harry repeated, half to himself.

Emma frowned playfully. "Well, yes! You're not expecting me to drive home in the early hours of the morning, full of bubbly, are you?"

Harry's heart was thumping. "Certainly not!" he replied, aware, but uncaring, that he was grinning like an idiot. "It's against the law. I couldn't possibly allow it!"

A geriatric, green Toyota appeared from the lane and pulled up behind Emma's Beetle.

"Here's Ollie!" said Adam, and turned to pick up one of his bags. Harry put down the champagne and picked up the other one. Catching his son's eye, he asked cautiously, "Well; now you've met her, what do you think?"

Adam's face broke into a grin at the sight of Emma's rear, clad in figure-hugging jeans, protruding from her car. "Way to go dad!"

Harry burst out laughing, and Adam curled an arm around his father's shoulders. "She's great, dad. Be happy!"

They could hear Emma and Ollie talking outside, as father and son squeezed one another in a bear-hug. Finally, releasing each other, sheepish and close to tears, they walked out to greet Ollie and load Adam's bags into the Toyota.

Knowing he would not see his son again for several months brought a lump to Harry's throat. But he steadied himself as Emma nestled against him and he felt her fingers entwine with his.

"Take care and keep in touch!" he said.

"No sweat!" Adam replied and slammed down the boot lid. Walking round the car, he nodded to Emma. "Look after him."

"No worries," she replied, and slipped an arm around Harry's waist.

Adam opened the passenger door, and with a broad smile, reached out to grasp his father's hand.

"Happy New Year, dad!"